Eyes in a Moon
of
Blindness

Carie Coulbourn

Green Ivy Publishing
1 Lincoln Centre
18W140 Butterfield Road
Suite 1500
Oakbrook Terrace IL 60181-4843
www.greenivybooks.com

Eyes in a Moon of Blindness/ Carie Coulbourn

ISBN: 978-1-946446-46-6
Ebook: 978-1-946446-47-3

Cassandra's Prophesy, translated, 1558 A.D.

Eyes in a moon of blindness
Endless sea of sun
Nothing as it should be
Prophesy undone

Three rework the future
Two transform the past
One the rule of knowing
Each must stay the last

Sight and shifting shadow
Veiled son of the sea
Snared by chains of fate
In their destiny

Prologue

The next few moments would be forever etched in Daemon's mind, burned there in fire and blood and adrenaline.

Jack took a little wooden box out of his pocket and turned it over in his fingers. Deirdre watched his hand from where her head rested on his chest and frowned. He stepped away from her, over to the chair, and sat down, drawing her with him with a hand on her waist so that she stood next to the chair with her hand on his shoulder. He opened the box and took out a tiny blade, no bigger than his finger; Daemon could smell the silver and bone and the faintest trace odor of old blood and death magic. Deirdre's eyes went distant, and her hand tightened on Jack's shoulder as Daemon felt her swift surge of alarm.

"Jack, wait—" she gasped as he sliced his finger with the knife and his magic surged. Lightning flashed outside the window, and Jack shuddered and clenched his fists and panic filled his eyes as he realized his mistake—like the straw that broke the camel's back, the magic was finally too much for his flesh; his eyes rolled up into his head and he fainted, slumping in the chair. The little box tumbled to the floor, and the ring and the knife skittered, clattering beneath the chair as they slipped from his limp fingers.

The vines that contained the vampire flickered and withdrew swiftly back into the salt, and the wide protective circle flickered and went out as thunder crashed through the room, rattling the windows. The electrical power died with Jack's spells and an ominous *snap-crackle*, and the distant sound of shattering glass, plunging them into darkness lit only by random flashes of electric lightning, like a demonic strobe.

Chapter 1

Deirdre

Thursday

"Deirdre!" She looked up involuntarily at the sound of her name and smiled as Jack caught up and put his arm around her shoulder. His hand was very warm through her thin shirt, and his brown eyes sparkled at her. "Hi," he said, and smiled down at her.

"Hi," she said, warmth creeping into her voice.

"How are you?" he asked as they walked together out to the parking lot. She fished her keys out of her pocket as they walked. He matched his long stride to hers and reached across their bodies to take her backpack from her hand.

"Good," she said, biting her lip and stealing little glances at him. His profile showed a bone structure an actor would kill for, smooth tanned skin just a little rough with blond stubble around his chin, a narrow pouty mouth, and dark eyelashes so long they cast a shadow on his cheek. They emerged into the bright sunshine and his dark blond hair caught the light, shining with bronze highlights.

"So, a bunch of us were going to hang out at the diner today. You want to go?" he asked. She didn't answer right away.

"When?" she asked, playing for time to think. A muscle jumped in his jaw, giving away his discontent with that answer.

"After practice. Around six, I guess." He shrugged, playing it casual, glancing over at her. She pressed her lips together. That would probably give her enough time. Just.

"Six-thirty be okay?" she asked, clicking the unlock button on her keychain, and her heart jumped at the pleased smile that crinkled the corners of his eyes and erased his irritation.

"Sure. Six-thirty is great," he told her sincerely, slowing as they reached her car. He pulled his arm from her shoulders and bent to open the door for her, slung the backpack to the passenger's seat, and stepped back to let her get in. She started the engine, and reached for the door and closed it, then powered down the window to say goodbye to Jack.

"See you later?" she said, looking up at him. He bent down and rested his well-muscled arms on the door. His face was just inches away.

"See you later," he confirmed, and leaned in. She gave him a light kiss, just a brush across his lips, before she pulled away.

"Bye," she said, blushing. He stood up, his eyes shadowed as he looked down at her, and stepped back.

She put the car in gear and checked her mirrors carefully, pulling out slowly and joining the general exodus. When she looked in her mirror again, Jack was still standing where she had left him, his hands in his pockets, watching. A slight smile curved her lips as she turned out onto the street, heading home. She drove carefully, like always; a year ago her twin brother had nearly lost his life in a devastating crash.

She wound her way up the long driveway, through the dappled shade of the forest that lined the well-maintained drive. She pulled into the spacious garage and jumped out, grabbed

2

her backpack, and went into the house. She entered the kitchen through the garage door, greeting Maria as she snitched one of the fresh cookies the housekeeper was moving from hot trays to wire racks to cool. The house smelled wonderful, vanilla and melting chocolate and sugar. The cookie was almost too hot as she bit into it, gooey and delicious. "Mmmm," she groaned with pleasure. "Maria, you make the best chocolate chip cookies *ever*," she sighed. Maria smiled with satisfaction.

"Is he awake?" Deirdre asked then, excitement making her eyes bright. A spark of compassion crept into Maria's eyes, and she nodded. Deirdre turned away, but Maria called her back.

"Here," she said, thrusting another warm cookie into her hand, on a crisp white napkin this time. "One cookie won't hurt," Maria said conspiratorially. Deirdre smiled.

"Thanks!" she said, and dashed off to her brother's room.

"I'll bring the dinner tray in a little bit!" Maria called after her. Deirdre waved her hand in acknowledgement as the door swung shut behind her.

Upstairs she knocked gently and pushed into the room. She put her backpack down on the floor at her feet and placed the cookie on the countertop, washing her hands thoroughly at the small sink, and drying them on disposable towels before she entered the room.

"Alastair?" she said, and smiled when he looked over at the sound of her voice. She studied him for a moment, making sure there was no change for the worse. It should have been like looking into a mirror. Her twin brother had the same dark blue eyes and wavy blue-black hair. The male version of her bone structure framed his face, the same generous mouth, almost the same narrow nose; his eyebrows were a little heavier, two dark slashes on his brow, while hers curved delicately above her eyes.

His skin was a shade lighter than her healthy ivory, stretched tight over his too-prominent bones. It was waxy with illness, and a long white scar stood out against his paleness, a thin jagged line that appeared from beneath his hair at his temple, ran down the side of his face to his jaw and down his neck, disappearing beneath the collar of his shirt. His striking dark blue eyes were framed with thick, long, carbon-black lashes, and he looked toward her, his gaze just slightly to the left of where she actually stood, blank, sightless. He would have been six or seven inches taller than her, if he could stand, and was strong across the shoulders where she was delicate. They both had a slender grace that belied their strength. The corners of his mouth turned up in a small smile.

"Deirdre," he greeted her. His voice was whispery, weak, but she would swear it was getting stronger by the day. His hospital bed was raised to a seated position, and the nurse had dressed him in a dark green button-down flannel shirt. His useless legs were covered by blankets. His hair had been washed and combed, but she noticed he needed a haircut; it curled over the tops of his ears and if he could see he would already have brushed it out of his eyes. As if in response to her thought, he raised his hand in parody of the familiar gesture of her memory to run his fingers through it. She looked down and blinked the moisture from her eyes. At least he was awake. She consoled herself with that thought and swallowed a few times so he wouldn't hear tears in her voice.

"Hey, there. Did you have a good morning?" she said brightly as she settled herself in the reclining chair that sat next to the bed, picking up the book there and opening it to the bookmarked page where she had left off the day before.

"Oh, sure. Same old, same old. Is Maria making cookies?" he said, a hint of anticipation animating his voice. Deirdre smiled.

"Yep. She sent one up for you." She placed the cookie with the napkin into his emaciated hands. His long fingers trembled as he lifted it to his lips and took a bite. While he ate it, so slowly, she shared the latest gossip from school. He listened intently, as he always did. He wiped his mouth carefully when he was finished.

"How's Jack?" he asked when she rambled to a stop.

She shrugged, then, realizing he couldn't see her, she said, "He's okay, I guess." He frowned a little.

"Just okay?" he probed. "Come on, Dee Dee, spill," he pleaded. She smiled at his old nickname for her. She had hated it to tears when he called her that a year ago. Now it was beautiful to hear it from his lips.

"He's… fine. Really," she hedged, not wanting to get into it. He heard the careful indifference in her voice and raised his eyebrows at her, prompting her for more. "A bunch of us are going to the diner later," she offered.

"Hmmm. Okay then." He sat back again and looked away, the short burst of energy already waning.

He plucked at the covers over his legs and she recognized the nervous gesture. There was something bothering him. She narrowed her eyes.

"What is it?" she asked. He looked over at her, frowning, and didn't answer. She waited him out, knowing him well.

"It's nothing," he said finally. "Just curious about him, that's all. He used to be my best friend, y'know."

"Yeah, I know. He's fine, Al. Promise," she reassured him. He relaxed.

She looked over at him, wishing as she always did that he were whole, could stand up and walk out of here, could look at her and see her, though even without his sight he still saw her more clearly than anyone else. Tears threatened, and she turned to the book on her lap, reading aloud until Maria came up with the dinner tray. Deirdre helped her arrange things on the little table that pulled across the bed and stayed with Alastair while he ate. When he was finished she took the tray back down to the kitchen. Maria looked at it critically and shook her head.

"You get him to eat twice as much as anyone else can," she said. Deirdre smiled sadly.

"Still not enough," she murmured, shaking her head. Slowly she returned upstairs. She didn't come all the way back into the room, but stood in the doorway, watching.

"Hey, Al, I'll see you in the morning, okay?" she said. The nurse was already changing him into his pajamas and would take care of his other nighttime routines. She picked up her backpack and slung it over her shoulder.

"'Kay. 'Night, Deirdre. Have fun," he said. He sounded so tired. It was barely even six.

She watched for a moment, then said impulsively, "I love you, Al." He turned his head toward her in surprise.

"I know, Dee Dee. I love you, too," he said. She watched for one more moment, then went to her room to change for her date.

She looked at the clock on the dash as she pulled into a parking space on the street near the diner. Six twenty-four; Jack would be pleased. As she walked the half block down the street, she thought about how much her life had changed. Alastair's accident and subsequent coma last year had put a lot of things in perspective for her.

Gone was the invincible teenager, gone the easy innocent assumption they would live and be young forever. Every time she turned around, she still expected to see Alastair standing near, his lips lifted in that crooked smile, more familiar than her own, his eyes full of mischief. Reality felt dark and cold and lonely; she was lost without her brother, her other half, withdrawn into herself, falling out of touch with everyone at school. Alastair had chided her about it just last week, complaining about the lack of information she could give him about the lives of their mutual friends and acquaintances during his absence. In the last month since Al had awakened she felt like she had awakened too, finally beginning to take an interest in things around her and in her own life again.

She took a deep breath, reveling in the sensation of her lungs filling with air. She had felt like her chest was in a vice for so long, an aching loss that never eased. Then he had awakened from the coma, finally, miraculously, and the doctors had informed her father two weeks later that Alastair could finally come home from the hospital. That same morning, Jack had asked her out.

She had been standing outside in the commons, leaning against the base of the statue of Thomas Jefferson that stood there in the center of the courtyard, talking to Courtney, laughing, really *laughing* for the first time in what felt like forever. Jack had just walked up and said, "I heard Al's coming home tomorrow. I was wondering if I could take you somewhere to celebrate?" She had just stared at him in shocked surprise, at the way his skin glowed in the sun and the velvet in his eyes, and nodded. "Great. I'll pick you up. Seven?" he offered. She nodded again and managed to speak.

"Seven would be great. Where are we going?" she had asked. He had shrugged.

"Dinner and a movie?" he suggested. She had accepted and now they had been dating for two weeks. She smiled as she remembered. It was odd getting to know Jack now, especially since she thought she already did know him; they had practically grown up together. He was different lately, though, without Alastair as a buffer. She supposed everyone was different one-on-one, but it seemed like more than that. And she was different too, since the accident. Shyer, more withdrawn; her emotions ran deeper now.

She smiled to herself again, anticipation warming her chest and putting a little bounce in her stride as she stepped up to the diner's doors. Jack must have seen her crossing in front of the windows, because he met her at the door, pushing it open for her with a warm grin of admiration on his face.

"You look beautiful," he told her. She smiled up into his eyes as he took her hand and led her toward the back of the room where their friends were already gathered.

He led her to a booth and pulled her in next to him, tucking her into his side and putting his arm around her waist. With his free hand he picked up his soda and looked at her with raised eyebrows, silently asking her if she wanted one. His knuckles were raw, like he had scraped them on something or been in a fight. She took the soda from his hand and went to trace the skin across his knuckles with her fingertips, but now under the light it was smooth and unblemished. She frowned at the discrepancy.

"Did you hurt your hand?" she asked him, suddenly unsure. He looked at her in surprise.

"No, why?" he said. She shook her head and laughed a little, turning his hand back and forth. For no reason at all she thought of Alastair's revelation, that Jack had a secret.

"Nothing. I just thought I saw... sorry," she released his hand and grimaced, feeling stupid. "Must have been a trick of the light," she murmured, glancing up uncertainly at the bright bulbs that lit the tables. Falling silent, she settled back against him; he tightened his arm around her reassuringly and caught the waitress's attention. Deirdre, still distracted, glanced swiftly at the menu and ordered the first thing she saw: a grilled cheese sandwich with fries and a Pepsi. The server took the rest of the orders and departed.

Deirdre looked around the crowded room, relaxing in the familiar atmosphere. Conversation ebbed and flowed around her and over her effortlessly. The couples at two of the next tables were part of their group; the guys played football with Jack, and she had known the girls a long time, even though they weren't particular friends—at least, not anymore. She was trying to change that, but it was hard. They had closed their ranks to her in the last year, resenting her withdrawal and antisocial behavior.

It was a little easier with Courtney; she had lost her mom a few years ago, and understood better than the others what that could do to a person. She was sitting across the table with her date, Kyle, who was tall and dark and sharply slender in sharp contrast to her friend's white-blond hair and curves. She had apparently been crushing on him since he moved into town a few months ago. Deirdre paid close attention so she could discuss the evening in detail with Courtney later. To her eyes it seemed to be going well. Kyle was attentive and funny, and Courtney was clearly enjoying herself. Deirdre flashed another smile at Jack; he met her eyes and gave her a slow smile back; her heart skipped. When he looked at her like that….

When her food arrived she realized she was ravenous. She licked her lips in anticipation and reached for the ketchup. Just as she opened it a rowdy scuffle broke out at the table next to her, jostling her elbow and spilling the thick red goo down the front of her denim jacket. Her plate was thrown from the table, shattering with a loud crash on the tile floor of the restaurant, sending her food flying everywhere.

She jumped to her feet and Jack pushed his way past her and grabbed one of the guys—Jason—by his collar. He yanked him to the side, glaring at him as one of their other friends grabbed the other one involved in the joking altercation. "Hey! Watch it, man!" he gave his friend a little shake and then turned toward Deirdre to survey the damage. She snatched up a napkin and began to dab the front of her jacket, and he handed her a few more.

"Do you want to go wash that off in the bathroom?" he asked her, worry at her reaction clouding his eyes. She looked up at him and managed a small smile.

"Yeah. I think I better." She wrinkled her nose and let out a little laugh at the relief in his expression.

"Relax, it's no big deal. It's just ketchup," she reassured him. He smiled hesitantly back at her. The girls at the next table stared at her in disbelief.

"If you say so. I know a lot of girls who would be freaking out right about now," he admitted, still eyeing her warily, as though she would decide to start 'freaking out' any second, and glancing at the other girl—Gretchen—who rolled her eyes and looked away. Deirdre shook her head.

"Nah. I *am* still really hungry, though," she said, eyeing the scattered food regretfully as she continued to wipe at her jacket.

"No problem," he reassured her. "We'll get a new plate." They looked up as the waitress bustled toward them, broom and dustpan in tow. She gathered up the majority of the scattered food and glass pieces in record time and tolerantly agreed to get a replacement dinner going. She eyed Deirdre's jacket with concern.

"You should wash that off right away so it doesn't stain," she said solicitously. Deirdre nodded.

"I know. I was just going to go to the bathroom and take care of it," she said. The waitress chewed her lip.

"There's actually a line at the bathroom right now. Tell you what. Why don't you come and use the employee restroom? Just this once," she offered. Deirdre smiled.

"Thanks!" she agreed. She put her hand on Jack's chest and smiled up at him. "Be right back," she promised, and followed the girl back to the kitchen.

Grease hung heavy in the air back there and Deirdre wasted no time in ducking into the bathroom and seeing to her jacket. She was able to get most of the stain out, but of course the jacket was wet when she finished. Still hungry, she stepped out, looking both ways in the narrow corridor, realizing she couldn't remember which way led back to the dining room. Biting her lip in embarrassment, she turned left and began to walk. She knew she had chosen wrong when she stumbled through a door into a tiny room that could only be the employee lounge. She sucked in a breath and flushed scarlet as she took in the room's other occupant.

A giant young man a few years older than her stood there in a pair of dirty jeans, black boots, and nothing else, a ragged black T-shirt in his hands. He was enormous, six foot six or seven, maybe taller, and powerfully built. It was like walking in on a granite mountain with smooth bronzed skin. As she raised her eyes to his face the room seemed, impossibly, even smaller. His nose was straight and slightly too long, his full lips slightly parted in surprise. His hair was a thick wavy mop, rich dark brown, above a high smooth forehead, falling in tangled waves to his shoulders. His cheekbones and jaw might have been carved of stone, but she saw none of that at first; all her attention was caught by his eyes. They were bright hot blue, blazing almost feverishly in his face, leaving her speechless. Her heart raced and she caught her breath in terror. Those eyes looked right through her, pinning her feet to the floor and she swallowed hard and shivered, suddenly chilled. He stared for a moment, then pulled his shirt on before he spoke.

"Lost?" he asked cryptically. He reached for the dark green cook's apron hanging on a hook nearby and slipped it over his head. She blinked and looked down at the dirty floor, sure the heat in her cheeks would start a fire. She could barely breathe.

"Um, yeah," she replied, tongue-tied. Her stomach flipped, clenching. It was ridiculous that she should be so stunned, unable to breathe and frozen in place. She clamped her jaw shut, fighting the alien feeling. No one had ever affected her like that before; no one had radiated such hidden menace.

"Back the way you came, past the bathroom, and hang a left through the door on the far side," he said, tying the fraying strings behind his back.

"Thanks," she said, still unable to think of anything else to say. His eyes released her and she turned and fled back down the hall, reaching the dining room still flushed and slightly out of breath. Jack looked at her strangely and she murmured some excuse about it being hot back there in the kitchen. He raised his eyebrows and let it go. Courtney gave her a look that Deirdre knew meant she wasn't buying it. Deirdre shook her head slightly—she wasn't going to describe the encounter with Jack there—and Courtney gave an equally circumspect nod, girl-speak for 'talk about it later.' When Deirdre's replacement plate of food arrived she ate every scrap, trying to fill the hollow space in her belly. Jack watched with amusement.

"You weren't kidding when you said you were hungry," he teased. She smiled and shrugged, sipping the last of her soda self-consciously. She noticed none of the other girls had eaten more than half of their plates, even Courtney.

"I skipped lunch," she said, by way of excuse.

Shortly after they finished their food, Courtney and Kyle rose to leave. Courtney waved goodbye to Deirdre and held her hand to her ear in the universal gesture for 'call me!' Deirdre nodded and smiled and leaned back against Jack's side, continuing their conversation, part of her mind worrying over Jack's secret, part still thinking about her encounter with the giant in the back room.

About an hour later they stood up to pay their tab. Jack got it, and she smiled her thanks as he added an extra tip for letting her use the employee bathroom. Feeling a chill as she stood by the open door, she realized she had left her jacket in the booth and went to retrieve it. Jack followed her. She frowned as she stared at the empty booth, still stacked with their dirty plates.

"I must have left it in the back or something," she said, glancing doubtfully toward Jack as she waved to the server.

"Do you mind if I go back and look for my jacket?" she asked politely when the girl came over.

"Knock yourself out," the waitress replied. Smiling at the girl's friendliness, Deirdre went back through the employee door and looked around the bathroom. Her jacket was nowhere to be seen. Deciding not to waste any more time she returned to Jack, glancing into the kitchen on her way back out. The man she had met before was bent over the grill, a spatula in his hand.

"It's nowhere," she said in response to Jack's questioning eyebrow.

"Huh," he grunted, "I guess we'll just tell the waitress. She'll probably find it later and we can come back for it tomorrow, if you want," he suggested. They did that, giving Deirdre's name and number, then left for the night.

Outside in the street she took a few deep breaths of fresh air, clearing the greasiness of the restaurant air from her lungs. It was already getting dark, and the sky was a deep sapphire blue, just starting to sparkle with the first stars of the night. Jack took her elbow lightly as they walked to her car.

"That was fun," she told him, shivering a little as the night cooled. He took off his own brown leather jacket and draped it around her shoulders, his hands lingering for a moment at her neck; heat tingled where his fingertips brushed her skin. She snuggled into the coat, still warm from his body heat and smelling of leather and his cologne. "Mmm, thanks," she murmured. Half a block later they reached her car. He leaned up against it and pulled her in front of him, his hands burning through her clothes at her waist, as though calling her blood to rush toward anywhere he touched. He looked down into her eyes, studying her.

"When do you have to be home, Deirdre?" he asked softly. She just looked at him for a moment and he bent down and kissed her. She slid her hands up his back, drawing him nearer. Kissing

Jack was like summer, hot and deliciously lazy; warmth spread across her skin. He pulled her closer and she sank into him with a sigh. He moved one hand up to tangle in her hair while his other pressed her tightly against him at the small of her back and moved his lips from hers. He angled her head just right and kissed the corner of her mouth down her jaw to her throat, his warm breath and the soft caress of his lips sending hot tendrils into her belly. She wished he would never stop.

"A-hem," someone cleared their throat nearby and they stumbled apart in surprise and embarrassment. Jack's jacket slid from her shoulders. She bent over and snatched it from the ground, then she stood and looked up—and then up some more. The man from the diner stood on the curb, strange burning eyes and all. He towered over both of them, and she revised her original estimate of his size; Jack was six feet tall himself. The stranger smirked at them in the dim light of the nearby streetlight. She pressed her lips together in irritation.

"Yes?" she asked, pulling Jack's jacket over her arm, trying not to fidget under his scrutiny. He just looked at her—through her—with those eyes for a too-long moment, and her heart began to beat harder. She felt her skin heat and she swallowed, unable to look away.

"Are you Deirdre?" he asked finally, and she stood utterly still, stunned at the soft caress he gave her name, involuntarily pulled into his atmosphere again.

"What?" she murmured.

"Are you Deirdre?" he repeated, focused entirely on her, as though Jack didn't exist.

"Yes," she said, a little breathless now. She felt like a gazelle that had inadvertently caught the lion's attention. Terror and something else skittered through the space behind her eyes and clenched her belly.

"Annabelle said you left your jacket. She asked if I would try to catch you before you left," he said, holding out a shapeless bundle. She reached forward and took it from him, then snatched her hand back, nearly dropping the jacket, when an almost electric shock raced up her arm. Startled, he reacted too, clenching his huge hand into a fist for a second before dropping it to his side. His eyes widened almost imperceptibly; if she hadn't been staring into them for the past few seconds she would have missed it. His throat moved as he swallowed. She clenched her hand too as it cramped from a sudden chill, brushing frost crystals from the ends of her fingers into her palm, as though she had thrust her hand into a snowdrift. They stood there like that for almost another full second before Jack grew impatient.

"Well, thanks, pal. We appreciate it," he said, breaking the spell as he moved closer to her, putting his arm possessively around her waist.

The stranger's eyes broke contact with Deirdre's for a split second, following the movement and meeting Jack's gaze. Jack narrowed his eyes and tightened his hold in reaction. "Daemon. My name is Daemon." The young man glanced back to Deirdre.

"Thank you… Daemon," she said quietly, tasting his name like snow on her tongue.

"You're welcome," he said, and smiled, even white teeth flashed against tanned skin. Her breath stopped. There was some-thing dangerous, almost predatory, in that smile. She just stood there, her pulse pounding, breathless, and then he turned and walked back toward the diner. As soon as his back was turned she felt a distinct sense of release and leaned a little harder against Jack, confusion and doubt clouding her eyes. What was wrong with her? She swallowed, uncomfortable.

After a moment Jack let out a breath. "What a weird guy," he said. He took both jackets from her and held hers so she could put it on.

"Yeah," she murmured absently, threading her arms through the sleeves, shivering from the cold spot the damp part of the jacket made where it rested against her shirt. Jack didn't notice this time. He put his own coat back on and reached for the door handle. Settling into the seat, she looked up as Jack bent down and leaned in. "Do you really have to go home, Deirdre? We could go for a walk or something. You could come over to my place," he offered, but the moment had passed, for both of them. Deirdre was still shaken up from the strange encounter, and if he would acknowledge it, so was Jack.

"I should go. I haven't even started my homework yet," she said, by way of excuse. He grimaced.

"Me either," he admitted. He leaned in for another kiss, lingering and sweet, and she almost changed her mind. She pulled away regretfully.

"See you tomorrow, Jack," she said. He smiled into her eyes.

"Goodnight, Deirdre." He stepped back from the vehicle. She flipped on the lights, illuminating his lean figure as she pulled out of the space into the street. He stood watching her for a moment, then turned and walked back toward the diner and his own car as she pulled away.

***

Jack

Thursday

Jack had a secret, and the only other person who knew about it was Alastair. He leaned over the bathroom counter, staring at himself in the mirror. Why couldn't Alastair have stayed in a coma? He felt instantly guilty for thinking it. He had wanted Al to wake up, didn't he? He had studied for a year in preparation for

16

it. Still… what would he eventually remember about that night? Or had he already remembered? That thought haunted him, made his blood run cold. Not that he wouldn't have faced the consequences if Al *had* made it home in one piece that night, but now that it had been nearly a whole year…. Jack shook himself and stood. He had lived with the possibility for a month.

He had finally asked Deirdre out, to try to keep tabs on the situation, or so he told himself. And then, just to complicate things, the more time he spent with her, the more he remembered how much he liked her. She was smart and great company and devastatingly beautiful, almost unapproachably so, and some-how… fragile. She made him want to take care of her, to protect her. Of course, he had always known those things about her, had always enjoyed it when she hung out with him and Al. Often more than he had enjoyed his own dates on those occasions, to the irritation of many girls. He left the bathroom and looked down the hall. Her long black hair hung down her back in thick waves to her slender waist, making her easy to pick out of the crowd. He called her name and his heart jumped when she turned and smiled at him.

Her dark blue eyes captured him as he caught up to her, and his skin tingled electrically when he touched her, even in the most casual way. He felt the now-familiar surge of frustration at the elusive feeling that he never quite had her undivided atten-tion. He wasn't used to girls being indifferent to his presence, but Deirdre… she always seemed distant, even while she walked and talked with him, as though her mind was elsewhere, thinking of other things.

He asked her to dinner and watched her carefully, unsure of her response; she turned him down as often as she accepted. A surge of warmth and anticipation filled him with pleasure when she agreed this time, adding an unexpected bounce to his step. He walked her to her car and bent to kiss her goodbye. She pulled away almost immediately. That was another thing. It hurt his pride to be so easily resistible, especially since even that small contact left him breathless, wanting her. He stared after her as she drove away.

Jason was waiting at his car. He looked at Jack's face as he approached, his eyes narrowing. "What's up?" he asked, noting his friend's frustrated expression. Jack just looked at him and shook his head, unwilling to answer. He unlocked the doors and stashed his backpack as he fished his duffle bag out of the mess in the back and walked with him to the locker room. He hoped the coach wouldn't be too hard on them today, but it was a futile desire. They had a game tomorrow, after all. Jason fished a football out of the bin by the door as they headed out onto the grass.

Jason jogged out to the middle of the field and raised his arm for a throw. He whipped it hard and fast but it was coming up short. Jack ran forward and jumped, his large hands closing over the ball and tucking it into his side as he landed in a crouch. He threw it back and Jason snatched it out of the air right in front of him. Back and forth they threw and ran until they were both breathing heavy and sweating. When they were warmed up coach had them running plays for another hour. Jack easily caught everything Jason threw at him, a well-oiled machine that had the coach smug and jovial by the end of practice. He made them run a few laps, just for kicks, and let them go. Jack rubbed his sweaty face on his shoulder and tossed his dripping hair out of his eyes, grinning at Jason.

"You ready?" he asked, taking air deep into his lungs as he tried to catch his breath. Jason gulped air and nodded, catching the already damp hem of his T-shirt and wiping his face with it.

"Yeah, I guess so. They won't know what hit 'em," he grinned as he followed Jack out of the locker room and to his car. They got in and Jack drove carelessly toward home. When they got there Jason walked with him from the car, teasing. "Better get cleaned up. Deirdre won't kiss you if you look like that," he ribbed as he leaned against the faded siding outside Jack's door. Jack's easy mood evaporated and he clenched his jaw, even as his heart thumped at the thought of her. Jason saw his expression and raised his eyebrows and shook his head.

"She's not coming?" he guessed. Jack looked away, unlocking the door.

"She's coming," he said.

"Then what?" Jason prodded. Jack shrugged.

"Nothing," he said. Jason just stood there for a minute, then shook his head and left, walking down the street to his own house to get cleaned up.

Jack stripped the rest of the way and stepped under the steaming hot spray. The heat and pressure of the water massaged his tired muscles and relaxed him, and he soaped down, trying to put Jason's words out of his mind. Whatever his friend thought, he was not in love with Deirdre. No way. It was just the weird situation. No matter what, he couldn't let Alastair tell anyone what had happened that night. That was all Deirdre was: a means to an end. The hot water caressed his skin and her haunting blue eyes floated through his mind and he closed his eyes, imagining her smiling up at him. His heart squeezed in his chest.

He shut the image out with a curse, throwing a punch at the tiles of the shower wall. One of the tiles cracked and fell to the tub at his feet and he looked at his hand, shaking it in surprise. Red blossomed from his knuckles, running down his arm and dripping off his elbow into the drain. He turned off the water and dried himself, wrapping the towel around his hand until the bleeding stopped. He got dressed, ran his fingers and some gel through his hair, and shaved swiftly but carefully.

He returned to the tub and frowned at the tile lying in the bottom of the basin and the naked brown spot on the wall with irregular knots of tile adhesive, long dried where it had been before he hit it. *Shouldn't leave it like that*, he thought to himself. He put out his hand and reached down inside himself and opened the conduit to his power the way his father had shown him before he was killed. Hot magic tingled along his veins.

He opened his eyes and directed a thin, controlled stream toward the broken tile, bending it to his will. Before his eyes it knit back together and he lifted it back into place, sealing it to the wall with a tiny bit more magic. He lowered his hand and examined his work. Good as new. He turned the magic on himself and held it over the cuts on his knuckles. After a moment he flexed his hand, testing it. Again, good as new, though it still hurt beneath the superficial healing. He turned away. A knot of anticipation curled up in his stomach when he thought of Deirdre, and he went to his car, not caring that he would be far too early.

At the restaurant, he chose a seat at a booth in the back where he had a good view of the street. Jason was holding down the next table for the rest of the group. A bunch of them were supposed to come, and they began to trickle in, a few at a time. Jack couldn't help glancing often at the clock above the counter, and he caught Jason smirking at him more than once. He glared at his friend. Courtney and her date, Kyle, came in and sat across from him; then everything faded as Deirdre walked past the windows.

She approached the door and before he realized it he was on his feet, getting the door for her. He couldn't help but smile at her—she was shockingly lovely and his heart thumped when her soft red mouth curved into a smile just for him; he muttered some inane comment and guided her back to the booth, pulling her in next to him. Her skin was warm beneath his hand and he could barely take his eyes off her. He was about to offer her a soda when she grabbed his hand and traced her fingers across his knuckles where the cuts would have been if he had not healed them.

The burn beneath the surface faded under the touch of her cool fingers, but his heartbeat raced in shock when she said, "Did you hurt your hand?" She seemed surprised that there were actually no cuts there.

He lied quickly, putting just the right amount of curiosity into his voice, "No, why?" and let her explain the oddity away herself. He had found that was usually the best policy when someone saw something they shouldn't have: deny and dissemble. She was further distracted when the waitress came over for their order. Deirdre took only seconds to order, still somewhat preoccupied. Jack took a few minutes to wonder how she could possibly have seen through the healing. She shouldn't have. A pang of worry pulsed through him. Had Alastair said something? But no, even if he had, that wouldn't explain it. He shook it off—time enough to worry about it later. He tightened his arm around Deirdre's waist, enjoying having her close. It felt good to have her there, right somehow. He thought back to what Jason had said, troubled.

Their food arrived and she reached for the ketchup, opening the bottle just as Jason jumped up from the next table trying to avoid the splashing soda he had tipped over. He stumbled into their booth, bumping Deirdre's arm and sending her plate over the edge of the table. Deirdre jumped up and Jack followed, grabbing Jason and dragging him back to his feet, steadying him as he glanced around for the waitress. She was already on her way with a towel, broom, and dustpan to help them clean up the mess. Jack turned to Deirdre. She was swiping at a large ketchup stain that dripped down the front of her jacket. He grabbed a few more napkins and handed them to her, wishing he could make the stain just disappear. She would probably stomp out and not speak to him for days.

"You should probably go wash that off in the bathroom," he suggested, bracing himself for her wrath. She looked up at him, and he was surprised to see that she was laughing. Her eyes crinkled at the corners and her mouth curved in a smile. Relief washed over him. She wasn't angry, or even upset. He sat back down in the booth, and picked at his hamburger and fries, waiting for her to return. Courtney had the ketchup bottle in her hand and was valiantly trying to extract some of the thick glop from the bottle.

"Typical," she said, exasperated as she hit the bottom a third time without result. "When you want it, it won't come out, and when you don't..." she waved a hand at Deirdre's retreating figure as Kyle handed her a knife, grinning at her mild tirade. Jack grinned, too.

Deirdre returned soon, uncharacteristically flushed and nervous-looking. He wondered what had occurred to shatter her composure. She claimed it was simply the heat from the kitchen, but he wondered. By the look in her eye, so did Courtney. The server brought her replacement plate and he watched in amusement as she finished it all. He wondered where she put it; her body was so slender and fragile-looking; all the other girls he had dated worked hard at starving themselves to keep such a figure. It was disconcerting to watch someone so small put away so much food. They sat comfortably for a while longer, then stood up to pay the tab. At the door, she wondered where her jacket had gone. He didn't remember seeing it since the ketchup incident.

She looked for it for a few minutes, but they ended up just leaving her name and phone number, hoping the server would find it and give her a call. Out in the street, she was shivering, her ivory skin erupting in goosebumps. He shrugged out of his jacket and laid it over her shoulders, his hands lingering at her neck for a moment, savoring the silken texture of her heavy black hair and the softness of her skin. When they reached her car his heart began to beat faster, anticipation heating his blood. He pulled her into his arms and she came willingly, all soft skin and smelling of raspberries and vanilla.

He kissed her slowly, hesitantly at first, then more confidently when she responded by pulling herself closer, leaning into him. Her hands caressed his back, and he gently opened her mouth with his. She tasted like honey and wine, and she made him hungry; he wondered if she could feel his heart race. He pulled her slender body more firmly against him and raised one hand to the back of her head to tangle in her glorious hair, kissing down the soft skin of her throat over her pulse, rewarded by her soft sigh of pleasure.

"A-hem." He released her suddenly, startled by the extremely unwelcome interruption. He fought to control his breathing, not to give away how much she moved him as he eyed the stranger. A young giant smirked at him from the curb, and Jack frowned in irritation. The stranger offered Deirdre her jacket, but instead of leaving after she took it, he lingered, staring at her. Jack narrowed his eyes and stepped forward, annoyed, just as the stranger shifted a little.

Jack paused, his awareness focusing. There was something extremely odd about him, wrong somehow. His aura was too thin, for one thing, almost non-existent, and, even more strangely, it was blood red. Also, there was the way he held himself, standing on the balls of his feet, his limbs loose and ready. Jack had seen posture like that somewhere before, but he couldn't quite remember…. Frowning in concentration, he put his arm protectively around Deirdre.

The stranger flashed a feral grin and finally walked away with predatory grace. Jack kept trying to put his finger on the elusive recognition he felt. Absently, he took the jackets from Deirdre and helped her back into hers. He put his own back on and opened her car door for her. Her deep eyes captured him, and suddenly she had his undivided attention again; he found himself unwilling to let her go.

He took her hand as she got into the car, and her fingers were icy. He massaged her hand for a moment, trying to warm it, then he had to let go so she could shut the car door. He leaned in and kissed her goodbye, lingering, wanting her to stay more than ever, knowing she wouldn't. He stepped back from the car and watched her pull out, then turned away, toward his own vehicle. She had mentioned studying, and his mind returned to the enigma of the stranger, Daemon. He couldn't help feeling that he should have recognized him, somehow—that there was some clue he had overlooked. Perhaps he should do some 'studying' of his own....

The house was dark, as usual. No doubt his mother was already in bed. She would be gone again in the morning before he got up; meanwhile, he needed to be very, very quiet while he asked Shasta about Daemon. His mother wouldn't appreciate finding out her son was a Sorcerer, and he would never allow it; for a mortal, that knowledge was incredibly dangerous. When a mortal knew, they tended to be more aware, to see things they shouldn't. The legacy was his father's, and his mother had never known about him either. She still thought his father had died in a fire. A pang of guilt hit him and he thought of Alastair.

Jack went straight to his room and closed and spell-locked the door. He shoved the rolled up towel against the crack at the bottom of the door to block out any light; if his mother woke up he wanted her to think the room was dark, that he was asleep. He took a small wooden box from his desk drawer and withdrew an oddly fashioned ring from it, slipping it on his finger. With a Word he invoked the circle he had drawn on the floor in white paint mixed with salt beneath his carpet. The circle would do many things, but usually he used it for silence. It was probably the first thing Shasta had taught him after his father had died when he was twelve. That, and hammering home the essential need for secrecy.

The familiar golden haze rose around him and closed in a dome just above his head. He sat cross-legged on the floor in the middle and slipped the ring on his finger. It was made of bone, pale and smooth and about ¾ of an inch wide, etched with odd designs and symbols, inside and out, and it held his only means of communication with a ghost: his tutor, Shasta.

After a moment the ghost appeared, sitting in front of him. Jack caught his breath. "Don't *do* that!" he snarled. The ghost had appeared looking just like Deirdre had looked tonight. The apparition smiled seductively. "As you command," it murmured in Deirdre's soft voice, then reverted to its usual form, a powerful middle-aged man in 1920s finery, with dark hair and eyes, high cheekbones, and thin lips. "She's on your mind again," he commented, still using Deirdre's voice. Jack glared and it smirked at him.

"Actually, I called you to ask about this one," Jack said, conjuring an image of his encounter with Daemon on the palm of his hand in careful detail, including, as far as possible, voice and mannerisms. The ghost looked bored.

"What about him?" he said.

"I feel like I recognized him..." Jack explained, "...or something about him."

"And so you should," the ghost replied, but didn't elaborate further. Jack sighed in exasperation.

"Well? Tell me," he prompted. The ghost curled his aristocratic lip.

"If I did that you would never learn," it prevaricated.

"I know I should know, okay? Come on. I've learned all this stuff in the abstract. No substitute for experience. Just tell me," he said, leaning forward across his knees. It shook its head.

"Catalog," it insisted. Jack rolled his eyes.

"Fine. Huge. Young. Intense eyes. Ready posture. Thin red aura. Satisfied?" he said. The ghost raised his eyebrows.

"Anything else?" it prompted. Jack frowned.

"Like what?" he said, sitting back and shifting his legs, exasperated. It was the ghost's turn to roll his eyes.

"I'll give you a hint. Any weirdness in temperature?" it prompted. Jack pursed his lips, trying to remember. He remembered Deirdre, who had been standing closer, shivering, and the chill in her hand after she had touched Daemon's fingers, and the answer came to him all at once. He froze in stunned silence. The ghost smirked at him nodding.

"Shapeshifter..." Jack breathed. Then in one smooth motion he leapt to his feet, pacing back and forth, restless from a swift surge of adrenaline, still careful not to break the circle. He stopped suddenly and wheeled on the captive spirit. "Did you know there was a Shapeshifter here? What's it doing? How can I tell what kind it is?" He reeled off the first questions that came into his head. The ghost watched his display of impatient energy with disapproval, but launched into scholar mode anyway.

"No. I hadn't sensed one, but as you know my range is limited, and they're extremely rare. I can't imagine what it wants here. He may just be wandering through. They're often nomadic, if you remember. Very few stay anywhere for long. You can tell what kind it—*he*—is by using your Mage sense. Next time you see him, alter your Sight like I taught you—extend your senses into the spiritual realm. His beast will show up there, like an afterimage superimposed over his physical form..." The ghost leaned forward intently then. "If you do that, make absolutely sure he doesn't catch you at it—his beast can see you there just as easily as you can see him. And *don't* touch him—he'll know what you are, if he doesn't already," he cautioned. Jack shook his head.

"I don't use magic outside the circle," he claimed, pushing the memory of fixing the tile deep where he hoped Shasta wouldn't pick it up.

The ghost shook his head, plainly disbelieving, but only said, "Good. Let's get to work." They practiced different permutations involving extending his Sight for almost an hour after that, his magic hot and tingling underneath his skin, until Jack felt stretched and drained. He had kept the circle up and consulted with the ghost long enough for one night, and it had been a long day. Shasta stirred, sensing Jack's fatigue.

"That's enough for now," he smiled, and a red sheen coated his eyes as he faded from view. "Don't forget to feed me," he reminded him, a veiled threat in his tone. Jack clenched his jaw distastefully.

"I won't," he said and walked toward his desk. The circle dropped as soon as he touched the translucent barrier, and the ghost vanished at the same time. Jack took a short thin-bladed knife about the size of his little finger, handle and all, from a small, plain wooden box on the desk. The narrow bone handle had the same strange markings as the matching ring. He inserted the silver blade beneath the ring and drew it back out, shallowly slicing his finger. Blood welled up beneath it, and he smeared the outer surface of the ring with it and twisted it on his finger, making sure the entire surface, inside and out, was coated with his blood. He waited a moment for the hot tingle of magic to die away, then removed the ring and placed it and the blade back in the box. They had soaked up his blood and were miraculously unstained, clean and white, and no cut marred his finger. He could still feel the burn of the cut beneath his skin, however, and he knew from experience it would take about a day for it to fade.

He shut the box and sealed it with a Word, putting it back in the drawer with a bunch of broken pencils and other miscellaneous junk.

***

Daemon

Thursday

Daemon slid his motorcycle into the slot behind the dumpster at the diner. He was late, again. His clothes were still grimy with sawdust and drywall powder mixed with sweat and water and oil from cleaning his tools. At least he didn't have to work that site anymore. He and half the crew were starting work on the new wing of the high school in the morning. He would no longer be late for this job: Annabelle would be pleased. He grabbed his pack from where it was secured with a frayed bungee cord just behind the black leather seat. He buzzed the back door and Annabelle let him in and ran off, in a hurry because she was doing it all since he was late. He scrubbed down his hands and face and put his tool belt in the locker in the break room. He stripped off his filthy T-shirt and extracted the fresh one before shoving his pack in there too. He was just about to put the clean but ragged T-shirt on when the door opened and the most beautiful girl he had ever seen walked in on him.

She was slender and fragile-looking, with perfect curves in all the right places and not very tall, but then, he towered over everyone. Her blue-black hair hung down her back in thick lustrous waves to her waist. Her skin was a dewy ivory, and her enormous eyes were sapphire blue framed by thick, carbon black lashes. Her oval face was graced by high cheekbones and a delicate rounded chin, high forehead, and generous mouth. She bit

28

her lower lip, reddening it and revealing straight white teeth. A rosy blush colored her cheeks as she stared at him. She smelled of raspberries and vanilla and herself, and his beast stirred, wanting a taste; before he could stop it his magic chilled the air and she shivered. After a moment he recovered, reining it back with an iron hand, pulling the shirt down over his head. She must have come from the dining room; he knew they hadn't hired anyone new and she for sure wasn't dressed for serving.

"Lost?" he guessed, and her blush deepened as she nodded.

"Yeah," she said in a soft breathless voice that grabbed him in the gut. Covering his reaction he grabbed his cook's apron from the hook and put it on as he gave her directions back to the dining room. He stood there and watched her walk swiftly away, wishing he would have asked her name. Her scent still lingered in the air and he inhaled it, memorizing. His beast stirred again and he shook it off and headed for the kitchen. Annabelle would be cursing his name if he didn't hurry.

He cooked food until almost closing time, when Annabelle stuck her head into the kitchen. "Hey, Daemon, would you do me a favor?" she asked. He turned and nodded. She held out a wad of denim. "Some girl was in here and couldn't find her jacket—would you see if you can catch her? She just walked out. Name was, um, Deirdre. Pretty brunette." He took the jacket, immediately recognizing the scent floating off it underneath the stronger odor of ketchup mixed with a faint hint of someone else, male. Deirdre. It suited her. He raised his eyebrow at Annabelle and she grinned. She was forever trying to fix him up, and he could never tell her why it would never happen. Still, that was one beautiful girl. Another glimpse wouldn't hurt.

He removed the apron and walked through the restaurant to the front door, tracking her easily. On the street she had turned left. He looked over and saw her at the edge of a streetlamp's glow, making out with a blond guy near a blue Toyota. Lucky jerk.

He walked up, perversely pleased to interrupt them, clearing his throat loudly. He held out her jacket and when she reached for it her fingertips almost brushed his. He was unprepared for the electric surge of magic that pulsed between them as his beast came alert. There was something... *different...* about her, something he had never encountered before. He stared at her, trying to figure it out. The blond guy grew impatient and stepped up, putting his arm around her slender waist. The beast growled within and Daemon wrestled it back down with an effort. What the hell was going on with it?

"Well, thanks, pal. We appreciate it," the blond guy said, momentarily breaking Daemon's concentration. He blinked and took a breath, which was a mistake, because he just inhaled more of her intoxicating scent.

"Daemon," he said, still staring at her, the boy all but forgotten again. "My name is Daemon." Her captivating eyes looked up at him.

"Thank you, Daemon," she said, and her voice caressed the night. He would have liked to stay and listen to her forever, and his beast agreed—it was practically purring. Instead, he tore himself away with a parting grimace and left them. He ducked between the buildings and watched them for a moment longer, cursing himself. Why the self-flagellation? A girl like that would never even look at him—especially if she knew what he was; why watch her kiss someone else? But he couldn't help it—she fascinated him, and any view was better than none.

The kid helped her on with her jacket and into her car—at least the make-out was over. He watched the waterfall of her long black hair as she freed it from the jacket, wondering what it would feel like to touch it. The boy leaned into the car for another long kiss and Daemon felt the growl rising from deep in his chest. He cursed softly, pulling back on his beast, but it was too little, too late. Coming after her had been a supremely bad idea, and the full moon wasn't helping, but it was too late for hindsight. He couldn't have known it would react to her so strongly. He had kept it chained for too long, and now it was coming.

The tremors took him and he fell to his knees. Swiftly he stripped with shaking hands, leaving his clothes behind some milk crates stacked in the alley. All control fled and his bones cracked and shifted. It felt good, like stretching after a long stiff night as his body settled into his other form, but it was terrifying, too. He would remember only snatches when the Change wore off, and he had even less idea than usual what the beast would do tonight. He could at least make sure it—he—wouldn't kill anyone. He used the last few minutes he had as himself to incant the spell his father had taught him before he left. It would chain the beast, at least a little, curbing its more violent tendencies. The beast would wander, and it might track prey, but with the spell locked in place it would not kill or eat. Also, it would remain unseen by anyone except another of the Tears of the Gods: a Sorcerer or other magical being like him.

Keeping the secret was paramount to his kind; they were almost wiped out because so many had failed to do so; they had been hunted almost to extinction by almost every other kind of Tear, simply because most could not control the beast, and the beast didn't care about secrets. Most chained themselves with iron when the beast came upon them, but that wasn't an option for Daemon. No chains would hold his other form, or even his human one. However, Daemon's father had been a friend to a Sorcerer, who had developed the spell for him, and he had passed it on to his only son. The spell and the beast: his father's bitter legacy.

With a low growl it was finished and he rose to his enormous feet, free.

***

Deirdre

Thursday

Deirdre walked into the dark house, grabbed an apple from the refrigerator and walked upstairs to her room. She paused to listen at Alastair's door for a moment, then, hearing nothing out of the ordinary, she continued down the hall. She made herself comfortable in the stretchy tank top and knit pants she would sleep in and got out her homework. She stacked her books on her desk and fished her cell phone out of the pocket of the jeans she had been wearing, then threw them in the hamper along with her damp jacket. She opened her notebook as she speed-dialed Courtney's number. The line picked up on the first ring.

"Deirdre! Hi!" the other girl greeted her cheerfully.

"Hey, Court. How's it going?" Deirdre asked, as she began working on her math homework and crunching on her apple. She hated geometry; unfortunately it was the bulk of her homework tonight.

"*Great*—I am *so* glad you called. I have to tell you *everything*. Hold on while I get off the line with Gretchen!" She was gone before Deirdre could respond. After a minute, the line clicked back open. "You there?" Courtney asked.

"Still here. So tell me—how was Kyle? You guys looked like you were having a good time—did he kiss you?" Deirdre asked, smiling.

"We had a *really* good time! After dinner he took me back to his house. He lives with his dad and two uncles—his dad's brothers—in this *gorgeous* little loft south of downtown. The main floor is all open, this *huge* living room with a fireplace big enough to *walk* into, I *swear*, and the *coziest* little kitchen. There are gigantic windows everywhere, like walls of glass looking out over the lake, you know?" Courtney paused for breath and Deirdre 'mm-hmmed' to let her know she was still listening.

"Anyway, you go up these totally open stairs—no railing, you could just fall right off—*seriously*! And then there's this *gorgeous* wrought-iron balcony, like, that looks over the downstairs, and behind that are these cozy little bedrooms. They all have their own space, right? And Kyle showed me his room—he has this *huge* skylight that *opens* in the slanted roof over part of his room, where his bed is, so you can just lay there and look out the skylight right from the bed. It's all gold and black—*so* cool.

"So, after he gave me the tour we sat around with his dad and uncles—apparently his dad and one of his uncles are architects, I'm not sure about the other one—but they have offices in Minneapolis, and they work all over the world and they can bring their work home whenever they want. I guess they designed this place and built it, and they'll live in it until they feel like building something else—Kyle's lived *everywhere*." Courtney paused for a moment and Deirdre took the opportunity to comment.

"Sounds amazing. So they're cool?" she asked, starting Courtney off again.

"Totally. And his dad doesn't look at *all* old enough to be his dad. He's totally hot—he looks like he could be Kyle's older brother or something." She giggled, and Deirdre made a mock-disapproving sound, then laughed with her.

"Anyway," Courtney continued her story, "after a while— actually it was almost an hour, they were really nice, like I said— but then Kyle said it was probably time to take me home, so we left. He drove me home, and he parked and got out of the car to walk me up to my door, right? I was about to walk inside—I had my hand on the doorknob and everything and I didn't think he was going to kiss me after all, so I was kinda bummed, y'know? Because it was a really great night. But then he said my name, and I turned back to him, and he just stepped up really close and he did!" Courtney sighed with pleasure, remembering.

"And how was it?" Deirdre asked.

"It was WOW," Courtney said, sighing again. Deirdre smiled.

"Awesome," she said. Courtney restarted after a short pause, homage to her first kiss with Kyle. "So tell, how was your night? And, oh yeah—what was the deal when you came back from the bathroom? You were all flustered or something," she prompted.

"Yeah, that was really weird," Deirdre said, and told her all about her encounter with Daemon. "Okay, so I went to the employee restroom, to clean off the ketchup. It was back in this little hallway between two doors that looked *exactly* the same, and when I came out, I couldn't remember which way to go. I mean, I wasn't paying attention when the waitress brought me back there—I was just worried about my jacket. So when I came out of the bathroom, I must have turned the wrong way, because I ended up in the employee break room. I guess it was the break room." Deirdre paused and took a breath, remembering.

"Anyway, there was a guy in there, the cook, must have been, and he was changing in there or something, because he was half naked—"

Courtney interrupted with a shocked noise and giggled, "Which half?" Deirdre rolled her eyes and continued.

"Courtney, *please*. The top half, okay? Anyway, he was *huge*, probably *seven feet tall*—I kid you not—and *built*, like a linebacker, you know, muscles *everywhere*. And he was *gorgeous*, too, his face—I mean, like Bradley James gorgeous, but dangerous somehow. *And* he had these blue eyes, these *eyes*, that were really strange, *burning*, hot—I can't even describe them. He was *terrifying*. I about peed my pants. Anyway, he told me how to get back to the dining room, and I just *ran*." Deirdre let an embarrassed laugh into the phone and Courtney made appropriately shocked and sympathetic noises. She turned Deirdre's story over for a moment.

34

"So, *gorgeous*, huh? Does Jack have competition?" Courtney asked. Deirdre snorted.

"Yeah, right. Did you not hear the part about how he was beyond scary?" Deirdre said. It was Courtney's turn to 'mm-hmm' this time, only she wasn't agreeing. Deirdre sighed, exasperated. "*No*. There is *no* competition for Jack. Jack is… well, he's *Jack*." Deirdre insisted, but Courtney kept teasing her. Deirdre eventually just stonewalled her for a minute, and she finally let it go.

"So, did *Jack*"—she put the same emphasis on his name that Deirdre had a moment ago—"kiss *you* goodnight?" Courtney asked. Deirdre smiled to herself.

"Yes, he did—when he walked me to my car," Deirdre told her.

"And?" Courtney prompted when she didn't continue right away.

"Come on, Courtney. You know I would be content to kiss Jack for *days*." They laughed together, then Deirdre continued. "I think he was going to ask me to come over or do something else, but then that guy interrupted us." Deirdre blushed, remembering.

"He *did*?" Courtney squawked in surprise.

"I know. He was just returning my jacket, which I accidentally left there, but he *totally* ruined the moment," Deirdre told her, a note of irritation creeping into her voice. Courtney giggled.

"I *bet*," she said, and Deirdre shook her head.

They continued to chat about other things, and Deirdre finished her math homework and moved on to language arts. She said goodbye to Courtney and got out her laptop and booted it up. She worked a little on her essay that was due in a few days, then sat back and rubbed her eyes. She looked over at the clock and rolled her shoulders, trying to loosen the cramp that had developed between her shoulder blades from leaning over the desk so long.

She closed her eyes for a moment, and then she must have fallen asleep in her chair, because she had a little dream. She saw her LA classroom, clear as day, and the look of panic on Courtney's face as the teacher smugly handed out vocabulary test sheets and told them to begin. She came back to herself with a start and looked around the room uneasily. No longer tired, she frowned to herself and got out her vocabulary list and reviewed it, just in case, feeling silly. It was just a dream.

Crawling into bed, she let her thoughts drift. She wondered what Jack was doing, if he was in bed too, or doing his homework, or maybe, just maybe, thinking of her. She smiled at the thought and closed her eyes. She dreamed again, of Jack this time, pacing back and forth within a dome of golden light, talking to a dark-haired man who looked a little blurry around the edges somehow. She woke up again, almost right away, according to the clock. What a weird image. She sighed and closed her eyes again, and slowly fell into a restless dream-filled sleep.

Chapter 2

Jack

Friday

Jack woke early, with the sun in his eyes. He threw on his sweats and stepped out for a run. His mother's car was already gone, leaving a telltale dry spot on the driveway; it had rained in the night. The air felt heavy but smelled clean. He stretched a little then began down the driveway, into the street. The sidewalks were uneven or non-existent, and the morning traffic was light, so he preferred to run along the edge of the road. He arbitrarily decided on a new route today, jogging left when he would normally have turned right at the intersection down the street. This way would take him toward the downtown area and along the lake.

He had gone a mile or so when he saw it, a man-shaped patch of ice frosting the ground behind a park bench. He pulled up short, breathing hard, and stared at it in shock. The Shapeshifter had Changed *last night*? He looked around carefully; the ice was already melting, and there was no sign of anyone nearby. He wished he would have checked the moon schedule. Most Changers locked themselves up when the moon was full, not that they *had* to Change, but because it was more difficult *not* to. At the very least he should have picked a less populated spot; there were miles of woods around the edges of town where he would meet no one. And how *had* he met no one? Jack's own magic safeguards would have awakened him if the Shifter's magic was making waves. So he hadn't killed anyone, but hadn't been locked up, had shifted *in town*... this was getting stranger by the second. How could he have let his beast loose around people without risking his secret—or worse, hurting someone? Who *was* this Shapeshifter? He wondered how he could get another look at him without him knowing; maybe the enigma had something to do with what kind of animal he became. Maybe he was something harmless, like a hamster. Jack grinned to himself.

Jack shook his head, decided he had run long enough, and turned back toward home to get ready for school.

Jack picked up Jason on his way in, as usual. He was yawning and looking a little scruffy around the edges.

"You okay?" Jack asked him after he yawned for the hundredth time.

"Yeah, man. I just didn't get much sleep," Jason said, stifling another yawn.

"How come?" Jack asked, turning into the lot.

"Umph," he yawned again before he answered. "Gretchen called late and she wanted to stay up talking and talking.... Girls are a lot of work, man." He ran his hand through his hair. Jack laughed at him, and Jason gave him an injured look.

"Well, hey, what about you? You look pretty well rested. Doesn't Deirdre demand a decent chunk of your time? Losing your touch?" Jason mocked. Jack grimaced.

"Maybe. And no, Deirdre's not like that," Jack said, scowling a little. Jason nodded.

"Well, in my humble opinion, *that's* a girl worth hanging on to," he mumbled, and stumbled out of the car and made a beeline for the pop machine and a heavily caffeinated soda. Jack watched him go, then levered himself out of the car and grabbed his backpack. He hitched it over his shoulder and walked toward the school, preoccupied. A girl worth hanging onto, indeed. Provided you could get hold of her in the first place.

He stared curiously as he passed several construction vehicles parked on the lawn near the side entrance he usually favored. Wasn't it kind of late in the year to start that kind of work? He put it out of his mind as he walked down the hall toward his locker. He rounded the corner and stopped short, just looking for a moment when he saw her, leaning against his locker, her backpack sitting on the floor by her feet. She was a vision in a casual knit dress that skimmed her tempting curves in a tan color that made her skin glow. Her black hair fell in smooth waves to her waist, and little black slippers encased her feet. His gut clenched and he felt a little breathless.

What if he really was falling for her? he thought as his heart pounded in his chest and the raw emotion surged through him. *Would that really be so bad?* he asked himself. *Yes! You're a Sorcerer, dimwit. A human girl? Not smart.* He tried unsuccessfully to shove the feeling away, no longer able to deny to himself the effect her presence had on him. Her attention was engrossed in the activity down the hall, where several burly construction workers were setting up do-not-cross lines of tape and unrolling huge sheets of plastic. He approached her and touched her shoulder; she jumped a little, then looked up at him and smiled. His heart thumped and the rest of the world faded away.

"Hey," he said, smiling back at her, finally getting around to wondering what she was doing there. She had never sought him out at his locker before.

"Hi," she said warmly, moving out of his way so he could open it. He made himself turn away, somehow soothed and stirred up all at once in her company. "I was waiting for you…." She laughed a little and looked up at him. "I guess that's obvious." A pretty blush colored her cheek. He shuffled his books around his locker, grabbed the ones he needed, and hitched it closed, heart pounding.

"Not that I'm complaining," he said, watching her curiously, "but why?" he asked. He looked down into her bottomless indigo eyes, just now noticing the dark smudges beneath them. She bit her lip and shrugged.

"I don't know. I just wanted to see you, I guess...." She blushed again. He raised his eyebrows at her and warmth flooded through him.

"Well, *that* is a great reason," he smiled at her, and he couldn't help himself, he reached out and touched her face, tracing her jaw with his thumb. Was it his imagination or did she tremble? He stepped closer, drawn by an invisible cord. "You look tired," he murmured, tucking a stray lock of hair behind her shoulder.

"I had a lot of strange dreams last night," she admitted with a shrug. He wanted to just leave with her, play hooky for the day, go somewhere, just the two of them. He was shocked at the strength of that impulse. He was on the verge of asking her what she thought of the idea when they were interrupted.

"Oh, geez, get a room!" Courtney barreled up to them and grabbed Deirdre's hand. "I have *got* to talk to you *right now!*" She tugged her away. Deirdre frowned and resisted, taking back her hand. Courtney scowled. "I'm serious! It's important!" she insisted. Deirdre sighed and glanced back up at Jack. She shrugged and entwined his fingers briefly with hers. His skin tingled at her touch.

"See you later?" she asked reluctantly.

"Lunch?" he asked, wondering if he could wait that long; he let her go when she nodded. She picked up her backpack and walked gracefully after Courtney down the hall. They didn't go far before Courtney stopped her and started talking rapidly and gesturing toward the construction crew. Deirdre looked uninvolved in the conversation at first, but Jack could see her posture change after a moment and suddenly Courtney had her undivided attention. They both focused on the construction crew and Deirdre suddenly gave a start of surprise. Jack followed her gaze to see what had made her react like that and gave a startled jerk of his own.

Standing in the middle of the corridor, just a few feet from Deirdre and Courtney, was Daemon. Jack stepped toward them protectively, but then stopped short. This might be the perfect opportunity to use his Sight and get some answers. The Shifter hadn't seen him yet, and Jack looked over his shoulder surreptitiously. No one was nearby—they wouldn't see anything even if they were. He reached inside for the warm well of power and channeled his magic into his Sight. Almost everything faded, but standing in the hall was an enormous… no, it couldn't be. *That's* not *a hamste*r.... He stared for a long moment, then someone slapped him on the back. He blinked and shut it down, returning abruptly to the real world. Kyle had his arm draped across Jack's shoulder.

"Hey, man. What are the girls so intent about?" he asked, chomping on a piece of mint gum. Jack managed a shrug.

"Not sure. I was just going to ask them," Jack said and began to walk down the corridor. Deirdre and Courtney had approached Daemon and were talking to him. He towered over Deirdre, and Jack increased his pace nervously. It looked like Deirdre was introducing Courtney, of all things. They spoke together for a few minutes, and then Daemon made a gesture like he had to get back to work. He walked away and they continued to watch him for a moment, turning back just as Jack and Kyle walked up.

"Hey, Court. How's it going?" Kyle asked. She looked kind of flustered; if Jack were honest, he would admit they both did.

Deirdre's cheeks were pink and her eyes were bright in reaction to the encounter, but the expression on her face when she saw him was relief, and he relaxed a little bit. He tried to identify the uncomfortable feeling in the pit of his stomach, and had to laugh at himself when he did; jealousy was unfamiliar territory. He put his arm around Deirdre's shoulders and she relaxed into him and sighed contentedly.

"Was that the guy from last night?" Jack asked her, though he knew full well. Deirdre nodded and shivered a little.

"Yeah. He's kind of..." Deirdre paused, looking for the right word.

"Gorgeous?" Courtney supplied, earning a glower from Kyle. Deirdre grimaced.

"I was leaning more toward 'terrifying,'" she said with a shiver and a glance down the hall after him. *Thatagirl*, Jack thought. His Sight had raised more questions than it answered. Terrifying was an understatement for the Shapeshifter, if that's even what he was. Jack wondered what had truly brought the strange creature there to their city, and what he wanted. Deirdre took a breath and turned to look at him.

"I better get to class," she said. Her exquisite face was lifted toward him and impulsively he bent and kissed her deeply, oblivious to the snickering crowd of students that ebbed and flowed around them. He was surprised by how hard it was to let her go. She laughed in pleased surprise when he released her and walked away down the hall with a smile and pink cheeks, glancing back at him before she was lost to the crowd. Kyle looked at Jack with an amused expression.

"So when's the wedding?" he quipped and clapped Jack on the back, pushing past him on his way to his classroom, following the girls. Jack rolled his eyes and walked down the hall in the opposite direction.

***

Deirdre

Friday

Language Arts was the first class of the day. Deirdre and Courtney took their usual seats and arranged their books and papers, ready for class. Deirdre's mind wandered tiredly, so she was a little startled when Courtney kicked her ankle thirty seconds after class started. She looked up, glancing around and blushing in embarrassment, wondering what she'd missed. Courtney was flashing her a panicked expression and the teacher was smug, handing out papers to the front person in each row. Déjà vu hit her hard; her fleeting dream from last night had looked exactly like this. She took a paper from the stack and passed the rest back, simultaneously glad she had studied and disconcerted by the coincidence. She did well on the test, she was sure, thanks to the visionary warning, but she couldn't concentrate on the rest, wondering uncomfortably about the oddity of dreaming something before it happened.

In the hall, she passed Daemon several times during the morning, feeling like she had been punched in the gut every time. It was like wading through thick, heavy gel each time she came near him, exhausting and disorienting; holding her breath seemed to help. Each time she made it past him she sighed with relief, settling into her classroom with a drained sense of something dangerous barely averted. During classes her attention wavered between the weirdness of the dreaming and thoughts of Jack and Daemon until her nerves were frayed and raw; by lunchtime she was a wreck.

She practically ran out to her car when the bell rang; as a junior she was allowed to leave campus for lunch and today she intended to make the most of it. Her heart leaped when she saw Jack leaning against her car, his face turned toward the sun, waiting for her with his hands in his pockets. She dropped her books on the back seat of the car and fell into his arms, breathing him in and letting his embrace smooth down her ruffled emotions.

"Hey, honey, what's wrong?" he murmured into her hair as he held her tightly against him. The endearment sounded sweet in her ears and his voice was gentle with concern. She just shuddered and hugged him tighter, burying her face in his chest. He stroked her back and her hair, just holding her close. When she felt a little better she loosened her hold enough to look up at him.

"Just get me away from here," she said, and handed him her keys. His surprise was palpable; she hated his reckless driving. Today she didn't care; she just knew she couldn't concentrate on driving herself. He pursed his lips and beeped the locks open as she walked over to the passenger side. He adjusted the seat for his long legs and shifted the mirror as she settled herself into the seat, her hands clenched on her lap and her posture stiff with tension. He turned the key in the ignition and the car purred to life. He turned toward her.

"Anywhere in particular?" he asked as he put his arm over the back of the seat and backed out of the slot.

"Anywhere that isn't here," she said, glancing back at the school with an unreadable expression in her eyes. He followed the trickle of cars toward the parking lot entrance, watching her from the corner of his eye as she visibly relaxed now that they were on their way.

He pulled out onto the street, making his way slowly downtown. She was silent as they drove, still and preoccupied, her eyes staring blankly at the thoughts turning round inside her head. He pulled into a parking space and killed the engine.

"How about something to eat?" he asked, nodding toward the restaurant.

She smiled tiredly, nodding. She ate slowly, preoccupied, not paying much attention to his attempts at conversation. When they were finished, he stood and followed her back to the car.

"Back to school then? Or would you like to tell me about it?" he asked, glancing over.

"*Not* back to school yet, please," she grimaced, shuddering. She could skip study hall without any guilt, and she knew Jack didn't have any more classes today at all.

"Okay," he nodded and put the car in gear. "How about we just drive around for a while?" he said, pulling smoothly out of the parking lot and into the congested downtown lunchtime traffic. That was another thing she loved about Jack; he never pushed. Replete with food and cocooned next to him in the car she felt very comfortable, and she finally felt like she *could* talk about it. It felt strange at first, confiding in Jack, but it grew easier as she spoke. He was a great listener.

"A few things have been weird today," she started, settling more deeply into the comfortable seat and absently watching him drive. His eyes checked the mirrors and watched the road, relaxed, and he reached over and took her hand, gentle reassuring pressure on her fingers.

"I'm just... all shaken up today," she began.

"Okay," he said encouragingly, rubbing his thumb softly across her knuckles.

She started haltingly, shifting in her seat, ill at ease. "I dreamed something last night, and today it actually happened just the way I dreamed," she laughed self-consciously. He stayed silent, and she went on.

"It sounds so crazy when I say it out loud, but I feel sometimes like this whole day has already happened, like I'm just living through it again," she continued rapidly, watching him closely, worriedly, for his reaction. His brow knit, a little line appearing between his eyebrows, but that was all. She settled back in her seat and was quiet for a moment, staring out the window for a few minutes before turning back. He eased the car to a stop as the light turned red and took the chance to meet her eyes but didn't speak. She looked so tired, the smudges beneath her eyes darkening them; her ivory skin was pale except for a pale pink blush highlighting her graceful cheekbones. Her red lips parted slightly as she took a breath, pausing for an extra moment before she spoke again.

"I dreamed of you, last night, too," she said. He raised his eyebrows slightly at that, the little line disappearing; then he had to turn back to the road as the light turned green. She continued, her voice quiet but clear. "It was just for a second, and it was very odd. You were standing inside some kind of golden dome made of light, and you were talking to a man, and he was all blurry, like he wasn't really there." He stared at her for a moment, then turned back to the road and had to apply the brakes sharply to stop in time to avoid hitting the car ahead of them. Her free hand braced on the dash. His hand tightened over hers briefly. She misinterpreted his reaction. "I know. Crazy, right?" she said, and sighed.

"Not what I was hoping for," he teased, grinning weakly, hiding his alarm as best he could. She laughed and a faint blush darkened her cheeks. He decided it was time for a distraction.

"So what happens next?" he asked. She looked confused. "You're re-living the day, right? So what happens next?" he looked at her facetiously. She looked out the window, a little put out that she had bared her fears and he was laughing at her. He squeezed her hand.

"Hey," he said. He waited to continue until she looked at him.

"I'm sorry. I'm not laughing at you, I swear. I would never do that," he said, sincerity ringing deep in his voice. She looked away again.

"I know," she said, but her voice was doubtful.

"I just want to cheer you up," he said, turning onto the main street, heading in the general direction of the school. She looked out the windshield, then sat up straight in her seat when she realized where they were, gripping his hand tightly in sudden panic.

"Pull over!!!" she said, her eyes wide with terror. "Get off this road!" In a split second he had merged into the outer lane, momentarily cutting off a dark blue sedan that honked loudly at them; ignoring it, he pulled into a side street, directly into a parking space.

"What is it?" he asked her, then jerked around as a loud explosion sounded nearby. In moments he was out of the car, standing there with the door open, leaning out into the street to see what had happened. A car at the next intersection along their previous route had run the red light, plowing into the blue sedan that had honked at them. Smoke and reverberations bouncing off the buildings filled the air as chaos erupted and traffic screeched to a gridlocked halt. He stared in shock, then slowly turned around and lowered his head to look through the doorway at Deirdre. She had tipped her head back in her seat and closed her eyes; tears leaked from the corners, soaking her lashes and beginning to fall down her cheeks. He closed the driver's door and walked over to her side. Opening the door, he crouched down beside her and reached over to pull the lever and push the seat all the way back.

Deirdre sat up, questions on her lips, but he just picked her up and slipped underneath her, holding her in his lap. She curled up there, arms around his neck. "I told you. I'm having the weirdest day," she said into his shoulder. He held her away from him for a moment, tilting her face toward him and wiping her tears away with his thumbs.

"I can see that," he agreed, still numb with shock, and tucked her back into his shoulder. "Thanks for saving our lives, by the way," he said.

"*I* didn't. This is exactly how it happened in the dream," she said, her voice a little soggy. Then she shifted a little and curled her hand around the back of his neck. "You believed me when I said to pull over," she said, her voice incredulous. He nodded, brows knit, eyes distant.

"I've seen stranger things," he said after a short pause, and his voice rang with truth. She wondered what he meant, but she didn't have the energy to ask right now. He held her, stroking his hand down her back and playing with her hair, soothing, while the sirens came and went and traffic restarted, and she slowly relaxed again.

She stirred and sat up a little, looking at him as he stared out the windshield, his brown eyes unfocused, the little line resting between his brows as he thought. She touched his face, smoothing away the line, and he blinked when her hand brushed his impossibly long eyelashes. His gaze focused on her face, studying her, and his expression was frustrated. She raised her eyebrows, unspoken questions filling her eyes. He shifted her a little on his lap, and raised one of his hands up to cradle her head.

"You okay?" he asked her, looking directly into her eyes. She held his face in her hands and nodded.

"I will be," she said. "Thanks for taking me out, today, Jack. It's nice to just get away sometimes," she said, meeting his gaze. His familiar warm brown eyes were flecked with dark gold and ringed with black. The little line reappeared as he smiled self-deprecatingly.

"I just want to fix it for you," he said, chuckling self-consciously. She smiled as she comprehended the source of his frustration.

Then she leaned close and whispered against his lips, "You did. You do," and she kissed him softly, looking into his eyes. He kissed her back but otherwise held very still, letting her be the aggressor for once. She had meant to just give him a little kiss and that was all, but watching his eyes darken with desire and feeling his heartbeat and breathing increase while she kissed him, knowing she moved him, was incredibly heady. Tasting him, she wanted more. She parted his lips with hers, deepening her kiss, and traced the shape of his lower lip slowly with her tongue.

A knock on the window shattered the moment and they pulled apart in shock. A plump meter maid looked down at them, tolerantly amused. They were both blushing deeply as Jack leaned forward and rolled the window down.

"Your meter is empty. You need to move it along, if you don't mind," she said, hands on her hips. They nodded breathlessly and Deirdre opened the door and stepped out onto the sidewalk, self-consciously straightening her dress and smoothing her hair as she walked around to the other side of the car and sat down in the driver's seat. She adjusted the seat and the mirror and pulled out carefully into the nearly empty side street, leaving the meter maid behind, staring after them with a bemused expression on her face.

Jack took a slow breath, and she snuck a look at him from the corner of her eye. He was looking at her the same way, and it suddenly struck her as funny. She began to laugh, and he joined her, his low chuckle rumbling beneath her lighter one. He stretched his legs out and leaned back in the seat as she drove. She pulled reluctantly into the school parking lot and cut the ignition, sitting back in her seat with a sigh and touching Jack's hand gently. He squeezed her fingers reassuringly, and she pulled herself together and exited the car. Deirdre opened the back door and gathered up her books. She shut the door and turned toward the school, squaring her shoulders. Jack came up behind her, resting one hand gently on the back of her neck. An echo of heat twisted down her spine and she sank back toward him, closing her eyes.

"You okay?" he asked her again. She nodded, and turned to look up to his warm eyes.

"Will I see you later?" she asked, and it was all she could do to pull away.

He released her and nodded, thrusting his hands into his pockets and rocking back on his heels. "It's Friday," he reminded her. Her eyes widened and she smiled.

"That's right; the game. I'll be there," she confirmed, and bit her lip as the image of him all decked out in his gear, grinning wildly, his hair dark with sweat, paraded through her imagination. He cocked his head at her as though wondering what she was thinking and his eyes glanced at her mouth, following the movement of her teeth against her lip. She lowered her eyes and began to turn away.

"Will I see you after?" he asked her.

"'Course!" she promised easily, a genuine smile lighting her face. He smiled back, reassured, and nodded his head.

"Okay, then," he said, and stepped toward his car.

"'Bye, Jack," Deirdre said, and he suddenly changed direction and swept her up into his arms and kissed her once more. He set her back down, breathless and shocked, and grinned at her.

"'Bye, Deirdre," he said, and jogged away. She watched him for a moment, then turned and went into the school, grinning like an idiot.

She was shockingly late; study hall was long over and Courtney would be wondering what had happened to her in Chemistry. The halls were empty as she hurried toward her classroom, hoping she could slip unnoticed into the back. She skirted around the construction materials, walking swiftly, when a metal stud that was leaning against the wall slipped, clanging to the floor right beneath her feet. She tripped, twisting and slamming her ankle against the heavy shaft, and dropped her books, scattering them across the hallway.

She would have fallen hard, but icy iron-strong hands caught her, and she jerked as an almost electric current ran through her body at his touch. She felt a lesser jolt when he shielded her as they half-fell against the wall. Shocked, she looked up into Daemon's blazing blue eyes and gasped in visceral reaction as his hands grew somehow *colder* around her waist and something *clicked* between them, locking into place, balancing. She heard a distant ringing chime, echoing in the back of her head. She blinked, wondering what had happened, and only then began to be aware of a knife-sharp agony in her ankle.

He tried to set her gently back on her feet, but when she put her foot down, she hissed in pain and fell back against him. He was hard as rock and as steady, and he smelled of sawdust and winter. She gripped his wrist hard in reaction to the pain and to keep from falling again. Somehow, the dangerous predatory atmosphere she had sensed around him only this morning had suddenly disappeared. He still had extraordinary *presence*, but strangely, she was no longer afraid. He… she tried to find a word for the feeling… *belonged* there, catching her, and she felt incredibly *safe* here in his embrace.

"Your ankle?" he asked softly. She nodded, her face tight with pain; the ankle had begun to throb.

"Is it broken, do you think?" he said. She tried to move it and agony shot up her leg.

"I'm not sure," she said, biting her lip and blinking away the tears that leapt to her eyes. His brow lowered in concern.

"Can I look at it?" he asked. She raised her eyebrows, and a tiny part of her wondered what a construction worker/cook knew about broken bones.

"I guess so…." she said, then yelped in outrage as he lifted her effortlessly into his arms and took a few steps down the hall, graceful as a cat.

"Hey!" she glared at him. He smirked at her.

"Chill," he said succinctly, and set her gently on a chair. She sat stiffly, uncomfortable with the intimate way he leaned in close as he kneeled in front of her, even though at the same time it felt like she should be used to having him in her personal space. The strange duality of sensation and the pain made her head spin, and she closed her eyes for a moment. When she opened them, the shock of his size hit her again; even sitting back on his knees he had to duck his head to look her in the eye. He reached for her foot and she pulled it away, beneath the chair. He looked up, into her eyes.

"Please, Deirdre," he said. She swallowed, overwhelmed by the power behind his stare. Someone not to be trifled with—but then she already knew that. Feeling like a chastened child, she grudgingly extended her foot again.

"Thank you," he said gravely; she had the feeling he was hiding a smile and she glared at him. He took her foot gently in his icy fingers; she flinched and bit back a cry of pain, gritting her teeth. He slipped off her shoe and tears flooded her eyes and she gripped his granite shoulder hard to stay upright, digging her nails in. He didn't even seem to notice, cradling her foot in the cool palm of one enormous hand and feeling around it gently with the other. Two tears escaped her eyes and dripped down her cheeks, and a single whimper escaped her lips. He looked up at her, concern clouding the fire in his eyes. She bit her lip.

"Is it bad?" she whispered.

"Bad enough," he told her. He took a deep breath and put his hands on either side of her thighs on the seat of the chair and looked down at the floor. Then he looked up at her from under his eyelashes. *Oh my God*, she thought, and swallowed hard again as her head swam and her stomach did a little flip; *Courtney was right, he is incredible.*

"I can fix it," he said softly.

"What?" she asked stupidly.

"I can fix it, but it will hurt. A lot." he said. She blinked at him.

"More than it already does?" she asked. He smiled, and the beauty in it knocked her breathless. She steadied herself with thoughts of Jack, and relaxed a fraction.

"Only for a second," he told her sincerely. She slid her gaze to the side and chewed on her lip again. His eyes followed the movement.

"Now?" she asked. He looked into her eyes.

"The sooner the better," he advised, then they both looked up as a shape loomed over them.

"Daemon, you're on the clock," another construction worker, an older man, reminded him, interrupting their intense conversation. Daemon got slowly to his feet. He towered over the burly man.

"John. I'm going to take a little break," Daemon told him. John narrowed his eyes.

"How little?" he asked suspiciously. Daemon glanced at Deirdre.

"Fifteen minutes," he said, folding his rock-hard arms across his chest. The other man looked at him, then at Deirdre, and shook his head.

"You can have twenty," he said, leering at them, then he turned away and walked back down the hall. Daemon bared his teeth at his back and Deirdre shuddered, hoping to never be on the receiving end of that look. Closing his eyes for a moment, he shook himself like a huge lion. Then Daemon turned back toward Deirdre, his eyes full of concern now.

"I think we should go outside. Maybe to your car," he said. She looked up at him in surprise.

"Why?" she asked. He pursed his lips, then his mouth pulled into a grimace and he looked away.

"You might scream," he said cautiously. His eyes were tight and a muscle jumped along his jaw. She swallowed, but met his eyes steadily.

"Okay," she nodded and began to stand up. Her face went white as a sheet as soon as her foot touched the ground. He flinched and bent to her side in an instant.

"I'll carry you," he said.

"No," she shook her head vehemently. He raised his eyebrows.

"Deirdre…." he said, exasperation coloring his smooth voice. She pushed his hand away—or rather, she tried to. She couldn't budge him an inch. He gave in to her intent, though, and moved back, but only a little. She struggled to rise, using only one foot and gripping the chair with both hands. He stood there watching her, his arms folded across his chest again. She looked away. There was no way she would make it two inches without help, much less all the way out to the car. Even holding her ankle in the air hurt, and what was she going to do? Hop or something? She sighed.

"All right," she looked up, defeated. To his credit he didn't gloat, just came over and scooped her up. He held her very gently against his chest, as though she were made of glass, and his even steps barely jarred her at all. Still, she was white faced and panting when they reached her car. She loosened her death grip around his neck to fish her keys out, and beeped the locks open. He held her easily in one arm like a baby as he reached down and opened the rear door, and set her gently on the seat inside. He let her rest there for a moment, kneeling on the pavement in front of her, poised to take her foot gently in his long hands. Before he touched her he looked at her and she met his eyes, heart thumping with dread.

"This is going to hurt. A lot," he warned her again. She pressed her lips together.

"So you said," she answered. Still he hesitated.

"Can you do it or not?" she asked, her voice sharp with anxiety. She unclenched her fists and wiped her damp palms on her thighs. He pressed his lips together and gripped her foot in both hands. She nearly cried out then, digging her nails into her legs when her hands tensed involuntarily.

"Hold onto my shoulders and be very still," he told her. She obeyed, fitting her hands lightly into the dips of his shoulders where his muscles overlapped. Her thumbs rested in the hollow just above his collarbones. His shoulders spanned the width of the car door and she wondered absently if he would even fit in her car. He glanced up, and his eyes blazed again, capturing her, just when she thought she was getting used to them, and her stomach repeated the weird little flip. She stared into his eyes and her breathing and heartbeat slowed just a little as she involuntarily relaxed, half-hypnotized. His eyes were the exact color of blue fire, she realized, and just then he did something with his hands and she threw her head back and screamed. She gasped and leaned forward, her forehead nearly touching his, panting and shaking as echoing waves of agony washed through her.

"Once more, now," he murmured softly, his face and voice tight with sympathy, and pulled and twisted simultaneously, his long cold fingers guiding things back into place, and she bit her lip hard to keep from screaming again. A tortured whimper escaped anyway and tears ran down her cheeks as she collapsed against him. He hesitated for a bare instant in surprise, then gathered her into his arms and held her. She crossed her arms tightly around his neck, crying softly as her ankle throbbed painfully in time with her pulse. She tasted blood in her mouth where her teeth had cut through her lip.

He stroked his hand down her back and murmured in her ear, "Hey, it's all right, it's done, you're okay." She took a shuddering breath against his cool shoulder, and he filled her senses for a moment, huge, with sculpted muscle and smelling of fresh snow and sandalwood, his chin smooth against her temple. She pulled back abruptly, disconcerted.

Her ankle still throbbed, and she moved it hesitantly back and forth. It hurt, but now it was a manageable pain rather than the screaming agony she had felt before. She looked at him and smiled tentatively into his eyes. An unreadable expression crossed his face, and then he smiled hesitantly back at her. He raised his hands to her face and wiped the tear tracks from her cheeks with his thumbs, and she let him.

His skin was rough against her cheek, but his touch was incredibly gentle, a cool whisper across her skin. She took his hands and moved them from her face, blushing at the somehow intimate moment. She colored even more deeply when she realized she had just hugged a virtual stranger. Her brows knitted when she realized he didn't feel like a stranger anymore, not at all.

He helped her get up, and she tested her weight gingerly. It was painful, but she could walk. Probably.

"It will bruise; you should get it wrapped and put some ice on it," he advised as she leaned on his arm and the door of the car. She nodded.

"I don't know what you did, but thank you," she said, and glanced up at him. He nodded.

"Anytime," he said with a crooked grin. A little laugh exploded from her lips.

"I hope not!" she shook her head, shuddering at the idea.

"I can walk you to the nurse's office," he offered when she wobbled unsteadily. She grimaced at the thought of walking through the halls on Daemon's arm—talk about attracting stares—but she wouldn't make it on her own. At least he wouldn't have to carry her. She stifled an unwelcome pang of disappointment and took a deep breath.

"Let's get this over with," she said, and held onto him as he slipped his arm around her waist, effortlessly supporting all her weight. He might as well have carried her.

***

Daemon

Friday

Daemon steadied the wood against the sawhorses with his left hand and cut expertly with the circular saw in his right. The screech of the saw echoed in the hallway. He put the cut piece with the others in the pile and tossed the extra end into the huge trash bin he would probably end up having to take out to the dumpster. He sensed her coming as soon as she entered the school. It was incredibly distracting, having her walk by all the time; he felt a pull toward her like he had never felt from anyone else; a backwards rubber band that strained between them, stronger when they were closer, creating uncomfortable tension when farther away. He braced himself.

She was walking swiftly and avoiding eye contact as she had all day. One of the guys bumped the stack of metal studs leaning precariously against the wall and one slipped out of place. He moved faster than any human, catching her as she fell, but still wasn't in time to prevent the accident completely. His hands closed around her and suddenly an electric shock coursed through him, throwing them back. He hit the wall and kept his grip and his feet only thanks to his unnatural reflexes, and when she gasped

57

and looked up into his eyes, another tremor went through him. His magic surged and his hands chilled where they touched her, but instead of ice forming around them and frosting everything he touched, she absorbed it somehow. He felt the chime of power as something *clicked* between them, locking into place, balancing, and the rubber band feeling *snapped*. He stared at her, wondering what had happened.

He went to let her go but as soon as her foot touched the ground she convulsed in pain and fell back against him. She dug her little fingers into his wrist and he steadied her as gently as he could, inhaling her intoxicating scent. He was annoyed that she smelled almost as much of the blond boy as herself—what had she been doing? Sitting in his lap? He was gratified that she seemed to be more at ease than she had ever seemed in his presence before, in spite of her pain. He frowned when he realized the strange pull he felt toward her seemed to have intensified; the rubber band may have snapped, but now the connection was deeper—an unbreakable cord that seemed hooked somewhere in his gut.

The muscles of her slender waist were taut beneath his hands and she held one foot in the air; her dazzling eyes were full of pain. He glanced at the other workers. John raised his eyebrows at him but said nothing, knowing the accident was their fault. Daemon could almost read his supervisor's mind: Maybe the good-looking young man could smooth things over before anyone got in trouble. Daemon pursed his lips and turned back to Deirdre. As it happened, he wanted to help her, though he really didn't understand why she was so compelling. Sure, she was beautiful, extraordinarily so, but there was something else. And how did she make his magic go all wonky? She didn't even seem to know she was doing it. Well, first things first: information.

"Your ankle?" he asked softly. She nodded, and her face was tight with pain.

"Is it broken, do you think?" he said. She tried to move it and her muscles jumped and she gasped.

"I'm not sure," she said, her voice tight and strained. His brow lowered in concern. If it wasn't actually broken he would be able to fix it; his ability would stretch that far. She was in a lot of pain, though; a break was the most likely cause. Looking into her eyes, he made his decision.

"Can I look at it?" he asked. She looked at him with questions in her eyes, but to his surprise she didn't ask any of them, or make any rude comments about him not being a doctor. She just agreed. He lifted her off her feet and into his arms and she yelped. She felt wonderful, soft and light and smelling of raspberries and vanilla and herself... and Jack. He stifled a growl and chastised himself. *Not mine, not mine at all*, he reminded himself, and his beast.

"Chill," he said, both to her and to himself. He smirked at his own inside joke, and set her gently on a chair. He kneeled in front of her, as close as he dared, reluctant to let go of her. He reached for her foot and she pulled it away, beneath the chair. He looked up, into her eyes. She stared back at him, her expression half defiant, half afraid. He wished she wouldn't be afraid. He was used to it—people nearly always sensed something strange about him, and then there was his size and his odd eyes. He knew it. But now, with her, he wished fiercely that it wasn't so. He sat back and forced himself to be slow and gentle. He made an effort to damp down the intensity of his stare and speak quietly.

"Please, Deirdre," he said. She swallowed, and looked at him uncertainly, but pressed her lips together and extended her foot for his inspection.

"Thank you," he said gravely, feeling triumphant. She glared at him and he wanted to laugh, but he realized that would hardly win him any points. He took her small and shapely foot gently in his fingers; she flinched and he heard her teeth snap together as she stifled her response to the pain he caused. He knew immediately what the problem was; no one was as familiar with the way bones should fit together as a Shapeshifter. He slipped off her shoe as carefully as possible, keeping his expression steady as she dug her tiny fingers into his shoulder in reaction to the pain.

He made sure, cradling her foot in the palm of one hand as he felt around it gently with the other. This would probably be less painful if it *was* broken; however, it wasn't, and he had a decision to make. Play doctor and invite a million questions he had no answers for, or simply carry her down to the nurse's station and have done with it, and her. Problem was, he didn't want to be done with her. He looked up. Two tears had escaped her indigo eyes and dripped down her cheeks, and his heart wrenched in his chest and he felt like someone had punched him in the gut.

"Is it bad?" she whispered.

"Bad enough," he told her. He took a deep breath and leaned close to her, taking an enormous risk, if she had but known it. He looked up at her and listened to her heart jump and stutter when he met her eyes. It was confusing and he wondered what it meant, but he didn't deviate from his course.

"I can fix it," he said softly. She frowned at him, not understanding.

"I can fix it, but it will hurt like hell," he said again. She blinked at him and raised one eyebrow.

"More than it already does?" she asked. He smiled. Brave girl, if she could make jokes while she was in so much pain.

"Only for a second," he promised. Her straight white teeth scraped across her lower lip. He wondered suddenly what it would feel like to have her teeth scrape across *his* lip, then pulled himself forcefully back to the matter at hand.

John interrupted them.

"Daemon, you're on the clock," he said. Daemon got slowly to his feet. He looked down on the burly man and told him he would be back in fifteen minutes. John leered at them and Daemon glared at the older man, almost daring him to say something. John lowered his eyes and slid them to the side, resenting Daemon though he wasn't really sure why, not realizing he had just lost a dominance contest.

"You can have twenty," he said, his voice thick with innuendo, then he turned away and walked back down the hall. Daemon bared his teeth at his back and let him go with an effort. John was clueless and it was better for everyone if he didn't die, even if he had insulted Deirdre. Daemon closed his eyes and took a deep breath before turning back toward Deirdre.

"I think we should go outside. Maybe to your car," he said. Her face registered surprise.

"Why?" she asked. He didn't want to explain, but gaining her trust meant being completely up front.

"You might scream," he said cautiously. Telling her was the right choice; he could see understanding and resolve crystallize in her eyes as she stared up at him. She swallowed, but met his gaze steadily.

He wasn't ready for it when she tried to stand up. She jarred the ankle and he could tell she could barely stay conscious she was in so much pain, but she kept on. He offered to carry her, and she actually tried to push him away with her tiny hands. "No," she shook her head vehemently. He raised his eyebrows.

"Deirdre...." he said, shaking his head in exasperation. What could she be thinking? He moved back, giving her space to come to the inevitable conclusion on her own, wishing she weren't so stubborn. He watched in disbelief as she actually was able to force herself to her feet. She stood there, panting and white-faced, and looked up at him in defeat. He stepped forward, careful not to show how much he liked being close to her. Anticipation sped his heart as he gathered her very carefully in his arms. He walked as smoothly as he could, enjoying the sensation as her slender arms wrapped tightly around his neck, her hot breath tickling his collarbone as she buried her face against his chest. It felt so *right* to have her there, holding her, protecting her. He wondered at the impression. He felt a pang of guilt when he looked down at her pain-filled face as they reached the vehicle.

She beeped the locks open and he set her carefully on the back seat, careful not to jar her leg in any way. He kneeled down on the pavement in front of her and waited until she was ready before he touched her. He looked into her eyes, full of suffering, and hated the necessity of causing her more pain.

"This is going to hurt. A lot," he warned her again.

"So you said," she answered. Resolve hardened her expression, and he watched her, fascinated by the contrast between her fragile beauty and the steel in her eyes. It hit him hard then that she had placed a lot of trust with no proof at all that he could do as he said. He suddenly wondered why, but was afraid to ask. What if he reminded her that he was a total stranger and she changed her mind? And anyway, they weren't strangers anymore. They hadn't been strangers since he touched her and looked into her eyes and she took his magic; was it only minutes ago?

"Can you do it or not?" she asked, her voice sharp with anxiety and impatience. He braced himself for her pain and took her foot in his hands as gently as possible. Her entire body tensed and she almost screamed right then. He looked away from the agony in her eyes, stealing himself to follow through.

"Hold onto my shoulders and be very still," he told her. She obeyed, and her touch was as light as a caress and his skin tingled beneath her hands. Involuntarily he glanced up again. She captured him, bottomless indigo eyes he could fall into, and his heart skipped a beat and his magic flared. She absorbed it again, and it seemed to calm her; her eyes dilated slightly, her breathing and heartbeat slowed just a little and she relaxed a fraction. It was impossible, but he wasn't going to question it; he moved his fingers, shifting the bones away to make space for the dislocated one to move back into place in one smoothly expert motion. He had learned bone manipulation long ago, but the technique came back swiftly, like a major league pitcher reentering the game after a short conference with the catcher. As he had predicted, she screamed, and it cut him like a knife in his gut. Her entire body convulsed and her fingers dug hard into his shoulders, strong enough to actually draw blood had he not been a Shapeshifter. She bent her head, oblivious to everything but pain, panting, her entire body shaking in agony. He hated himself, but pushed on.

"Once more, now," he murmured softly, and didn't wait. He pulled and twisted simultaneously, guiding things back into place. To his surprise she didn't scream again, although the sound she did make was almost worse, a tortured whimper, and he smelled her blood where her teeth had pierced her lip. His beast flared at that, wondering what her blood would taste like; he stifled the gruesome idea. Unaware of the direction his thoughts had taken, conscious only of the lessening of pain and that the ordeal was over, she fell into his arms, clinging, tears running down her cheeks. Shocked and hardly knowing what to do, he closed his arms gently around her fragile body and stroked his hand down her back, savoring the fact that he was allowed, even for a moment, to touch her marvelous silky hair and feel her arms around his neck. Her tears were wet and hot against his shoulder. Instinctively he murmured soothing words in her ears.

"Hey, it's all right, it's done, you're fine." He held her until she broke the embrace, sitting up abruptly. She looked into his eyes with her tear-stained face and smiled shyly, and his heart tried to leap from its cage. He froze, clenching his jaw, hiding his reaction; here was an angel, impossibly beautiful, and her tears were awful, wrong. Angels shouldn't ever cry. He carefully echoed her smile, and hesitantly raised his hands to her face and wiped the tear tracks from her cheeks with his thumbs, trembling when she permitted his touch. Her skin was as soft as it looked, warm and smooth. He swallowed.

She took his hands and moved them from her face, holding them in her lap for a moment, and a gentle blush brought color back to her pale cheeks. He blinked and, barely aware of anything else, he helped her get up. She tested her weight on her ankle gingerly, and he tried to get hold of himself.

"It will bruise; you should get it wrapped and put some ice on it," he advised as her fingers pressed gently into his arm, balancing between him and the door of the car.

"I don't know what you did, but thank you," she said, her voice warm and sincere as she glanced up at him. He nodded, recovering a little. He hoped she wouldn't start asking questions. He could never explain what he had done or how he had done it, and he didn't want to lie to her.

"Anytime," he said, teasing. A little laugh escaped from her lips.

"I hope not!" she shook her head, shuddering at the idea.

"I can walk you to the nurse's office," he offered when she wobbled unsteadily and winced.

"Okay. Let's get this over with," she said; bravely, he thought. He slipped his arm around her slender waist, enjoying her closeness for a few minutes more. In spite of the danger, he was glad he had helped her. He left her at the nurse's office reluctantly, reflecting on the last half-hour as he returned to the job. *She's not afraid of me anymore*, he thought to himself. He smiled, surprised by exactly how content that made him.

Chapter 3

Deirdre

Friday Evening

She stepped out of the car gingerly, favoring her left ankle. Courtney stepped out on the other side and jogged over to her. "You okay?" she asked, hunching against the chill breeze that hit as soon as she exited the car. Her fine white-blond hair whipped around her face and she tossed her head to clear her vision. She took a red cap from her jacket pocket and pulled it down over her head, securing the fly-away halo. Deirdre nodded and began walking slowly with the rest of the crowd toward the stadium. The mob bottlenecked at the ticket counter and they eased their way into the line. Deirdre's ankle began to throb and she kept her weight off it as much as possible. The tight wrapping helped; the school nurse had done a good job.

They finally passed through the ticket booth and made their way up into the stands, finding their usual spot right behind the bench just above where the players would sit. Deirdre sat in relief and put her ankle up on the edge of the wall that ran around the stadium and looked out over the grassy expanse through the chipped and rusty bars of the railing. Excitement and expectation filled the air, and she watched the supporters of the other team as they filed in and took their seats across the field.

Courtney leaned over. "What happened to your ankle?" she asked, having just now noticed the bandage. Deirdre took a breath and wondered what to tell her. It was such an odd story; she still didn't really understand what had happened herself. She decided on the bare minimum.

"I tripped over some of the construction stuff in the hallway when I was coming back from lunch today," she said. Courtney raised an eyebrow at her, as though sensing there might be more to the story.

"Is that where you were during study hall?" she asked. Deirdre shook her head.

"No; during study hall I was with Jack," she said, an involuntary smile curving her lips as warmth shot through her at the memory. Courtney grinned at her.

"Do tell," she said. Deirdre blushed scarlet and lowered her eyes.

"Nothing to tell," she stated, shaking her head at Courtney, unwilling to feed the gossip mill with kiss and tell about Jack. Courtney frowned at her, annoyed but resigned.

"Come on, Deirdre, not even one little detail?" she begged, her eyes wide. Deirdre rolled her eyes.

"We went out for a long lunch and then drove around for a while… talking," she told her. Courtney latched onto her hesitation.

"Just talking?" she asked archly. Deirdre blushed again and pressed her lips together.

"No, okay? But not *much* else, either! Now hush—it's starting!" The band started up and the players from both teams streamed onto the field. She picked Jack out immediately, recognizing his tall leanness and easy loping run. She lost track of him in the crush as they took their seats. The band played on and the cheerleaders took the field and did their thing; the excitement of the crowd was contagious.

Deirdre looked along the bench for Jack, and tension she hadn't even noticed eased from her shoulders as she watched him. He sat on the bench next to Jason, almost right in front of her, leaning over, his elbows resting on his knees and his helmet dangling in his hands. She filled her eyes with him, just watching him talk to Jason, discussing who knew what. He flashed his easy grin at his friend and her heart jumped. Just then, Kyle and Gretchen reached them and Deirdre pulled her ankle in to let them through. Gretchen plopped down on the bench next to Deirdre and flipped her long blond hair back over her shoulder. She was wearing the cutest denim skirt and Deirdre complimented her on it; she smiled back at her, pleased.

"Thanks! I didn't expect to see you here!" she said. Deirdre looked at her in surprise.

"Why not?" she asked.

"I saw you with that incredibly hot construction guy earlier—was he actually *carrying* you?—and then you weren't in Chemistry. I figured you and Jack broke up or something," she said, carelessly laying waste to Deirdre's life all in one sentence. Courtney stared at her, hurt in her eyes. Deirdre leapt instantly toward damage control.

"We did *not* break up! Daemon was just carrying me because I hurt my ankle really bad. And that's why I wasn't in Chemistry, too—I was in the nurse's office!" Deirdre protested. Courtney looked slightly mollified.

"Daemon carried you?" she asked, disbelieving. Gretchen chimed in again, obviously pleased at having information the other girl didn't.

"Yeah, and she had her arms around his neck and everything; he made it look so easy—he must be really strong." She shivered and added with a note of cattiness, "How did it feel? He looks like he would be hard as a rock!" She looked at Deirdre expectantly. Deirdre narrowed her eyes at the other girl, wondering if she was actually trying to make trouble or if she was really that oblivious. She glanced over at Courtney and Kyle. Kyle had an amused look on his face and Courtney looked at her with sardonic interest.

"Yeah, Deirdre, how did Daemon's muscles feel while he was carrying you around today?" she asked sarcastically, obviously still hurt that Deirdre hadn't given her the whole story first.

"His name is Daemon? Mmm," Gretchen giggled. Deirdre blushed and looked away, remembering *exactly* how it had felt to be held firmly in his strong arms, irrational guilt clouding her eyes as she stared at Jack. She stamped it down. She had done nothing wrong. She sat up straighter and cleared her expression, knowing from experience that if they saw any sign of embarrassment or guilt they would tease her mercilessly and spread it through the entire school in no time.

"Please. I barely know him. He just helped me when I sprained my ankle," she blew off the other girls with a wave of her hand and breathed an inward sigh of relief when the players stood up to jog out onto the field for the kickoff, giving her a reprieve. Jack stood up and turned then, searching the crowd for her and looked up into her eyes. She grinned widely in response to his smile when he saw her and he turned and jogged out onto the field, pulling his helmet down over his blond hair and fastening the chin strap as he ran. Ignoring the others for a moment, she studied the other team; they were playing West High tonight and their blue and white uniforms couldn't hide the fact that several members of their team were noticeably bigger than theirs. Deirdre bit her lip as a pang of worry shot through her belly.

"I hate this, sometimes," Gretchen said softly, and Deirdre looked over at her in astonishment. She looked surprised and a little embarrassed that she had spoken aloud and gave an embarrassed half-smile as she looked at Deirdre. *She must be as worried for Jason as I am for Jack,* she thought, feeling an unexpected kinship with the other girl. She smiled understandingly.

"I know what you mean," she said, and turned just in time to see Jack catch the ball and begin running. He didn't make it very far; blue number thirty-four slammed into him and knocked him to the ground at their own twenty-first yard line. Her heart leaped to her throat until he rolled gracefully to his feet and tossed the ball to the ref. He was moving easily and she breathed a sigh of relief as they took their positions around Jason. Gretchen laughed a little in sympathy with her, and the roller coaster of the game began.

Gretchen's nervousness peaked as soon as the ball was snapped and lasted until it left Jason's hands; then Deirdre's heart kicked into high gear as Jack caught Jason's passes and raced down the field always just ahead of the other team. West High with their larger players shut down their running game early on, so as wide receiver, Jack had the ball often. Her heart kept up its staccato rhythm every time he was hit and her fingernails dug little crescents into her palms. When they switched to defense and Jack jogged in from the field, she breathed a sigh of relief and collapsed into a jelly-like blob on the bench, echoing her friend's tension.

She could almost feel the frustration coming off the blue players in waves as they failed time and time again to upset Jason and Jack's coordinated effort; hours of long practice had made their timing perfect—it was as though they could read each other's minds, and it was clearly driving the other team crazy.

Just before halftime, the score was tied and the other team had the ball. Jack stood up and began to pace the length of the bench, staying loose until he had to go back on. He looked up at her as he passed, his hair and the slight blond roughness on his chin damp with sweat, his eyes bright and his face flushed with adrenaline.

He stopped for a moment, just looking at her, and gave her his slow smile, and suddenly everything faded and they were all alone. Her heart pounded and she caught her breath, remembering his lips on hers, his hands on her waist, in her hair.... She felt her eyes widen and her face flush; she caught her lip with her teeth. He smiled wider and she could see him chuckle, almost like he knew what was in her mind; then the moment was broken and he kept walking, rejoining Jason at the bench. Courtney looked at her with a raised eyebrow.

"What was that?" she asked curiously. Deirdre was still breathless.

"That was Jack being Jack," she told her, and laughed lightly.

"I see," Courtney said cryptically, shaking her head. Deirdre laughed again, adrenaline and desire making her feel a little giddy. She stood up.

"I'm going to the bathroom," she announced and walked as swiftly as she could past the other spectators until she reached the stair. Once there she slowed in deference to her ankle and made her way carefully up and onto the concourse. She walked past the crowd at the concession stand and stepped into the inevitable line that led into the girl's bathroom. The line moved swiftly, and she had her chance. She went to the bathroom and stood at the sink washing her hands for a moment.

She looked into the mirror and something happened when she met her own eyes. She felt for a moment as though she were pulled inside out, and something seemed to *stretch* inside her skull; she gasped and gripped the edges of the sink in both hands, trying to keep her balance as the world flipped sideways and her veins filled with ice.

She stared into the mirror, her face frozen as she watched the scene playing out in her head. She was on the football field, right in the middle of the action as she had never been before.

The clock was ticking—there were almost two minutes left in the game. Jason stood off to her right and he looked over his shoulder at Jack, making eye contact right through her, as though she wasn't even there. She followed his gaze and watched Jack crouch down and freeze in place, readying himself for the snap. He looked tired; his shoulders sagged a little and she could see him taking deep regular breaths, resting for the fraction of a second it took for the others to be ready. As she heard the ball thump into Jason's ready hands, Jack dug his toes into the grass and shot forward with perfect coordination.

She lost sight of him for a moment as he cut through the West High defense and bodies flew around her, the red players shielding Jason from their larger counterparts as best they could. She flinched when one of them passed right through her, hitting the dirt hard but bouncing back to his feet and diving back into the fray. Miraculously, Jason stood unmoving in the eye of the storm, his gaze riveted down the field, following what could only be Jack's progress. A blue player made it through the red ones just in front of him and, out of time, he ducked swiftly to the side and threw the ball just before he was brutally slammed to the ground.

Even Deirdre could see that the pass was short, and she watched Jack break and turn, racing back for the ball, leaping between two enormous blue uniforms to snatch the ball out of the air. He landed still running and turned on his toes to sprint back down the field, but the path had closed behind him during his split-second detour. He ran forward anyway, slipping through gaps she couldn't even see and gained another two yards before he dodged to the right and two blue-clad titans slammed into him on both sides simultaneously, crushing him between them. She heard bone crunch and in the vision she screamed; the hit was brutal, and when they got up, he lay there, limp and too still on the torn grass.

The vision faded and she almost fell, clutching desperately at the slick white porcelain as her knees failed her. She had never felt so *cold*. Blind panic overcame her shock, and strength returned with a shot of adrenaline to her system. It hadn't happened yet. *Not yet, not yet*, her mind clung to that as she trembled in front of the mirror and wondered what on earth she could possibly *do*. She had never tried to get Jack a message during a game; she wasn't sure she even could. The coach wanted girlfriends and their distracting influence as far away from his team as possible, and mostly the team agreed with him.

She took a deep breath. She had time; she could figure this out. She replayed the images in her head, searching for a way out. What kind of message could possibly change the outcome? She thought of the way he had maneuvered the car out of traffic within moments of her say-so this afternoon, and hope steadied her. If she got him a message, he would believe her. Her mind raced as she splashed cold water on her face and patted it dry with paper towels. She walked out of the bathroom as fast as she could on her gimpy ankle and back up to the stands. She had to find Gretchen. She and Jason had been dating a while; if anyone knew a way to get a message to one of the players she would. She fought through the half-time crowd to her seat, but when she got there, her friends were missing.

She squashed down the panic that threatened to paralyze her and looked around, finally spotting them on the stairs going up opposite the ones she had just come down. Courtney spotted her and waved her toward them. Deirdre waved back and followed them, catching bare glimpses through the milling crowd. She reached the place she had seen them last and looked around, finally spotting Courtney and Kyle standing against the wall near the bathrooms on this side. She ran up to them, ignoring the throb of her ankle.

"Where's Gretchen?" she asked breathlessly as she caught up to them.

"Bathroom," Courtney said, waving her hand at the crowded doorway. Deirdre gritted her teeth in frustration, searching the line for her and realizing she must be among those already inside. It would take her forever to get out of there in this crowd. She turned back to Courtney.

"Do you have pen and paper?" she asked urgently. Courtney frowned at her.

"Maybe," she drew her purse in front of her and began to dig through it. "Why? What's the matter?" she asked. Deirdre was staring at the bathroom door again, willing Gretchen to come out. She turned back to her friend.

"What?" she stalled, trying to think of an explanation for her behavior that didn't involve explaining how she could suddenly see the future.

"What's wrong? You look a little frazzled," Courtney repeated, as she triumphantly handed her a black and white zebra striped pen from the depths of her purse. "No paper, sorry," she shrugged.

"How about one of the sheets from your check register?" Deirdre asked, desperate. Courtney blanched.

"Seriously?" She looked like she was about to refuse, but Deirdre glared at her, and she pressed her lips together and dug through her purse again.

"Deirdre…." Courtney said, irritation coloring her voice.

"I'll tell you about it later, I promise," Deirdre said, and snatched the paper and pen from her friend's hands.

"You better," Courtney warned, and Deirdre could tell she was thinking about her earlier reticence concerning the incident with Daemon.

"I will. Everything," she promised rashly, and grimaced inwardly, wondering if she could come up with something that could explain any of this. The sound of Jack's crunching bones flashed across her memory and her heart seized in renewed panic. She had nearly lost her brother to an accident; she couldn't bear it if Jack was badly hurt and she could have done something—anything—to prevent it. She bent her knee and placed the torn out paper on it and thought carefully about what to write. She was relieved when Courtney turned back to flirting with Kyle, both of them all but ignoring her.

The images played out in her head again as she hesitated and she closed her eyes and forced herself to *see* what the vision showed her. She steeled herself, watching him get hit again and again, and finally, she had an idea. It might work. It was simple enough, but would he be able to do it? He had dodged right out of sheer instinct—could he think fast enough to change that response? He had to. She wrote quickly and straightened up just as Gretchen rejoined them.

"Hey, Deirdre," she said. "I should have just gone with you—that took forever," she commented. Deirdre glanced over at Kyle and Courtney. They were still deep in conversation at the wall. Kyle leaned over her friend and she looked up at him with her wide blue eyes; neither of them were paying attention to anyone else at the moment. Deirdre grabbed Gretchen's arm and drew her slightly away.

"If I needed to get a message to Jack, how could I do it?" she asked her intently. Gretchen frowned at her.

"A message? Like a note?" Her brow furrowed. "Why not just text him?" she asked.

Deirdre shook her head. "He turns his phone off during the games," she said, trying to keep the panic from her voice.

The other girl pursed her lips, thinking about it. "Well, I suppose you could get a guy to sneak it into the locker room. Or maybe one of the cheerleaders could give it to him—Andrea? She would love an excuse to get Jack in trouble, because that's what would happen—he would get in big trouble—maybe kicked out of the game! What are you *thinking*?" she glared at Deirdre in disbelief. Deirdre glared back.

"It's *important*, Gretchen. *Really* important. I would *never* get Jack in trouble for nothing. *Never*," Deirdre asserted fiercely. Gretchen just looked at her for a moment then backed down a little.

"Okay. I believe that. But still...." she said, shaking her head. "Okay. I think your best bet would be to ask Kyle to go into the locker room. We better do it fast, though. Half-time will be over soon." Deirdre nodded and folded the note in half. They turned back toward Courtney and Kyle. They were gone. Deirdre gritted her teeth and cursed. Gretchen raised her eyebrows.

"What do we do now?" Deirdre was getting even more frantic. Once he was on the field again he would be impossible to reach.

"All right. All right," she said. "You go hang out near the locker rooms. Maybe you can find someone else who will sneak in and give it to him. I'll go see if Kyle and Courtney went back to our seats. If they did, I'll send Kyle down to you. 'Kay?" she offered. Deirdre nodded gratefully. Gretchen started to walk back toward the stairs that led into the stands. Deirdre called her back.

"Gretchen." The other girl turned back to her, eyebrows raised. "Thanks," Deirdre said.

"Thank me if it works. Go!" Gretchen said and waved her off.

Deirdre hitched her way down the hall as fast as she could, adrenaline and worry making her shaky and emotional. She camped out in the hallway that led to the boy's locker room, as close as she could get without calling too much attention to herself. She leaned heavily against the wall, favoring her aching ankle, watching the passersby closely for anyone who would and could pull off her errand.

***

Daemon

Friday Evening

Daemon flipped his spatula on the end of the meat fork, executing a complicated maneuver over the empty grill. He was dead bored; the diner was empty. Annabelle sat at the bar, studying her Basic Anatomy homework. Suddenly his stomach dropped into his shoes, and the utensils clattered to the floor.

"You okay in there?" Annabelle called, glancing up through the pass-thru window. He looked at the clock.

"Umm, no..." he said, and began to remove his apron. "Hey, Ann, I forgot something. I'm gonna have to leave you here for a bit—think you can handle it?" he couldn't help teasing her a little bit. She rolled her eyes at him.

"Gee, I don't know," she said. He grinned and raced toward the back door.

"Be back by the time that high school game gets over!" she shouted after him.

"I will!" he yelled back, as the door shut and clicked behind him. He jumped on the bike and raced out of the parking lot. He didn't know how he knew, or where she was or what the problem was, but somewhere, Deirdre was in trouble.

He paused at the intersection, waiting for the light. By the time it changed he knew where he was going. It was as though an invisible thread connected them; he was unaware of it until she twanged it, and now it was vibrating somewhere near the middle of his spine, pulling him toward her like a fisherman with a smallmouth bass.

He had a few minutes to think about what he was doing on the ride toward the stadium, and his outlook was grim by the time he arrived. He had heard of this kind of thing before, of Shapeshifters magically entrapped, forced to do the bidding of another. He wondered how she had managed to put her magical handcuffs on him without him even knowing. He stalked through the now-unmanned gate and into the stadium, homing in on her unerringly.

He saw her before she saw him, and her beauty seemed less compelling now that he knew what she had done. He was about ten feet away when she turned and saw him. She looked up, and up again, until she met his eyes and he watched the emotions play across her face: genuine shock that he was there, hope that he might help her, and then, after reading his body language and expression, uncertainty and finally fear crept into her bottomless eyes, and then despair. She turned away, scanning the crowd and clenching her little hands into fists. He paused, trying to puzzle it out.

She didn't expect him to be there, that much was clear, even though she had called him. And she needed something; that was also clear. But she seemed to have no intention whatsoever of asking him for anything at all. He watched her duck her head and blink back tears, her delicate shoulders hunched as though in pain. He considered the implications carefully, watching her. Earlier today she had clearly not realized the effect she was having on his magic. Perhaps she didn't know she had done it. The idea stunned him.

How could she work such complicated magic without even knowing it? Unless... well, he still didn't know what she was, except that she clearly wasn't a Sorceress—he would have known as soon as he touched her if that were the case. Maybe… maybe she didn't know what she was either.

He walked closer and her scent hit him, made stronger by her agitation; he was pleased that the blond boy's scent was nowhere on her now. He loomed over her.

"Can I help?" he asked. She stared up at him, and her eyes were full of unshed tears.

"You—you want to help me?" she asked, disbelieving; her voice was thick with need, and he suddenly wanted fiercely to touch her, to comfort her. He forced his hands to stay by his side; he had frightened her again, he could see it in her eyes, and he couldn't bear it if she flinched.

"Yep," he said casually. "I saw you over here, and you looked… worried, so…" He shrugged.

She bit her lip.

"Well, as it happens, I do need something," she looked up at him from under her eyelashes, and his heart stuttered. Nope, he had been wrong. Her beauty was just as devastating as he remembered, magical Shackles or no. He waited quietly.

"I really hate to ask you to do this," she said and looked, of all things, embarrassed. He raised his eyebrows. She took a deep breath and straightened her shoulders, and then held out a paper. He took it, and his fingers brushed hers. Ice crystals formed on her fingertips and she shivered. She held up her fingers, watching it melt, and stared up at him in disbelief. He braced himself for the inevitable barrage of questions, but they never came.

"Can you please take that into the locker room and give it to Jack?" she asked him. He blinked at her. *You have got to be kidding*, he thought. She read the thought in his eyes and glared at him.

"It's *not* anything like that. It's *important*, Daemon, I swear. He could *die*. I saw it," she said, and she laid her hand on his arm, leaning into him as she pleaded. "Read it if you want," she offered. Her glorious hair swung forward and her scent swirled up to him again; her hand was hot against his cool skin.

"Okay," he agreed, overwhelmed, and relief filled her eyes. He looked up at the doorway she had indicated.

"In there?" he confirmed. She nodded.

"And Daemon?" she added as he stepped away. "Don't get caught. Please." He glanced back at her and pressed his lips together. She looked back at him and bit her lip, and he cursed himself for a sucker. Running errands for a teenager and her boyfriend like some lapdog. What was the world coming to? He walked up to the doorway and inside just like he belonged. Nobody noticed.

When he got inside he opened the note and read it. Well, she had said he could, hadn't she? He frowned at it, confused. It didn't seem to make any sense. Shrugging, he worked his way into the room, following the sound of voices, using all his considerable skills—including magic, of course. He could walk up to someone and cut off a lock of their hair without them ever knowing, so Deirdre's request that he not get caught was no problem. The problem would be getting Jack alone long enough to give him the note. That had to be done face to face, to make sure he received her message, no matter how obscure. He could only think that it wouldn't be as obscure to Jack as it was to him.

He located the boy on the other side of the third row of lockers. They were about to return to the field, strategies finalized and encouragement complete; Daemon made his move. He reached out with his magic and pulled a little, and smiled to himself as Jack cursed when he discovered his shoelaces were untied. He waved his friend out when he offered to wait while he tied them.

79

"Go on ahead, I'll be there in a second," he said, and Daemon heard him bend toward his shoes. He walked around the end of the lockers and was surprised to find Jack standing there with his arms folded, as though waiting for him to appear, his laces still loose.

"What do *you* want?" he asked, curiosity and reserve overlaying his voice. Daemon studied him for a minute, just looking. Jack just waited, looking back, unmoved. Daemon was unwillingly impressed; most men couldn't look him in the eye for long, but the boy was as comfortable as Daemon.

A twinge of suspicion flickered through his mind, but he just held out Deirdre's note and said, "Deirdre asked me to give you this." Jack's surprise was palpable; he frowned and took the note from Daemon's fingers, handling it by the edges. He opened the paper and read it, and his frown deepened. He handed the note back to Daemon.

"What does it mean?" he asked. Daemon re-read the note and shrugged, perversely pleased that Jack didn't seem to know any more than he.

"I don't know. She seemed pretty desperate to get you that message, though," he said. "She was really worried." He glanced back over his shoulder, toward the door, ready to go. Jack bent and tied his shoes, thinking.

"Hmm. Well, tell her I..." Jack stopped. He looked up at the other man. "Tell her I got it, and I'll see her after the game," he finished. Daemon wondered what he had been about to say. Tell her... what? I love her? *That's what I would have said, if she was mine,* he thought, and closed his eyes and just nodded. *Not mine, not mine. His.* He turned and left abruptly.

Deirdre met him in the hall, her eyes bright with hope. He nodded and watched as relief flowed through her entire body. Her posture straightened and she smiled dazzlingly up at him, making his heart stutter. He looked down at her. "He said to tell you he got the note and that he'll see you after the game," he passed on the message.

She put her hand on his arm again and said, "Thank you so much." Her eyes looked down and then back up into his. "That's twice now," she reminded him. "I owe you." She took her hand from his arm and put both her hands in her pockets, chilled. She owed him, huh? He liked the sound of that. At the least he hoped that meant she wouldn't disappear from his life anytime soon; then he remembered the chains she had placed on him. No, she would be in his life for a while. He grimaced to himself. Maybe it wasn't all bad. Maybe he could figure out how to break out of the magic without her figuring it out; if she truly didn't know, then it was possible. In the meantime…

"Where are you sitting?" she asked him as they walked away from the locker area.

"Sitting?" he asked.

"Well, yeah. To watch the game," she peeked at him from the corner of her eye. "You could sit with us, if you want," she offered.

"Us?" he asked.

"Yeah. My friends and I," she clarified, then an unreadable expression flashed across her face. "Unless you're here with someone?" she glanced over at him. He quirked an eyebrow at her, and found himself wishing it would bother her if he was.

"No," he assured her. She smiled. They walked for a moment in silence.

"So, do you want to tell me about all that back there?" he asked. Her face fell and worry clouded her eyes. He regretted the question instantly even as his desire for an answer ratcheted up three notches. Anything that made her look like that…. She slowed to go into the stairwell.

"Are you coming?" she asked. He hesitated. Watch her watch Jack? Sounded like slow torture, actually.

"Yeah," he found himself following her down the stairs. She made her way to the bench and sat down next to a pretty girl with thick hair, artfully streaked blond. He smirked at the girl's stunned expression when he followed Deirdre to her seat and sat down next to her on the other side.

"Gretchen, Daemon. Daemon, this is my friend Gretchen," Deirdre politely introduced them. He nodded at her curtly. Gretchen raised her eyebrows at Deirdre and gave her a meaningful look. Deirdre explained.

"He took the note to Jack," she said. The girl turned her raised eyebrows on him.

"Oh. That was nice of him," she said slowly, glancing uncertainly between them.

Deirdre looked around. "I take it you didn't find Courtney and Kyle?" she said. Gretchen rolled her eyes.

"No. Courtney texted me—they left," she said. Deirdre looked at her, eyebrows raised.

"Oh, really?" she said, fishing out her own cell phone and checking the display. She had a message. She swiped the phone open and checked it. 'gon wit Kyl dnt wait up' she read aloud, and looked back at her friend. Gretchen smiled and they laughed a little together. Daemon sighed to himself. Ah, teenage girls. How had he forgotten?

The band played the final notes of the school fight song and the cheerleaders strutted off the field. Daemon watched Deirdre watch for Jack in the line of players coming back. Jack looked for her as he approached the bench, his gaze focused. She met his eyes and something intensely private passed between them. She bit her lip, and he nodded slightly, eyes dark. She sat back a little, somewhat more relaxed. Then Jack saw Daemon sitting there with her and his brows furrowed. He looked back at Deirdre, his eyes full of questions. She just shrugged, and he looked back at Daemon. Daemon just looked back at him until Jack's attention was called back to the game. Daemon shifted his weight, inexplicably feeling slightly guilty when Deirdre looked over at him.

"What was that about?" she asked, frowning in suspicious disapproval. It was his turn to shrug. *Your boyfriend doesn't like me sitting here with you*, he thought but didn't say. She knew, or she would if she thought about it for half a second. She narrowed her eyes at him, then turned away, her attention back on Jack. Defense was playing, so Jack was just resting, leaning over with one foot up on the bench. Daemon turned the words of the note over in his head, along with everything Deirdre had said, worrying at it like a dog with a bone as the game progressed. The third quarter passed with neither team making any headway against the other, and the fourth was half-over; he was growing restless, wondering what was supposed to happen. Something was, he was sure; at least, Deirdre was clearly afraid something would happen. She kept glancing at the play clock and wiping her hands nervously on her jeans.

They were on defense again when Deirdre and the entire crowd gasped and sat forward suddenly. Daemon's attention sharpened as he followed her gaze toward the center of the field, where a boy in a red uniform sat holding his arm, every line of his body taut with pain. The medics quickly braced the arm and shoulder and helped him off the field. The coach checked on his player, then turned and surveyed the rest of the team.

"Jack!" he yelled, and hooked his thumb toward the field. Jack looked up and acknowledged the coach with a wave. He ran out onto the field. Stress filled Deirdre's face and Gretchen flashed her a sympathetic look. Daemon leaned forward, wondering what bothered her in this chain of events.

"What is it?" he asked. She answered him absently.

"Jack will play both offense and defense now; probably for the rest of the game," she said. He would have sworn she looked worried, but he didn't really understand why she would be.

"Why Jack?" he asked, fishing for more information.

"Jack can catch anything and he's really fast—Coach is probably hoping for an interception," she told him, her eyes riveted on the field, a note of pride filling her voice. He frowned, unsatisfied, and sat back again, watching. A few minutes later, Coach got his wish. Jack plucked the ball from the air right in front of the stands and ran out of bounds; the crowd went wild. His grin was triumphant as he took off his helmet and ran over for a quick mouthful of water before turning around again to play offense. Daemon watched him meet Deirdre's eyes and drink in the admiration he saw there. He winced. Slow torture, just like he thought. She glanced over at him and smiled widely, a stab through his gut, but her eyes were so bright with excitement he couldn't help but smile back.

Moments later he saw her glance at the play clock and watched her face go white with shock. She leaned forward and gripped his knee with one hand. With the other she grabbed Gretchen's hand in hers. Her little hand was hot on his leg, her pulse pounded in her throat, fluttering like a trapped moth beneath her delicate skin, and he could smell her terror. Fear for the blond boy dumped adrenaline into her veins and Daemon flinched. She smelled incredible when she was afraid, and the beast stirred as his magic reacted to her intense surge of emotion. She was tugging the line again, completely oblivious. He clamped down on himself, jaw clenching. It was almost physically painful, sitting close to her while she was like this.

Jack was on the far side of the field, and Daemon watched him crouch, ready for the snap. It came and the boy was off, dodging through the blue-suited players like they weren't even there. During this last half they had really been gunning for him, trying to break up the smooth team he made with the quarterback. It hadn't worked so far, but... Daemon glanced at Deirdre's white face and felt the pounding of her heart through her hand on his knee. What had she seen?

The quarterback was taking too much time. The crowd was going crazy, cheering them on, and Jack was nearly clear of most of the blue crush when one of them finally broke through Jason's circle and leapt toward him. Gretchen yelped as he threw the ball just as the huge boy hit full on, slamming Jason into the dirt. Deirdre's hand was white-knuckled around Gretchen's and she dug her fingers into Daemon's knee. He could tell she was holding her breath, frozen, watching the scene play out.

Jason's pass was short, but not by much, and Jack turned abruptly from his clear path to meet it. He jumped into the air and captured the ball against his chest, and came down still running. Agilely, he dodged past a couple of surprised defenders, but the deviation had cost him precious moments. All the blue players were converging, openings closing even as they appeared, cutting him off. The huge blue cornerback appeared right in front of him and Jack ducked beneath his swipe and swerved to the left around him just as two other players dived in front of the cornerback from the right, bringing all of them down. One of them caught Jack's leg and screamed when his hold on the moving limb wrenched free. Daemon wouldn't be surprised if the kid had a broken arm after pulling that stunt, but it had worked. Jack hit the dirt, rolling a few times before he lay still, panting and staring up at the opposing team's stands. Incredibly, he had kept hold of the ball.

Deirdre still didn't move, though the crowd around her was going crazy. It wasn't until Jack rolled tiredly to his feet and handed the ball to the ref that she took a deep, shuddering breath and buried her face in her shaking hands. After a moment she dropped her hands to her lap and breathed a shaking sigh of what could only be relief. *In the fourth, cut left not right!* *—Deirdre.* The note had made sense after all. If he had cut right instead he would have been smack in the middle of that brutal pileup. He really *could* have died. Daemon stared over at her, mind churning. Somehow, she had known.

How?

Her eyes blazed exultantly, though damply, and her hands clenched into fists. She turned toward Gretchen and gave the other girl a tight hug, though Gretchen was still staring out at the field, watching the quarterback. He was holding his arms tight to his chest and seemed to be having trouble getting his breath. He limped toward the bench and collapsed on it, waving away the concerned medic until he had conferred for a few moments with the coach. They sent in the back-up quarterback, and the game continued. Jack managed to finish what he had so spectacularly started and made what would be the winning touchdown after a couple more plays, but for Deirdre, and for him, he realized, the game was over. Daemon touched her hand.

"I'm gonna go," he told her. She stared up at him for a moment.

"I'll come with you," she decided abruptly. She turned to Gretchen.

"I'll see you by the locker room in a minute, okay?" Deirdre told her. The other girl nodded. Daemon could feel her eyes following them as he helped Deirdre up the stairs. It seemed she could suddenly feel her ankle again; pain hovered behind her eyes with every step. They paused at the top of the stairs; then Deirdre began walking toward the locker room hallway where he had first seen her. He followed, after a few steps placing one hand under her elbow, taking some of her weight as she limped slowly along. He walked unhurriedly, matching her pace, and silently, just letting her think the thoughts inside her head while he thought his. It was restful after the emotional rollercoaster they had ridden tonight.

They were approaching the locker room when she slowed even further. A few other people milled along the hall, waiting for their players to emerge after the game, coming down early to avoid the crush of people that would inevitably fill the passage just minutes from now. Speaking of which… He stirred restlessly and took his hand from her arm. She looked up at him, leaning against the wall now. She didn't say anything, just looked, and he found himself sinking into her dark blue eyes. He swallowed and pulled himself out with an effort.

"I've got to get to work before all these people start arriving there," he said softly. She nodded slowly, still not breaking eye contact. She took a breath and he could guess what she wanted to say; it was written so clearly in her eyes.

"Thank you, Daemon. If…" she looked away, then back at him with an embarrassed little smile. "I was going to say if you ever need anything, call me, but it seems so… inadequate… after everything you've done," she laughed a little. "Was it only this afternoon you set my ankle?" she asked rhetorically. She was quiet for a long minute.

"It feels like a lifetime ago," she murmured, almost to herself, and silence stretched between them, filled with unsaid things. She tried again.

"If I could think of a way to repay you… any way… well, you know." She flapped her small hand in the air, unable to find the words she wanted. He looked down at her and, unable to stop himself this time, he touched her delicate jaw with his fingertips. She didn't flinch. Snow crystals formed on her eyelashes and she shivered and sighed beneath his touch, her breath forming a frozen cloud between them. Both their eyes widened in surprise, and she laughed incredulously, her hand flying to her face where he had touched her as he dropped his arm to his side. *How the hell does she keep doing that?* he thought in consternation. The thought crossed his mind then that he could think of a way to repay him. Several.

But he remained silent. The things he wanted had to be given freely or they meant worse than nothing. And now was not the time, standing out here waiting for Jack. Her boyfriend. His heart felt suddenly restricted in his chest, caught in a vice, and he clenched his jaw and stepped away. It was time to go.

"Goodnight, Deirdre," he said, and turned and left abruptly. She was surprised to stillness, and he could feel her standing there exactly where he had left her. Was it his imagination, or did he actually hear her whisper, "Goodnight, Daemon," underneath her breath?

***

Deirdre

Friday Evening

Deirdre felt the emptiness beside her when Daemon left. The concrete hallway was suddenly dingier, dirtier… colder. Which was strange, because he always seemed to carry a chill with him. She thought about what had happened when he touched her face tonight. Snow on her eyelashes and her breath had frozen, but inside heat had tingled underneath her skin.

"Goodnight, Daemon," she whispered to the air, tasting snow on her tongue as she breathed his name. She swallowed and closed her eyes and banished him from her thoughts as far as possible. Jack. She had managed to save Jack. He had done it. He had believed her and they had changed it. Relief washed through her again, a cleansing release of tension and fear. Her heart throbbed in her chest. Several members of the team burst through the door, and she looked up, hoping for Jack. Usually he took a shower first. Usually she preferred him to, but tonight was different. She needed to see him, to touch him, to make sure he was really okay. She watched the door.

She had almost given up when he finally appeared, still in all his gear, holding his helmet in one hand, supporting himself on the doorframe with the other. He dripped with perspiration and dark circles smudged his eyes; he looked somehow thinner than he had when he had teased her from the field a few hours earlier. Her ankle forgotten, she ran to him. She stepped up to him and stared up into his exhausted eyes.

"Jack," she breathed, and felt somehow... whole. He looked down at her, swaying with fatigue, and took her in his arms. He held her tightly, and laid his cheek against the top of her head. They stood there for a long moment, until she pulled back enough to look up into his face again. He moved his hands to her face and cradled her jaw in his palms, his fingers tangling in her hair, and what she saw in his eyes left her breathless. He bent his head and kissed her softly, almost chastely at first, then more deeply. He was here. Really *here*. Something snapped inside her and she lunged for him suddenly, tackling him against the doorframe, kissing him passionately. He froze, startled for a split second, then his arms tightened around her and he gasped.

"Jack, Jack," she whispered in between kisses. He yanked her away from prying eyes and into the shadow of the doorway just inside the locker room and held her tightly, crushing her against him, and returned her passion with interest. She slowed finally, panting for breath, and just stared up at him. She didn't want to let go of him, but she had to; at least temporarily. He disentangled himself gently from her embrace.

"I'll hurry," he promised and kissed her again. He groaned when he pulled himself away a second time. "I'll hurry," he repeated and disappeared into the depths of the room. She stood there catching her breath for a minute, straightening her hair and clothes and brushing grass and dirt from his uniform off herself; then she peeked out the doorway. Seeing no one watching she snuck back out into the hallway to wait while he showered and took care of his gear. Gretchen was still there, pacing. She walked up to the other girl.

"Hey," she said. "Any news about Jason?" she asked, remembering vaguely that he had sat out the rest of the game after Jack's narrow escape, that he had taken a hard hit as well. Gretchen looked tense.

"Bruised or cracked ribs they think. He got hit pretty hard on that last play," she said, worry clouding her eyes. "When he comes out he has to go to the hospital for X-rays—make sure it's nothing worse," she told her. Deirdre cringed.

"Gretchen, I'm so sorry," she sympathized. It could so easily have been Jack; she remembered the vision of the hit and the sound of his crunching bones and shuddered. Gretchen stared at her intently.

"You knew. About Jack, I mean. You knew something was going to happen, didn't you?" she accused. Deirdre bit her lip.

"I had a really bad feeling, so I warned him, yeah," she admitted.

"That note? It was a warning?" she asked incredulously. Deirdre shrugged and nodded, trying to downplay it.

"Well, lucky you, *Jack* is fine," Gretchen almost spat the words. Deirdre winced, wishing she could have helped Jason and Jack both. But it had been impossible. She didn't explain; she just walked away to the other side of the hallway to wait for Jack.

Chapter 4

Deirdre

Saturday

Deirdre had just stepped out of the shower late on Saturday morning when Maria called up on the intercom that someone was on the telephone for her. She wrapped a thick towel around herself and took another one with her into the bedroom. She limped over and picked up the phone, cradling it against her shoulder as she took her heavy mop of dripping hair in her other hand and squeezed it with the other towel.

"Hello?" she said.

"Hi." It was Jack. Warmth flooded through her body at the sound of his voice. "I was about to give up on you," he said.

"Sorry," she replied with a smile. "I was in the shower." He was silent for a moment and she squeezed her hair some more.

"I was just wondering if you had any special plans today," he said. She raised her eyebrows, curious. She wanted to spend at least an hour or two with Alastair, but seeing Jack would be very nice, too.

"Nothing really *scheduled*," she said. "I wanted to spend time with Alastair, but... what did you have in mind?" she asked, reaching for her detangling spray and comb.

"Oh, nothing really. I just wanted to see you," he said. She thought for a moment as she sprayed her hair with the detangler. Jack and Alastair had actually been best friends before the accident. Al would enjoy his visit, and he had been cleared by the doctor to have more visitors just this past week.

"Well... do you want to come over here?" she asked Jack hesitantly. "You could visit Al for a little while and then we could... do something else," she suggested. The horses needed exercise, and there were always movies to watch or games to play. She had a feeling Jack would prefer something outdoorsy, though; at least, he and Al had always done athletic boy things when he had come over before. She was pretty sure her ankle was up for it. The end of the line was silent for another moment.

"That sounds great, Deirdre. What time should I come?" he finally answered. She smiled.

"Whenever you want. I'll be here," she answered. She would be dressed and ready by the time he arrived even if he left right now.

"Okay, then. I'll be there soon," he promised, and hung up. She set the phone back in its cradle and finished combing through her hair, then got out the blow dryer. It took forever, but eventually her hair was mostly dry. She pulled it up in a ponytail; if they were doing outdoor things she was putting her hair up. She wrapped her ankle tightly and tested it out, walking around the room. Wrapped up, it felt almost as good as new. Amazing. She dressed swiftly in jeans and a stretchy dark blue v-neck shirt that matched her eyes. The towels went into the hamper and she pulled up the covers on her bed, then padded downstairs in bare feet and walked into the kitchen.

She poked her head into the fridge and called to Maria, "What's for lunch today?" Deirdre was starving, having slept through breakfast.

"I was thinking sandwiches," Maria said, entering the kitchen from another door.

"Sounds great," Deirdre said. "Hey, Maria?" she turned toward the maid. Maria raised her eyebrows. "Jack is coming over, so would you make sure there's enough for him, too, if he wants any?" Maria smiled at her.

"Jack, huh? And is handsome Jack coming to visit Alastair or you?" she asked teasingly. Deirdre blushed.

"Well, both, actually," she said firmly. Maria nodded sagely.

"Uh-huh. I bet," she teased and waved a towel at her. "Go on, get upstairs. I'll bring him up when he comes, and the sandwiches too, okay?"

Deirdre grinned at her. "Thanks Maria! And Cokes? For me and Jack?" Al would have milk—colas were off his diet. Maria nodded, and Deirdre went to see Alastair.

He was dressed in blue today, too, and he laughed when she told him they matched. She told him about her date Thursday night, and about meeting Daemon. He enjoyed hearing about how she had clumsily spilled ketchup all over herself. Then she told him about yesterday. He was silent, letting her talk it out. When she finished, he sat very still for a moment. She watched him impatiently, waiting for a reaction. Finally, she grew impatient.

"Well? What do you think?" she prompted him finally.

"What did you say? I spaced off…" he said and she stared at him incredulously until he grinned and she realized he was teasing her. He shook his head.

93

"It's like a made-up story," he observed. "Seeing the future? I mean, come on. And who the hell is this Daemon guy? Or should I say *what* the hell is he? Snow when he touches you? Fixing your bones? It's crazy, Dee Dee." She sat back in her chair, waiting for the rest. She could tell he wasn't mocking her; the whole thing sounded impossible, even to her, and she had lived through it. There was a minute of silence while he thought.

"Have you seen anything else? Any other future events sneaking up on us I should know about?" he asked.

"Nothing today," she shook her head. "Nothing since Jack, last night," she shivered, still disturbed by the whole chain of events.

"Maybe it was a fluke…. You know, just one really weird day, and it won't happen anymore…" he speculated.

She shifted in her seat, turning the idea over in her head. "That would be fabulous," she said, but her voice wasn't quite sincere. Would it really? What if she *hadn't* seen what would happen to Jack—and hadn't been able to prevent it? Alastair looked at her like he could see what she was thinking. She ducked her head. "Well, I guess it came in handy. Twice at least," she admitted. He shook his head and raised his eyebrows.

"My sister can see the future…" he murmured, still trying to wrap his head around the idea.

"We don't know that. We only know I could do it yesterday," she clarified.

"My guess is that these kinds of things don't go away," he asserted. She looked at him. He seemed awfully willing to believe.

"You seem to be taking this awfully well," she said suspiciously. To her surprise a guilty look flashed across his face.

"Yeah, well, about that… I've seen stranger things," he said, his thoughts seemingly turning inward. She frowned at him.

"That's funny," she said.

"Funny?" he asked.

"Not funny ha-ha, funny strange. That's exactly what Jack said," she told him. He looked at her with an odd expression in his unseeing eyes, like he felt a little sick.

"Really?" he said, and laughed weakly.

"Yeah... hey, listen, about Jack..." She paused. He raised his eyebrows.

"He's coming over today," she announced. Alastair froze in the bed and the lines on his heart monitor sped up. She frowned at him.

"What's wrong, Al?" she asked him. He sighed.

"It's nothing really..." he stalled. "It's just, I'm not sure I'm ready to be seen yet, like this, I mean." He gestured toward himself. Deirdre bit her lip, wishing she would have asked first, but not agreeing. Al was the one who was always bugging her for news—how much better if their friends would call or come see him on their own? But Alastair wasn't finished. "And also, Jack was the last person I was with... that night...." He trailed off and she flinched, remembering.

They had been drinking that night. It had taken her a very long time to forgive Jack for that, even though the blood tests showed that he had not been drunk at all; with only traces in Al's blood stream it had been ruled out as the cause of the accident. Actually, his right front tire had blown out as he was going around a curve; the car had pitched through the wire guide rail and rolled three times down the incline beyond; Alastair had been thrown clear just as the car blew up. Alcohol had nothing to do with it; just very, very bad luck. Still, he shouldn't have been drinking—he was only sixteen, and Jack had only been seventeen at the time. Deirdre knew Jack himself had never had a drink since that night, and that he still hated himself for his part in what had happened to Al.

"Do you want me to tell him you don't want to see him yet?" she asked. He thought about it for a minute.

"No. No, actually it will be good. Bite the bullet, you know?" he gave her a weak smile.

"Yeah… I guess. But only if you're sure," she said, watching him carefully. He nodded firmly. Moments later Jack followed as Maria entered the room, holding a tray full of lunch. She put it on the bedside table and arranged Alastair's sandwich on the tray in front of him while Deirdre went to greet Jack and explain about the hand washing procedure. He had slept well, she thought, relieved that the dark circles beneath his eyes were gone; he had been asleep on his feet last night after he had gotten cleaned up, and she had followed him in her car to his house to make sure he got there without falling asleep at the wheel. She had unlocked his front door for him and walked him to the door of his bedroom. There, she had kissed him goodnight and left him looking after her, his eyes unreadable, as she let herself out.

He looked wonderful in worn blue jeans and a cream-colored sweater that brought out the golden tone of his skin and hair—and did nothing to hide the breadth and strength of his shoulders. Her stomach flipped and she looked away, melting into his embrace in greeting. He put his fingers under her chin and guided her gaze back to his. He smiled his slow smile and touched her cheek with his thumb, the velvet in his eyes and caress sending heat throughout her body.

"Hey," he said, filling the casual greeting with deep warmth. She smiled into his eyes. He released her and washed his hands as she instructed, and she led him into the sickroom.

He knew all the details of Alastair's condition of course, but she could tell the reality still shocked him. She was pleased that he hid it well, greeting Al with a normal voice, full of life. "Hey, man. Lookin' good," he said, gently smacking Al on his shoulder exactly like he would have a year ago. He settled into a chair next to Deirdre's and accepted a plate with a thick sandwich on it from her. Al shook his head in response to the comment.

"Yeah, sure," Al said, his eyes following the sounds as they settled in. He flashed a mischievous grin in Deirdre's direction. "According to Deirdre, you're the one who looks good," he teased. Deirdre choked on her sandwich for a moment and Jack barked out a surprised laugh, with a pleased glance at Deirdre. She could tell her face was bright red as she recovered, closing her eyes in embarrassment. Al looked smug and took a careful bite of his sandwich.

"Al…" Deirdre chided, refusing to look at either of them. Jack squeezed her hand until she met his eyes. He winked at her and handed her a Coke. She popped the top and took a sip, cheeks still flaming.

"Well, I'm no competition for you, apparently," Jack said. When Alastair raised his eyebrows in confusion Jack explained, "It's all I can do to tear her away from you, these days."

Al grinned. "Yeah, well, she just hangs around me because I'm a captive audience," he said. Deirdre pressed her lips together and cleared her throat in mock irritation. Jack laughed.

"So. What else does Deirdre say?" Jack asked and took another bite. Al grinned and slid his blank gaze Deirdre's way again.

"Don't you *dare*," she hissed, eyes narrowed, although, truthfully she was so thrilled to see him joking around and eating like normal he could have said just about anything in that moment and she would have forgiven him.

"Wouldn't you like to know?" Al said, waggling his eyebrows. Jack grinned appreciatively and chuckled good-naturedly, but his eyes slid to Deirdre again and she could see the spark of curiosity in them. She resolved not to leave them alone together. Alastair had been her confidant far too often recently. They talked and ate for about a half hour and Deirdre watched in thrilled disbelief as Alastair finished his entire sandwich. A few minutes later Maria called up.

"Deirdre? Would you bring the tray down when you're finished, please?"

"Okay!" Deirdre called back, and stood to gather the lunch things. So much for not leaving the two guys alone. She would have to hurry. She hefted the tray and carried it down to the kitchen. Maria was putting some cookies and Cokes into the top of an insulated backpack.

"I thought you and Jack might want to take a walk or something later," she said, a mischievous twinkle in her eye. Deirdre blushed and smiled.

"We might..." she agreed, laughing. Maria glanced at the empty tray and stopped in surprise.

"Did Alastair eat his whole sandwich?" she asked, staring at Deirdre. Deirdre grinned smugly.

"Yep," she confirmed. Maria smiled at her.

"Well, I guess we'll have to have Jack over at mealtimes more often..." she hinted. Deirdre laughed and blushed again then escaped back upstairs. Jack was standing next to Alastair's bed, and they looked to be deep in conversation. She knocked on the door as she entered, and they both jumped in surprise.

"Sorry," she said, curiosity coloring her tone. "I didn't mean to interrupt. You guys okay?" Jack looked at Alastair as he answered.

"Yeah, we're fine. Al's getting tired of me, though," he grinned at her. She looked past him in concern, hearing the truth beneath the banter. Alastair did look tired.

"We should get going... let you rest," she said. Al looked simultaneously disappointed and relieved.

Jack turned to Alastair and said, "It was good to see you, Al. Really good. Pick up the phone some time, will ya?"

Alastair nodded. "Yeah. Yeah, I will. You guys have fun," he laid his head back on the sheets and closed his eyes.

"Bye, Al," Deirdre said quietly, pausing to look at him for just one more moment. Then she led Jack out into the hall.

"What should we do now?" she asked him. He shrugged and looked down at her, catching her to him with an arm around her waist.

"I don't know. It's your house," he said, "What do you suggest?"

"We could... ride the horses, or go for a walk, or watch a movie..." she proposed, twining her arms around his neck.

"Whatever you want," he said.

"Okay, then... horses?" she said.

"Sounds great," he grinned and released her, allowing her to lead him down the stairs and through the kitchen for Maria's bag, then through the great room and out the back door. At the stable, Deirdre led Jack to Alastair's horse, a gelded bay named Mandarin, and gave him Al's saddle and other equipment. Her father had wanted to get rid of the horse, since Al would obviously never ride again, but Deirdre kept stalling. It was a piece of life before the accident she wasn't quite ready to let go of yet.

"You know everything?" she asked, making sure he could get the horse ready on his own.

"Sure," Jack said. He had been riding with Al a million times, though he had usually ridden their father's horse on those occasions. She watched him for a moment as he greeted the animal, rubbing his nose and patting its strong muscular neck, saying hello to an old friend. He untangled the bridle and threaded it onto the horse's head with ease. She tore her gaze away and went to saddle her own horse, SarahBell. Jack was finished first and came over to help her.

They led the horses out to the yard and he held her horse's head while she climbed agilely into the saddle, her ankle barely twinging as she threaded her toes into the stirrups. He mounted Mandarin and leaned down to readjust the stirrups to accommodate his long legs. She led the way toward the trail, around the edge of the corral fence and through the gate. Jack followed a few yards behind, until they got to the trail. There, it was wide enough for two and he trotted up next to her. The horses were excited and jumpy, but they were both experienced enough riders that it was fun. In the cool outdoor air with Jack, Deirdre felt free and her spirits soared, all burdens forgotten. They walked and talked for a while.

"Where did you learn to ride?" she asked him. He was startled by the question.

"Actually, Al taught me everything I know about horses," Jack told her. She smiled.

"Really?" she laughed. "Al and I used to ride together all the time," she sighed, her eyes suddenly no longer seeing the trail. Jack wondered what she was remembering.

"Yeah, me too," he said. "But you and I have ridden together before," he reminded her. She smiled.

"You remember that?" she asked, laughing. He just nodded, looking over at her as they rode.

In the spring at the end of the fifth grade, Alastair had invited Jack over to go horseback riding. Deirdre had been excited to go shopping and to a festival in a nearby town with Gretchen and Courtney. Just as Jack arrived, Maria had come out of the kitchen to tell her that Courtney had called and her mother wouldn't be able to take them after all. Deirdre had been devastated. Jack had watched the whole exchange from the hall, just behind Al. He had nudged him and whispered something in Al's ear. Al had frowned at him, then rolled his eyes when Jack leveled his stare at him.

"Hey, Dee Dee," he had said, earning a scowl from her through the blurry moisture in her eyes at the irritating nickname. "Do you want to come out to the meadow with me and Jack?" he asked. Her vision cleared instantly in surprise at the unexpected offer and she stared at him, shocked. She remembered shifting her gaze to Jack, and his sweet, shy grin. She had nodded and gone with them to the stable. Her horse then had been Kylie, a gorgeous palomino pony. They had saddled up and she had followed the boys down the trail toward the meadow. The trail was damp, and she let the pony pick her own way, soon falling behind. Jack had glanced behind them eventually, noticing her lagging, and gestured for her to catch up. She had clicked her tongue and squeezed her legs into Kylie's ribs, urging her to a trot, when Alastair had yelled out his challenge.

Al and Jack kicked their horses, racing into the meadow; a split second later Deirdre kicked Kylie too, recklessly joining the game. She was already at a trot and Kylie was fast—she blew by them just at the opening into the wide, almost flat clearing, laughing breathlessly. She turned to look back over her shoulder to see Jack laughing and Al's grimace at being beaten by his twin sister, when Kylie had put her foot in a deep rabbit hole and stumbled, breaking her foreleg with an audible snap.

Deirdre had fallen off horses before, and she braced herself, throwing her arms over her head and curling into a ball and trying to roll with the impact, but this was by far the hardest she had ever fallen.

She heard but didn't feel—yet—the snap in her forearm on impact, and felt the world spinning around her as she rolled, the sharp tightness in her chest as the breath was knocked out of her, the warm wetness that leaked over her stomach and gathered in a puddle under her back from the ragged hole in her gut where a sharp stick had stabbed her, slashing through her light shirt and leaving a deep painful gash behind when her momentum tore it free. Her scream was cut off when she came to an abrupt halt against a hidden rock, striking her head sharply.

The next thing she remembered was waking up to find Jack bending over her, worry tightening his mouth into a thin white line, his beautiful brown eyes wide and scared. His warm hand clenched around hers was the next thing she felt, and then the renewed agony of the puncture in her abdomen. She realized he was shirtless, and looked down to find his other hand pressing the missing garment, now soaked with her blood, into her stomach, restricting her breath further. She struggled, whimpering, panicking as she fought to breathe. Jack called to her, leaning over her, his warm eyes boring into hers. His voice sounded very far away.

"Deirdre! Calm down! Breathe slowly, now, breathe with me," his gaze burned, and she focused, instinctively trusting him. He squeezed her hand gently and held it to his chest so she could feel him breathe, taking slow exaggerated breaths, and she focused on putting the pain aside, concentrating on Jack, really seeing him. She breathed with him, pretending the pain belonged to someone else, distancing herself until she could hardly feel it at all. He sensed it when she began to relax, as the tightness of having her breath knocked out of her faded and she shunted the pain away. The tension in his posture eased slightly, but his eyes still blazed with concern.

"Where's Al?" she asked softly after a moment. Jack's eyes darkened and he glanced behind him, over his shoulder.

"He went to get help," he told her tightly. She frowned. It wasn't *that* bad, was it?

"I'll be fine," she said, and tried to sit up. Fire screamed through her gut when she moved and she gasped as the pain returned in spades.

"Lie still!" he said roughly, dropping her hand and pushing her shoulder back down into the dry fragrant grass and shoving his other hand more firmly against her stomach to slow the bleeding she had re-aggravated. She nodded.

"Yeah. I think I will," she murmured and passed out again for a moment.

"Deirdre!" Jack snarled, coming back into focus slowly. Her head rang with his shout, and she winced.

"Okay, okay, I'm awake," she groaned. "Quit yelling." He barked a sharp, relieved laugh, his head falling toward his chest, and she grimaced. She breathed for a minute, trying to get back to the place where the pain was someone else's, where her insides weren't on fire; now she could feel her arm, too. When she could speak again, she reached for Jack with her good hand, wrapping her hand around his forearm where he still held his shirt against her wound. He leaned over her again and brushed her hair gently back from her forehead with his other hand.

"How bad is it, Jack?" she asked softly. His warm eyes turned bleak and he looked away. She pressed her lips together.

"Oh," she whimpered, closing her eyes as fear washed through her.

"Deirdre!" he growled, and she could hear the undertone of alarm in his voice this time. "Stay with me! Stay awake!" he commanded.

"Yes, Jack," she murmured, forcing her eyes open, staring up into his, only inches away now. She smirked suddenly, and he blinked at her and pulled back a little, eyebrows raised.

"What are you smiling about?" he asked her, half-incredulous.

"I won," she said smugly. He raised his eyebrows.

"Won what?" he asked. She tried to laugh and grimaced in pain.

"The race, silly," she said when she caught her breath again.

"It doesn't count if you almost kill yourself," he said. She rolled her eyes.

"That was an accident!" she scowled. He smirked.

"Duh," he rolled his eyes back at her, "but it still doesn't count." She glared at him.

"Yes it does! Admit it," she said, narrowing her eyes. He narrowed his eyes back at her.

"No," he said stubbornly, an unmistakable challenge in his gaze. She stared at him for a moment in disbelief as her temper flared; then she decided to change her strategy. She widened her eyes and stared up at him, beseeching, and blinked slowly.

She saw it in his eyes when he began to waver and she pleaded softly, "Please, Jack?" He bit his lip, but finally huffed in exasperation and rolled his eyes.

"Fine. You won," he admitted, and she smiled widely at him and was surprised by the sudden softness in his expression. He smoothed her hair back again. It felt nice, comforting. She shivered as a wave of cold washed over her and fought the lead weights on her eyelids.

"I'm cold, Jack," she whispered. She opened her eyes in time to catch a glimpse of his panicked expression before he schooled it back to forced calm.

"Stay with me, Deirdre," he pleaded, and she nodded.

"Stay with you..." she murmured, and she tried, she really did. Her arms and legs felt thick and heavy and numbness was spreading from her extremities. He took her hand and kneaded it in his and cursed softly.

"Talk to me," he suggested desperately.

"'Kay. 'Bout what?" she asked. He bit his lip, thinking furiously.

"Who do you have a crush on?" he asked suddenly. Her eyes flew open and she glared at him.

"M'not telling *you* that!" she protested, her words slurring tiredly. He grinned at her, pleased he had pulled her back a little, and her mouth curved up involuntarily at him.

"So there is somebody?" he teased. She huffed and refused to look at him. "Okay. Who was your first kiss?" he asked next. She rolled her eyes.

"Haven't yet," she admitted. He raised his eyebrow at her.

"Oh, really?" he smirked. She frowned at him.

"Yes, really, geez," she said. "Anyway who was yours? Your mom?" she teased back. He looked at her speculatively, then leaned over her.

"What are you doing?" she asked, her heart suddenly pounding in her chest.

"What do you think I'm doing?" he asked, and pressed his lips to hers for a long, breathless moment. Her heart stopped and then restarted double-time. He pulled back a few inches and she stared up at him in astonishment, suddenly painless.

"My first kiss is you," he told her, smiling his irrepressible grin. Her jaw dropped.

"Was not!" she protested. He raised an eyebrow and just looked at her. She studied him. "Really?" she said, unable to hide the smile that crept into her expression. He grinned again and put his hand over his heart.

"As God is my witness," he said theatrically. She looked at him suspiciously.

"You probably say that to all the girls," she muttered. He frowned at her and narrowed his eyes. Then he stood and walked out of her line of sight and her chest tightened in panic. He wouldn't leave her alone, would he?

"I'm sorry, Jack!" she tried to call out, but her breath was short and it was barely a whisper. She closed her eyes as tears stung them, and clenched her good hand in a fist. He knelt swiftly beside her when he came back and her eyes flew open.

"Don't *do* that!" she whimpered, grabbing his hand in a death grip, and his eyes widened when he saw her tears. He lowered his eyebrows and cradled her face in his warm hands.

"Hey, don't worry; I won't leave you, Deirdre. Never," he promised, and wiped her tears away with his thumbs. She blinked at him, comforted, and relaxed a little. Then he smiled again and picked something up. "I just went to get a few more witnesses, since God wasn't enough for you," he said, and closed her hand around a thick bundle of daisies. She raised an eyebrow at him in confusion, fighting a relieved smile.

"See, look," he said, taking one and pointing to the center. "It's like a little golden eye, watching you," he said. She couldn't help it—she giggled, then whimpered and winced.

"Oh! No laughing, no laughing," she pleaded. He looked chagrinned.

"Sorry," he said, checking the wound in her stomach. His expression was unreadable as he looked back at her face. He glanced over his shoulder, back into the woods the way they had come. When he looked back at her he was unable to hide the worry in his eyes. She raised her hand to his face, noticing the contrast of her pale skin against his tan and she grimaced.

"What?" he asked softly.

"I'm like a ghost next to you," she said, putting her palm on his chest to illustrate her point. He grinned.

"Nah. You're too pretty to be a ghost. What *you* are, is a perfect little porcelain doll," he said. She smiled again but it was tired and her heart wasn't in it. She had never felt so weak, so cold, or so thirsty.

"Do we have any water?" she asked, moistening her parched lips. He frowned in consternation, and then his expression cleared.

"Pretty sure Maria put some in Al's and my saddle bags," he nodded and was about to go in search of it, but she grabbed his hand and pulled him back.

"No. You'll never catch the horse. Just stay with me," she pleaded instead. He nodded, and held her hand for a minute, studying her face. She watched him, so glad he was there. If not for Jack... She didn't want to think about what might still happen. He had managed to help her hold back the darkness for a while, but she could feel it closing in on her, cold and heavy and black.

"Jack?" she whispered, and he bent closer to hear her.

"What is it, Deirdre?" he asked, almost as softly.

"Thanks for staying with me," she said, and fainted.

"What are you thinking?" he asked her. She stirred and shifted in her saddle, then turned and grinned at him mischievously.

"I'm thinking… rematch!" she called and squeezed her knees and lowered herself over SarahBell's shoulder in a smooth long-practiced motion.

Taking the signal, SarahBell snorted and broke into a gallop. Deirdre laughed, ignoring the twinge in her ankle as they raced down the familiar trail, glancing back over her shoulder to see Jack's surprised expression change into a wild grin as he raced up behind her. SarahBell ran full out along the trail, her hoofs beating in time to Deirdre's racing heart. About a mile down the trail she pulled the horse back to a walk, laughing and panting, out of breath.

"I win!" she called triumphantly over her shoulder. Jack pulled up beside her and, swifter than thought, reached over and picked her bodily up off her horse and sat her down in front of him on his.

"Gotcha," he said chuckling as she glared at him over her shoulder, speechless with surprise at his action and shock at his strength. He caught up SarahBell's reins and they continued down the trail. Jack's torso was warm against her back, and she found herself relaxing into him. Up ahead the trail forked. She put her hands over his on the reins and steered Mandarin toward the right-hand trail, which switch-backed up the steep side of the tall hill in an uneven zigzag. SarahBell followed docilely. He gathered the reins into one hand and the other crept around her waist.

"Where are we going, Deirdre?" he asked in her ear. "Up to the guest house," she told him, half turning toward him and looking up to see his face.

"The guest house?" he asked curiously.

"Well, sure," she paused, frowning at the unexpected question. "You mean Al never took you this way?" she asked, surprised. She felt rather than saw Jack shake his head no.

"No. We always rode in the meadow or around the lake," he said, gesturing back toward the other fork. Deirdre turned that over in her thoughts for a moment, trying to identify the reason that information pleased her. She decided it was because it felt nice to have some parts of Jack that were only hers, not Alastair's.

"Oh. Well, it's not really a guest house. Al and I just started calling it that when we were little. It's this old ruin that sits at the top of the cliff that overlooks the lake. We're not supposed to go inside, but it has the most amazing view from up there," she explained. "This trail goes all the way around the lake, too—it joins up with the paved trail on the far side," she continued, waving her arm in the general direction as she spoke.

"Why do you call it the guest house?" he asked. She smiled to herself, remembering.

"We used to make up stories about people who would come visit us there. Magical people, like elves and kings and Sorcerers," she laughed. "They would always have to stay at the guest house, so no one would find out their secrets. When you see it, you'll understand why we came up with stories like that. It used to be a mansion." They came around a bend and there it was, silhouetted against the sky. Jack's arm tightened involuntarily around Deirdre's waist and he inhaled sharply. She smiled, pleased with his response. Watching Jack's reaction to the house for the first time, she saw it with new eyes, a sprawling, impressive ruin, the rounded turret thrusting toward the sky, jagged with crumbling brick where the roof had fallen in. Chunks of fallen stone littered the area, and ivy and moss thrived in every crack and crevice.

He lifted Deirdre down and jumped after her. They tied their horses to a tree branch with easy access to a thick patch of grass. Deirdre went to SarahBell and untied the bag Maria had packed. Jack followed and took it from her, hitching it up over his own shoulder.

"What's this?" he asked, indicating the backpack. Deirdre shrugged.

"I'm not exactly sure. Maria packed it for us," she smiled. Jack smiled back at her and took her hand. She looked over her shoulder at him and wound her fingers through his.

"I can definitely see why you guys made up stories like that. This place is amazing..." he said, staring up at it, clearly awed.

"Come on. We can explore it later. I want to go down to the beach," she said, and led him away from the sprawling, broken edifice.

The path was steep, overgrown and littered with loose rocks and slick piles of dead leaves, and they picked their way down, going slowly, Deirdre favoring her ankle. She caught him looking at the bandage where it peeked through between her jeans and her shoe as she walked and remembered she still hadn't told him about what had happened yesterday. He didn't ask, yet, just let her lead the way, surefooted on the unfamiliar path, shortening his longer stride to match hers. At the bottom, the trail widened and forked, one path leading toward a dock peeking through the trees, the other disappearing into the woods.

Deirdre walked toward the beach and the dock, stepping up carefully onto the old slippery wood. Jack followed, pausing at the edge of the dock and looking out over the water. Little wavelets washed at the shore; the sound of the placid water was soothing. Deirdre walked out to the end of the pier and sat down at the edge. She took off her shoes and socks and carefully unwrapped the bandage around her ankle. She rolled up her pants, dangling her feet over the edge, letting the cool water caress her toes and ease the ache from her injury. The wind stirred her hair and she lay back, turning her face to the sun. She sighed, deeply relaxed, and eased herself all the way back, putting her hands behind her head and looking up at the sky. Wispy clouds floated high above her, and a bird floated on the breeze at the edge of her vision.

A shadow blocked the sun for a moment; Jack had joined her at the edge of the dock. He gazed down at her for a moment, looking very tall from her angle. She closed her eyes. She felt the wood squeak and shift a little beneath her back as he sat down beside her. He shifted around for a minute and she guessed he was taking off his shoes and socks, too. She smiled to herself, and her thoughts went to Alastair. It had been over a year since they had been here together. He would have been getting out his fishing pole, or throwing rocks that he had gathered from the beach far out into the water. Sudden grief washed through her and a single tear escaped from her eyes, hanging on the end of her lashes. A shadow blocked the red glow of the sun behind her eyelids, but she kept them shut.

"Deirdre, don't cry..." Jack whispered, and she heard a roughness in his voice as his fingers brushed the moisture from her lashes. She opened her eyes and looked up into his, blinking the blurriness from her vision. She gave a small embarrassed smile.

"Sorry. I just really miss him sometimes," she said, "The way it was, I mean." Jack's face was serious.

"Yeah," he sighed and reached around her, pulling her into his arms so that her head was pillowed on his shoulder. "Me, too," he said. They lay there looking up at the sky for a while, kicking their feet in the icy water. It felt good, to be held like this, and Jack was very warm.

"Let's go walk on the beach," she suggested softly.

"Mmm, okay," he agreed, levering himself up to sitting. She sat up and gathered her shoes and socks, pulling her bare feet out of the water and onto the dock, and began to rewrap the brace. He took her foot carefully in his hand and traced the bruises, so gently she barely felt it.

"You didn't have this yesterday. What happened?" he asked softly. She looked up, meeting his concerned eyes, and told him the story, unsure why she felt hesitant to do so, but knowing her reluctance had something to do with Daemon. She couldn't explain why she suddenly felt he belonged in her life, and she didn't want to hurt Jack, as she felt it might.

"After you dropped me off at school yesterday, I went inside and I was walking down the hall. A metal stud from the construction fell as I walked past, tripping me and slamming into my ankle. Daemon fixed it," she said. "Now it hardly hurts at all," she shrugged and took it back, slowly re-winding the brace. He looked at her curiously.

"What do you mean, 'Daemon fixed it'? How?" His eyes were clear, with no trace of the jealousy she had feared. She looked out over the lake for a moment, then back at her ankle and continued wrapping while she talked.

"I'm not sure, exactly. When it first happened it hurt like crazy; I couldn't even touch it without almost passing out, it hurt so bad. He said it was dislocated, and that he could fix it. It would hurt like hell, he said, but only for a second. I wasn't going to miss your game, and it already did hurt like hell, so I said okay. I figured he couldn't make it worse. He carried me out to my car, because he thought I would scream when he did it, so he didn't want to work on it there in the hall. Then he did something to it with his hands, and I did scream, the first time. It felt like he was moving my bones around," she shuddered at the memory of agony. Jack was silent, listening. He continued putting on his shoes as Deirdre went on.

"Then he did something else, like twisting and pulling everything back the way it was supposed to be. I didn't scream that time, but it was close. As soon as he finished the pain was gone—well, almost gone. It just felt like it does now, bruised and a little sore. It was... amazing, really. Then he walked me to the nurse's office, and she wrapped it up with ice." She ended the story with another shrug and finished putting on her shoes and socks. Jack just looked at her, and she wondered what he was thinking.

"That *is* amazing," he said, and helped her to her feet. She stood easily, and he followed her to the end of the dock. She hardly limped at all. She lowered herself to the rocky beach and he jumped down beside her.

He kept his gaze out over the water, occasionally checking his footing by glancing down at the sand, and she wondered where his thoughts were. The sand was coarse and pebbly, crunchy beneath their shoes, ending at enormous smooth boulders that formed the base of the cliff where it met the lake. The water was louder here, splashing more roughly against the rocks than it had on the gentle slope of the sand. She turned and led him into a hidden crevasse. Finding the familiar hand and footholds, fissures and divots worn smooth by the wind and rain, Deirdre began to climb. Jack watched her for a moment, memorizing her path, then followed.

It was an easy climb and she scrambled onto the flattened top, about twenty feet in the air, after only minutes of effort. She stepped away from the edge, running her hand against the rough cliff as Jack pulled himself up after her. He sat and dangled his feet over the edge. She stood a few feet behind him and put her hands on her head, letting the steadily rising wind lift and twist her ponytail as it stirred the waves roughening the surface of the lake.

The free fey feeling caught her again, as it had on her horse, and she threw her hands out and spun in place, eyes closed. She stopped suddenly, and her hair whipped around her face as she laughed out loud. Jack jumped to his feet and caught her waist, dragging her away from the edge, fear clouding his eyes, and she caught his forearms, gripping hard.

"Jack..." she gasped, her breathing ragged. Something felt wrong inside her head, *stretching,* and her body cramped with sudden cold from within. She gasped.

"Deirdre?" he said, his voice rough with worry.

She blinked as he held her close, warm and solid for one instant, and suddenly the world… *flickered*. One moment she was standing there with Jack on the top of the boulder, in the early afternoon, under the sun. The next, it was night, a storm was raging outside, and she was in Alastair's sickroom. Lightning struck nearby, arching through the sky behind the window, and a moment later the lights sputtered. Deirdre blinked again and she was back with Jack. Her eyes widened with fear, and she clutched at him. It was happening again, only this time it *hurt*. Dread blossomed in her chest, and then something icy cold clawed at the space behind her eyes. She screamed as agony filled her skull; something *stretched* inside her again and she jerked, throwing her head back and forth, trying to rid herself of the searing, throbbing pain. She gasped as her body fought to drag in air that felt suddenly thick and sticky.

"Deirdre!" Jack shouted, holding her upright by sheer brute strength as she writhed in his arms, one arm locking around her waist and the other cradling her head.

"Help me, Jack…" she pleaded through gritted teeth and her hands closed on his arms again, digging her nails into his skin. He winced but held her body tightly against his, bracing her upright. The thing *expanded* inside her head again, reaching, and suddenly, like turning on a tap, she felt a soothing warm flow of force from Jack into her through every point of contact. Very soon it was no longer warm and soothing, but hot and tingling along her nerves, subverting the pain with exquisite pleasure, melting the cramping ice in her veins with dazzling heat, like a mainline to the sun.

She felt Jack's long, strong body tense and tremble against hers and he tightened his hold around her. Whatever the connection was with him she embraced it like a lifeline as it strengthened; it erased the pain and tingled hotly through her body as whatever it was *stretched* again, and she *saw*. As though superimposed on the rest of reality, she saw through Alastair's blind eyes. He gazed in agony out on his sickroom, unable to move, unable to breathe.

114

The monitors were going wild and the nurse was rushing into the room with controlled urgency, a full routine already in place for emergencies like this. Then the lightning struck again, and the lights flickered and died in a shower of sparks. Alastair knew then, and Deirdre knew, as they were plunged into darkness, that it was time. He had held on for an extra year, had had a few more days with Deirdre. He was glad of that, but now it was finally time to go. The lights wouldn't ever come back on again. Not for him.

The pain and pleasure faded slowly and Deirdre went limp in Jack's arms, her hands clenching convulsively on his arms as they fell toward the edge of the rock. He managed to keep them from actually going over, more by guiding the fall than by preventing it.

He stared at her, breathing hard. "Deirdre?" he whispered, picking up her frail body and holding her in his lap. "Are you all right?" he asked, stroking the damp strands of hair back from her face.

"Jack?" she looked up at his dark, worried eyes. "Jack..." she breathed and clung tightly to him, her relief palpable. He held her close until she eventually stopped trembling. She tried to sit up and he helped her but didn't let her leave the circle of his arms. She leaned her head on his shoulder and breathed deeply. "That was... different..." she said breathlessly. He stroked her hair and shook his head, still shaking in reaction.

"Yeah," he agreed. He looked down at her and she stared into his eyes.

"Jack, it's getting worse..." she said; she felt all loose and tingly, like her bones were all squishy and her muscles were made of hot jelly. "The things I saw yesterday... well, it was nothing like this. At first, they were just flashes, like snapshots, and then, when I saw you during the game, that was really intense, like I was actually there in the middle of it, but I couldn't actually *feel* anything." She shuddered a little as the agony in her memory broke through the daze.

"So that was a vision?" he asked her. "And you could...*feel* it? Like you were part of it?"

"Yeah, but..." she took a deep breath and told him. "Something is going to go wrong with Alastair," she said intently, hopelessly. Her grip was weak but she held him as tightly as she could. "He's going to die soon, during a thunderstorm," she said, burying her face in his shoulder, tears flowing silently, dampening his shirt. The wind chose that moment to pick up, whipping around them as a cloud covered the sun and they shivered, huddled together on the exposed rock as she clung to him.

***

Jack

Saturday

Jack woke late. He felt a little stiff from sleeping so hard, and sore from his exertions at the game last night, but nothing like it could have been. He had made the coach show him the video right after the game. He might have been killed if he had landed in that pileup. The kid who had grabbed him had broken his own arm. And Deirdre had known it.... How? He tried to wrap his mind around it, but couldn't.

He looked over at the clock on the bedside table. It was nearing lunchtime. He wondered what she was doing today, wanting fiercely to see her, wishing he hadn't been too tired to see straight last night and had thought to make plans. *A human girl...* what was so bad about that, really? After all, his father had married one, right?

He knew he was rationalizing, but he suddenly didn't care anymore. He couldn't think of anything he wanted more than to be with her. He picked up the phone and dialed her number. Maria answered. She warmly told him Deirdre was busy and asked if he

116

would like to wait. He agreed. Several minutes passed and he was about to hang up and try again later, imagining that Maria had forgotten about him, when she answered.

Her voice sent a thrill through him, and he said, "Hey, I had almost given up on you." He could hear the smile in her tone when she answered, pleased he had called.

"I just got out of the shower," she told him. He tried to think of a casual way to ask her to spend the day with him.

"I was just wondering if you had any special plans today," he said. Her turn to pause. He waited, aching, hoping she wasn't busy with Courtney or something. That would be just his luck.

"Nothing really *scheduled*," she said. "I wanted to spend time with Alastair, but... what did you have in mind?" she asked. His heart thumped, but he acted casual.

"Oh, nothing really. I just wanted to see you," he said. She paused again, and he forced himself to be quiet, to just wait and see what she wanted to do.

"Well... do you want to come over here?" she asked. He could hear the hesitation in her voice, and he wondered about it until she said, "You could visit Al for a little while and then we could... do something else." Visit Alastair? He had almost forgotten that was the whole goal of asking her out: making sure Al kept his secret and finding a way to heal him that wouldn't attract too much attention. It seemed so secondary now, almost trivial. Being with her was the only thing he cared about lately, as Jason had so grumpily pointed out. Still, it would be nice to see his friend again, really see how he was doing, talk to him. And then, he and Deirdre could *do something else...* a nicely open-ended invitation, promising hours of time with her. He smiled to himself.

"That sounds great, Deirdre. What time should I come?" he finally answered.

"Whenever you want. I'll be here," she responded. He wondered how fast he could shower.

"Okay, then. I'll be there soon," he promised and hung up, jumping out of bed. He went to the kitchen and poured himself a glass of orange juice and drank it in one gulp. He was putting his glass in the sink when he saw the note on the refrigerator. He sighed as he looked at it, then scrambled some eggs and made some toast. When he was done eating he washed his dishes and went to his room and threw on some old sweats and his shoes and went out to the garage to get the lawn mower started. At least the lawn was small and it only took him half an hour. He chucked the mower back in the garage and flew into the shower. He threw on some jeans and a shirt and ran his fingers through his damp hair, then jumped into the car.

He blasted the radio and drove too fast, slowing as he pulled up the long dappled drive to the magnificent house, feeling a strange sense of déjà vu. It had been over a year since he had been here. Everything was familiar, but different too, and suddenly he felt like a stranger. He had forgotten how imposing the property was, rolling lawns and stands of trees, grand buildings, all red brick and marble and sparkling glass.

He lifted the knocker twice; Maria answered the door almost instantly and greeted him warmly. She led him back to the kitchen and picked up a large tray full of sandwiches and drinks. His stomach rumbled; he was already hungry again. He was always ravenous the day after a game. She waved him away with a smile when he offered to take the tray from her and led him up the stairs. She came to an open doorway near the top of the stairs—not Alastair's old room, but the room that used to be their father's home office. Just inside the door there was a sink with a little counter now, and Deirdre appeared there from the depths of the room.

She took his breath away, as always, and when his eyes met hers warmth flooded through him and he moved closer, drawn by an invisible force. She wore a simple long-sleeved T-shirt and jeans that hugged her curves, and her hair was bound up in a ponytail, revealing the graceful line of her neck and shoulders. She glanced away shyly, and he hugged her gently, enjoying the way she fit against him, the slight pressure of her head against his chest, of her arms around his waist. He touched her chin and raised her face to his and ran his thumb across her soft cheek. She blushed and her lips parted slightly, and she whispered his name in greeting. His heart skipped and stuttered.

"Hey," he said, inadequately, a deep warmth loosening his muscles, relaxing him. She smiled into his eyes and he released her finally, unwillingly. He washed his hands as she instructed and followed her into the sickroom.

He knew all the details of Alastair's condition from talking to Deirdre, but the reality was shocking. He was a pale shell of the Alastair he had known. A pang of searing guilt tore through him, but he hid it well, forcing himself to greet his friend normally, as he would have before the crash.

"Hey, man. Lookin' good," he said, gently smacking Al on his shoulder. Al smirked at him and shook his head. It was odd to see the way Alastair's old mannerisms had changed slightly, like a distorted echo, just recognizable enough to remind Jack constantly of what had happened. It was an uncomfortable feeling. And there were the new things: the sightless eyes, unsteady hands, and, of course, the long, thin white scar that ran down the left side of his face. It was a little like watching an actor do an impression. Some things were uncannily dead on, and some things were the actor's own.

"Yeah, sure," Al said, his eyes following the sounds as they settled in. He flashed a mischievous grin in Deirdre's direction. "According to Deirdre, you're the one who looks good," he teased. Jack laughed in surprise at the joke and glanced with amusement at Deirdre, then winked at her and handed her a Coke.

"Well, I'm no competition for you, apparently," Jack said. When Alastair raised his eyebrows in confusion Jack explained, "It's all I can do to tear her away from you, these days." He tried not to sound annoyed.

Al grinned. "Yeah, well, she just hangs around me because I'm a captive audience," he said. Deirdre pressed her lips together and cleared her throat in mock irritation. Jack laughed again. This was easier than he had thought. The twins were back, teasing each other with the easy banter of people who knew each other better than anyone else. He had forgotten how it was with them. It was nice to see Deirdre so at ease, and he watched her closely, wondering how much of her reticence this past year was related to this. Not anger or grief or accusation, but simply missing her other half. He stifled a wistful pang of jealousy.

"So. What else does Deirdre say?" Jack asked and took another bite. Al grinned and slid his blank gaze Deirdre's way again.

"Don't you *dare*," she hissed, eyes narrowed, though a gentle light floated in them. Jack looked at her speculatively. What exactly did Al know that might provoke such a reaction? He grimaced to himself as he thought about how that question might apply to him as well. Apparently, Alastair knew the innermost secrets of quite a few people.

"Wouldn't you like to know?" Al said, waggling his eyebrows. *Actually...* Jack grinned appreciatively and chuckled good-naturedly, but his eyes slid to Deirdre again curiously. Did she really talk to Al about *him*? He suddenly wanted fiercely to know what she might have said. He pushed the feeling aside and steered the conversation to more general topics, and they talked easily as they ate, taking their time. They were just finishing when Maria called up.

"Deirdre? Would you bring the tray down when you're finished, please?"

"Okay!" Deirdre called back, and stood to gather the lunch things. Now was the chance he had been waiting for, and he took it. As soon as she left the room Jack stood and came around to stand near the head of the bed.

"Hey, man. How's it going really?" he asked. Pain flashed across Alastair's face, but he answered bravely, Jack thought.

"It's okay. It's strange, almost like my old life was a dream, and this is the reality, you know?" he said. He laid his head back against the sheets. Jack paused for a moment, suddenly unwilling to broach the subject he had worried about since he had heard that Alastair had awakened from the coma. Al spoke.

"You must be wondering if I remember anything. I do. I remember it all. I haven't said anything to anyone, Jack. And I won't—ever. Not even to Deirdre," Al said, the old familiar strength of personality coming through his weak voice. Jack bent his head, relief and grief warring inside him. Al went on. "She'll be back in a minute, but I have to know something, Jack," he said. Jack nodded, then realized his friend couldn't see the gesture. He forced his voice to sound normal.

"Anything," he answered.

"What are your intentions toward my sister?" Alastair asked, his voice serious, his expression intent. Jack grinned in surprise and almost teased him, but then… He paused for a second and thought about his answer. He braced himself and decided to tell Al the truth.

"I think I love her," he said softly. Al looked surprised, then, shockingly, he smiled.

"Good," he said. "She'll need you…" he didn't finish. Jack's jaw tightened in grim understanding. Before he could say anything else, a light knock on the door interrupted them and they both looked up toward the door.

"Sorry," she said, curiosity coloring her tone. "I didn't mean to interrupt. You guys okay?" Jack looked at Alastair as he answered.

"Yeah, we're fine. Al's getting tired of me, though," he forced himself to smile naturally. Actually, that was true, he realized, as Deirdre's attention sharpened on her brother. Alastair did look tired. She came in and took Jack's hand. His pulse jumped beneath her fingers as his heart beat faster with anticipation. *Deirdre, all to myself...*

"We should go," she said.

Jack turned to Alastair and said, "It was good to see you, Al. Really good. Pick up the phone some time, will ya?" Alastair nodded. Jack hoped he really would. He missed his friend.

"Yeah. Yeah, I will. You guys have fun." He laid his head back on the sheets and closed his eyes.

"Bye, Al," Deirdre said quietly, pausing to look at him for just one more moment, and Jack felt an irrational pang of jealousy at the love he saw in her eyes, and another twist of guilt at the sadness that mingled with it there. Then she led Jack out into the hall.

"What should we do now?" she asked him, visibly shaking off the sickroom. He shrugged and looked down at her, catching her to him with an arm around her waist, loving the way she felt in his arms, and that he was allowed to hold her.

"I don't know. It's your house," he said, "What do you suggest?" he looked down at her, perfectly content. *What am I doing?* he thought, but didn't try to break away.

"We could... ride the horses, or go for a walk, or watch a movie..." she proposed, twining her arms around his neck.

"Whatever you want," he said, wondering what she would pick.

"Okay, then, horses?" she suggested.

"Sounds great," he grinned and released her, allowing her to lead the way to the stables. She paused there and he watched her decide which horse he would ride, finally leading him toward Mandarin, Alastair's horse, a strong brown gelding. She brought Al's saddle and other equipment over while Jack greeted the animal. It was almost like meeting an old friend. He and Al had ridden often, although he used to always ride her father's horse. He was surprised they had kept him after the accident, but he saw the look in Deirdre's eyes when she looked at the beast and thought he could guess why they had.

"You know everything?" she asked, handing him the saddle and half-turning toward her own horse, SarahBell.

"Sure," Jack said, expertly threading the bridle over Mandarin's ears and the bit between his teeth as she watched. He put the saddle on the horse's back and tightened up the girth, not bothering with the stirrups yet. He led the horse over to where Deirdre stood and lifted her smaller English style saddle into place and buckled it on tightly for her. He remembered Al telling him long ago what a superb rider his sister was. He smiled, looking forward to riding with her, remembering with shock that they had only ridden together once before, long ago. That had been quite a day....

He followed her outside and he held her horse politely while she mounted. When she was settled he got up on Mandarin, following as she led the way toward the familiar trail, then moved up beside her when the path widened beneath the trees. The horses were jumpy, needing the exercise; Deirdre clearly knew what she was doing. He watched her covertly; she looked at home on SarahBell's back, calm and sure and strong. They talked as they rode.

"Where did you learn to ride?" she asked him. He was startled by the question.

"Actually, Al taught me everything I know about horses," Jack told her. He had assumed she already knew that. She smiled.

"Really?" she laughed. "Al and I used to ride together all the time," she sighed, her eyes suddenly no longer seeing the trail. Jack wondered what she was remembering.

"Yeah, me too," he said. "But you and I have ridden together before," he reminded her. She smiled.

"You remember that?" she asked, laughing. *Oh, yeah, I remember*, he thought, but just nodded, looking into her eyes. She stared at him and her eyes got a faraway look, and she blushed and looked down at the ground.

"What are you thinking?" he asked her. She stirred and shifted in her saddle, then turned and grinned at him mischievously. He had barely registered the look when she took off, bent low over the saddle, galloping swiftly away. Laughing, he kicked Mandarin and went after her.

She ran full out along the trail, and he cursed the fact that he hadn't been on a horse since Al's accident—he was out of shape and out of practice. A thought crystallized in his mind as he chased her: when he caught her he wasn't going to let her go. About a mile down the trail she slowed the horse back to a walk, and he pulled up beside her, laughing and panting, out of breath. As soon as she let him get close enough, he reached over and slipped his hands around her slender waist. He plucked her off SarahBell and sat her down in front of him.

"Gotcha," he said chuckling at her surprised glare, feeling triumphant. He caught up SarahBell's reins from her hands and they continued down the trail. After a minute she leaned back into him, and he breathed in the scent of her hair and skin and felt content. Just ahead the trail forked, and his skin tingled when she put her hands over his on the reins and steered Mandarin with a light caress toward the steeply winding right-hand trail. He realized he had never taken the right-hand fork before.

"Where are we going, Deirdre?" he asked in her ear.

"Up to the guest house," she told him, half turning toward him and looking up to see his face.

"The guest house?" he asked curiously, gazing down into her blue eyes.

"Well, sure," she paused, looking surprised. "You mean Al never took you this way?" she asked, turning back toward the trail. He shook his head.

"No. We always rode to the meadow or around the lake," he said, gesturing back toward the other fork. Deirdre shifted in the saddle in front of him, and he saw the edges of her smile. For some reason, that pleased her. He wondered why. She began to tell him about the place, and he listened, captivated by the memories she shared.

Magical people, like elves and kings and Sorcerers... he thought wryly. He wondered what Al would think if he knew Deirdre had been planning to take him, a real Sorcerer, up here. There had to be a punchline in there somewhere. They came around a bend and there it was, silhouetted against the sky. Jack's arm tightened involuntarily around Deirdre's waist and he inhaled sharply, awed in spite of himself. Her raspberry shampoo and the scents of the forest filled his senses.

The house was enormous—a ruined mansion indeed. It looked like a castle, complete with a hollow-windowed, decaying tower; it was covered in ivy and moss, and half the roof had fallen in. Debris littered the grounds. He lifted her gently down, enjoying the way she clung to him a little, and jumped after her. He tied their horses to a tree branch in easy reach of a thick patch of grass while Deirdre went to SarahBell and untied the bag she had brought. Jack followed her.

"What's this?" he asked, as he took the pack from her and threw it over his own shoulder. It was surprisingly heavy. Deirdre shrugged.

"I'm not exactly sure. Maria packed it for us," she smiled and he felt his own lips turn up in automatic response. He took her hand and let her tug him down the path after her. She looked over her shoulder at him and wound her fingers through his.

"Come on," she said, walking toward the other end of the ruined patio. "Let's go down to the beach."

She led the way, going slowly over the treacherous ground. After a moment he noticed she was favoring her ankle slightly, and watched her more closely. He caught a glimpse of an ace bandage peeking from beneath the hem of her jeans and narrowed his eyes. He tried to remember if she had been limping last night at the game, but he couldn't—he had been too tired. She caught him looking at least once but didn't explain. His curiosity increased but he decided to wait until she felt like telling him about it and concentrated on just enjoying her company. It wasn't hard. At the bottom, the trail widened and forked, one path leading toward the beach, the other disappearing into the woods.

Jack followed her down to the beach and across to the long, narrow wooden platform. He watched her step up and walk slowly down to the end, sit down and take off her shoes and socks and unwrap the bandage. She moved with natural grace, confident and unselfconscious. He walked down to the edge of the dock, removed his socks and shoes and joined her, dangling his feet in the water and looking out over the lake. The water rippled quietly, washing back and forth with a gentle soothing rhythm, and he found himself relaxing. He looked down at Deirdre, her eyes closed, her head pillowed on her arms as she lay back on the dock. Her mouth curved into a gentle smile as he watched, and then he saw a glimmer of tears on her lashes. He leaned over her in an instant, concern quickening his heart.

"Deirdre, don't cry..." Jack whispered, his voice rough as his fingers brushed the moisture from her lashes. She opened her eyes and looked up into his, blinking the blurriness from her vision. She gave a small embarrassed smile.

"Sorry. I just really miss him sometimes," she murmured. "The way it was, I mean." Jack just looked at her, imagining what it must be like for her in this place of so many memories. He sighed and lifted her gently to put his arm beneath her head. She rolled toward him and curled up into his side, her arm draped across his stomach.

"Me too," he agreed, thinking of all the times he had wished Al was well himself.

He lay holding her there, the dock cool against his back, Deirdre warm and soft against his body. She sighed gently, and he wondered what she was thinking of now.

"Let's go walk on the beach," she suggested.

"Mmm, okay," he murmured, sitting up with a groan. He watched her as she sat up and gathered her shoes and socks, carefully not looking at him. She pulled her bare feet out of the water and onto the dock and began to rewrap the brace. He stared at her ankle, black and blue and yellow. He took her foot carefully in his hand and traced the bruises with the barest touch of his fingers, curious. They looked older, more completely healed, than he knew they could be.

"You didn't have this yesterday. What happened?" he asked softly. She looked up, meeting his eyes, and he was surprised to see reticence there. She didn't want to tell him. *Why not?* he wondered, watching her carefully as she spoke.

"After you dropped me off at school yesterday, I went inside and I was walking down the hall. A metal stud from the construction fell as I walked past, tripping me and slamming into my ankle. Daemon fixed it," she said. "Now it hardly hurts at all,"

127

she shrugged and took it back, slowly re-winding the supportive bandage. He looked at her curiously.

After a minute he figured out why she might have hesitated to tell him about it. She must realize that he didn't particularly like Daemon. He wondered what she would think if she understood why that was so. Apart from the way the guy looked at her, that was. He ought to be used to it. He wondered why it bothered him more when Daemon did it. It was interesting that she didn't seem to be afraid of the Shapeshifter anymore. Her fear before had been so instinctive, so automatic. He wondered how the Shifter had gotten around it.

"What do you mean, 'Daemon fixed it'? How?" he asked gently, careful to show no trace of jealousy. She looked back at her ankle and continued wrapping while she talked, a little frown of concentration and mystification on her face. He began to put his own shoes back on, watching every nuance of her body language carefully from the corner of his eye.

She told him, and Jack was silent, riveted. *Shapeshifter bone manipulation.* He cursed to himself. *He must be* old…. The shock of that didn't quite distract him from the pang of emotion he felt when he pictured Daemon *carrying* her. He fought to keep his expression neutral, continuing to casually put on his shoes as Deirdre went on.

When she finished, he just looked at her for a moment, digesting the story. He was sure there had been more to it, but he was equally sure that whatever else there had been, she hadn't consciously realized it.

He wished he would have been there to see the Shifter's magic in action, and wished just as intensely that he hadn't opted to use it on Deirdre. Daemon was more dangerous than Jack had given him credit for. She clearly felt a connection with him now, a trust that hadn't been there before. Jack wondered if he would feel more or less jealous if he knew how she actually felt about

128

him. It was a strange feeling. He had never been jealous before, had never felt like there was someone he couldn't bear to lose. He swallowed the feeling, buried it deep. She wouldn't appreciate it. She was watching him, expecting a response.

"That *is* amazing," he said, and helped her to her feet. She stood easily, and he followed her to the end of the dock. He noticed that she hardly limped at all and wondered how extensive the original damage had been. She had said dislocated, right? Even the mildest dislocation usually took weeks to recover from. *Incredible,* he thought, genuinely impressed.

She lowered herself to the beach and he jumped down beside her. She looked up at him and became suddenly shy again, withdrawing, but not completely. They turned and walked down the beach toward the bottom of the cliffs and he kept his gaze out over the water, occasionally checking his footing by glancing down at the sand, giving her space to think, to decide what she wanted from him today.

The water was louder here; spray filled the air, smelling of algae and mud. She turned and led him into a crevasse, and stopped for a moment, studying the sloping wall of rock. He wondered why she had led him here to this dead-end spot when she began to climb nimbly up the rock face. He watched her in shock.

She was full of surprises; he wondered if Alastair had taught her to climb like that or if it was something that just came naturally. He was awed again at the quick results of the Shifter's magic. Deciding to try it, he began to follow her up. She made it look easier than he found it, but he dragged himself up over the edge not too far behind her.

He sat on the rim and looked down. The place where the crack in the rock led back to the beach lay about twenty feet below. The wind ruffled his hair. He turned just as Deirdre closed her eyes, threw her arms out, and began to spin around. He leapt to his feet, half sure she would laugh at him for overreacting and half terrified

129

she would fall. He caught her as she stopped and the strange look in her eyes when she opened them and looked into his made his heart stutter with fear. He pulled her tightly into his arms in panic as her eyes flashed silver; she gasped his name and her skin was suddenly icy cold. *Magic,* his mind stuttered in panic. It wasn't a kind he recognized. That made it worse.

"Deirdre?" he said, his voice rough with worry; her eyes had gone distant and she was white as a sheet.

She blinked as he held her close, and then her eyes went wide with fear and agony and she clutched at his arms, digging her nails into his forearm. She jerked, throwing her head back and forth, as though trying to rid herself of sudden pain, and she screamed, the wind whipping the sound out over the lake. She gasped and he felt her body fighting for air, fighting something unseen inside her.

"Deirdre!" Jack shouted, grunting with the effort of holding her as she writhed in his arms, one arm locking around her waist and the other cradling her head. She was much stronger than she looked and it took all his strength to keep them upright. He bent to look into her eyes, only slightly reassured that they were blue again. She focused hard on him, clenching her jaw.

"Help me, Jack..." she pleaded through gritted teeth, and her hands closed on his arms again, digging her nails into his skin.

Fear had him reaching into his well of power, not sure what he planned on doing, not knowing what else to do. He held her body tightly against his, bringing his power up, bracing her upright, when suddenly she seized that golden stream, drawing from his source and taking it into her, feeding a ravenous hunger he could feel deep in her core once they were connected. His eyes widened and he nearly fell; it felt incredible, like she had a direct line to every nerve in his body and poured pleasure along all of them at once. Realizing it was helping her somehow, raw and unfocused as it was, and hardly able to see straight from sheer sensation overload, he opened the channel further, pouring it into her; it tingled hot along his nerves, and he gasped for air and trembled in reaction, fighting to stay standing against the waves of magic that coursed through them.

After an interminable time she went limp in his arms, and the power drain slowed and stopped. He felt weak and his nerves felt raw and over-stimulated as he fought for breath, heart pounding in his chest. He nearly dropped her as her hands clenched convulsively on his arms and they fell toward the edge of the rock. He managed to keep them from actually going over, barely.

He stared at her, breathing hard. "Deirdre?" he whispered, picking up her limp body and holding her in his lap. "Are you all right?" he asked, stroking the damp strands of hair back from her face.

"Jack?" She looked up at him and her eyes were dark black, her pupils dilated so wide only a thin ring of blue was visible. "Jack…" she breathed and clung tightly to him, her relief palpable. He held her close until she eventually stopped trembling. She tried to sit up and he helped her but didn't release her from the circle of his arms. She leaned her head on his shoulder and breathed deeply. "That was… different…" she said breathlessly. He stroked her hair and shook his head, still shaking in reaction.

"Yeah," he agreed. He looked down at her and she was looking up at him with those bottomless eyes.

"Jack, it's getting worse…" she said, and he wondered what she meant. What was getting worse? "The things I saw yesterday… well, it was nothing like this. At first, they were just flashes, like snapshots, and then, when I saw you during the game, that was really intense, like I was actually there in the middle of it, but I couldn't actually *feel* anything," she shuddered and a shock went through his body as he understood, and then another shock shook him as he processed the rest of her words. Fear for her rocked him and he asked for more information.

"So that was a vision?" he asked her. "And you could...*feel* it? Like you were part of it?"

"Yeah, but..." she took a deep breath and told him. "Something is going to go wrong with Alastair," she said intently, hopelessly. Her grip was weak as she clung to him tightly. "He's going to die during a thunderstorm," she said, burying her face in his shoulder, tears flowing silently, dampening his shirt. The wind chose that moment to pick up, whipping around them as a cloud covered the sun and they shivered, huddled together on the exposed rock. They were both too weak to climb down yet. He thought of the food and drinks in the backpack he had left near the horses. They might as well have been on Mars.

Jack's mind suddenly caught what she had said.

"You *felt* Alastair die?" he asked, looking down at her. Her eyes went totally black and he pressed his lips together in concern.

"It was more like... I *was* Alastair as he died," she said, her voice falling flat, dead. He felt a spark of power draw through him again, just a hint of what had come before as she closed her eyes, shuddering. He frowned at her. Shasta had never said anything about Deirdre being *Tear*, but there was no way any of this could have happened if she wasn't. Following a hunch, he channeled his Mage sense, looking down at Deirdre with his Sight. Curiously, the first thing he saw was a thin silver thread that stretched away from her across the lake, seemingly anchored near the middle of her spine. He had no clue what *that* was. Then the girl herself faded from his vision until only her eyes were visible—all *three* of them, two of them open wide and staring up at him, the third, located centrally where her forehead would be in the real world, barely open a crack, just a sliver of indigo blue. He gasped and blinked the Sight away.

Deirdre is a Seer. A Seer.

The knowledge hit him hard in the gut, implications spiraling through his mind as he tried to get a handle on it. She was staring up at him.

"What did you just do?" she asked him slowly. His gaze slid away while he thought about how to answer her. On the one hand, if she was part of his world, then he could legitimately tell her. Part of him was simultaneously relieved and elated to finally have someone to share his world with, his real world; part of him was exultant that it was Deirdre. He loved her, pure and simple, and he realized suddenly that he would have told her soon anyway; after all, her brother already knew. He wanted to share everything with her. Part of him apprehended how dangerous the world had suddenly become for his beautiful and gentle girl. Seers were prized, and if anyone found out about her they would want to use her. Oracles throughout history were preserved in isolation by the most powerful, or hounded to their madness-induced deaths to give prophecies for anyone who asked. Then he laughed internally to himself. He was actually contemplating keeping the truth from a *Seer*. What an idiot.

He wondered suddenly if she had ever *seen* before. If not, if this was the first time, the sudden onset of her power might account for the strangeness yesterday, warming up almost, and the tremendous draw on his power today. She was about the right age. From what he could remember from his studies, the opening of the third eye typically occurred gradually and required copious and continuous amounts of both power and time. He would have sworn even a few hours ago she was nothing more than human. He frowned, wondering about it. She didn't appreciate his delay.

"Jack, what did you just do? Your eyes just glowed *gold*," she asked again; she was looking at him doubtfully. He raised his eyebrows in surprise that she could see him use his Sight now; then sighed and began to tell her.

"Deirdre, you know those stories you and Alastair used to make up about the guest house?" he asked, trying to decide exactly how to word it. She nodded, frowning in confusion, and started to speak. He stopped her with a finger over her mouth. "I'm answering your question, I promise," he said. She looked at him for a moment, then nodded again and settled back into his shoulder. He tightened his arms around her and drew his knees up, tucking her head beneath his chin and holding her closer as she shivered against him.

It was a little easier without watching the reactions in her strange stoned gaze. She must be high on the power drain, he thought. And no wonder if she was; that had been an incredible amount of magic. He wondered what his own eyes looked like. He shook his head to get his scattered thoughts back on track. "Well, there actually are things like that in the world. Sorcerers, for one. Like me," he tensed for her reaction. She lay still in his arms, and he drew his head back to look at her face. Her eyes were closed and her face was relaxed; she was asleep. He began to laugh softly as a wave of exhaustion swept through him as well. He leaned against the rock face and laid his head back. He locked his arms around Deirdre and just held her, watching over her while she slept.

They had been sitting like that for only a few minutes when Daemon pulled himself up over the edge of the rock. They stared at each other in shock before Daemon lunged at them. He flew to Deirdre's side and studied her closely as though looking for damage. His hands twitched, like he wanted to rip her from Jack's embrace.

"What did you do to her?" he growled, so close his shoulder brushed Jack's, and he saw Daemon's skin ripple and his eyes flash silver in reaction to the touch. Jack narrowed his eyes and sat without flinching, knowing the cat was out of the bag now. Daemon knew what he was. Thankfully the Shifter got hold of himself and managed to stay human.

134

"*Nothing*. What are you doing here?" Jack asked sharply. Daemon eyed him warily and didn't answer.

"What's wrong with her?" he asked instead, slightly calmer. Jack glared at him. There was something weird going on here. What was the Shapeshifter doing here, and, more importantly, how had he found them in this remote spot? How had he known, as he seemed to, that something was wrong with Deirdre? Too many questions. And Daemon wasn't talking.

"If you must know, she's high on magic," he told him. Give a little, get a little, right? "Now, *what are you doing here?*" he asked, and his voice was low and dangerous now. Daemon stood, towering over him. Jack didn't care. He could take the Shifter, even drained as he was and holding Deirdre. Especially if the creature stayed human.

"She *called* me," he said abruptly. Jack frowned.

"What do you mean, she *called* you?" he said. Daemon glared at him.

"Use your Sight, Mage," he said bitterly. Jack's frown deepened, but he did as the Shifter asked. He opened his Sight and saw again the silver thread attached to Deirdre's center, only now, instead of stretching out across the lake, the other end was right in front of him, disappearing into Daemon. He blinked the Sight away.

"*What the hell is that?*" he asked fiercely, furious now. Daemon glared back at him, equally enraged.

"*Shackles*," he hissed at him. Jack's eyes widened in disbelief.

"You put *Shackles* on a human girl?" he asked, horrified.

"Of course not! *She* put them on *me*. And she's not quite human, is she?" he scoffed.

135

"She was yesterday," Jack asserted. "And it wasn't there in the morning, because that's when I used Sight to figure out what *you* are. She hasn't seen you today. So how the hell did it happen?!" Jack asked, fury sharpening his voice. Daemon wilted a little.

"Actually, I've been trying to figure that out myself. It was there last night, though. She called me then, too, to help her save your ass," Daemon told him. Jack blinked at him in surprise.

"So that's why you were there with her. I wondered," Jack admitted. His anger flared again. "But the Shackles look like they go both ways, Daemon. How is *that* possible?" he asked. Daemon frowned at him.

"What do you mean, they go both ways?" he asked.

"They go both ways. You could call her, if you wanted," Jack said, then balked at the thought. "But you'd better not," he warned, eyes flashing. Daemon rolled his eyes.

"Please. Why would *I* call *her*?" he mocked. Jack ignored him. He was thinking furiously.

"You never know..." he murmured, preoccupied. Wasn't there a story about Seers and Shapeshifters... some kind of mythical connection—the Guardian story—that was it. *Oh, God, no, nononono....* Daemon saw the shock in Jack's eyes as the realization hit him.

"She took your magic, yesterday, didn't she?" he breathed softly. Daemon frowned again.

"So?" he said defensively. Jack glared at him, and his eyes were full of rage and grief.

"You bastard. You son-of-a-bitch goddamn bastard. Don't you know *anything*?" he said. Daemon glared back at Jack.

"Be very careful what you say next," he warned, and his eyes flashed silver again.

"That's not the Shackles spell. She's a *Seer*." Jack put a hand over his eyes for a moment and swore softly, and Daemon froze in place, his expression revealing the depths of his dismay.

"Oh my God, no," he said, and fell to his knees. "Oh my God," he whispered, and silver scales erupted along his skin.

"Don't you *dare!*" Jack hissed at him, but it was too late. Deirdre gasped and stiffened in his arms and he held her tightly while Daemon, unable to help himself, siphoned off some of the magic Jack had given her to support his Change. She twitched in his arms and moaned as though in pain. He cursed the Shifter creatively under his breath, though he knew Daemon couldn't stop it now even if he tried. Daemon stripped swiftly, and Jack could hear him talking softly in a ritual cadence under his breath. Jack listened. Was he reciting a spell while he shifted? He had never heard of a Shifter who could work verbal spells. The enchantment chimed into place, something about hiding and binding, just as Daemon's jaw began to shift. Jack watched the entire process in fascinated horror.

It *looked* like it had to be incredibly painful, but Daemon didn't act like he was in pain; in fact he melted into it, anticipating each stage before it happened and flowing easily with it. *So fast*, he thought, grudgingly awed. *Is it always so fast?* Jack resolved to ask him about it sometime. Deirdre went still and stiff in his arms and he tore his eyes from Daemon to glance down at her. She stared, wide-eyed, as Daemon finished his transformation and an enormous silver dragon stood in front of them, balanced precariously on the too-small perch, then he leapt into the air, beating his giant diamond wings and stretching out in the air as he flew, flashing in the sun.

He returned almost immediately to the beach and curled up on the sand, dazzling the eye. *He's beautiful*, Jack thought in unwilling surprise. Deirdre stirred in his arms.

"Jack?" she said softly, and turned his face to hers with gentle fingertips on his jaw. Her eyes were clearer now, though she still seemed a little spacey. "Daemon is a dragon?" she asked, slightly shocked—but nowhere near as much as he had expected. He sighed.

"Yes. Daemon is a dragon. And I am a Sorcerer. And you, my darling, are a Seer." She stared at him and laughed a little.

"Very funny," she said. "I'm dreaming again, aren't I?" she said, then frowned and shook her head. "Why don't these dreams ever involve kissing?" she murmured to herself, sounding disgruntled. He smiled down at her, amused in spite of the situation.

"We can do that, if you like," he said, and bent his head.

"Yes, please," she whispered and met his lips. He kissed her softly, grief and fear for her making him especially tender. She pulled back after a few minutes with a contented sigh, staring up into his eyes. Her brow furrowed a little and she stroked her fingertips down his cheek.

"What's wrong?" she asked curiously. He stared down into her eyes and his heart wrenched in his chest, pounding with grief, fear, and the overwhelming desire to make and keep her safe, to hold her forever.

"I love you," he said; the words tumbled from his lips of their own accord. Her breath caught and her eyes widened in shocked surprise. She stared at him for a long moment, heartbreakingly beautiful, her expression indecipherable. He held his breath, waiting for her response.

Her mouth curved into a slow smile. "I love you, too, Jack," she breathed. He smiled down at her, suddenly light as a feather. *She loves* me, he thought incredulously, feeling suddenly like the luckiest man on earth, holding the most incredible treasure anyone had ever imagined. The feeling lasted until the dragon growled and flashed sunlight in his eyes and reality came crashing down on him again. She wrinkled her brow again at the grief in his expression.

"Can you stand?" he asked her. She stirred, moving stiff muscles.

"I think so," she said, distracted as he intended from asking again what was wrong. They would get to that soon enough. He helped her to her feet and stood himself, stretching his arms above his head for a moment. He grinned when he caught her watching him and she blushed. They walked together toward the edge of the stone, and she winced when she put her weight on her ankle. She caught his hand, squeezing hard and he looked down at her. She looked shocked again as she stared out across the beach at the dragon. She took in a deep, ragged breath.

"My ankle hurts…." She sounded surprised. "This…Jack…" She shook her head and blinked. "This… it isn't a dream, is it?" she said breathlessly, holding her free hand to her stomach, hunched over like she felt someone had punched her there. He sighed.

"Nope," he confirmed, and she sucked in a deep breath.

"*Not a dream, not a dream,*" she chanted to herself, as though trying to make sense of it, still clutching her stomach and his hand, staring out at the dragon.

"Do you think you can climb down?" he asked her. She looked uncertainly down the sloped face of the rock. The dragon stirred and lifted its huge head, watching them with silver-grey eyes, slit vertically like a cat's. Then it stood, shook itself off, and padded closer to them.

"Daemon says he'll lift me down," she said. It was Jack's turn to feel like he had been punched in the stomach. *Telepathy? What next?* He glared at the beast.

"Don't touch her," he warned, and raised his hand toward Daemon, prepared to use magic if necessary. Deirdre frowned at him, but Daemon backed off, lying back down and staring up at them sullenly.

"Daemon wouldn't hurt me," she told Jack, her eyes hurt and confused. He winced inside.

"Maybe. But he shouldn't touch you, all the same. Come on, I can get you down," he said gently, and held out his arms. She stepped close, questions in her eyes, and trust. He picked her up and held her against his chest. She felt wonderful cradled there, and she put her arms around his neck and laid her head on his shoulder, breathing softly against his neck and sending shivers across his skin. Her long, heavy hair tickled his arm, escaping strands stirring in the wind that chose that moment to pick up again. He stepped off the rock and her arms tightened convulsively as her whole body tensed. When they didn't plummet to their death she looked around in amazement, and then up at him with a wide smile. He grinned at her, realizing he was showing off a little. He saw the dragon roll his eyes as they floated gently down to the beach and stifled a pang of irritation.

"*That* was cool," she said, when he set her on her feet. The dragon huffed. She and Jack laughed. Her eyes slid over to Jack.

"A Sorcerer?" she said, eyebrows raised. He nodded slowly. "So you can do magic? Like, actual magic spells and things?" she looked at him curiously. He nodded again slowly. "So that's what Alastair was hiding," she said under her breath. He narrowed his eyes at that but didn't say anything. Al hadn't told her everything, but he had told her *something*. Oh, well. He studied her. She seemed to be taking all this rather well. He began to relax until she stepped toward Daemon.

"And you can turn into a silver dragon." Jack could hear the awe in her voice. He swallowed a stab of jealousy, wondering how much of her thoughts Daemon could hear. The legends disagreed on many of the specifics of their link. There weren't very many occurrences of them, and even fewer properly recorded; they

140

tended not to last long. Grief and fear surged within him again. He damped it down and tried to enjoy her wonder at discovering his secret world.

"Whenever you want? Not just at the full moon or something?" she asked the dragon. It chuckled, a low rumble that sounded like a distant avalanche. Jack was just glad she was talking aloud. At least he could hear one side of their conversation. And at least she didn't seem to have that connection when Daemon was human. He closed his eyes for a moment, hating the situation. She was a Seer. And she should have been his. She *was* his. But he had to share her, and the sharing might kill her or drive her insane. Dread made him feel sick. When he opened his eyes she was standing next to the beast, stroking his shoulder. He could swear the dragon was grinning smugly.

"Deirdre…" he said, watching, fear for her skittering through his stomach.

"I told you. He won't hurt me," she said, and her voice was tight, unhappy with him. He stepped closer to them to explain, eyeing the beast with frustration.

"I know he won't hurt you on purpose, but his magic… Deirdre, his magic can hurt you. And when you touch him, or he touches you, his magic can touch you, too." He put his hands on her shoulders, rubbing gently. "Tell her," he ordered Daemon, his voice sharp with irritation. After a moment, she ducked her head, listening intently to a voice he couldn't hear. After a moment Jack was relieved to see her jerk her hand from the beast's hide as though it burned. She whirled on Jack, her eyes wide.

"Is he right, Jack? Are we… connected?" He was gratified that she clearly hated the idea, but winced at the betrayal in her eyes. He was just glad it wasn't directed at him.

141

"Daemon assures me it was an accident, and I believe him. No one could have known. Even I didn't know you were a Seer until today," he told her carefully.

"It's because I'm a… a Seer?" she asked, her expression confused. He hated that he didn't have all the answers. Or any, really.

"I think so. There are legends. Of Shapeshifters and Seers forming this kind of bond. But I don't really know. I don't remember them clearly—I studied them a long time ago—and some of the details contradict each other. One thing is clear and consistent. If you feed your visions on Daemon's magic, you will either die or go insane. It's like… alcohol instead of water. Both liquid, both thirst-quenching, but one is technically a poison, and one is necessary for life. You need Sorcerer magic, Deirdre. Mine," he said, watching her eyes, trying to gauge how she was taking what he was telling her. Then he thought of something and let her go abruptly. What if she didn't want his magic? After all this insanity, she might not.

"That is, you can take mine if you want it, and it will feed your gift and sustain you. Or we can look for another Sorcerer, though I don't know of any here," he said. She looked at him for a second, then a little smile curved the corners of her mouth and heat flashed in her eyes, knocking him back a step.

"Is that what that was before? That…" She slid her eyes toward Daemon and took Jack's arm and drew him about twenty feet away, then lowered her voice. "That incredible hot tingling under my skin that I could feel everywhere you touched me? Was that your magic?" she asked, blushing furiously and looking at him from underneath her eyelashes. His heart squeezed in his chest. Was it possible it had felt the same to her? He smiled his slow smile at her.

"Yes," he answered, and heat flooded through him as he allowed himself to think of it, of her sharing that feeling again. No wonder Sorcerers fought over Seers, apart from the power play…

hot desire pulsed through him. She took a deep breath and closed her eyes for a moment, then stepped very close to him and twined her arms around his neck. He slipped his hands around her slender waist, anticipation zinging through his veins and making his heart race.

"You mean to say," she asked, her voice low and silky, "that I can have that, *and* this?" she asked, looking up at him with heat blazing behind her eyes.

"I mean to say," he confirmed, watching her eyes as he spoke.

She pulled his head down to her level, looking him right in the eyes, and then, just before she kissed him, she said, "Then don't be an idiot. Of course I want you," and she pulled his lips to hers, her mouth warm and eager. He pulled her soft and supple body more tightly against him and kissed her hungrily. She melted into him, and when she opened her eyes again they were dark and full.

"Say that again," he whispered against her neck, as she kissed along his jaw, sending trails of fire across his skin. He felt her smile as she said, "Don't be an idiot," and laughed softly when he growled against her throat.

They spluttered and fell apart as they were suddenly drenched with cold lake water. The dragon huffed and sniggered and flicked its tail across the surface of the lake, sending another sheet of water toward them. Deirdre shrieked and ran up to the dragon, sheltered by his scales. Jack clenched his jaw and flicked his magic at the water that came toward him and it dropped back into the lake. She slapped Daemon on the knee, which was as high as she could reach. Jack's jaw dropped in shock and then he had to laugh at the image of the slender girl scolding the massive twenty-foot dragon. Not surprisingly, it was the dragon that backed down, hunching his shoulders and lowering his elegant head toward her. She glared for a moment, then relented.

"Okay, okay, you're right," she said, answering some un-spoken remark, and caressed the graceful beast's nose. Jack raised an eyebrow. Did she really have to pet him? He shook the water out of his hair and strode toward them. Deirdre ducked her head, listening. She nodded. "I know, Daemon. It's okay. We'll figure it out. Don't worry," she said. She scratched the ridges along his eye and the bastard sighed with pleasure and nudged her when she stopped.

"Knock it off, Daemon," Jack warned.

"Don't worry," Deirdre said, leaning against the great beast and scratching his eye ridges again absently. "I'm full of your magic right now. I feel kind of sloshy, even," she said. Jack pressed his lips together and he would swear the dragon smiled smugly. Jack folded his arms across his chest.

"Don't you have somewhere to be?" he said.

Deirdre answered for the Shifter, which was surprisingly irritating of her. "It's his day off," she said.

"And you want to spend it as a dragon?" Jack said. Deirdre stopped scratching; whatever he had said inside her head had sur-prised her. She started scratching again after a moment, her eyes distant and thoughtful. Jack sighed and sat down in the sand, a long-suffering expression on his face. She looked at him frowning.

"What?" she asked him. He raised his eyebrows.

"I'm having trouble sharing you today," he admitted with a wry smile. She smiled at him, and her eyes were full of promises.

"He'll change back soon, and then he'll go," she assured him. Jack relaxed and lay back in the sand. The dragon flicked his tail again, halfheartedly splashing water at Jack again. Jack magicked it back into the lake.

"So what did he say a minute ago, when you went all qui-et?" he asked after a long silent minute. She looked at him for a

144

moment, then back at the dragon, conferring. Asking his permission before she shared something private? Jack wondered. Finally she answered.

"He said his human self probably won't remember much of this, and he has to... recharge, kind of, before he can change back," she told him. Jack raised his eyebrows.

"Really?" He was surprised Daemon wouldn't remember. He had thought only very young Shapeshifters had trouble with remembering their time as the beast. But Daemon had to be... hmm. "Daemon, how old are you?" Jack asked.

"Twenty-one," Deirdre answered for him casually. Jack froze in surprise.

"He's only twenty-one years old? But..." he said in surprise.

"Why does that surprise you?" Deirdre asked, curious about the stunned tone in his voice.

"Where did you learn bone manipulation?" Jack asked. The dragon laughed, a deep rumbling in his sinuous throat.

"From my father," Deirdre said, speaking for him again.

"Your... *father*?" Jack said, shock running through him yet again. He gave up trying to relax and sat up. This was one unusual Shifter. Most Shapeshifter fathers didn't stick around. And a *dragon*? There couldn't be that many of those to begin with, and they usually preferred ancient and inaccessible mountain ranges, like the Himalayas and Karakoram ranges in Asia.

"Daemon, who was your father?" he asked slowly. After a long moment of silence he glanced at Deirdre. She just looked at him and shook her head and shrugged. No answer. Jack wondered what secrets the answer would reveal and understood the Shifter's reticence. Jack didn't go around telling people who his father was, either.

"Hey, man, don't worry about it," he let it go. The dragon blinked, almost in surprise.

"He says thanks…" Deirdre said, her eyes confused. Jack gave her a little shake of his head that meant 'I'll explain later,' and she nodded slightly. If Daemon noticed the exchange he gave no sign.

Deirdre leaned back against the beast, far too comfortable, in Jack's opinion, and her eyes were distant, talking to him on their own private wavelength. Jack hid his frustration, standing up and brushing sand off his jeans. He looked up just as she suddenly broke out into a wide sunny smile.

"You would? Really?!" she laughed delightedly. She turned toward Jack, and her gaze turned pleading.

"He'll let us fly with him!" she said, her excitement palpable, her blue eyes bright with anticipation. Jack frowned in disapproval, but he felt a stab of curiosity of his own. How many people got to fly on a dragon?

"Please, Jack? He says it's too dangerous for me to do it on my own. You'll have to strap us down, so we don't fall off. Please?!" she begged. How could he resist her? And flying on a dragon, really, who hadn't dreamed of doing that at least once? He rolled his eyes and barely caught her as she jumped on him, wrapping herself around him in a full-body hug; her legs and arms clung to him for a delicious split second before she dropped away.

"Thank you!" she said, as he steadied her on her feet and she grabbed his hand and dragged him toward the dragon's shoulder. She climbed nimbly up Daemon's forearm and planted herself between his shoulder blades, just in front of his wings in a little dip that seemed made for the purpose. Jack followed her up and sat just behind her, holding her against him as he bound them both with magical straps to the beast. The bands were sparkling gold against his silvery hide, and Jack guided her hands, showing her how to grip so they wouldn't cut into her skin. She twisted around and planted a kiss beneath his chin, and he grinned at her. Her enthusiasm was catching.

"Do we need a spell so no one will see us?" he asked Daemon, an afterthought that should have been a before-thought. The dragon shook his head.

"All taken care of," Deirdre translated, almost bouncing with excitement. Then she gripped and hunched a little.

"Brace yourself," she passed on the warning, and he tightened his grip on her just as the dragon leapt into the air.

The world spun and in moments the lake was nothing but a tiny jewel in the landscape beneath them. Deirdre gasped and stared, and it truly was breathtaking. The wind tore at their hair and Jack twisted Deirdre's bountiful tresses into a magical binding that was far more comfortable for both of them. The golden light glimmered in her hair and she grinned wildly back at him and laughed. Daemon pumped his wings, sending them higher. He flew through a cloud and it froze at their passage, dusting them with snowflakes, then banked and swooped over the town and past it to the forest and beyond, then spiraled down in lazy circles, working his way slowly back toward the lake. He flew close over the town and down, flying just a few feet above the surface of the shining water, the gusts from his vast wings filling sails and ruffling the hair of the boaters. Incredibly, the wind of his passing was all they noticed. He landed gently back on the little strip of beach, barely jarring them at all.

Jack released the magical binding and climbed down, helping Deirdre. She slipped off Daemon's knee and Jack caught her in his arms, her cheeks red with cold and her eyes shining. He looked down into her eyes and released her hair, watching it cascade over her shoulders and down her back; her beauty in that moment, with the sun setting behind her and the diamond wings of the silver dragon casting golden sparks over the sand, took his breath away, and he stared. She looked up at him watching her, gazing back into his eyes, her lips parting slightly. Finally he tore himself away and walked back toward the beast's head so he could look him in the eye. He stroked the silvery neck, and it left a chill on his skin that wasn't unpleasant, like touching scales of icy-slick granite. They tugged on his skin, sharp on the edges, and he was careful not to rub against the grain, certain the beast's hide would slice his hands to ribbons if he did.

"Thank you, Daemon," he said sincerely. "That was... incredible," he said. Daemon inclined his majestic head in acknowledgment.

Deirdre came up behind Jack and took his hand, tangling her fingers with his. With her other hand she rubbed the dragon's nose, communing with him silently. She nodded wordlessly, then turned to Jack. "He's going to change back now," she told him.

They politely turned away, looking out over the lake, tinted orange and pink under the spectacular sunset. Jack put his arms around Deirdre, holding her back against his chest as they waited. He rested his chin on her head and she leaned back into him, shivering with cold. He drew on his well of power and put out his hand and lit a fire a few feet away. She gasped, her eyes wide as it blazed without any sign of a fuel source, but she bent toward the warmth, holding her hands out and relaxing more and more as she warmed up. After a few minutes, Daemon joined them at the blaze, dressed once again in his black T-shirt, jeans, leather jacket, and black boots. He didn't linger, just paused for a moment, nodded silent acknowledgment, his eyes lingering on Deirdre, and walked away toward the deeper darkness surrounding the trees.

Deirdre paused a moment, then disentangled herself from Jack's embrace and went after Daemon. Jack stayed by the fire and put his hands in his pockets. He thought about how it probably wasn't polite to watch them, and did it anyway. Daemon heard her footsteps and turned around and waited. Jack couldn't hear what she said, but he could see Daemon's face. She spoke as she reached him, and he smiled down at her, and the look in his eyes…. Jack pressed his lips together and looked away. When he glanced back, Deirdre was coming back to him, her eyes on the sand at her feet.

Daemon stood still and silent, watching her walk back, and Jack met his eyes over Deirdre's head, and something passed between them, a kind of accord.

They both loved her. And they would both protect her, however they thought best.

It was an uneasy alliance, but it was a beginning. Daemon turned and walked into the forest, taking the path along the lake. A few minutes later they heard the faint roar of his motorcycle as he headed back into town.

Deirdre took Jack's hands in hers and looked up at him, her back to the fire. "I should get you back," he said softly, noting the tiredness in her eyes. He brushed her hair back from her face, tucking a strand behind her ear in a soft caress. He couldn't decide right away if this had been a good day or a bad one. He thought of her words on the cliff, and sharing his magic with her. *A good day*, he decided. *Maybe the best day ever*. He turned toward the upward path, waving his hand over the blaze to quench it as they passed. They walked hand in hand along the beach, the edges of the sun blazing at their backs, the air cooling swiftly toward night. They worked their way up carefully, the shadows playing tricks in the swiftly fading light. At the top, they sat on the ground a little distance from the horses, and he lit another fire.

They opened the backpack and ate Maria's cold fried chicken and apples, licking their fingers and talking, watching the stars come out. Deirdre finished her cookie and took the last sip of her soda, then rose to her knees and began to pack everything up. Her hair swung in front of her face, and he caught it and brushed it back behind her shoulder. His hand lingered there on her back and she looked down at him.

"Mmmm. I don't want to, but we should get back," she breathed. He reined himself in with an effort.

"Okay," he said, his voice rough. He cleared his throat and released her and stood.

She finished packing up and he put out the fire with a wave of his hand. The moon had not yet risen and the starlight was weak; it would be difficult to ride back without light. Jack conjured a radiant blue-white ball that floated in the air in front of them. Deirdre looked at him with awe.

"I don't think I'll ever get used to that. Is it… you make it look so easy, but it can't be…" she said. It wasn't really a question, but he answered her anyway.

"It's not, really," he admitted. "You're looking at the fruits of about sixteen years of practice and study," he said. She stared at him.

"You started studying and practicing when you were *two?*" she said, shocked.

"Sure," he shrugged. "When did you start walking? Or talking? The power manifests just as early as that, and we have to learn how to use it or… well, bad things will happen," he told her, turning away. They picked their way down the rocky path to the horses, still talking.

"There was this one time I remember when I was about four. I got so mad I exploded my toy fire truck," he chuckled a little. "I was heartbroken. I really loved that truck. And my dad freaked out. My mother doesn't know, and that was a tough one to cover up." Deirdre's pause stopped him.

"Your mother doesn't know?" she asked in surprise as she resumed walking. He shook his head.

"No. It's… dangerous. For people to know," he told her softly. When she didn't respond, he drew her back to the story.

"So, I worked extra hard on my lessons after that—I didn't want to ever do something like that again unless I meant to." Deirdre tied Maria's sack on the back of SarahBell and went around to mount up when Jack stopped her. He slipped his hands around her waist from behind her and spoke softly in her ear.

"Will you ride with me again?" he asked her. She leaned into him.

"All right," she agreed, looking up at him over her shoulder, and he took SarahBell's reins from her fingers and drew her over to Mandarin with him. He got up first, then lifted her up in front of him again. He held both sets of reins and they followed his ball of light back down the path. The horses were a little skittish of it at first, but after a while they got used to it and were calm and easy again.

"Jack…" Deirdre began, then stopped. He waited quietly, one arm around her waist, just enjoying holding her close for the little time they had left. Finally she went on.

"What do you think I should do about… Alastair—the vision?" she asked. He didn't answer right away, considering her question carefully, which she appreciated.

"I'm not sure. What exactly did you see?" he asked finally. She told him everything she could remember, and he asked a few clarifying questions before he gave his advice.

"It seems like, in the vision, the power outage causes some extra problems with his care that night, right?" he asked. She nodded.

"Maybe," she said.

"Well, I think you should find out if they have a plan if that happens, like a generator or something, and make sure they either get one, or double-check it," he said. Deirdre nodded.

"Okay," she agreed. She could do that easily enough.

"Also… this sounds morbid…." He shifted behind her, uncomfortable. She squeezed his arm where it rested across her middle and he went on. "You could check the weather forecast and make sure he has extra care that night, or maybe even stay with him yourself. Sometimes seconds make a difference…" he suggested. She nodded, and he shifted again, this time in relief, and went on.

"Also… I might be able to do something," he said, and she jerked in his lap and twisted around to stare at him.

"What?!" she said. "Like… magic?" She barely choked out the words and Mandarin got a little skittish at her agitation.

"Deirdre, relax, please," he said, letting go of her so he could use both hands on the reins. She took a deep breath and forced herself to calm down. Jack got the horse under control again and they resumed their leisurely walk beneath the trees. She took carefully slow, deep breaths and he explained.

"My magic can heal, but not everything. I'm no Master. Severe injuries like Alastair's… I just don't know how much I can do. What I know is still mostly superficial. Nothing like Daemon's bone magic. But… you remember the other night, at the diner?" he asked, and she nodded, a little smile playing across her lips.

"When you first got there, you thought I had some cuts across my knuckles," he reminded her. She frowned, trying to remember.

"That's right… but there was nothing there…" she said.

"Yes, there was. I had just healed it, but not very deep. You saw through it, probably because of what you are… or what you were becoming…" he explained. She was silent for a long minute, warm and relaxed in his arms. He held her and breathed in the scent of her hair, and the horse plodded along the trail, following the dim blue mage-light.

"Al knows what you are, doesn't he?" Deirdre said finally. Jack tensed and nodded against her hair. He braced himself for the inevitable question. He had decided long ago, before he told her what he was, long before he realized he loved her, that if she ever asked about Al and that night, he would tell her as much of the truth as he could. Now he could tell it all—if she asked. Dread tightened his stomach.

"So, how did that happen? I'm guessing if your mother doesn't even know, that's some pretty heavy information," she observed.

"Yeah…" he said, and paused so long she wasn't sure he would answer. She simply waited, allowing him to decide. Finally, he did. His voice was soft and full of grief and regret.

"I hoped you wouldn't ask," he admitted softly, then paused again, feeling the tension in her back as she sat against him.

"It was that night… the night of his accident," Jack said. It was Deirdre's turn to shift uncomfortably. He went on quickly, fearing he wouldn't have the courage to get it all out. What if she couldn't forgive him? Fear of losing her twisted his gut.

"Deirdre… you have to know… Al's accident was my fault," he said, his voice tight and low. She tensed and turned toward him, her face stricken with shocked horror and grief. The horse skittered. Jack pulled the gelding to a halt. "Maybe we should stop for a minute," he said unwillingly. *Please, please, Deirdre, if I could change it…* he thought desperately. He wondered what his chances were for forgiveness, and he thought his chest might crack in two as his heart pounded heavily against his bones. She slid to the ground and stood there, her back to him. He followed her down and tied the horses to a nearby branch. He took a deep breath and told her everything, wishing he could see her face, and at the same time relieved that he couldn't watch the damage he was inflicting. He wasn't sure he could take it if she hated him after this.

"How much did Al tell you?" he asked first, hoping she already knew most of it, hoping she had already made her peace with it and had chosen him anyway.

"Nothing," she said and his faint hope died. His only consolation was that he wasn't that guy anymore. Al's accident had changed him, too, had been a wake-up call like no other. Hopefully she would see that. He took a deep breath and stuck the knife in, hoping it would lance the wound and not do more damage.

"We were drinking that night. You probably know that. What nobody knows is that Al was drunk. *Really* drunk. I took a full bottle of Jack Daniels from my mom's cabinet, and we had most of it; Al had more than me." Jack took a deep breath and stepped closer to Deirdre. She stiffened, sensing his intent to touch her, and he dropped his hands, shoving them in his pockets. She spoke and her beautiful voice was cold… dead. He had never heard it so empty, so dark.

"The police said he wasn't," she said. He winced.

"I'll get to that part," he said softly, just glad she was still talking to him. He went on with an effort.

"We were goofing around over by the ravine on the other side of town, just like I told the police," he said. "There's that ancient wooden bridge there—Farin's Bridge—the one that's practically falling apart, it's so rotted." Deirdre nodded. She knew the place. And how dangerous it was. She folded her arms in front of her protectively. He swallowed as his throat tried to close, and continued hoarsely.

"We had been out in the middle of it, throwing rocks over the edge, into the stream, having a grand old stupid time. Anyway, we were heading back, walking toward the east bank, when Al stumbled and fell against the railing. It split and he fell, but not into the water at the bottom. He fell about fifteen feet, onto the rocks," he said, and she shuddered and her breath hitched. His

154

heart stuttered and he closed his eyes, wishing for all the world that he was not the one who had caused her this pain, wishing she would accept his comfort in this moment, knowing she wouldn't.

"I panicked," he admitted. "I used my magic to burn off the alcohol and floated down to him. He was bleeding all over, and his leg was broken and he was knocked out. I just felt lucky he wasn't dead," Jack said, lost now in the tragic memory. "I conjured a light, and I healed him as best I could. The cuts were easy, but his leg and his head… I healed the cut on his head, but I wasn't sure about underneath…his brain… I just couldn't tell. He woke up as I was healing his leg. At that point it was either explain, or knock him out again, and I couldn't do that. I figured he probably already had a concussion. So I swore him to absolute secrecy, and I just… told him. I healed his leg, and it was enough for him to walk on it, and then I sobered him up. I had been planning to do that anyway, without him knowing. I wouldn't have let him drive drunk, Deirdre. But…" He shook his head, trying to clear it.

"I went home. I didn't hear about the accident for days, and by then, he was already in the coma, had been since the accident. There was nothing I could do for him," he said, grief thickening his voice. "I always wondered about the concussion. If he did have one… It might be why he fell asleep at the wheel… oh, God, Deirdre, I swear to you, I didn't know. I really thought he would be okay. Maybe sore for a few days. I'm so, so impossibly sorry. And when he woke up, I was… well, worried about what he would remember… Oh, God, I'm so sorry." His words stumbled to a stop, finally finished, spent. He waited silently for her reaction, eyes on the ground.

After a long, heavy silence, she said softly, her voice thick with tears, "Thank you for telling me." She walked over to SarahBell and climbed up. He closed his eyes; it hurt to breathe, and he couldn't feel his heart beating anymore. To be so close to her and then lose her all in one day… It was… worse than anything he had ever felt. His eyes felt scratchy and hot, and he couldn't move. She drew the horse up next to him and reached down and touched his shoulder. He opened his eyes and looked up into hers, wide and wet with unshed tears. Damp trails marked her cheeks and her mouth was full and red. His breath left him like he had been punched in the gut. He had done this. Him. She spoke.

"Take me home, Jack," she said. He nodded silently and walked stiffly over to Mandarin and pulled himself up. The night felt icy cold without her near, and he ached to hold her. He led the way down the trail on Mandarin, and she followed on SarahBell. They stabled the horses in terrible silence, and he let the light go out when they entered the well-lit yard near the house. He walked a few steps behind her up to her home, craving her touch, her smile, her forgiveness like he had never wanted anything before.

She went up the stairs onto the back porch and put her hand on the knob of the door. He stayed on the ground. Earlier she might have invited him in, but now... She paused for a moment, hunched over, then turned back toward him. "I'm going to need some time, Jack," she said. He nodded. She looked at him for a moment, then turned and went into the house. He just stood there for a minute, trying to bind the pieces of his heart back together, and finally gave up and just settled on getting through the next few minutes. He began to walk around the house, toward the front driveway where his car was parked in front of the garage. He stepped up to the vehicle, oblivious to anything but the agony inside his chest and behind his eyes, when iron-strong hands grabbed his hands and twisted them behind him and slammed his chest against the car. He didn't resist.

"*What did you do to her?*" Daemon hissed in his ear. Jack didn't deny it this time.

"What? Have you been watching us all night?" he asked the Shapeshifter, hardly able to care. Daemon growled.

"*No*. She just *called* me *again* about a half hour ago, and it was…" the pain in his voice was noticeable. He slammed his forearm into Jack's back again, knocking him against the car. *God, he's strong*, Jack thought, slow with aching regret. The pain almost felt good, like punishment: fitting.

"What did you do to her, you son-of-a-bitch?" Daemon hissed in Jack's ear again, the threat unmistakable. Jack laughed, half crazed, and Daemon actually flinched from the hopelessness in the sound.

"Tonight? Nothing," Jack said. Daemon's hand tightened on Jack's wrists with a grip like steel, binding them more surely than handcuffs, straining his shoulders painfully. Jack's breath hitched in his chest, his grief nearly getting the better of him and Daemon growled again, his disbelief palpable. Jack explained, wrenching the agonizing words past stiff lips.

"Last year I nearly killed her twin brother. Tonight… to-night she found out about it," he said, his voice trailing off at the end, almost inaudible. Daemon heard him, of course. Jack could feel the shock in his posture as his grip tightened, the iron bar of his forearm against Jack's burning shoulders a five-ton weight. Unable to breathe, Jack had had enough.

He spat a Word: "*Release*," and Daemon flew away from him, stumbling back, arms wide, catching his balance swiftly as a cat and launching himself back at Jack. He swung his fist and caught Jack across his jaw, slamming him back against the car. Daemon readied himself for another swing and Jack got up in his face, arms spread wide, spitting blood from a fresh cut inside his mouth.

"Take your shot, Shifter. You think you can hurt me to-night?" Jack challenged and laughed desolately again, then doubled over in pain, but not from Daemon's fists. Daemon paused, eyeing him doubtfully. Jack kneeled on the ground, bent over, his breath hitching in his chest. Daemon hesitated where he stood, then folded his arms and cursed. Jack pulled himself together and got slowly to his feet, still fighting for breath, like he had holes in his lungs. He pulled his keys out of his pocket.

"I'm going home now. Got a problem with that?" he asked, half hoping Daemon might take another swing. It might feel good to get in a fight. But he could think of less suicidal punishment than fighting the giant without magic, and there was a slim chance Deirdre might forgive him. He needed to live for that to happen. He clung to the idea, closing his eyes, and his breathing eased for a second. Daemon glanced up at the dark and silent house and sighed in annoyance. He held out his hand.

"Keys," he demanded. Jack swayed, then frowned, not understanding.

"Give me the damn keys, Sorcerer," he insisted. "You're in no shape to drive and she would hate it if you died before she could forgive you," Daemon said grudgingly. Jack let Daemon take his keys, surprised how closely Daemon's thoughts had followed his own.

"You think she might?" he asked the Shifter, his hope warming the icy hole in his chest.

"Geez," was all Daemon said, rolling his eyes, and shoved Jack into the passenger seat. He went around to the driver's side and cursed when he found the seat was already back as far as it would go. He drove out of the driveway and to Jack's house, not stopping to think about how he knew where that was. Jack leaned back in his seat and let him drive, taking absolutely no interest in the process.

"Oh, God, Daemon. Such a stupid mistake. So long ago. I love her. I *need* her. Do you think she might forgive me?" Jack babbled. Daemon sighed, and put the car in gear and shut it off. They just sat there for a moment, listening to the clicks of the engine.

"What do I know?" Daemon finally answered. "I've known her all of three days. You've known her... how long?" he asked, longing and envy in his voice.

"Since kindergarten," he murmured, emotional exhaustion making his head spin. Daemon stared at him, his expression bleak.

"Well, then. You'd be a much better judge, wouldn't you?" he said crossly. He levered himself out of the cramped car and crossed to Jack's side. He dragged the Mage from the car.

"My advice? Pull yourself together. Fight for her. She won't forgive you unless she thinks you're worth it. So *be worth it*, asshole. She needs you, remember? Unless you *want* to go track down another Sorcerer," he growled, and propelled Jack up to the dark house and unlocked the door. He hauled Jack to his room and threw him down on the bed.

"Get some sleep, jerk. And if you don't call her in the morning, I'm going to come back here and finish what I started," he said. Dropping the keys on the dresser, he left.

Jack obeyed, too exhausted to do anything else.

***

Daemon

Saturday

Daemon slept in. *Saturday*, he thought apathetically, waking up unhurriedly. The last few days came back to him gradually, as he lay there. He wondered if he could somehow manage to see her today. Deirdre. How had she captivated him so completely, so quickly? He had never met anyone like her, had never met anyone he wanted. She would have owned him without the spell. He wondered about that again, wondered how he could break it,

159

wondered if he actually even wanted to. Without it, he would have no connection to her at all.

He got up and scrambled some eggs and made some toast for breakfast. He thought about how he could fill the rest of his day. He could ride for a while, explore the little city some more. The weather was perfect for riding and he headed north toward the lake, then west, driving past the park he had awakened in the other night, along the lakefront marina where people were taking boats out onto the water, and following the winding road out of town.

The road grew quickly rural and nearly empty, and his bike ate up the miles, wind in his hair, almost like the snatches he remembered of flying under the moon. He stopped for gas in the next town, barely large enough to be a blip on the map, and turned north again and then east, circling around, heading back toward home. It must be past lunchtime by now. When he got back to town he drove by the diner and grabbed a burger and fries to go, and took it back to the park to eat it. He lounged on the bench when he was finished, stretching his long legs out in front of him and watched the little sailboats try to take advantage of the light, steady breeze.

He was completely unprepared when his stomach turned inside out and his heart wrenched in his chest. He doubled over in pain as Deirdre pulled on him hard. Some of his magic escaped along the line and it burned deliciously, icy hot along his veins. He swore crudely as he surged to his feet and raced for the bike, oblivious to the reactions in his wake. Startled people stared in shock as the striking young giant sprinted across the park in his black leather jacket, jeans, and steel-toed black boots, swearing creatively. He leapt on the bike and kicked it into life, knowing immediately where to go.

He found the place where the paved path joined up with the dirt one that wove around the north side of the long lake and forced himself to go slower over the uneven ground. It wouldn't do him much physical damage, but it would definitely slow him down if he wrecked the bike. He considered changing, but figured he would probably be more use to her human. He wondered darkly if it was her boyfriend again. He might have to do something about that, and the idea cheered him.

He knew immediately when she was near, and he pulled the bike out of sight into the trees. He jogged up the path and onto the beach, looking for her, not seeing her but scenting her... and the blond boy. He felt a growl in his throat. Just the two of them, and no visible danger. What had happened? He tracked them swiftly down the beach and into the huge boulders that met the cliff at its base. He wondered vaguely what Deirdre was doing climbing on her ankle, eyeing the rough rock doubtfully, but he climbed up anyway, certain of her location.

He saw Jack sitting there, Deirdre limp in his arms, and he bolted toward them, a growl in his throat. He wanted to tear her from the boy's embrace, but he noticed the relaxed lines of their posture and caught himself just in time.

"What did you do to her?" he growled, and bent to study her more closely, searching for damage. Her call had been full of pain, and he was relieved but confused to find her sleeping peacefully. He was so close he brushed against Jack's shoulder and hot magic burned through him from the touch. Recognition and shock swamped him and he struggled for a moment against the Change the instinctive threat triggered. *Sorcerer.* He stuffed the beast back inside and eyed Jack warily. No doubt Jack knew what he was; he scowled at the Mage.

"*Nothing.* What are *you* doing here?" Jack answered sharply. Daemon eyed him suspiciously and didn't answer.

"What's wrong with her?" he asked instead, forcing his words to be slightly calmer. Jack glared at him but finally answered.

"If you must know, she's high on magic," he told him. Daemon frowned. *How had that happened?* he thought, even as relief washed through him. A magic high wouldn't hurt her. He wondered uneasily what kind of games the Mage had been playing, and remembered the pain in her call. He shifted worriedly. He wouldn't get far against a Sorcerer, especially when he was human. Still, he was willing to try, for her. He would make sure it was needed first, though.

"Now, *what are you doing here?*" Jack asked again, and his voice was low and dangerous. Daemon stood, towering over him. The boy wasn't intimidated. No wonder he had been able to meet Daemon's eyes in the locker room—no wonder he had been ready, waiting. He had obviously sensed Daemon's magic. Then, another thing occurred to him. What if Jack could break the bond? He wouldn't want Deirdre bound to Daemon, of that he was certain, and if anyone could break the Shackles spell, it was a Sorcerer. Then again, what if he had taught it to her? But that made no sense. For what purpose? And how had she executed it? Deirdre had no magic of her own—at least he didn't *think* so. It was all too confusing. He needed more information. He decided to play it straight.

"She *called* me," he said abruptly, watching Jack's reaction closely. Jack frowned.

"What do you mean, she *called* you?" he said. Daemon glared at him. How could he not know? But he didn't, that much was clear.

"Use your Sight, Mage," he said bitterly. Jack's frown deepened, but he did as he asked. Daemon watched his eyes flash gold and the odd flicker as he opened his sight to the other realm. He came back almost shaking with rage.

"*What the* hell *is that?*" he asked fiercely. Daemon glared back at him, reacting to Jack's anger with his own.

162

"*Shackles*," he hissed at him. Jack's eyes widened in disbelief.

"You put *Shackles* on a human girl?" he asked, horrified. Daemon would have rolled his eyes if he wasn't so pissed. And how had the Sorcerer not sensed Deirdre's *otherness*?

"Of course not! *She* put them on *me*. And she's not quite human, is she?" he scoffed.

"She was yesterday," Jack asserted, and continued before Daemon could contradict him, "and it wasn't there in the morning, because that's when I used the Sight to figure out what *you* are. She hasn't seen you today. So how the hell did it happen?!" Jack asked, fury sharpening his voice. Daemon wilted a little. It was nice to have the time frame narrowed down. It must have happened when he fixed her ankle. Hurt zinged through him, the sharp sting of betrayal. He swallowed, hiding it with the ease of long practice.

"Actually, I've been trying to figure that out myself. It was there last night, though. She called me then, too, to help her save your ass," Daemon reminded him bitterly.

"So that's why you were there with her. I wondered," Jack admitted. His anger flared again. "But the Shackles look like they go both ways, Daemon. How is *that* possible?" he asked. Daemon frowned at him, perplexed.

"What do you mean, they 'go both ways'?" he asked in confusion.

"They go both ways. You could call *her*, if you wanted," Jack said, then balked at the thought. "But you'd better not," he warned, eyes flashing. Daemon rolled his eyes, but he felt a little better. It was becoming more and more certain she hadn't meant to do it at all. And the Mage's reaction amused him. Call *her*? *Interesting…*

"Please. Why would *I* call *her*?" he mocked. Jack ignored him. He was thinking furiously, his gaze turned inward. Daemon hoped he was coming up with a way to sever the cord.

"You never know…" he murmured, preoccupied.

Daemon saw shock and horror blossom in Jack's eyes as something new occurred to him and Daemon tensed, instinctively reacting to the boy's body language.

"She took your magic, yesterday, didn't she?" he breathed softly. Daemon frowned. What did that have to do with anything?

"So?" he said. Jack glared at him, and his eyes were full of rage and grief.

"You bastard. You son-of-a-bitch goddamn bastard. Don't you know *anything*?" he said. Daemon flinched inwardly at the open censure he saw in the Sorcerer's eyes, but outwardly he just glared back at Jack.

"Be *very* careful what you say next," he warned, feeling the Change pushing at his vision, giving everything a reddish tint.

"That's not the Shackles spell. She's a Seer, you asshole." Jack put a hand over his eyes for a moment, and Daemon stood frozen, unable to move as the information sunk in. A *Seer*. Deirdre was a Seer. He felt as though someone had punched a fist through his gut and pulled out his innards. The greatest of all taboos: *never, never*, touch a Seer.

"No. Oh my God, no," he said, and fell to his knees. "Oh my God," he whispered, and silver scales erupted along his skin. *My fault, my fault, my fault…* the mantra drove his Change like a hammer's assault, and he *knew* then the exact moment it had happened, that fateful split second when he had wrapped his hands around her slender waist and caught her as she fell. He almost didn't hear the Sorcerer through his distress.

"Don't you *dare*!" Jack hissed at him. It was too late.

Deirdre gasped and stiffened and Daemon felt the hot burn of Sorcerer magic in his veins, sucked along their connecting magic, speeding the Change and burning across his skin, clashing violently with his own icy power. Daemon stripped swiftly, automatically, and began to murmur his spell under his breath, all without thinking about it. All he could think of was Deirdre and what would happen to both of them now. *I didn't **know**!* he inwardly protested his own towering guilt, anguish burning through him as hot as the foreign magic. The familiar enchantment chimed into place just as his jaw began to shift.

Daemon flowed and melted into his transformation, reveling in the sensation as the beast emerged. *So fast!* he thought in shock, almost exploding from his flesh, and he stood for a bare moment, balanced precariously on the too-small perch, then leapt into the air, beating his giant diamond wings and stretching out in the air as he flew, flashing in the sun. *Ahhh, freedom*, he thought. But wait. He shook his head and returned almost immediately to the beach, curling up in the sun, slightly dizzy. Dual sensations warred in his head. A sweet-hot thread thrust exotic thoughts into his mind, and he concentrated, trying to follow the fragile-seeming filament back to its source. He felt external amazement, awe, fascination, and he saw an enormous silver dragon—himself, he realized with shock—as though through another's eyes.

He blinked slowly and realized with mixed incredulity and discomfiture that he could *hear Deirdre's mind*. His great heart twisted in his chest and he tensed with the onslaught of emotion, hers and his, as they both realized what had happened. Deirdre accepted the oddity with surprising aplomb, but Daemon realized after a moment that she still thought she was only dreaming as her mind floated, still high on the Sorcerer's magic. As for his own emotions, they were so mixed up he could hardly catalog them all: wonder, shock, horror, embarrassment, attraction, incredulity... He had never imagined being so close to anyone, and he was painfully conscious that she wasn't *his* to be close to, which made him feel like a voyeur when she spoke to Jack and he could hear all the things she thought but didn't say.

"Jack?" she said softly, musically, with all the undertones of emotion his name brought to her mind. He felt her inner shock as she asked, "Daemon is a dragon?"

"Yes. Daemon is a dragon. And I am a Sorcerer. And you, my love, are a Seer." Her surprise was muted and he heard her thought: *This is a very strange dream.* Daemon couldn't help grinning to himself as she laughed. He wondered how Jack would convince her.

"Very funny," she said. "I'm dreaming again, aren't I?" she said, then frowned and shook her head. And Daemon wished fervently he could turn off the surround sound when he felt her longing and she asked Jack grumpily, "Why don't these dreams ever involve kissing?"

"We can do that, if you like," Jack said, and bent his head.

"Yes, please," she whispered and met his lips.

Daemon tried again not to listen or look, and his relief was strong when they stopped. It was wrenching torment to feel what she felt while she kissed Jack when he wished… well, better not to think of it. Her emotions went sad and curious as she realized from Jack's demeanor and expression that something was very wrong. She asked about it, and Daemon wondered what Jack would tell her. He was unprepared for the words he spoke, or for Deirdre's visceral response.

"I love you," he said, and Deirdre's world spun dizzily. Her longing for this to not be a dream was almost physically painful, her deep and abiding love for the Sorcerer a tangible thing, and her thick desire for him lay inseparably entwined within the deeper emotions. Daemon bore it as best he could, realizing with anguished misery that she had been lost to him long before he ever met her.

"I love you, too, Jack," she breathed, and her mouth curved into a slow smile. The emotion was both gentle and fierce in her mind, deep and joyful and selfless, and completely overwhelming. Daemon growled, no longer able to hold it back, hating his unwilling intrusion on their private moment. *To be loved like that...* Longing and loneliness warred within the dragon.

"Can you stand?" Jack asked her. She tried, moving stiff muscles that felt somehow disconnected from one another.

"I think so," she said, distracted from asking again what was on Jack's mind. She watched Jack as he stretched and Daemon caught the echo of her hunger and her sweet shyness when he caught her looking. They walked together toward the edge of the stone, and she winced in pain when she put her weight on her ankle. Daemon stirred when he felt the deep shock of realization go through her; he felt it when she suddenly knew this wasn't a dream at all. Her thoughts hit a brick wall as she processed the idea and he could feel her body react to the stress in her mind.

"My ankle *hurts*..." She sounded surprised. "This... Jack..." She shook her head and blinked. "This... it isn't a dream, is it..." she said breathlessly, holding her free hand to her stomach, hunched over, feeling as though someone had punched her there. *He really **does** love me, he loves **me**.* Her heart soared and Daemon was pulled along for the ride. And then she looked over at Daemon, and he could feel the shock go through her again. *Daemon is a **dragon**,* she thought, clear and sharp. *He's magnificent.* He felt her genuine admiration and awe through the link.

Thank you, he said in her head, a little wryly, and she sucked in a deep breath.

"*Not a dream, not a dream,*" she chanted to herself, as though trying to make sense of it, still clutching her stomach and Jack's hand and staring out at Daemon.

"Do you think you can climb down?" Jack asked her. Vertigo hit her as she stared down the rock's surface and felt the weakness in her limbs. *I can lift you down, Deirdre*, he sent, standing up and walking closer.

"Daemon says he'll lift me down," she told Jack. It was almost worth the earlier torture to see the Sorcerer's face when he realized Daemon could talk to Deirdre's mind. Daemon gloated just a little, and she sent disapproval across the link.

"Don't touch her," Jack warned, and he raised his hand toward Daemon, an unmistakable threat. Even in this form Daemon didn't want to take on a Sorcerer. Especially not in front of the girl who loved him. The rejection stung, though. He would *never* hurt her, and anyway, the real damage was done. Barn door, horse, and all that. *I will **never** hurt you*, he sent, and Deirdre recognized the sincerity behind the promise. She turned her confusion on Jack.

"Daemon wouldn't hurt me," she told him confidently. Daemon winced at how it would sound to the Sorcerer; knowing, of course, that in reality, he already *had* hurt her, more than anyone else probably could have, simply because of what they were. Grief welled up inside him and he hid those thoughts from her as best he could. Jack was gracious, in a way. He didn't immediately condemn, at least, and he distracted Deirdre long enough for Daemon to hide his regret. *Still, what a show-off.*

"Maybe. But he shouldn't touch you, all the same. Come on, I can get you down." He held out his arms and picked her up, holding her against his chest. Deirdre wrapped her arms around his neck and leaned her head on his shoulder. Daemon remembered how that felt with a pang of envy. A moment later Jack stepped off the rock and floated gently toward the ground as she clung to him in awed surprise. Daemon rolled his eyes and huffed, and they both laughed. Well, could he blame Jack, really? He had been showing off when he set her ankle, too. Well, a little.

"*That* was cool," she said, when he set her on her feet. She straightened her clothes and hugged herself for a second before she spoke again.

"A Sorcerer?" she said, eyebrows raised. He nodded slowly. "So you can do magic? Like, actual magic? Spells and things?" She cocked her shapely head, looking at him curiously. Jack nodded again. "So that's what Alastair meant," she whispered to herself. Daemon wondered for a moment who Alastair was and what he was to her—he was all mixed up in her mind; love and pain and regret and care and a sense of long close history together... *Oh, her brother. A twin? Interesting. But he was an invalid....* His thoughts were interrupted as her attention turned back toward Daemon.

"And you can turn into a silver dragon." He could hear the awe in her mind, and the curiosity. Old legends traipsed through her thoughts for a moment.

"Whenever you want? Not just at the full moon or something?" she asked him. He had to laugh at that. *Not just at the full moon, although it is easier then*, he answered. She smiled, and came closer, and reached out and stroked his shoulder. The dual sensation was amazingly pleasant, the way it felt to her to stroke his hide, cold and smooth and sharp beneath her hand, and the light caress of her tiny, warm fingers on his shoulder. She smelled incredible from this form, warm and sweet and mouth-watering.... He stifled the thought as soon as it occurred, doubly thankful for the restrictive spell.

"Deirdre..." Jack warned, watching her with fear in his eyes.

"I told you. He won't hurt me," she said, not understanding Jack's reservations and unhappy with him a little for it. He explained kindly, Daemon thought. He could have been much harsher, and been perfectly justified. An unusual person, Jack. His respect for the boy went up a notch.

"I know he won't hurt you on purpose, but his magic... Deirdre, his magic *can* hurt you. And when you touch him, or he touches you, his magic can touch you too," he put his hands on her shoulders, rubbing gently, and Daemon cringed from her pleasure at his touch.

"Tell her," Jack ordered Daemon, his voice suddenly harsh. And Daemon did, speaking carefully, mind to mind. *Yesterday, when I caught you as you fell, something happened. Shapeshifters and Seers... I never should have touched you. I didn't know, Deirdre, I swear it. But now, it's too late, and there's a connection between us, a magical bond. It's how I can hear your mind, and how I know when you're in trouble. That's how I came to you last night at the game—it's why I'm here now. I felt your pain. But Deirdre, my magic isn't good for you. You need his. Sorcerer magic is the only thing that will keep you sane and whole through your visions.* He braced himself for her wrath, but when her reaction came it was much worse than anger. She felt... violated. He retreated, feeling sick, hiding deep inside his mind from the force of that emotion, and his own grief and anger welled up again. He hadn't asked for this either, after all.

"Is he right, Jack? Are we... connected?" She turned to Jack. Again, the Sorcerer was generous. Daemon would almost rather he had attacked. Punishment felt more fitting than forgiveness, and it would have felt good to lash out. Still, the only punishment that would change anything was death—according to the legends, at least. He wasn't ready to go that far yet. Jack's reticence was looking more and more like wisdom. Daemon and Deirdre would be bonded possibly for the duration of their lives. How long did Seers live anyway? Maybe it was a moot point. The bond itself would kill her far earlier than her natural lifespan, whatever that was. He felt sick again. He listened miserably while the Sorcerer explained.

"Daemon assures me it was an accident, and I believe him. No one could have known. Even I didn't know you were a Seer until today," he told her carefully.

"It's because I'm a... a Seer?" she asked, her expression confused, and an inkling of resentment of her newly discovered power flashed through her mind so quickly Daemon almost didn't catch it. He frowned to himself. Jack was talking.

"I think so. There are legends. Of Shapeshifters and Seers forming this kind of bond. But I don't really know. I don't remember them clearly. The only stories at all are ancient and corrupted, and some of the details contradict each other. One thing is clear and consistent. If you feed your visions on Daemon's magic, you will either die or go insane. It's like… alcohol instead of water. Both liquid, both thirst-quenching, but one is a technically a poison, and one is necessary for life. You need Sorcerer magic, Deirdre. Mine," he said, and Daemon heard the longing in his voice, though Deirdre didn't—she was too preoccupied. Then his attention focused with surprise as Jack's tone changed.

What is he doing? Daemon thought, incredulous.

"That is, you can take mine if you want it, and it will feed your gift and sustain you. Or we can look for another Sorcerer," he said. *That is one clever bastard*, Daemon thought in reluctant admiration as he felt Deirdre's reaction to Jack's words. In two sentences he had given her choices, respect, and selflessness. She remembered sharing Jack's power earlier. *Whoa*, Daemon thought, and then he put two and two together, momentarily sidetracked. *So that was why she called me—she had a vision*, and he hated that using his Shapeshifter magic at first had caused her such pain.

Her reaction to her memories dragged his attention back; her raw desire rocked him and he blocked her off as best he could. She and Jack walked away, and that helped a little, but it was still like listening to passionate lovers at a door that was slightly ajar. He tried very, very hard to think of other things and not put himself in Jack's place, imagining her whispering those words in *his* ear… He turned his thoughts to flying. Soaring high above the earth, riding the wind… He withstood it as long as he could, then flicked his tail across the surface of the lake, drenching them in cold lake water.

They spluttered and fell apart, and he huffed and sniggered at the shocked expressions on their faces. Just for kicks, he did it again, sending another sheet of water toward them. Deirdre shrieked and ran close to him, sheltering in his shadow. Jack clenched his jaw and flicked his magic at the water that came toward him and it dropped back into the lake. Deirdre slapped Daemon on the knee, which was as high as she could reach, and he ducked his head apologetically. *I'm sorry!* he thought at her. *You guys are just so... loud? It's impossible to ignore*, he said. She glared for a moment, then relented.

"Okay, okay, you're right," she said, awkwardness coloring her thoughts as she caught the echo of what it was like for him to have to listen to them be in love. She caressed the sensitive skin of his nose and he sighed with pleasure, half at the sensation of her hands on him, and half at the expression on Jack's face.

I really am sorry about everything, Deirdre. I didn't know what it would do... Well, I didn't know you were a Seer. I just—I couldn't let you fall. I'll try to stay away from you, if that helps. And maybe your Sorcerer can break the bond.

She nodded. "I know, Daemon. It's okay. We'll figure it out. Don't worry," she said. She scratched the ridges along his eye and he treasured the gentle touch and the softness of unexpected forgiveness in her thoughts. He tried not to love her more for it, or at least not to let it show in his thoughts. She stopped scratching and he nudged her gently to continue. He had forgotten how pleasant it was to be touched. His father had scratched and petted him like this sometimes, but it had been years since anyone had even known he was around in this form, thanks to the spell. And he hadn't been close to anyone in his other form either. Too many lies had to be told to be close to a human, and other Tears carried their own set of dangers. He had missed it more than he realized.

"Knock it off, Daemon," Jack warned.

"Don't worry," Deirdre said, having followed Daemon's thoughts shyly. She leaned against him and scratched his eye ridges again absently. She addressed what she thought was Jack's concern; Daemon could have told her that magical incompatibility might

172

not be the real problem the Sorcerer had with her getting so comfortable with him, but what fun was that? "I'm full of your magic right now. I feel kind of sloshy, even," she said. Jack pressed his lips together and Daemon smiled smugly to himself. Jack folded his arms across his chest.

"Don't you have somewhere to be?" he said.

It's my day off, Daemon told Deirdre, laughing to himself when she echoed him for Jack's benefit, annoying the Sorcerer further.

"And you want to spend it as a dragon?" Jack said.

Why not? I won't remember much anyway, he thought. Deirdre stopped scratching, and her thoughts were surprised.

You won't? Why not? she asked.

Don't really know. Too young, or something. It takes a long time for a Shapeshifter to be able to control their other half. That's why I use a binding spell. I might hunt in this form and never remember. His thoughts shuddered and flashes of horror stories that felt like reality flickered in his mind. She started scratching again after a moment, her thoughts distant. Jack sighed and sat down in the sand, a long-suffering expression on his face. She looked at him frowning.

"What?" she asked him, picking up on his annoyance. He raised his eyebrows.

"I'm having trouble sharing you today," he admitted with a wry smile. She smiled at him, and her thoughts were full of promises. Daemon winced.

I won't stay much longer. I'm recharged enough to change back soon, he thought. He had had about as much of the two of them as he wanted. Deirdre by herself, on the other hand… But no. There were a hundred reasons why that wasn't a good idea. He tried to stifle the thought so she wouldn't catch it.

"He'll change back soon, and then he'll go," she said. Jack relaxed and lay back in the sand. The dragon flicked his tail again, halfheartedly splashing water at Jack. Jack magicked it back into the lake with a thought. *Show off*, Daemon thought. Deirdre smiled.

"So what did he say a bit ago, when you went all quiet?" Jack asked her after a long silent minute. She looked at him for a moment, then back at Daemon, conferring.

Is it all right if I tell him? she thought. He was surprised at her consideration.

Sure. He probably already knows, he thought. She answered Jack's question aloud.

"He says his human self probably won't remember much of this," she told him. Jack raised his eyebrows.

"Really?" he sounded surprised, but then asked, "Daemon, how old are you?"

"Twenty-one," Deirdre answered for him casually. Jack froze, and Daemon wondered at the Sorcerer's obvious surprise. Yes, he was young for a Shapeshifter, but why had Jack assumed he was older?

"Why does that surprise you?" Deirdre asked, curious about the stunned tone in his voice, echoing the direction of Daemon's thoughts.

"Where did you learn bone manipulation?" Jack asked. The dragon laughed, a deep rumbling in his sinuous throat.

Oh. Of course. Only the very old Shapeshifters remember that; it's considered a lost art, he told Deirdre. *I learned it from my father.*

"From my father," Deirdre said, speaking for him again.

"Your *father*?" Jack said, sounding, if possible, even more shocked. He sat up.

"Daemon, who was your father?" he asked slowly. Daemon abruptly shut down his thoughts, thinking again of flying. He had already said enough; maybe too much. That was a very penetrating question—he had underestimated the Sorcerer again. Deirdre sensed his reluctance and didn't pry, just shrugged at Jack, conveying Daemon's non-answer.

"Hey, man, don't worry about it," Jack let it go. The dragon blinked, surprised and grateful that he didn't ask Deirdre to push for an answer. She could probably find out if she wanted to, what with her carte blanche access to the inside of his head.

I would never do that, she told him, responding to his uncomfortable thoughts of another searching through his mind. He felt her sincerity, and echoed it with his own.

Feeling strangely reassured, he said, *Thank him for me, please.*

"He says thanks..." Deirdre said, her thoughts confused by the exchange, but willing to let it go for now.

Deirdre leaned back against him, and he enjoyed the warmth and gentle pressure of her weight against his skin; her scent filled the air. He was getting hungry. It was very close to time to change back. He hid the gruesome urge by thinking of flying again. She followed his thoughts this time, and Daemon was surprised to feel her longing to follow him into the sky.

Would you like to fly with me? he offered tentatively, unable to hide his pleasure when the idea caused her heart to stutter and her blood race with anticipation.

"You would? Really?!" she laughed delightedly. She turned toward Jack, and her gaze turned pleading.

"He'll let us fly with him!" she said, her excitement shining in the front of her mind.

He has to use his magic to bind you; it's too dangerous unless he comes along, Daemon warned, his own longing for the sky building with her enthusiasm.

"Please, Jack?" she begged. Jack agreed, but even his presence could not spoil this. Deirdre's experience would be Daemon's in a way it would never be Jack's, and Daemon held on to that.

"Thank you!" she said, and she climbed nimbly up Daemon's forearm and planted herself between his shoulder blades, just in front of his wings. Her weight was almost unnoticeable. Jack followed her up and sat just behind her, and he bound them both with magical straps. The bands tingled hot against his hide, but it wasn't unpleasant, and he could feel Deirdre's excitement expand as the moment drew closer.

"Do I need a spell so no one will see us?" Jack asked Daemon. He shook his head. *All taken care of*, Daemon thought as he readied himself to spring.

"All taken care of," Deirdre echoed, almost bouncing with excitement. Then she gripped and hunched a little, gripping onto him with her legs.

Here we go, he thought.

"Brace yourself," she passed on the warning, and Daemon leapt into the air, watching Deirdre's reactions and feeling her thoughts, closer than he had ever thought to be to another person.

His diamond wings caught the air and he flapped them powerfully, rising swiftly higher, instinctively using the flowing air currents and his icy magic to speed his ascent. The wind whistled past them, warm to Daemon but crisp and cold to Deirdre, exhilarating, and she laughed recklessly. Daemon flew higher, until the lake was nothing but a tiny jewel in the landscape and they could see a faint curve in the horizon, partially obscured by clouds in the east and the flaming ball of the lowering sun in the west. The air was light up here, making her feel lightheaded and making

Daemon work harder for altitude; he flew slowly lower, gliding through a cloud, dusting them all with snow with a faint pulse of his magic, rewarded by Deirdre's soft breath of incredulity in the back of his mind.

He turned west, toward the sun, past the town far below, and over the seemingly endless forest of trees, flying for miles, retracing his motorcycle route of this morning through the air. Her wonder and joy was like ambrosia in his thoughts, and he could have flown like that forever, but he could feel her beginning to feel the chill past the adrenaline, and the trace of tiredness that she fought against. Regretfully, he turned back, flying in lazy dizzy-making circles, enjoying her roller-coaster high and delighted laughter when he managed to make her feel weightless, held down only by magical straps of gold. She was getting truly cold when he flew low over the town and lower over the lake, teasing the few sailboats that still floated there. He landed as gently as possible on the sand of the beach.

Her fulfilled contentment was all the reward he had hoped for, glowing in the front of her thoughts. He was surprised to feel the hot touch of the Sorcerer on his neck, and even more surprised when Jack thanked him, his voice full of awe and respect.

Daemon inclined his head in acknowledgment.

Deirdre came up behind Jack and rubbed the sensitive hide of his nose, her touch cool and gentle this time with the chill of the flight still on her skin. *That was the most amazing thing I've ever done... so... free... I had no idea. Thank you, Daemon*, she sent; her warmth and appreciation, and the depth of her understanding was overwhelming.

You're welcome, Deirdre, he sent, and he was unable to hide his longing for her in his thoughts, this time. Her thoughts scattered in surprise, and he closed his eyes, readying himself for her scorn. He should have known better; her thoughts were as gentle as her touch.

Oh, Daemon. You know the way I love Jack, she thought, and he felt it then, her love for Jack making him ache.

I do, he said, the tight pain coming through.

But, she continued to his surprise, *I am linked to you, in some ways closer than to him, and I don't know what it means, other than that you both tell me it's wrong, dangerous. But it doesn't feel wrong to me, Daemon. Because of it you helped me. Because of it I know what I am, and what you are, and Jack. You fixed my ankle. You showed me what it's like to fly. I have never had a friend like you, and I think... I think you're supposed to be part of my life.*

His thoughts spun away, stunned, awed, and he stared at her, his enormous dragon eyes unable to see the true color of her blue ones, able to see so much more. The exact curve of her jaw, the lissome line of her slender body as she stood before him, the way her hair caught the fire of the sunset and took it, kept it, the heat of her, radiant, the vitality in her pulse.

Is it enough? she asked him, waiting patiently for his response. Enough to be her friend? To come to her aid when she called? To fly with her? To be part of her life? He wondered if he would regret his answer, but was unable to keep it from her.

Yes.

What else could he say?

Understanding and thankfulness flowed through her thoughts, and he knew it was time to go. She smiled softly at him and stepped back, dropping her hand and turning away.

"He's going to change back now," she told Jack.

He moved across the sand a little way as they turned their backs, and embraced the Change. It was always harder to stuff the dragon back inside than it was to let it out; hence the patch of ice he left on the rocky beach when it was finished. It took longer than usual too; he was much too preoccupied, and he made himself do it without accessing Deirdre's store of magic with difficulty. He didn't need any more Sorcerer magic in his system, thank you very much. The severance of their close telepathic link was a sudden silence inside his head and a sense of something missing, lost. He reached inside for it, tracing her along the connecting magic, and there she was. He felt a strange sense of relief, knowing that he could contact her if he wished it, that she was still there, just not as immediate. He had to laugh at himself then, missing something that had been so totally alien only hours before.

He rose stiffly to his feet and jogged back to the rock for his clothes. He dressed up there, then climbed down and returned to them, walking slowly, watching Jack hold Deirdre as she warmed herself in front of his magical fire. He paused for only a moment as he passed them, nodded silently, and turned away. It was harder than it should have been to leave her there alone with the Sorcerer. Then he heard her footsteps behind him, and he stopped, his heart quickening as she walked toward him.

"Daemon," she said, gazing up at him with her bottomless eyes. *Enough, Deirdre*, he thought, aching as she filled his senses again, imagining taking her in his arms and... *Enough. Not mine. Never mine.*

"I'm sorry," she said. He stared at her in surprise, wondering guiltily if she could still read his thoughts.

"For what?" he asked carefully. She smiled sadly up at him.

"You apologized for creating the link, and I... reacted badly. The way I see it, now that I've had time to think, you're trapped, too. And not by your own choosing. Maybe I asked too much, to hope you will be my friend after that. If you don't want to, I understand. So, I'm sorry," she finished. A swirl of mixed emotions crashed in his chest and he wanted fiercely to touch her, but he wasn't sure what his magic would do—he didn't have the most secure hold on it right now, and the Sorcerer stood only a few feet away.

Later, when he tried to pin down the instant when attraction became love, this was it, this impossible moment: she stood in front of him, breathtakingly lovely and powerful and incredibly desirable—and not even knowing it—and *apologized* for putting a magical hold on *him*, a Shapeshifter, the bottom of the *other* food chain; a hold, no less, that had the power to kill *her* slowly. He stared at her long enough that her cheeks colored and she lowered her eyes, imagining he was rejecting her apology.

"I'm not," he said softly. She looked up at him swiftly, her expression confused. He clarified. "I'm upset that the bond could—will—hurt you. I'm upset that I can't touch you. But being magically and telepathically tied to you? For my part, I'm not sorry about that at all." He smiled down at her and kept his hands firmly in his pockets with difficulty. It was her turn to stare and she was blushing furiously.

She finally raised an eyebrow at him and said, "Scoundrel." He thought he saw pleased amusement in the set of her lips but she turned away and walked gracefully back to her Sorcerer before he could be sure. He looked past her to Jack, who was looking back at him, and a strange kind of understanding clicked into place between them. He nodded his head slightly in acknowledgment, and turned and melted into the forest.

His motorcycle was where he had left it and he pulled it from the trees onto the path and kicked it to life. He drove slowly in the twilight, carefully trying to keep his thoughts on the path and not on Deirdre. It was a losing battle, and when he reached his apartment it was with no real memory of how he had got there.

He was ravenous as usual; the Change used physical energy as well as magic, and he never ate as the beast. Unseeing, he threw a steak under the broiler and sliced up two potatoes and fried them American style over the stove until they were soft in the middle and crispy on the outside. He took them outside to his tiny balcony to eat, sitting at the rusty cast iron table and chair that furnished it.

He ate without tasting the food, and sat for a long time as evening darkened into night, his thoughts re-living the day, trying not to wonder what she and Jack were doing. Speaking of which…

That idiot, Jack. That made twice now that Deirdre had tugged his line for that bastard. As soon as he had the thought he felt guilty, knowing it wasn't true. This afternoon had been because of her vision. Still, watching the two of them together… it was like rubbing sand into his eyes. His thoughts moved unbidden on other aspects of the day.

The telepathy thing was interesting. Her mind was as beautiful as the rest of her. He actually remembered the whole time he had been a dragon with them at the beach. He wondered if the link somehow strengthened his human perceptions, even while he was a dragon, somehow bridging his two selves. He savored the memories. Flying with Deirdre had been heavenly. It was strange that she seemed to be more comfortable with him as a dragon. Her thoughts of him as human were all tangled impressions mixed with fear; how odd that she had been afraid of the man but not the beast. He smiled. After today, she didn't fear him at all. His smile faded.

And after today, he knew her heart was taken. No chance that kind of love would change. A crush he would have had a chance against, but that? She would only ever think of Daemon as a friend. She had asked him if that was enough, and he had agreed. But he hadn't agreed not to love her. He shifted in his chair and sighed. Apparently, he was a glutton for punishment. He stood up and took his dishes to the kitchen and washed up, then flopped on the couch and started channel surfing to distract himself.

When his stomach dropped as she tugged the line *again*, he debated just staying there, not answering. The Sorcerer could deal with it, surely. He mused on that, unseeing as the screen flickered in front of him. Jack was unusually powerful, even for a Sorcerer. Deirdre had been full of his magic, high on it even, but he hadn't seemed weakened at all. How much power could a Seer take in one drain? In most of the legends, it took a whole Circle—at least three Sorcerers—to sustain a Seer; sometimes more for a young one, new to her power. He wondered what Jack's limits really were. He would have to not only feed her magic, but be able to protect her as well. A Seer… Well, he would have Daemon's help for her protection. He wondered if the two of them would be enough and resolved to talk to Jack about it very soon. With that thought he returned to her *call*; the pain of it still tugged at his spine. About ten minutes had passed. It wouldn't hurt to check it out, surely? He stood up and went back out to the bike.

He made good time to Deirdre's house, the hook in his stomach guiding him all the way. When he got there, all was quiet. He got off the bike and looked around a little, but there didn't seem to be any activity at all; even the house was mostly dark. He waited, frowning. After a moment, Deirdre and Jack came walking from the direction of the barn. He swallowed his pang of envy and just watched. She seemed fine. Even her ankle wasn't bothering her—her walk was straight and steady—her footsteps a sharp visual staccato against the ground. Then he noticed their body language.

Jack trailed, slouching, several feet behind Deirdre, his hands in his pockets, head down. Daemon's attention focused, shocked. He had never seen the Sorcerer anything but confident. And Deirdre… her face came into the light from the porch and her eyes sparkled with unmistakable moisture, and the tracks of her tears shone dully on her cheeks. Rage shook him, and despair. He should have stayed with them. With her. *Too late to prevent it, but…* He growled the threat in his throat. He stayed back, watching a little longer. What had that jerk done, that she would *call* Daemon? What travesty had made her look like that? Jack stayed on the grass as she walked up the steps. He looked up at her, his face full of grief, and she stopped at the door, staring down at the doorknob, hunched over with her pain. Daemon's heart broke for her and fury welled up again. She turned back and murmured something softly to Jack. Daemon had no trouble hearing it.

"I'm going to need some time, Jack," she said. Daemon watched Jack's eyes tighten even more, and he hunched a little, as though she had hit him, but he just nodded. She looked at him for another long second, then turned and went into the house.

Jack just stood there for a moment, looking like he was trying to catch his breath. Then he began to walk toward his car, parked near the garage. Daemon fell soundlessly in behind him, stalking. When he reached his car, Daemon moved. He caught his wrists in a lock with one hand and threw him against the car with the other. Jack's magic was hot beneath his skin, making him feel feverish and slippery to Daemon's touch. The whoosh of breath as it left Jack's lungs was extraordinarily satisfying.

"*What did you do to her?*" Daemon hissed in his ear. He waited for Jack to resist, bracing himself for any number of vicious spells, but none came. The Mage stood passively in his hold.

"What? Have you been watching us all night?" Jack asked instead, his voice full of grief. Daemon tried to control his rage. Apparently, that was what he *should* have done.

"*No.* She just *called* me *again* about a half hour ago, and it was…" even he could hear the pain in his voice as he remembered the anguish through that intimate link. He saw red, and slammed Jack against the car door again, fighting for control as the beast tried to look out of his eyes. Still Jack did not resist, and Daemon asked again.

"What did you do to her, you son-of-a-bitch?" His voice was low and dangerous, the threat unmistakable. Jack laughed, and the sound was creepy, half crazed. Daemon flinched, wondering with horror what Jack had done to make him sound so hopeless. He almost dropped him and ran up to the house, just to make sure she actually was okay, but Jack answered.

"Tonight? Nothing," Jack said. Daemon growled at the obvious lie and tightened his bone-crushing grip on the Sorcerer's wrists. Jack took a shallow breath and explained tonelessly, lifelessly.

"Last year I nearly killed her twin brother. Tonight... tonight she found out about my real part in it," he said, his voice trailing off at the end, full of despair, almost inaudible. Daemon heard him, of course, and reflexively the pressure in his grip increased and he leaned harder on the boy. Jack was responsible for Alastair's condition? Hope soared in his breast for one delicious second, until he remembered sensing Deirdre's feelings for the Sorcerer. She would forgive him, no doubt. Still...

Finally, Jack began to fight back.

He murmured something sharply under his breath and Daemon flew away from him, stumbling back, arms wide, as the spell hit him, turning his own force against him. He caught his balance swiftly as a cat and launched himself back at Jack, but his heart wasn't in this fight any longer. Frustration, not rage, fueled him as he swung his fist and caught Jack across his jaw, slamming him back against the car. Daemon readied himself for another swing and Jack met him halfway, startling him. He didn't expect the Sorcerer to try to take him physically, and he didn't, not really. Jack got up in his face, arms spread wide, spitting blood from a cut inside his mouth. His eyes were wild, despair and self-loathing vying for dominance. He growled at Daemon.

"Take your shot, Shifter. You think you can hurt me tonight?" Jack challenged, and laughed desolately again. Suddenly he doubled over in pain, but not from Daemon's fists. Daemon paused, eyeing him doubtfully. He kneeled on the ground, bent over, his breath hitching in his chest. Daemon wondered what it would be like, knowing you had hurt Deirdre so badly that she couldn't wait to get away from you, so badly that she might never speak to you again, so that she looked at you like you were a monster. *Oh, wait,* he reminded himself wryly, *I know exactly what that feels like.*

Daemon paused where he stood, folded his arms, and growled. Jack pulled himself together and got slowly to his feet, still fighting for breath, like he had holes in his lungs. He pulled his keys out of his pocket.

"I'm going home now. Got a problem with that?" he asked. Daemon glanced up at the dark and silent house and sighed in annoyance. The Sorcerer was out of his mind at the moment. He held out his hand.

"Keys," he demanded. Jack swayed drunkenly, and frowned, not understanding.

"Give me the damn keys, Sorcerer," he insisted. "You're in no shape to drive and she would hate it if you died before she could forgive you," Daemon said grudgingly. Jack let Daemon take his keys, blinking uncomprehendingly.

"You think she might?" he asked the Shifter, his hope almost pathetic.

"Geez," was all Daemon said, rolling his eyes, and he shoved Jack into the passenger seat. He went around to the driver's side and cursed when he found the seat was already back as far as it would go. Stupid tiny foreign cars. Jack leaned back in his seat and let him drive, taking absolutely no interest in the process.

"Oh, God, Daemon. Such a stupid mistake. So long ago. I love her. I *need* her. Do you think she might forgive me?" Jack babbled. Daemon sighed, and he put the car in gear and shut it off. They just sat there for a moment, listening to the clicks of the engine. **Yes** *she'll forgive you, idiot. After all, she forgave* **me**, *and I've only known her for three days.* He didn't reassure him. After all, it wasn't like they were friends. In fact, the bastard had been kissing the girl he loved all day. And he didn't like to speak for Deirdre anyway. There was always a chance… Daemon frowned. He couldn't really think that way and stay sane.

185

"What do I know?" Daemon finally answered. "I've known her all of three days. You've known her... how long?" he asked, unable to keep the longing and envy out of his voice. What if Daemon had known her first? *Stop it*, he told himself.

"Since kindergarten," Jack murmured, sounding exhausted. Daemon stared at him, his expression bleak. *Kindergarten...* He pictured Deirdre at age five, and couldn't help but smile. Then he pictured little Jack, probably carrying her books for her, and mirth faded.

"Well, then. You'd be a much better judge, wouldn't you?" he said crossly. He levered himself out of the cramped car and crossed to Jack's side. He dragged the Mage from the car, his thoughts bleak. Deirdre wanted Jack. Apart from that, she needed him, his magic. Daemon spoke grudgingly, wishing he could just let the wedge between the two grow into a chasm. Instead, he had to help them fix it. For her. He forced the words from his lips.

"My advice? Pull yourself together. Fight for her. She won't forgive you unless she thinks you're worth it. So *be worth it*, asshole. She needs you, remember? Unless you want to track down another Sorcerer," he growled, and propelled Jack up to the dark house and unlocked the door. He hauled Jack to his room and threw him down on the bed.

"Get some sleep, jerk. And if you don't call her in the morning, I'm going to come back here and finish what I started," he said, dropping the keys on the dresser and leaving.

Outside, he sat down on the stoop and put his head in his hands. Back to Deirdre? Or home to sleep? She didn't seem able to get along without him, and she was hurting. And his motorcycle was there anyway. He got to his feet and began the long jog back to her house. His body soon found the rhythm of his long, tireless, mile-eating stride. He could run like that for hours, days even, fueled by his magic, and it was exhilarating, running through the cool, crisp night.

He reached her house in about an hour and walked carefully up the long drive, subconsciously avoiding the hidden motion sensors that would trigger the large spotlights onto the lawn and trees. The house was dark when he reached it, and he gazed up at it, feeling gently and experimentally along his link to Deirdre, checking on her. He could tell, barely at the edge of his perception, that she was crying, at that last exhausted stage before sleep. Her pain, his pain. He sent her the barest spark of magic, soothing, easing her over the edge, into healing oblivion. He stood motionless for another hour or so, staring up at the house from the corner of the garage, listening with all his senses to the surrounding night. After he was sure that all was quiet, he retrieved the bike and walked it down the driveway, waiting until he was well along the street before he started it up and headed home to sleep. After he left, a shadow detached itself from the side of the house and glided away.

Chapter 5

Deirdre

Sunday Morning

Deirdre slept fitfully and woke up with scratchy, bloodshot eyes and a splitting headache. She remembered several snippets of dreams and wondered if they had actually been visions, but she was too tired to care. There was only one vision she was concerned about: Alastair. She had a few ideas of her own to add to Jack's... *Jack...* oh, God. The pain hit like an anvil to her chest, leaving her breathless and bruised. How could he? Alastair... lying forever blind and broken in that bed... oh, God. Tears flowed silently from her eyes, soaking the pillow. The phone rang and she looked at the caller ID. *Jack.* She couldn't talk to him. Not yet. She hung up on him and left the phone off the hook. Her cell phone rang next, vibrating across the dresser where she must have left it. She pulled her pillow over her head and screamed into it, and felt slightly better.

After a while she got up and took a cold shower, trying to wake up and face the day. She dried her hair, then stood shivering in front of her closet. She got out a soft cream-colored sweater and her black yoga pants. She dressed quickly and went down to the kitchen. The thought of solid food made her feel sick, but she wanted something to ease the thick feeling in the back of her throat. She opened the cupboards one by one, searching for hot chocolate, wishing Maria was there. She would make some of her delicious creamy hot cocoa from scratch, but Sunday was her day off. Deirdre felt suddenly dizzy and the stretchy feeling inside her head heralded another vision. She gripped the counter with both hands and held on for the ride.

Maria and her five-year-old boy, Matthias, were playing in the park. Deirdre smiled in response to their joyful laughter. Suddenly he ran in front of a swing and got clipped in the face with a red tennis shoe. The little boy was thrown to the ground, his nose bleeding profusely, sobbing in shocked pain. Maria's face was stricken as she held the little boy's T-shirt to his nose and scooped him up and put him in the car. The scene switched to the hospital; Matthias looked forlorn and miserable, his face swollen and bandaged, lost in the huge hospital bed. Maria was shaking her head in dismay, and the doctor was telling her his nose was broken and there was nothing more they could do without health insurance.

The vision faded, and Deirdre sank slowly to the floor. When her breath came back, she snagged the phone off the counter and called Maria at her sister's house where she stayed when she wasn't at work. She didn't answer, but Deirdre left a message anyway. "Maria, it's Deirdre. If you and Matthias go to the park today, be really, really careful near the swings. I... just have a really bad feeling that he might have an accident near the swings today. Be careful. Bye," she said, and hung up, feeling horribly inadequate. What if Maria didn't get her message? What if she did and it wasn't enough, and the little boy got hurt anyway? But what else could she do? She suddenly felt like screaming. What good was this... What? Curse? Gift? If she couldn't *change* anything? She put her head in her hands and tried to get a grip. She had changed it once. She had saved Jack... *Jack*.... And the pain hit again, wracking waves of anger, despair, betrayal, and grief.

She rode them out, huddled on the kitchen floor, wishing for the comfort of arms around her and perversely glad no one was here to see her like this. Al's nurse would stay upstairs with him, and it was just the three of them, anyway. *Al.* She had to find a way to save him, too. She focused on that goal and pulled herself to her feet. She gave up on the hot chocolate and just poured herself a glass of water from the tap. She drank it down and poured another, drank it, and felt a little better. She rubbed her eyes on her sleeves and went up to see Alastair, and his nurse.

The Sunday nurse was a chatty woman named Candy, about forty, plump and motherly, with wise brown eyes. Deirdre entered the room with a soft knock on the door. She was changing Al's shirt and getting him cleaned up for the day, doing all his morning routines. She looked up with a smile when Deirdre entered after washing her hands, then frowned when she took in her appearance.

"You look terrible, dear. Are you feeling all right?" she asked kindly. Al raised his eyebrows at her and Deirdre went around to the other side of the bed and took his hand, squeezing reassuringly. He relaxed.

"Hi, Candy. I didn't sleep well..." she began, then realized she could use the remark to get the information she required. "I've been worried about Alastair," she admitted. His brow furrowed, but not with concern, more like wondering what she was up to. He knew her too well; she felt a pang of loss.

"Worried about him?" the nurse prompted.

"Yeah. Like sometimes when we get bad storms, the power goes out. So what happens if all these machines lose power?" she asked the efficient woman.

"Well, that would be difficult, but we could handle a short power outage, if nothing else was wrong," she said. "Actually, I thought your father had ordered a generator," she frowned. "You know, my dear, that's a very good question. If I were you, I would ask your father what the delay is," she advised. Deirdre felt the knot of worry in her gut tighten. So there *was* something to worry about. She thought about the vision, about how she had felt like she couldn't breathe.

"And I noticed that Al was having a little shortness of breath the other day," she said. "Is that something to worry about?" she asked. The nurse's attention sharpened and she looked up.

"Really? Oh, that's not good, dear," she shook her head and gazed with concern at Alastair, as though coming to a decision.

"I'd better report that to the doctor right away. We may need to adjust his medication," she shook her head. Al just sat and listened, but Deirdre could almost feel his impatience as he waited for the nurse to leave so he could ask her what she was doing. She squeezed his hand again.

"What does that mean, Candy? Why is it bad?" she asked. The woman pulled Al forward slightly and helped him put on his shirt. Deirdre took a look at his chest before they covered him. He was muscular and well-formed, but far too thin. A long white scar marred the side of his chest, linked to the one that curved down his temple, along his jaw and down his neck. It continued down his shoulder and the far left side of his chest, along his side, and disappeared beneath the covers that preserved his modesty. She knew the scar wove its way all the way down his left leg, finally ending on his anklebone. He had been split open along his whole left side, bleeding and broken. Even too thin and scarred, he was beautiful. Rage and grief turned her vision dark for a moment, and she choked and bit it back, hating it, hating that he lay there, broken.

He gripped her hand, feeling her swift surge of emotion and trying to comfort her, even though he didn't understand it. She clutched his hand like a lifeline. Finishing her ministrations, Candy went over to the sink to remove her gloves and wash her hands again before she answered. Deirdre just waited, holding

Alastair's hand, riding the waves of her emotions and trying not to drown in them before she got what she needed.

"When someone is in an accident, or bedridden for any length of time, there is always a risk of the blood forming clots. Sometimes the clots get loose and break away into the blood stream, and get stuck in the smaller capillaries, like in the lungs. That can cause a shortness of breath, or even, sometimes, block things off so completely that the person feels like they can't breathe at all, and since the blood in the lungs is blocked… well, it can be fatal," the nurse explained. Deirdre swayed and felt the blood drain from her face, feeling like she might faint.

The nurse came swiftly over to her and lowered her into a chair and tried to reassure her. "Don't worry, my dear," she said. "We have procedures in place, and Alastair takes a blood thinner to help prevent it. We may need to up the dosage if you saw some symptoms, but I'm sure we can deal with it if anything were to happen. There's nothing to worry about," she patted Deirdre's shoulder reassuringly before she bustled out of the room to call the doctor. As soon as the door closed behind her, Al started in.

"What was that all about?" he asked, in the tone that meant he expected the truth, and all of it, right now. She closed her eyes and sat back in her chair, but didn't let go of his hand. And she told him, slowly, with many pauses.

"Yesterday, after… J-Jack… and I left you, we took the horses up the trail to the guest house. We walked on the beach a little and then something really weird happened. I had another vision. Of you. Dying." He froze, lying very still, and the heart monitor recorded the stutter in his heartbeat. She pushed on.

"It was really… intense, and … Jack… apparently fed me a ton of his magic to sustain it," she said. Alastair took a deep breath.

"So you know," he said softly. She nodded.

"Yes. He told me, after. Daemon came just then, too, and Alastair, he's a Shapeshifter, a *dragon*." Alastair's eyes flew wide open, and he stared sightlessly in Deirdre's direction.

"A *dragon*?" he echoed in stunned disbelief. She laughed; this was a good memory.

"Yes, the most *gorgeous* silver and diamond monster you've ever imagined, twenty feet long, at least, and Al, he let us *fly on his back*. It was *spectacular*," she sighed and paused a moment, remembering that feeling, before she came back to the reality of now.

"Al, Jack says I'm a Seer," she told him. He frowned.

"A Seer? Like a fortune teller?" he asked. She smiled at the image he conjured of herself sitting in front of a crystal ball under the dark folds of a gypsy tent.

"Sort of, I guess. I have visions," she said. "Like Friday's weirdness. Apparently, that's how it starts," she said, and her voice hitched in her throat. "This morning I had one of Maria and Matthias," a tear trickled down her cheek and Al tugged on her hand, pulling her up and into his embrace. He held her for a long moment, letting her get it all out, and she drank him in, leaning over the edge of the bed and tucking her arms in between them while he wrapped his arms around her and held her tightly.

"I called and left her a message," she murmured, "but what if it isn't enough? What if I can't save them? Or you? God, Al, I hate this, I hate it. I don't want to see everyone I care about almost die and have to rush to save them and—and what if I can't, Al? What if I *can't*?" She coasted to a stop and just rested against his chest, feeling safe and comforted for the first time since Jack had confessed. *Jack*.

"And then there's... Jack..." she said, hardly able to say his name. Alastair's arms tightened protectively, sensing unerringly that here was the true source if her acute distress.

"What about Jack?" he said, and his voice was hard. "Deirdre, what did he do?" he asked.

"*Nothing.* He didn't *do* anything. He told me about... that night... your accident. My God, Al, why didn't you ever tell me?" she said. He shrugged and stroked her hair.

"I guess... I was... ashamed," he admitted, and she closed her eyes. "But why are you all of a sudden so upset with Jack about that night?" he said, genuine confusion in his voice. She had begun to relax a little, lulled by the warmth and security she felt in his arms. She was so tired....

"He said it was his fault you had that accident, because you got a concussion when you fell," she said softly. Alastair shook his head.

"No way, Deirdre... well, I guess he might feel like that, but..." he paused for a moment, thinking about how to word it so she would understand—and accept.

"I've had a *long* time to think about this, Dee Dee. I have to take responsibility, not him. I was the idiot that drank almost a fifth of whiskey and fell off a bridge. Me. He didn't force it down my throat or anything. He didn't push me off the bridge either. Jack tried to *help* me. He risked the thing that mattered most to him to help me, to do everything within his considerable power to make sure I was okay." He paused, and stroked her hair. She hadn't thought about it like that before, about what it had cost Jack to help Alastair. His secret. She didn't understand what the true significance of that was, really, but it clearly meant something huge to Jack. His own mother didn't even know. Alastair took a deep breath.

"And, Deirdre, I didn't have a concussion. When I left him, I felt perfectly lucid. The cut on my head stung but I didn't have a headache or any disorientation or anything. I wasn't sleepy. The only thing that bothered me was that my leg hurt like the dickens.

194

When he healed it with magic, it fixed the problem, but the pain of it didn't really go away. So I guess that was a distraction, but it was my left leg, so it wasn't like I couldn't drive. No, Deirdre. It was the tire. If that tire hadn't blown out *exactly* when it did, that accident would never have happened. Just like the police said," his voice rang with truth. He was completely convinced. She wanted to believe it. She really did, but… He patted her head and planted a kiss on her forehead.

"Deirdre, even I can see you're exhausted," he joked, and she chuckled half-heartedly. He released her and she stood up, swaying slightly. Actually she did feel terrible. "Get some rest, Deirdre, and then we'll call Father about that generator. Together," he suggested. She nodded, even though he couldn't see her.

"Okay, Al. Okay," she murmured and left the room. She barely made it to her bed before she was curled up on top of the covers, fast asleep.

***

Alastair

Sunday Morning

Alastair frowned as he listened to his sister's slow retreating footsteps. That was some story. He rang for the nurse. When she came to ask what he needed, he said, "Candy, I need to make a phone call." She raised her eyebrows but brought him the cordless phone from across the room. He waited until she left before he dialed the number. Strange how familiar it still felt, even though it had been over a year since he had actually pressed those numbers. Familiar enough that he didn't have to see the keypad to make this call.

"Deirdre?" the voice on the other line was as familiar to him as his own.

"You're an idiot," Alastair said to Jack.

***

Jack

Sunday Morning

Jack woke from his nightmare with a jolt, only to realize that the dream was real. He had hurt her. Who cared if the actual events happened over a year ago, before he had known how he would care for her? She had cried because of him, and he felt every tear like a drop of searing acid on his skin. He winced as he touched his jaw, swollen and bruised from the Shapeshifter's attention, and turned his magic on it. It healed swiftly, but still felt a little stiff. He was probably lucky that blow hadn't removed his head from his shoulders. Shifters could do things like that. Daemon had pulled his punch.

He rolled over and picked up the phone. He dialed her number but it cut off after the third ring and when he dialed again it was disconnected. He tried her cell phone, knowing it was a lost cause, and it shunted him over to voice mail. He lay there for a second but finally hung up the phone without saying anything. He ached to hold her, to look into her eyes and know she was still his. He put the phone down.

If she forgave him... what could he do to make it up to her? His thoughts turned to Alastair. What if he *could* heal him? Now, rather than later? Her vision gave him an earlier deadline than he had hoped for. Shasta would know if he was ready. But it was too soon to ask, wasn't it? The death magic that allowed him to talk to the ghost was incredibly draining. Still... could he go the week without her? The empty ache filled him again. He wasn't sure he could go the *day* without her. He replayed yesterday, before his awful confession. She had said she loved him. She had said she wanted him. His heart squeezed in his chest. He pulled himself out of bed; he had to try. He ate a bowl of cereal without tasting it and took a quick shower, dressing carelessly in jeans and a T-shirt. He stared at the phone again, willing it to ring. Suddenly to his shock, it did. His heart pounded when he saw the number on the ID and he snatched it up, hope cracking his ribs.

"Deirdre?" he asked, his voice full of anguish.

"You're an idiot," Alastair said from the other end of the line. Disappointment rocked him and he sat heavily on the edge of the bed.

"So I'm told," he said dryly, remembering Daemon's reaction last night.

"Why the hell did you tell her the accident was your fault? It *wasn't*, Jack. I *didn't* have a concussion. You made sure I wasn't drunk. The *only* thing that caused anything was that damn tire," Alastair berated him. Jack closed his eyes and lay back.

If only it were true… He was silent, unable to respond.

"Jack?" Al said, disconcerted by the silence. "You there?" he asked. Jack sighed heavily.

"I'm here. But Al, how can you be sure?" he said.

Al snorted in exasperation. "Jack! You have to get over this, you *have* to. She needs you to get over this. My accident was *not your fault*. Not the one on the bridge, and not the one in the car. You didn't force me to drink with you. You didn't push me off that stupid bridge. You didn't slash my tire while I was going around that curve. You did everything in your power to help. *Everything*. So drop the guilt trip already! She loves you, and she's in really bad shape over this. Don't make her feel like she has to choose between us. It will tear her apart," Al protested eloquently.

Jack paused. He hadn't thought about it like that, that he was making her choose between him and her brother with his guilt. And there was some truth in Al's words. He *hadn't* meant for any of it to happen. A weight he had carried for a year lifted slightly from his chest as he realized that Al himself didn't blame Jack at all.

"Is that really how you feel about it, Al?" he asked. "You don't… blame me?" Al snorted.

"If blame has to be assigned, and I really don't see why it does, I blame myself, and maybe the basic unfairness of the universe," Al insisted dryly. Jack felt his lips twitch into an unwilling grin at that.

"Maybe I can go along with that," Jack said slowly. Al sighed.

"Good. Great. Now when are you coming over so you can convince Deirdre that you're still the guy she fell for in fifth grade? I highly recommend actual face to face for this," Al said. Jack's breath caught in his chest. *Fifth grade?*

"What do you mean, fifth grade?" Jack asked tightly. Al chuckled.

"I guess you guys probably don't spend much time talking when you're together," Al teased. Jack growled into the phone, blushing in spite of himself. So *not* something he wanted to talk to Al about. His friend continued. "She's been in love with you since the fifth grade, dimwit," he laughed. Warmth flooded through Jack and he just lay there, stunned and breathless, and feeling very much like the idiot Al had called him earlier. All that time, he could have…. Al was speaking again. "So, when are you coming? I'll try to help out, but it's pretty much going to be up to you," he said. Jack thought furiously. How much time would it take him to review the healing magic one last time, and to recover from the training? It seemed even more important that he try to heal Al now.

"I… have a couple of things I have to do first," he said slowly.

"Okay. She went back to sleep anyway. She's really upset, Jack. You should probably bring flowers. Maybe this evening? We could order a pizza or something, like we used to," Al said, and his voice held the first note of loss Jack had heard in it.

"Okay," he said. "So, maybe, five-ish?" he suggested. Al agreed.

"What kind of flowers, Al?" he asked, feeling a little sheepish at the question. Al laughed.

"Don't you know?" he could almost see Al shaking his head at Jack's stupidity. He frowned in thought.

"Should I?" he said, unable to come up with anything. Al chuckled again.

"Fifth grade, Jack. That's the only hint I'm giving you—I can't carry you all the way," and he hung up. Jack stared at the phone for a minute before he sat up and set it back on the dresser.

He walked to his desk and got out the little box that held his link to his ghost tutor. He spell-locked the door and invoked the circle. The bone ring felt slimy to his touch when he slipped it on. The ghost appeared, refined and elegant and surprised. "Hello, Jack. Back so soon?" the ghost read his thoughts and sneered. "Ah, first love. So sweet, so desperate—so doomed," he mocked. Jack glared at him.

"Will you finish teaching me the healing magic, or not?" he asked. Shasta rolled his eyes. "I will teach you. But do you not remember her vision? The boy will die anyway," he shrugged scornfully.

"Maybe," Jack said tightly. "She changed *my* fate," he told the ghost. The ghost frowned.

"Odd. That should not have happened." He tugged on his lower lip with a perfectly manicured thumb and forefinger, thinking. After a minute he shook himself and turned back to Jack. "So, anatomy," he began, and they got to work. After two hours Jack was exhausted, his eyes felt scratchy and dry, and he had sweated through his T-shirt. His head pounded and his magic burned under his skin. Shasta was looking at him with something like awe. At least, that's what Jack thought the expression looked like.

"What?" he asked the ghost, as he conjured an image of the exact structure of the eyeball again.

"Two hours of the death magic, and only three days ago you sustained a full hour of it, and lessons and practice on top of that. And yesterday you fed a *Seer*. Don't you feel it? How are you even still conscious?" the ghost asked him. Jack frowned.

"What do you mean?" he asked, concentrating on refining his magic into the hair-thin delicate stream the operation would require and matching it to the difficult healing frequencies, all at the same time.

"Isn't your well low? Your magic should be used up, should have been an hour ago—hell, should have been before we *began*. How are you doing this?" the ghost asked, waving his arms at the circle, at Jack's hands, at himself. Jack let the stream go, and checked his magic, deep inside. It felt the same as always, maybe a little hotter. Only his body was tired. He frowned at the ghost.

"It can run dry?" he asked. The ghost stared at him.

"Yes. It can run dry," he said, his voice full of shocked sarcasm. Jack shrugged.

"My well feels like always," he admitted. The ghost actually flickered in its shock, then conjured an old-fashioned armchair and sat down when he stabilized. Shasta didn't speak for a full minute. Jack just stood watching him, arms folded across his chest, resting. His shirt felt clammy and damp against his skin and his pulse pounded like a piston in his forehead. Finally, Shasta spoke, and his voice was careful.

"Did you know it usually takes several Sorcerers to sustain a Seer, even for one drain?" he asked. Jack slowly shook his head. Shasta closed his eyes. "I have only allowed you to take an hour's instruction a week because that's the maximum most Sorcerers could do. And I do mean maximum. Even your father could not do what you have done." The ghost opened his eyes and looked at Jack, who still stood there, listening in surprise to what the ghost was telling him. "You and your Seer need to be extraordinarily careful. Between the two of you, the power…" he shook his head and sat a moment longer. Then he stood and the chair vanished as though it had never been.

"Well, you are ready. You can heal your friend. Probably. With the help of the dragon. Make *certain* you use a circle. *Always. Especially* when you feed your Seer. That kind of magic is like a beacon for *others*." He paused, shaking his head and his mouth twisted into a leer. "A *Seer*… the stories—is it true?" Jack's eyes narrowed and he glared at the ghost. Shasta grinned lecherously. "Lucky bastard," he shook his head, then spoke his parting words of advice. "Also, as I have told you before, do not ever reveal to anyone the extent of your power. Always act as though it is a great effort to do what you do." The ghost waited until Jack nodded in acknowledgment of his warning, then disappeared.

Jack stood there for a moment, lost in thought, then turned and stepped from the circle. He fed the ring with blood, put the resealed box in his pocket, and stripped off the soaked shirt. He sat down on the bed as a wave of exhaustion hit him hard. He glanced at the clock and lay down. He had hours before he could leave to see Deirdre.

He slept.

***

Jack

Sunday Evening

When he woke, his mind was clear. He stepped in the shower again, rinsing the dried sweat from his skin. When he stepped outside, the wind and overcast sky heralded rain on the way. He flung himself behind the wheel and drove to the flower shop downtown. There he stood in front of the display cases, undecided, staring at all the bright blooms. What had Alastair meant: fifth grade? What did that year have to do with flowers and Deirdre? He ran through his memories. The main event that included Deirdre that year was… he smiled.

The girl at the counter wrapped up his purchase with a skeptical but professional smile. "Anything else?" she asked, and her eyes slid to the profusion of roses that filled the cold cases along the near wall. He shook his head, smiling to himself at her dubious expression.

"Okay… good luck," she called after him as he left the store. He turned out into the street, and walked along the sidewalk to his car. He paused in front of the jewelry store. What could it hurt to look? He went inside and walked carefully through the artfully lit display cases. He knew it was meant to be hers as soon as he saw it, tucked away behind some children's jewelry. He raised his head and looked around and an elderly man came slowly toward him. He opened the case and handed the piece to Jack for his inspection.

"It's perfect," Jack said, and the man nodded and took it back, walking carefully back toward the counter.

"Would you like to have it engraved, sir?" the man asked politely. Jack considered: What could it say? Suddenly, he knew.

"Sure."

He left the store, agreeing to come back in an hour to pick up his purchase, and went to his car. He put the flowers on the passenger seat and headed for the diner. It was nearly empty when he got there, much too early for the dinner rush. The only people in there were an elderly gentleman reading a paper and the waitress, the same one from the other night. He sat at the counter and ordered a cheeseburger from her, and asked if Daemon was there. She glanced up at the clock.

"He should be here any minute," she told him, looking at him curiously.

"When he comes in, would you tell him Jack is here and ask him if he'll talk to me?" he asked her. She raised her eyebrows at him.

"Okay," she said, and he watched her hesitate while curiosity got the better of her. "Do you want me to tell him what it's about?" she offered. He smirked.

"He'll know," he answered. She nodded and walked away to refill the old man's coffee. She went back to the kitchen to make his food, and he sat at the counter and played with his fork and sipped at his soda, fidgeting while he waited. Daemon arrived before the food was ready. The giant stood in front of him across the counter, arms folded, his stance hostile. Jack looked up at him, his face serious.

"Hey. I didn't have your number," Jack explained his presence there. Daemon nodded silently. "I… wanted to ask you if you would do something for me," he began. Daemon raised an eyebrow. Jack sighed. "For her," he clarified. When Daemon didn't react, he shifted in his chair and glanced out the window, unseeing. He hadn't expected this to be so difficult.

"Look, do you want to sit down or something?" he asked finally. After a moment, Daemon looked down and shook his head at the floor. He came around the corner, leading the Sorcerer to a table that would be out of earshot of the old man and the kitchen. He sat down and stretched his long legs out into the aisle, and refolded his arms across his chest. Jack took his soda and sat down across from him, leaning forward with his elbows on the table. He took a deep breath.

"Deirdre's brother, Alastair, was my best friend for more than ten years. About a year ago, after hanging out with me, he was in a really bad car crash." Daemon's eyelids flickered, but that was his only reaction, so Jack continued. "He was in a coma afterwards, but about a month ago, he woke up. He's blind now, and his legs are paralyzed." Daemon's eyes narrowed. "I want to heal him, but it would be a lot easier if you would help with the bone part," he said. Daemon considered, and Jack tried not to fidget. Finally, Daemon spoke, his deep voice rumbling softly.

"There's not much I can do for broken bones. Especially an old break," he said. Jack nodded.

"I know. But you can tell me what's wrong inside. It's… my magic doesn't work like that. Well, it's very difficult to make it work like that, especially if I'm trying to fix it at the same time. It's like I can't see it unless I already know what I'm looking for. And the healing magic is very difficult anyway. Draining. It would help a lot," he explained.

"You want me to help you fix your screw-up," Daemon said, summarizing. Jack narrowed his eyes.

"I want you to help me heal Deirdre's twin brother," he clarified. Daemon paused, then leaned forward.

"Last night you told me you almost killed her brother. How was a car accident your fault?" he asked. Jack's expression darkened. He had finally begun to come to terms with that night, thanks to Alastair, but the old guilt lingered, waiting to strike at unexpected moments. He looked at the Shapeshifter for a minute, studying him. Did he need Daemon's forgiveness as well? Perhaps he did, he thought: not for the accident, but for last night. For hurting Deirdre.

Just then, the waitress brought his food. He nodded his thanks and reached for the ketchup, waiting until she left to start speaking. "Okay. Here's the deal. If I tell you the whole story, will you help?" he asked. Daemon shrugged and leaned back in his chair again. Jack glared at him, and slowly and deliberately took a bite of his cheeseburger. He chewed and swallowed, waiting the Shifter out. Daemon rolled his eyes.

"Fine. I'll help," he said. Jack hid his momentary gloat of triumph and simply began.

"That night, Al and I were out drinking at this old wooden bridge just north of town." Daemon nodded. He knew the place. It was a death trap. "We were pretty far gone when Al stumbled into one of the side rails. It broke, and he fell, over the edge and fifteen feet down onto the rocks. He hit his head and broke his leg. When I got down to him, he was unconscious. I sobered up quick and healed the cut on his head, and his leg, and sobered him up, and let him drive home." Jack grimaced as guilt woke up and prodded him again, and pushed it away. He took another bite of his burger before he continued. Daemon waited patiently, unmoving.

"On the way home, his car tire blew while he was going around a curve; he jumped the rail and rolled the car three times. He was thrown clear at some point, but when they found him he was in really bad shape. I found out almost three days later, when there was nothing I could do. Until he came out of the coma they weren't even positive what the extent of his injuries really were, and I'm not much good at diagnostic magic. I always thought he might have had a concussion from the fall, and that the accident was my fault," he finished. Daemon stared at him, and a muscle jumped in his jaw.

"So last night you decided to—to what? Come clean? Tell Deirdre all that?" he said, leaning forward again, his expression full of disgust. "You are such an idiot." His tone was sharp and accusing.

"So I'm told," Jack growled. He was getting pretty sick of that consensus. "Anyway, s*he asked.* And I wasn't going to *lie* to her. What would that make me? I thought for a year that I *had* caused it." He shook off the guilt that tried to surface again and continued. "But this morning, I talked to Al. He convinced me that it wasn't my fault," Jack explained, unable to hide the thick relief in his voice. Daemon raised his eyebrow again. The question was clear.

"He said he was positive he hadn't had a concussion, but even if he had, the accident was caused by the tire, and nothing else. He didn't blame me at all, even for the rest, earlier that night. He asked me if I had poured the alcohol down his throat. And he told me I was forcing Deirdre to choose between him and me by blaming myself for it," Jack explained.

"So now you want to fix it," Daemon said. "Why did you wait?"

Jack shrugged. "Deirdre didn't know about the magic until yesterday. I couldn't get to him without her—" Daemon snorted, interrupting. The unspoken comment was clear: the Sorcerer could do whatever he wanted. Jack glared at him and continued. "—*and,* he's been too weak to even have visitors until recently. The first time I saw him was yesterday, right before we went to the beach and Deirdre… had a vision… the one that called you. The vision that Al would die…." Jack finished. Daemon sat back in his chair, shock clear in his expression.

"Let me get this straight. You're not only healing old injuries with magic—which is not recommended, by the way, in case you didn't read the back of the box—*and* you're trying to prevent a Seer's Prophecy?" Daemon whistled softly and the old man and the waitress turned to look over at them. Jack glared at him.

"She's done it before," Jack reminded him. "You were at the game." Daemon shook his head. Then he stopped and nodded instead.

"Okay, I'll give you that. But you know you stand as much chance of *making* a prophecy come true as stopping it when you try to mess around," Daemon pointed out.

"We'll ask Deirdre first. If it doesn't feel right to her, we'll wait. But this will work, Daemon. If you help, that is." Jack was leaning forward, his intensity almost palpable. Daemon shook his head.

"I don't really know what you think I can do," he said doubtfully. Jack frowned.

"Actually, I'm not really sure either. Only that my... teacher... said I needed you there," Jack told him. Daemon frowned, staring down at the table.

"All right. When and where?" he asked finally, and relief washed through Jack, making him realize uneasily how much he was counting on the dragon.

"Deirdre's. How soon can you get off?" Jack asked. Daemon raised his eyebrows.

"Tonight? You're doing this tonight?" he asked, taking a deep breath. Jack nodded as he swallowed the last of his burger.

"Since we don't know for sure when the prophecy is going down, I figured the sooner the better," he said. Abruptly, Daemon stood and walked away without a word. Jack had finished his fries and was sipping on the last of his soda when he returned.

"Annabelle says she can let me go around eight, if it dies down like usual," he reported. Jack nodded and got out his money as he stood. "Give her a big tip," Daemon ordered, and walked back to the kitchen. Jack grinned at his back and left extra cash on the table.

He headed back to the jewelry shop, which was just about to close, and picked up his purchase. Then he stopped back home for a minute. His mother had just come home from doing the grocery shopping, and he helped her bring the bags in.

"Thanks, honey," she said, stepping close and touching his cheek affectionately with her small, cool hand. Her blond hair was pulled up into a ponytail that curled against her neck, and her blue eyes were faded and tired.

"Are you going back out tonight?" she asked, when she saw him getting his jacket.

"Yeah. I'm going to Deirdre's," he grinned, unable to completely hide his nervous excitement from her. She raised an eyebrow.

"Deirdre, huh? I've always loved her. And Al, too. Is he any better?" she asked. Jack shrugged.

"A little, I guess. I saw him yesterday," he told her. She turned away, toward the bags of food on the table.

"All right. Have fun, Jack," she said. He put a hand on her shoulder and when she turned, he gave her a hug. She laughed into his chest with pleased surprise, and when he released her she put her hand on his cheek again.

"You remind me so much of your father," she said, joy and sadness warring in her eyes. She patted his cheek lightly.

"You should shave before you go," she scolded gently.

"Maybe Deirdre likes the rugged look," he said, smirking. His mother smirked back.

"Maybe she does, but I guarantee she'd rather kiss a man whose beard won't irritate her skin," she said. He frowned.

"Hmm. You may be right. Thanks, Mom. Any other hot tips?" he teased, retreating toward the bathroom and his razor. She waved her finger at him.

"Just one. Remember who you are and treat her respectfully," she said.

"That's two, Mom," he pointed out, grinning. She laughed again and waved him off, and began unpacking the groceries.

He left shortly after that, heart in his throat, a million questions racing through his mind. What would Deirdre do? What had Al said to her? Should he have called before he came? And of course, the million-dollar question: Would she forgive him? His tension grew the closer he got, his jaw clenching and unclenching, his hands doing the same on the wheel. *Relax*, he told himself ineffectively over and over. What had Daemon said last night? *Be worth it*—that was it. Well, he would try. He remembered her face last night and despair clouded his vision. What if it had been too much, bringing all that back up again?

He turned up the long drive, and parked in front of the garage, in his usual spot. He sat there for a moment and wiped his suddenly sweaty palms on his jeans. He took a deep breath and grabbed the flowers. The other package was in his jacket pocket, and the little box that held Shasta's bones was in his jeans pocket. He was as ready as he would ever be. Just as he exited the car, the rain began in earnest, buckets of icy water falling from the rapidly darkening sky. He ducked his head against it and the vicious wind whipped it into his face and down the back of his neck.

He hadn't reached the porch yet when she was suddenly there, heedless of the rain, staring at him. She stood on the edge of the top step in front of him in a creamy ivory sweater and stretchy black pants that hugged her shape. Her little feet were bare. Her eyes were huge and dark in her pale face, and on her cheeks were two hectic spots of red. Her hair blew wildly around her in the wind for a moment until it became soaked and heavy from the rain, and she stood motionless, staring at him for almost a full minute.

He stared back at her, filling his hungry eyes with her, waiting, oblivious to the weather. Finally, she stepped back and beckoned him forward, leading him into the house. He followed and she closed the door behind him and led him deeper into the foyer. His footsteps on the tile felt loud in the silence and left wet tracks behind him. He handed her the flowers wordlessly, and she took them the same way, looking at them for a long moment before she turned her gaze back on him.

She shivered in the air conditioning and dripped all over the elegant circular rug. He took his hand from his pocket and held it out, closed, until she put her small hand out underneath it. He dropped the bracelet into it, and withdrew. He ached to touch her, to hold her, but he forced himself to wait. Whatever happened now, it had to come from her. She held the bracelet up in the light, and looked at the inscription on the back. Her eyes widened slightly and he thought he saw something warm flicker in the back of her eyes. His heart pounded in his chest, trying to break free, to go to her.

"You remembered?" she said softly, half question, half incredulous statement. He smiled.

"Of course," he said. "It *was* my first kiss, and it's not every day I get to rescue a beautiful girl," he said. Her mouth curved into a slow smile and then she laughed. His heart stuttered and swelled in hopeful response to her smile. If she looked like that, he had a definite chance.

"That was a great day," she murmured, her eyes going distant, remembering. He laughed and contradicted her.

"It was terrifying. You were in pretty bad shape," he reminded her.

"I hardly felt it, when you were there," she murmured, holding the simple bouquet of daisies to her face and inhaling their fresh clean scent.

"That's because you were going into shock," he pointed out. He swayed slightly forward, wanting desperately to go to her, and she met his eyes, holding him there, rooted to the floor as she glided forward until she stood only inches away, gazing at him with her bottomless indigo eyes. She raised her hands to twine around his neck and lifted herself into his arms with a little jump, curling herself tightly around him and melting into his hungry embrace. He caught her and hugged her securely to him, leaning back a little to take her slight weight, her legs wrapped around his waist, her arms around his neck, her breath hot against his rain-chilled skin.

The flowers she still held crinkled in their cellophane wrapping, and he just held her, heart racing, aching with relief, suddenly weightless. He shrugged awkwardly out of his wet jacket and hung it on the newel post, and she laughed low in her throat but didn't release him. He carried her into the living room and sat down in the leather recliner and pulled the soft ivory blanket off the back and draped it around them. He leaned back in the chair and held her close, and ran his hand down the length of her back. She stretched her legs out along his and snuggled into his embrace, and he felt her relax with a deep contented sigh.

She rolled slightly over then and put the flowers down on the nearby table, and held up her bracelet. "This is beautiful, Jack. Thank you," she said. He took it from her and fastened it around her slender wrist. She held it up to the light and the amber gems set as the eyes in a chain of silver daisies winked and caught at the dim light, glowing in the gloom. "And for the inscription, too," she said softly, turning her face up to his. He glanced down at her, and, finding it uncomfortable, pulled her on top of him instead, so he could look into her eyes.

A warm glow suffused her cheeks, and her eyes shone with their own inner light. Her hair was still wet, hanging in dark tangles across her shoulders. He caressed her jaw with his thumb as she gazed down at him. A dark lock fell in front of her eyes and he pushed it back behind her slender shoulder.

"*In your eyes I see my heart,*" he quoted softly, gazing at her, his emotions crashing around in his head. She lowered her head and kissed him softly, gently. Then she scooted down a little and curled up into his side, laying her head on his shoulder, and he felt her relax, her body going all soft and boneless. He adjusted the blanket over them again and hugged her against him.

"So I guess I'm forgiven," he murmured, pressing his lips against her hair.

She laughed low and light, her breath a soft whisper against his skin, and ran her gentle teasing fingertips up his shirt and cupped her hand around the base of his neck at his shoulder. She pressed a kiss against his chest and traced the sensitive skin of the dip between his collarbones with her thumb as she murmured, "Al insists there was nothing to forgive." He grunted.

"Yeah. That's what he told me this morning, too. I'm still sorry, though. For putting you through that," he said softly. She hugged herself against him and he felt her sigh.

"I'm only sorry we didn't have more time last night," she murmured drowsily. He stilled and his heart jumped ahead a few beats before it slowed back into rhythm with hers. She laughed softly again and he knew she had felt his response. He decided it was probably time to tell her about his ideas for Alastair.

"Deirdre, I want to ask you something, and I want you to think about it before you answer, okay?" he asked carefully. She froze for a moment, and he could almost hear the reservations in her voice when she answered.

"Okay..." she agreed, then pushed up on her elbow, watching his face as he continued.

"I want to try to heal Alastair," he said hesitantly. She froze and stared down at him, the raw shock on her face turning swiftly to a desperate kind of hope.

"You can do that?" she asked, breathlessly, her small hand clutching at his shirt. He watched her seriously.

"I think so. It might not work. I don't *think* it's dangerous to Al, and I want to try," he explained. "I'll need Daemon to help," he added. "I already talked to him, and he's willing," he said. He slid his eyes away. "I was wondering if you might... if you might try to *see*," he said. Her eyes widened perceptibly, and he could see her thinking furiously behind them.

"How do I do that?" she asked, not committing, just curious.

"Well, I do have one idea..." he grimaced. She raised an eyebrow, questioning his obvious discomfort.

"It's a little weird," he said, shifting in the chair beside her.

"Weird?" she prompted curiously. He made a face.

"Yeah. You see, I know this ghost..." he said, half-mockingly. She looked at him uncertainly. He waited, and her expression turned to disbelief.

"You know this ghost...?" she repeated, as though trying out the words to see how they tasted. He grinned, then pulled her onto his lap as he refolded the recliner. He stood up and set her carefully on her feet.

"Is there somewhere we will be completely undisturbed? Where I can work some magic?" he looked down at her. She considered.

"I suppose..." she paused and looked at him. He could almost see her making a decision, and he wondered what it was.

She bit her lip and blushed, and he was even more confused. What would cause her to look like that? "Come on," she said, and walked back to the foyer. He followed her up the stairs and down the hall to her bedroom door. She opened it and he paused and looked at her for a moment, suddenly guessing what might have been in her mind a moment ago.

All the times he had fantasized about being locked alone in her bedroom with her paraded through his mind, and he took a deep breath, fighting to manage the heat that rose inside him with those images as he crossed her threshold. She followed him in and closed the door behind them. The soft snick-click of the lock seemed loud. He turned around, and she leaned back against the door, trembling, looking down at the carpet. He swallowed and was unable to resist slipping his hands around her waist and drawing her close.

"I can think of better magic to do in here," he said, only half joking, and she looked up at him with a smoldering longing that darkened her eyes and made his breath catch in his throat.

She stared up at him with those glorious eyes then lowered her gaze and took a deep, steadying breath. It was all he could do to let her walk away, leading him deeper into the room. He pulled himself together with an effort and applied his sudden surfeit of energy to the matter of healing Alastair. He stood back and surveyed the area.

"Can I move your furniture around a little?" he asked her, trying to concentrate. "Temporarily," he qualified when she looked at him in surprise. She shrugged.

"I guess so," she agreed, fidgeting a little with her hands. He stared at her. She never fidgeted.

"Do you need any help?" she asked. He shook his head at the offer, still studying her.

"No. I'll do it. I just need a large central area—the bigger, the better," he said, and stepped over to her bed. She followed him with her eyes, then hooked a finger over her shoulder.

"I'm going to change…" she said. He tried not to picture that, didn't succeed, and took a deep breath instead.

"Okay," he said, his voice huskier than usual. *Get a grip*, he told himself. He looked around her bedroom slowly, taking it in. A beautifully carved sleigh bed and matching cherry dressers dominated the room. The carpet under his feet was thick and soft, a rich dark blue, the color of her eyes. Her bedspread was embroidered blue silk in a slightly lighter shade, and soft white cotton sheets peeked out from beneath it. Her desk stood before the window, her homework spread out on its surface. The gauzy white chiffon curtains were pulled back, exposing the room to the gloom of the sky and the rain that poured in a constant staccato against the individual panes, making the view hazy and blurred. The walls were painted a creamy warm white, and an overstuffed chair that he guessed she used for reading from the books stacked next to it sat in the corner. He saw another door that he guessed was her bathroom from the slice of tile flooring he could see through the open wedge.

Another door led to the closet, which was where she was now, finding something dry to wear. He ignored that thought and began to move the heavy bed as far over as he could. When it was as close to the window as it could go, he stood in the center of the room and figured out how he would draw the circle. She emerged from the closet and took her clothes across the room to the bathroom, presumably to change. He caught her arm, and electricity zinged through him at the touch. She dropped her clothes and stared at him, so lovely that his heart almost stopped. He pulled himself forcibly back to the reason he had stopped her.

"Do you have any salt?" he asked her in a hoarse voice. He cleared his throat as she nodded stiffly.

"It's in the kitchen," she said, never looking away from his face. "I'll go get it," she offered after a moment, and turned away.

"Thanks," he said, and shoved his hands into his pockets as she left. *I need a cold shower. This is impossible*, he thought. *At this rate I'll never be able to concentrate long enough to heal Al. Get a grip, get a grip, get a grip...* He actually found himself wishing for Daemon's arrival, if only to dilute the atmosphere. He had never felt this out of control before; it was disconcerting.

She returned, re-locking the door behind her, and handed him a nearly full canister of salt, careful not to touch his fingers. She didn't look at him again as she gathered up her change of clothes and walked to the bathroom. He tried to steady the shaking of his hands as she turned on the light and closed the door behind her, hiding her eyes under the still-tangled curtain of her hair. It was slightly better with the door between them, and he paced out the circle, walking it three times to set it in his mind and in his magic, starting at due north and working clockwise as his father had taught him. She emerged from the bathroom and his attention scattered.

She walked slowly over to the bed and sat down in the middle of it and began to brush her hair. She was wearing a black sweater that zipped down the front, identical to the creamy one she had been wearing earlier, and her long, slender legs were encased in blue jeans. Her small delicate feet were still bare, and she tucked them under her knees to sit cross-legged in the center of her silk duvet.

All his senses felt raw and open, and he seemed aware of her in a way he had never imagined. Her scent filled the room, vanilla and raspberries and herself; in his view she seemed to be at once more vibrant and clearer than anything else, radiant. He could see every strand of her hair, every eyelash, every curve and shadow; he could hear the raspy pull of the brush through her hair, hear her shallow, rapid breathing and even the racing tempo of her pulse. He knew that her ivory skin would feel like silk beneath his fingertips, could feel the play of her supple muscles beneath, could taste her on his tongue, honey and wine. She finished brushing her hair and came off the bed toward him, almost as though pulled.

"Jack…" she breathed, and he pulled himself forcibly from his almost-trance, blinking and averting his eyes, shaking.

"Stay there," he told her, and forced his hands to be steady as he poured the salt in a perfect circle around them with the confidence of long practice. With a Word he invoked the circle, and she gasped and stared around her. "What is it?" she asked, and the simple question helped him focus a little.

"It's a protective circle," he told her. She held out her hand toward the protective barrier and hesitated, glancing back at him. He nodded. "Go ahead and touch it. You can't—" she gasped as a spark arced from her fingertips into the golden glowing dome and it hissed like a bug zapper. He grunted at the echo of that spark in his magic, like she had touched the base of his spine with an electric charge, zinging through his body. "Um, that shouldn't have happened…" he said, shaking in reaction. She smiled and closed her eyes, cocking her head to the side.

"It tastes like you," she murmured softly. He stared at her in shock for a moment, then pulled the little box out of his pocket and slipped the ring on his finger. Shasta appeared with a flourish and the temperature dropped abruptly then rebounded. Deirdre gasped and opened her eyes, staring at the ghost in shock.

"Deirdre! How lovely! It is about time we met, yes? I am Drake Brandon Arlonshasta, Sorcerer of the First Circle, Master of the White, the Violet, and the Black, Holder of the Firelancer's Lantern, and Jack's tutor. You may call me Shasta. I have heard so much about you, my dear," he said in clipped, well-schooled tones. The solid-shouldered, well-dressed, and handsome man took her hand and lifted it to his lips. His touch was cold and ephemeral, as though a gust of the north wind had taken hold of her. Jack watched the ghost perform sardonically, his arms folded across his chest. The ghost stepped back and Jack accidentally met Deirdre's eyes again. He stayed his ground with an enormous strain of will, clenching his fists tightly as she shuddered and dropped her eyes. Shasta looked from one to the other of them, his keen eyes and keener telepathy having missed nothing of the exchange. He grinned.

"So it *is* true," he cackled and folded his arms across his chest. Jack clung to the distraction.

"What?" he asked.

"The Sorcerer-Seer thing. So interesting to see it in action," the ghost said. Jack frowned at him, and the ghost shook his head. "Ignorance is not bliss, I see. Feed your Seer, Jack. She's hungry." Jack stared after him in sudden shocked comprehension as the ghost disappeared. He ripped the knife from its box and cut himself clumsily, rubbing the blood on the ring almost as an afterthought. He shook as he waited impatiently for the magic to finish and flung the ring and the knife back in the box and dropped it in his pocket. He crossed the circle to her and took her in his arms, shuddering at her touch as the gritty raw awareness of her returned; she burned like a bonfire in his mind, derailing every other thought. She gasped when he touched her and cried out when he opened his magic wide to her, clinging to him as the sweet-hot stream poured into her. She melted against him and when his lips touched hers this kiss was like nothing he had ever felt.

Magic charged, her skin threw sparks that tingled hotly against his skin, and every sense was heightened. He could feel her inside him, and for an exquisite moment they were joined as one. She breathed and his lungs filled with air; his own heart kept time to the cadence in her veins; he felt the fire inside her at his touch, all the nuances of her emotions as he held her tightly to him, her longing and her laughter, her pleasure and, most of all, her love for him, deeper and more constant than he had dared to dream. He shook with ecstasy and nearly stumbled into the edge of the circle, sheer instinct keeping him from touching it and collapsing their safety. He picked her up and held her soft, boneless body close, dropping to his knees on the floor in the center with a breathless groan. He sat back on his heels with her in his lap, as the all-consuming fire of his magic raged through them. After uncountable staggering minutes, the drain began to slow, and he began to come back to himself.

He hugged her to him and she trembled in his arms as she took the last little sparks and dribbles. He felt her heart pounding in her chest, her ragged breathing, and her little burst of pleasure at the last small surge before it abruptly cut off and she was sated. She went limp and heavy in his arms, unconscious, and he felt his own muscles shaking in exhausted reaction. He lowered himself the rest of the way to the floor and pulled her close, breathing deeply and feeling slightly dizzy. He brushed her hair back from her lovely face and watched her blink drowsily for a moment when she regained consciousness. She froze for a moment when she woke, then sank into him and sighed in satiated contentment.

"That's probably illegal," she murmured, and he laughed. He rolled over and pinned her gently beneath him, holding his weight on his elbows and staring down into her eyes. He was relieved that this time they sparkled clear dark blue instead of the black of overdose, and he wondered why that was.

She smiled up at him, bubbly with leftover euphoria. She wrapped her arms around his neck and stretched a little beneath him, arching her back and curling her toes; the sensation of her supple body moving beneath him was mouth-wateringly provocative. She took a deep breath and let it out in a burst and said, "I feel incredible. Like I could fly, or something." He laughed and brushed her hair from her face with his fingertips again.

"Me, too," he said, and kissed her softly.

"Yeah, but you probably *can* fly," she pointed out, drawing another chuckle from his lips.

"You're funny like this," he said, and this time she laughed.

"Keep it up then, and I'll be the star of Saturday Night Live. All I need is my daily dose of the delectable Jack," she said, and pulled him down for another kiss.

He kissed her back, and then raised one eyebrow and asked, "Delectable?" She grinned and laughed low in her throat.

"Mmmm, you have *no* idea. You taste like... I don't know... sunshine in the summer... or wind across a field of wildflowers.... It's mouth-watering...." She stole his breath as she kissed him hungrily, and when she stretched beneath him again he groaned and ran his hand down her side to the swell of her hip and back up.

"You need to stop doing that if you want me to be able to pay attention to healing Al," he whispered against her lips.

"I have to make sure you don't forget about me again once you get him back," she teased, laughing, and sent her hands down the length of his back. He shuddered at her electric touch.

"Fat chance," he returned breathlessly, and rolled off her and began to stand up. She sat up and allowed him to pull her gently to her feet.

He took a deep breath and brought out the ring again. She stepped closer and looked at it curiously.

"What is that, exactly?" she asked. He raised an eyebrow.

"The first thing you ask me about sorcery is death magic?" he teased.

"The *first* thing I asked you about was the blue ball of light," she corrected him. "What's death magic?" she asked.

"Death magic is just what it sounds like. Ghosts, vampires, zombies..." He shrugged. "Necromancy." He held up the ring.

"This is made from one of Shasta's bones. It lets me contact him, and I have to pay for the privilege in blood. Most Necromancy requires blood price." She wrinkled her nose in disgust. He grinned. "I know. That's why I don't do it. Except this. My dad gave me this ring. In case I had any questions he couldn't answer." She stared at it.

"Can anyone use that? Or only a Sorcerer?" she asked. He closed the evil object inside his palm. "I suppose anyone with magic could access it, as long as they followed the rules," he said.

"Rules?" she asked.

"Yes. Blood price is… dangerous. Each time I use it, I have to soak the ring in blood before I take it off, or Shasta could ask whatever task he wishes of me, at any time, and I would be compelled to obey," he explained. "And Shasta was… notorious," he added.

"Notorious?" she prompted. He hesitated, his expression growing slightly grim, sickened.

"Well, he made this ring himself…" Jack told her. She stared at him for a moment.

"But… didn't you say it was made from one of his own bones?" she whispered. He nodded grimly. She searched his face for any sign that he was pulling her leg, but found none.

"That's…" she stopped, at a loss for words, feeling a little sick.

"That's Necromancy. Black magic," he said, shrugging.

"And he's your teacher? That your dad gave you?" Her voice was laced with faint disapproval. He grinned.

"He knows lots of other things. Healing, for example," he pointed out. She nodded and relaxed a fraction, reminded of the task ahead.

"Have you ever asked him a question he couldn't answer?" she asked. He looked at her skeptically.

"Do you remember all those titles when he introduced himself?" he asked. She blushed and lowered her eyes.

"Not really," she said, and he chuckled as he followed her thoughts back to those moments.

"Mm. Well, now we know. We won't let it get so out of control again," he promised; then his eyes darkened hungrily as he thought of something. "Unless you want it to..." he finished. She flushed more deeply and looked up at him from underneath her lashes.

"Alastair..." she reminded. He smiled and slipped the ring back on his finger. Shasta reappeared in all his old-fashioned glory.

***

Shasta

Sunday Evening

He looked at the two of them.

"Ah yes, much better," he said, looking speculatively at Jack.

"And you are still... fine?" he asked. Jack nodded, but Deirdre frowned.

"What do you mean?" she asked the ghost.

"Jack did not tell you?" he asked, and she had the feeling his surprise was feigned, though she couldn't see the purpose of the deception.

"Tell me what?" she asked. Jack shook his head at the dead Sorcerer, but Shasta waved his concerns aside with a flick of his wrist.

"Seers usually require *several* Sorcerers to sustain them. Especially young, new Seers," he began to explain. She frowned. He continued. "Our Jack might be the most powerful Sorcerer I have ever heard of," Shasta finished. She looked at Jack in astonishment and he folded his arms over his chest, annoyed. Shasta just stared back, not intimidated in the least.

"She needs to know, Jack," he said. Jack frowned and looked at the floor, then nodded and looked up to meet her eyes. He smiled self-consciously at the flicker of admiration he saw in them, then redirected the conversation.

"Deirdre and I were wondering if you can teach her more about seeing," Jack asked. Shasta considered.

"Very well. Powers of the mind fall into the Violet," he began to explain. Deirdre frowned. Shasta saw the expression and sighed. "Back to the beginning. All right. Sorcerer magic is divided into several different categories. Each category is assigned a color. Powers of the mind—such as telepathy, telekinesis, prophesies, and foretelling—are Violet. If a student wishes to learn, they must find a master in that discipline and apprentice to them until the master sees fit to release them, usually as masters in their own right. It ensures the safety of the students while they learn, and allows Sorcerers to keep track of one another. Except for Jack here, who owns his master, and thus can operate outside the guild and under the radar. Which is very, very lucky for you, my dear. If the Sorcerers knew there was a new Seer... well," he shuddered, and then stopped and considered, thinking to himself for a moment. Then he shook his head and continued.

"Back to your powers. No one knows *how* Seers *see*. There have never been very many—perhaps one or two every thousand years, and you are far too valuable to experiment on. However, I may be able to help a little.

"First, the more power you hold within you, the easier it will be to have the vision you require, the more control you will have over what you see.

"Second, you will most easily have visions of those you care for or who are close to you—close in relationships and also close in proximity. That is why people have to travel to the Seer if they want a vision—unless they know you personally, long-distance visions are unheard of. Often, simply touching the supplicant's hand or face can trigger a vision about them.

"Third, never, never touch a Shapeshifter. Their primal magic will make your visions exceptionally vivid—able to affect you physically, in fact—and there is also the danger of forming a bond that can actually siphon magic away from you, making you hungry, which can be, as you experienced earlier today, actually quite dangerous, both to the Seer and the Sorcerers around her...." He trailed to a stop as he sampled the atmosphere around him. He actually flickered out of sight for a moment when he realized its import.

"You have bonded to the dragon?" he said softly in disbelief, staring first at her, then at Jack's stony expression. He conjured his chair and sat down, staring off into space, thinking furiously. She wondered what he would have to say about the situation. He shifted in his chair and crossed his legs.

"Not much is known about these bonds. With the scarcity of Seers and the rarity and private nature of Shapeshifters, it is very infrequent for them to come into contact. In fact, the only documented cases are so ancient that they are legends even among us. One thing is known: if he dies, you will die, and vice versa." Jack and Deirdre exchanged a leaden glance. Shasta thought again, then pursed his elegant lips. "I find it curious that you were so hungry just now that you were both half crazed; in the legends you can take the dragon's magic through the bond." He looked at her and the question was clear. She frowned.

"I can, I think," she murmured. "At least, I think I *did*, yesterday, just before that vision of Al." She paused, remembering. Jack nodded, remembering the terror of the silver flash in her eyes and the icy skittering of unfamiliar magic. "I felt... something... like ice in my veins, but burning—it *hurt*—" she touched her forehead in subconscious memory. "Daemon always feels cold to me, like I'm standing in front of the refrigerator on a hot day..." She paused, and they nodded their understanding. She continued, "And that vision... I felt like *I* was the one dying...." She shuddered, and Jack came over to stand behind her and put his hands on her shoulders, rubbing them gently. She leaned back into him, and the ghost Sorcerer nodded.

"Then the question is, why did that not happen today? You were hungry enough..." Shasta said.

"No imminent vision?" Jack said. Shasta raised his eyebrows.

"Possible. The vision itself triggered the drain of the Shapeshifter's magic, and then, when you touched Jack, it switched over to the preferred source," he nodded. "It fits. That does not make it correct, but I think we can work from it." He looked over at Deirdre. "And have you taken any of his magic since then?" he asked her. She frowned again.

"I... I'm not sure..." she said. She glanced up over her shoulder at Jack, then back at Shasta. "Last night Jack and I... I guess we sort of had a fight." She shifted uncomfortably at the memory and he tightened his grip on her shoulders, squeezing gently, and rubbed her upper arms soothingly. "I *think* I called him, and I *might* have taken a little of his magic when I did. Maybe," she sighed, frustrated.

"You called him," Jack confirmed wryly, rubbing at his jaw. Shasta raised an eyebrow and Deirdre turned toward him in surprise.

"The dragon *hit* you?" the ghost said; it sounded like a rebuke.

"He did *what?*" she gasped in disbelief. Jack shrugged uncomfortably.

"I deserved it, and he pulled his punch," he told them. Shasta grunted.

"If he hadn't, you wouldn't be standing here. You'd be keeping me company in the Grey," the ghost said sharply, and Deirdre swayed and passed her hand over her eyes. Jack shrugged.

"Maybe," he said. Shasta spoke sharply, his voice like ice.

"Make no mistake, Jack. If he wanted to, he could dismember you with one hand unless you stopped him with your magic. Remember Sampson?" Jack grimaced, and nodded. "A dragon would be ten times stronger than a lion, even in human form," Shasta warned. Deirdre's concern for Jack morphed into incredulity.

"Sampson? From the Bible?"

"Was a lion, yes," Shasta bit off impatiently.

"And we're getting off topic," Jack said with an edge in his voice. Shasta looked at him for a moment more, as though there was quite a bit more he wanted to say, but then he nodded acquiescence.

"Yes. If you did take the dragon's magic last night *after* Jack had… fed you, that could explain why you were so hungry today. Shapeshifter magic would be used up much faster, in essence burning you out—they don't mix well. Jack's magic, pure, should last the week, even for a young Seer. But that still doesn't explain how you managed not to do that today," Shasta said. She frowned again, considering.

"I think I've called him three times…" she mused, thinking aloud. "Friday night I was panicked about the vision I had of Jack. Yesterday, the vision of Al triggered it, and last night, I was… distraught," she said. Jack winced and she turned and put her arms around him, seeking and giving comfort. He held her for a moment, resting his chin on her head, then released her as she turned away again, back toward the ghost.

"And all three times he came?" Shasta asked curiously. She frowned and nodded.

"Apparently. I didn't know about last night," she said. He shook his head and waved for her to continue, but she shrugged, having nothing more to say. Jack filled in.

"So maybe the link is triggered automatically by magical or emotional distress," he suggested. Shasta frowned, dissatisfied, tapping on his lower lip with a long finger.

"Perhaps. Deirdre, can you tell where Daemon is right now?" he asked. She stilled, and her gaze turned inward. She pointed north and a little east. Jack closed his eyes and clenched his fists behind her back as a wave of jealousy washed over him. The ghost saw him, but only nodded at Deirdre. "And can you tell what he's doing?" he asked. She cocked her head a little, concentrating.

"He's cooking. And watching the clock," she said. Jack winced and confirmed her statement.

"When I spoke to him earlier he had to work but he thought he could get here around eight or eight-thirty," he said tightly. Deirdre looked over at him and read his unhappiness in his expression. She lowered her eyes and guilt flashed across her face. She bit her lip and crossed her arms across her chest.

"Can *he* do that too?" Jack asked the ghost.

"What? Tell where she is and what she is doing?" Shasta asked. Jack nodded rigidly. "Without a doubt, I would say, if he cared to," Shasta said. Jack folded his arms across his chest and paced a few steps around the circle.

"But the point is that she *didn't* call him earlier, when she clearly *was* in distress," the ghost pointed out. "The dragon is going about his business as usual. He doesn't even know she was hungry. If he had, he would probably be here already," Shasta pointed out. Jack gradually relaxed at his words. "It *can't* be automatic," the ghost said, and turned back to Deirdre.

"What were you doing earlier today, before Jack came?" Shasta asked. She shrugged.

"Sleeping, mostly, I guess. I didn't feel very well," she admitted. "I talked to Alastair for a while." Shasta looked at her speculatively.

"What were you doing *just* before he came? What were you thinking about today?" the ghost asked her. Her eyes slid toward Jack and she flushed.

"Um, waiting for Jack. And Jack," she answered in soft embarrassment.

"And did the dragon even cross your thoughts?" Shasta asked her then. She shook her head.

"No," she answered. "Well, maybe when I was remembering yesterday, but not really, no." Her voice was matter-of-fact, but Jack's heart flew into his throat. He felt instant remorse at his behavior over her connection to Daemon. He lowered his eyes in shame and ached to go to her, but he felt constrained by the ghost's presence. He looked up and met her eyes. They pleaded with him for understanding, and his face softened and he was suddenly standing in front of her with no memory of taking those steps. He reached out and caressed her throat and jaw with his hand, cradling her cheek in his palm and sliding his hand back to tangle in her heavy hair. She shivered at the touch, and a flash of heat shot through him.

"Sorry," he mouthed, and she nodded her head and leaned into his hand.

Shasta paced around, vanishing his chair and ignoring them.

"All right. Let us move on. We cannot test their bond until he gets here, and it might not be wise to do so anyway. Deirdre needs to learn how to have visions of what she wants, when she wants. Correct?" he asked. When they were silent, he turned around and looked at them, staring soulfully into one another's eyes, completely oblivious to anything else. He rolled his eyes in irritation and stepped between them, trusting the cold draft created by his presence to get their attention.

"Can we focus, please?" They separated in swift chagrin, and he paced away, muttering under his breath while they recovered themselves.

"People used to respect the death magic, but no, I have to get the one Sorcerer who can keep it going indefinitely, so he feels free to pursue whatever captures his attention at the time… Although, who can blame him? A *Seer*, for God's sake…." He turned and they were staring at him, obviously having overheard his mild tirade. He cleared his throat and clapped his hands.

"Controlling your visions, yes?" he asked. She nodded, and Jack conjured two simple wooden chairs and helped her sit down. She lifted her bare feet up to the turned wooden bar that braced the two front legs and leaned forward with her elbows on her knees. Her fine-boned face rested on one palm, the picture of relaxed attention. She looked so young in that pose, like a child, completely unaware of her power. No wonder the Sorcerer was entranced. She was lovely, and innocent. He stifled a sigh. A Seer wouldn't stay that way for long, no matter how powerful her protectors. It was simply the nature of their power; they saw far too much. He smiled at her. She smiled sweetly back and he recreated his own chair and hitched his slacks up to sit down across from her.

"All right, Deirdre," he said. She wiped her hands on her jeans and sat up, her mysterious dark blue eyes wide and eager, with only a trace of trepidation in them. She clasped her hands in her lap and focused on him. *Enchanting*, he thought. *And her mind is just as lovely.* He searched her surface thoughts, surprised that he could not see more. A thick silver fog obscured anything deeper. *Her bond with the Shapeshifter?* he thought, noting the color of the haze. *Interesting…*

"Let us start with Jack. You have already had at least one vision of him," he began. Her mind closed off completely as she abruptly sat back in her chair and her eyes slid to Jack and she flushed; her knuckles turned white as she squeezed her hands together in her lap.

"I don't think… my visions of Jack won't be… helpful…" she stammered out. He cocked his head at her in confusion, then watched the heat in her eyes as she gazed at his apprentice. He chuckled. *He is in for an exciting time… lucky bastard*, he thought. Jack shifted in his seat, his expression puzzled and curious.

"All right. Who do you suggest?" Shasta said. She relaxed slightly.

"How about… my father?" she proposed. He nodded.

"Perfect. Blood tie will help with the distance," he approved. "Now, close your eyes and visualize him, as clearly as you can. See the color of his eyes, the way he combs his hair. What is he wearing? Does he have anything in his hands? Is he sitting or standing?" As he prompted her, her mind opened up a little again, and he could see her building the image of a tall, powerfully built man, with thick blue-black hair combed back from a high forehead—no gray, he noticed—brown eyes that were somehow cold and dark without any inner fire, high cheekbones and pale skin forming in her thoughts.

He wore an expensive and exquisitely tailored black suit, crisp white shirt, black and burgundy silk tie, Italian shoes. He carried an elegant black briefcase and stood straight and tall, a confidence that bordered on arrogance in his demeanor. The image flowed directly into a vision, lost to him in the gray fog, and Deirdre gasped and her eyes flew open. She sat frozen in her chair, the only sign she gave was a gradual tightening of her grip on herself as her fingers dug into her knees, white and stiff. After a moment she blinked, coming back to herself.

"Very good," he said, pleased that she had had such clear success her first time out. She trembled, and Jack was suddenly by her side. He lifted her up and sat down himself in her chair, changing it into a stuffed armchair as he did so. He settled her in his lap and she curled into him, gripping him tightly.

"Do you want to tell us about it?" Jack asked her, murmuring into her hair. She shook her head, and he petted her, stroking one hand over her hair and down her back, massaging slow circles into the back of her hand with the other. "Okay. That's fine. But you did it, right? You had a vision?" he asked. She nodded and got a hold of herself, visibly drawing on his strength to regain her equilibrium. Shasta watched them with an unreadable expression. The unexpectedly desperate intensity of their relationship was suddenly no longer amusing. He shook off the odd premonition and tried to draw them back to the task at hand.

"All right. Check your energy levels. Try to feel your magic," he instructed. She frowned at him slightly, a little line appearing between her finely shaped dark eyebrows. Her gaze turned inward. After a minute, she shrugged.

"It seems okay," she said.

"It will get easier with practice and time. Do not forget to keep an eye on your magic. If it gets too depleted, and you cannot reach Jack, the Shapeshifter's magic will sustain you for a while, but it should be used only in dire emergency. It will burn through you much too quickly, it may become addictive, and it will kill you both if you rely on it for very long. His magic cannot recharge fast enough to sustain you both, and if he Changes he will take it back from you—he won't be able to help it—which could kill you. And, his magic will make your visions exceptionally vivid, perhaps even fatally so, depending on what you see." He stood up and vanished his chair, looking down at the impossibly beautiful girl curled in his apprentice's arms. She had a long, hard road ahead. He hoped she was strong enough.

"Take care, my dear. It has been a privilege to meet you. Remember, you are not responsible for the things you see. Everyone has their own path; your role is to set them upon it, perhaps to point out danger ahead. That is all. It is not your responsibility to rescue people, and it is definitely not advisable to try to change the things you see." He patted her arm, causing her to shiver in reaction to the clammy feel of his insubstantial hand on her skin—or perhaps it was the warning that made her tremble—and vanished.

***

Jack

Sunday Evening

Jack rubbed her back and relaxed back in the chair for a moment, and she leaned into him, tucking her head against his shoulder. He got out the little box and fed the ring, while she watched curiously. He put the kit back in his pocket and she looked at his hand, amazed that there was no mark where he had cut himself. "Deirdre, what did you see in the vision of your father?" he asked her. She sighed.

"I saw him attending Alastair's funeral this Tuesday," she told him, her voice tight and small.

"Hmm. And what do you see in your visions of me?" he asked, unable to resist finding out what had caused her odd reaction earlier. He was surprised when she laughed low and soft and went all boneless in his arms.

"Can't tell you that," she told him, watching his face for his reaction; he shifted beneath her uncomfortably. He chuckled quietly.

"Good or bad?" he asked. She smiled up at him.

"More like great," she admitted. He groaned.

"Why can't you tell me?" he asked. She lowered her eyes.

"When the time is right, believe me, you'll be the first to know," she said, and kissed him gently. He looked down at her with velvet in his eyes. She trembled, and her eyes filled with the secret inner fire that made him want to conquer the world and throw it at her feet. She blinked it down and pulled him back to the task at hand.

"What else do we need to do to be ready when Daemon comes?" she asked, and he sighed.

"We should probably talk to Alastair. He definitely has a say in all this. And I'll need to make a circle in his room, too, around the bed. And we should probably eat," he suggested. She sighed and left his embrace with visible reluctance, tugging on his hand when he didn't stand up right away.

"Let's order some pizza and then we can talk to Al," she suggested.

"Sounds good," he said, then pulled her back to him as he stood.

"It isn't really fair," he mock-complained into her hair as he drew her arms around his waist. She laid her head against his chest as he wrapped his arms around her.

"Actually, it's kind of like torture," she murmured, and he looked down at her, unsure what she meant. "To wait, I mean, after *knowing*," she said softly, her voice and eyes suddenly remote. She lifted her hand to touch the barrier, and it went right through, leaving the circle intact. He gasped and dropped his arms, staring at her in disbelief as she withdrew her hand and the sensation curled around his spine like someone trailing their fingertips in a hot bath, stirring up swirling curls and eddies.

"It's warm," she murmured in surprise.

"It's not supposed to let *anything* through—except me," he told her incredulously.

"Maybe it's because I'm full of your magic?" she mused.

"Maybe. Do it again. See if you can go all the way through this time," he suggested. She held out her hand and pushed it through ahead of her, stepping slowly forward. Her head cleared the dome first as it tapered toward the edge, then her shoulders, waist, knees, and finally her bare feet. It felt like walking through semi-solid sunshine, a warm pressure on her skin as she passed. She turned and looked back at him from the outside of the circle.

"See if you can come back in," he mouthed at her, but she couldn't hear him. His 'come here' gesture was clear enough, though, and she touched her toe to the barrier, testing it like water to see if it would let her back in. She met no resistance as she walked slowly back to him.

"*That* is cool," he said. She laughed.

"See if it makes a difference how fast you go through. Hit it," he said. She curled her hand into a fist and punched it into the dome. It went right through, but the sensation this time was hotter, more like flames than sunshine. She drew her hand back more slowly. He shivered. She raised an eyebrow at him.

"It feels like you're running your fingers down my spine," he tried to explain the sensation. She smiled.

"It feels to me like I'm pushing through thick warm molasses," she told him, and he grinned back at her. After a moment more, he shook himself.

"Time for food. I'm starved," he said. She laughed.

"Me too," she agreed, and they exited the circle. She reached for the phone on the dressing table.

"What do you want?" she asked. They agreed on the toppings and Deirdre placed the order. He flashed back to other nights, when they had ordered pizza with Al and one of her friends and sat around in the home theater in the basement. He wondered for a moment how those nights would have been different if he had asked Deirdre out before. He tried to remember if she had ever dated anyone else. He searched his memory, but he couldn't remember ever seeing her with another guy, not in all the time he'd known her. Not that they didn't want her. How many dates had Deirdre turned down? She had to be on everybody's top-five list. It was just that she was somehow… remote. Alastair's impossibly beautiful sister, the unattainable goddess.

He recalled Jason's shock when he had mentioned that he was taking Deirdre to the movies. For her, he was suddenly sure there had only ever been Alastair, and her girlfriends, which were sometimes Al's girlfriends, or his. He wondered uncomfortably how many girls she had seen him with. A lot. They chased him— there was always one hanging around. He had dumped Andrea to ask Deirdre out, for Pete's sake. He wondered if Al was right. Had she really wanted him since the fifth grade? Been just waiting for him to wake up? How much time had he wasted?

She leaned against the table after she hung up, and he gazed at the graceful line of her body, the tilt of her elegant head. "What are you thinking about, Jack?" she asked him softly. He looked at her a moment longer.

"You," he admitted, and she smiled and raised her eyebrows. He wanted to question her, but the clock was, unfortunately, ticking. He suddenly wished for a spell to suspend time, a spell that would give him the hours alone with her he craved.

"Time to go talk to Al?" he asked. She lowered her eyes.

"Yeah," she said, "I guess it is." Jack was suddenly nervous.

"Any idea what he'll say?" he asked her. She chortled.

"None," she admitted. She unlocked the door and went out, and he followed her down the hall. She paused at Alastair's door and knocked softly, then pushed it open and entered the room.

She paused at the sink and washed her hands; then continued to his bedside.

"Hey, Al," she said. He smiled over at her.

"Hey, Dee Dee," he said.

"Jack's here, too," she told him as Jack finished washing his hands and came up behind her. He slipped around her and began to walk around the room, trying to figure the best way to do the circle.

"Hey, man. Everything okay?" Alastair followed the sounds of Jack's footsteps with his sightless blue eyes. Jack smiled, and winked at Deirdre.

"Oh, yeah," he answered suggestively, and she glared at him as Al raised an eyebrow in disapproval.

"Oh, hey now, watch it, man. That's my sister," Al warned, but his eyes twinkled and he had to fight to keep his frown. Deirdre sighed and shook her head.

"Jack has something he wants to ask you," Deirdre changed the subject. Now it was Jack's turn to glare. She glared back and tapped her wrist, reminding him of the shortage of time. It was already seven-thirty. He flashed her a worried look, and she shook her head and smiled, urging him on.

"Okay… I'm listening," Al said when the silence stretched a little too long. Jack took a deep breath.

236

"I… I want to try to heal you. If you agree," Jack said. Alastair's heart monitor began to freak out as he gripped the rails of the bed with white-knuckled hands.

"You want to… you can do that?" he gasped out, fighting for breath. Deirdre flew to his side and Jack looked a little sick.

"Relax, Al, or you'll get the nurse in here!" Deirdre hissed in his ear, but her touch on his arm was reassuringly gentle. He took a few slower breaths and unclenched his hands from the bed. The heart monitor calmed a little. Jack stepped closer.

"I think so. I want to try. Tonight. What do you say?" he said. Al fought for control.

"Is it risky?" he asked, his voice unsteady. Jack hesitated.

"I'm not sure, but I don't think so. I'm pretty sure the worst that could happen is it won't work." He watched his friend closely.

"If that's true, then why the wait, Jack?" Al asked after a few minutes.

"You had to be strong enough. It will be hard on you. And training and practice were needed. For me, I mean. It takes decades to master this stuff, and I've only had a year. I had to know exactly what your injuries were so I could practice the right things," Jack pointed out. "And now we have Daemon," he added. Al swallowed and looked over at Deirdre.

Chapter 6

Deirdre

Sunday Evening

"What do you say, Dee Dee?" he asked. She stared into his sightless eyes, and tears filled her own. She leaned over and put her arms around him, and he held her for a long minute.

"I think I would do *anything* to get you back. All the way back," she whispered. "And I think Jack wouldn't put us through this if he couldn't deliver. And Daemon's going to help. I told you about my ankle, right?" she continued, talking softly in his ear. He hugged her tightly.

"Okay, Deirdre. Okay," he whispered. She hugged him tightly back and released him. Someone knocked on the door downstairs.

"I'll get it. We ordered pizza," she said as she left. She walked swiftly down the stairs and opened it. An attractive young man stood there, older, maybe twenty-three or -four, with soaked dark hair that hung in his green eyes and stood out in stark contrast as it dripped down his pale skin, almost blue with cold.

He was obviously uncomfortable, hunched against the still-pounding rain and cold wind that swirled in unpredictable gusts, whipping long strands of Deirdre's hair around her head. He was holding a heat-retaining cover that contained the pizza boxes.

"Hi," she said. She had forgotten to grab the money on her way to the door. He looked miserable out there. "Will you come in for a minute?" she asked, stepping back to give him room. He looked surprised.

"Sure. Thanks," he said gratefully and stepped gingerly across the doorstep, wincing at the dirty puddles he was tracking across the tile.

"Great. Can you just wait here? I have to go grab your money," she said, and began to walk away as he nodded. She paused and turned back toward him. "How much was it, again?" she asked. He fumbled with a paper under one of his hands.

"Um, thirty-two seventy-nine," he said. She nodded her thanks and padded into the kitchen in her bare feet. She reached across the counter for the cookie jar and pulled it toward her. Suddenly, strong hands grabbed her from behind, pinning her arms together behind her and clamping over her mouth, cutting off her scream. He lifted her off her feet and turned her around, strong enough that she had no chance of making any move he didn't allow. He held her tightly against him and she glanced up into his bright green eyes. Terror shot through her at the menace she saw there, and she tried to fight him, throwing her head back and forth and straining against him. Her efforts were laughable.

Instinctively she reached through her link for Daemon, trying to be careful not to touch his magic; he was already on his way, driving through the downpour. She felt him push the pedal all the way to the floor, but fear filled her belly, cold and solid; she doubted he could possibly be there in time. Tears threatened as she wondered how long it would take before Jack came looking for her. Jack would hear her scream, but she had no chance of that with the way the man held her. He pinned her hard against the counter, his lean body heavy and taught with contained power, bruising her forearms that he still held behind her, and he hissed at her.

"Look at me," he commanded. She stalled, fighting still with tears leaking from her eyes from the strike of the bruising, rounded edge of the countertop pressing into her arms and back; he yanked on her wrists so hard she thought her elbows and shoulder joints might break. A low whimper escaped, and she opened her eyes in reaction to the pain, glaring at him as her bewildered defiance turned slowly to rage. She met his eyes and she was caught. His eyes were mesmerizing, like bright green flames; they flickered and glowed, and against her will she began to relax as a tranquilizing effect seeped into her mind. She fought the sensation even as her body went limp and he had to catch her weight as her knees gave way.

"Much better," he muttered, and let go of her mouth long enough to slap a piece of duct tape across it. Inside her head she screamed and fought, panicked, enraged, unable to make her body respond, and she reached inside herself for anything that could help her circumvent his crawling mental chains. She found Jack's magic. It sat within her, still and thick, too serene to be of any help to her, but it gave her an idea. She cast further and purposely grabbed Daemon's wilder icy magic. It hit her like a riptide, mixing violently with Jack's, dragging her out from under her attacker's hypnosis. The release of the mental constraints whiplashed in her mind, cracking against her skull like an explosion. She recovered slowly, realizing after a moment that he didn't know she was free. How could he? Her head felt like it lay in pieces on the floor and she still couldn't move.

After a minute he let go of one of her hands to bring them in front of her. Enough feeling had returned and she made her move. She curled her hands into claws and dragged her nails across his face with all the strength she could muster, kicking and thrashing, trying desperately to make enough noise to call Jack. He cursed in surprise and hit her across the face with a brutal backhanded slap that made her head ring and effectively put an end to her struggle as she fought to stay conscious. She must have blacked out for a

240

moment, because the next thing she knew she was lying on the cold tile floor and he had slipped a prepared loop of slick nylon cord around her wrists and tightened it cruelly. She glared at him and began to struggle again, if somewhat feebly, and he glared at her with his feral gaze. She froze and her eyes widened in disbelief when she saw his face.

The bleeding gashes her nails had left across his cheeks were already closing. She stared, watching them heal right before her eyes, and his expression turned gloating as he got her feet tied together and bent over her. He stroked her hair back from her eyes and she shuddered in revulsion at his touch. And then he was gone. The refrigerator rocked with the impact and he crumpled to the floor in a tangled heap.

***

Daemon

Sunday Evening

Daemon walked over to the twitching figure and systematically broke a few more bones while he was still unconscious. When Daemon was satisfied with his work he went over to the counter and swiped one of Maria's knives from the block; in a moment Deirdre was free. He pulled her carefully to her feet and she fell into his arms and hugged him tightly, shaking and trying not to cry. He just held her, stroking his hand down her back, and she gradually calmed down, soothed by his touch and the steady sound of his heartbeat.

"Thanks," she said in a soggy voice, looking up at him as she stepped back. A faint smile was his only answer; his eyes were still full of concern.

"Let's get Jack," she said, and turned toward the kitchen door. Jack stood there, leaning against the frame, and she flew toward him as relief flooded through her. She stopped short when she took in his stony expression and hostile posture. Hurt and confused by his attitude, she looked back over her shoulder at Daemon. He went over to the refrigerator and picked up the broken body and tossed it on the table.

"You in the habit of inviting vampires into the house?" Daemon asked coolly. Jack's expression cleared and he stumbled toward it, looking back and forth between them in disbelief. Daemon bent and picked up the pieces of rope from the floor and tossed them on top of the body. Jack looked over toward Deirdre, taking in her disheveled appearance and the tear stains and hurt in her expression. He saw the bruise beginning to form across her cheek and the red welts on her wrists and cursed. He went to her and reached for her chin, and she flinched away from his touch. Agony seared his insides and he froze. She had *never* flinched from him before.

"Sorry," he whispered. She stared at him and after a moment he saw tears fill her eyes and begin to spill down her cheeks as she swayed forward and allowed him to draw her into his embrace. He clutched her close as she cried, cursing himself for an idiot, wondering how he would ever be able to bear letting her out of his sight again. This was twice the dragon had been there for her when he had not. Three times if he counted last night. Her tears burned into his shoulder through his shirt. Finally, they slowed. He took her shoulders and held her in front of him, staring into her face.

"Can I heal you, Deirdre?" he asked her. She nodded, but her eyes were still bleak.

"Watch that for a minute, will you?" he asked Daemon, nodding toward the still body of the vampire. The Shapeshifter nodded and folded his arms across his chest. Deirdre frowned a little and glanced back at Daemon as Jack took her hand and led her from the room.

"But he's dead, isn't he?" she asked. Jack glanced over at her as he led her up the stairs.

"Well... technically. But I have some questions for him," he said grimly.

"But..." she glanced back down the stairs and stumbled a little as dizziness struck her.

"Deirdre," Jack gasped and caught her to him.

"Dizzy," she murmured, and fainted. Jack's heart stuttered with the alarmed surge of adrenaline and he caught her up and practically flew to her room, mindful still of the nurse who could interrupt at any time. He shut and locked the door and laid her down in the center of the circle. He invoked it and brought out Shasta again. The ghost was getting a workout tonight. He appeared and knelt immediately on her other side.

"What happened?" he barked, and Jack gave him the images, not bothering with words. The ghost ran his cold hands through her body, head to toe, concentrating, feeling for trauma.

"All right. Head first." Jack concentrated, feeling the swollen wrongness of the bruise under her chin, the torn soreness of her cells. Then he felt something else, something in her mind, a dark shadow of the broken thrall that nearly made him retch in panicked terror.

I need Daemon, he thought at the ghost, and dropped the circle. He ran from the room, oblivious to his tutor's surprised cry. He threw open the kitchen door and caught Daemon munching on the pizza they had ordered.

"Bring him," he snapped and flew back, trusting the dragon to follow. He did, the broken vampire still unconscious, slung over his shoulder like a sack of dog food. Jack gestured toward the circle, and Daemon knelt by Deirdre's too-still form, taking Jack's former place. He threw the body unceremoniously on the floor a few feet away, just inside the edge, and barely blinked at the scent of cold rot the ghost put out. It was a measure of his anxiety that he barely registered that this was her bedroom.

Jack re-conjured the circle and snapped out, "There's something wrong in her head. I think the vamp must have had her in thrall, and she somehow broke it. You have to check, Daemon. You're linked to her. You have to look inside her head and tell me what's wrong." The Sorcerer's hands shook and he wiped them on his jeans, the burning intensity of his stare scorching Daemon's heart. He nodded once, sharply, and closed his eyes and felt along the link. It felt cold and limp, and he swallowed convulsively and his eyes fluttered open for a second. Whatever Jack saw in them made him go white beneath his tan, and he moaned, a tearing agonized sound, and Daemon could feel him summon his magic.

It filled the air inside the dome, almost visible, like dust in the sunlight, hanging in the air with the promise of violence. Daemon swiftly put his hands on the sides of her head and leaned over her, feeling along the link. Desperately, experimentally, he sent a tiny spark of his magic along the line, and it was like a torch in the dark. He followed it into her head. Pain. And a sort of rushing feeling, like standing next to a small, fast-flowing stream, only this one pulsed and gushed in spurts. Pressure, building with each throbbing stab of pain. He gasped and pulled back, carefully, gently, and opened his eyes.

"She's bleeding into her brain," he told them as soon as he was able.

The Sorcerer shoved Daemon's hands roughly out of the way and replaced them with his own, sliding his fingers along her scalp and into her hair.

"Shasta!" he snapped, and the ghost attended him. He threw his head back and closed his eyes and settled himself swiftly into a healer's trance, concentrating, following the ghost's whispered instructions intently. All Daemon could do was watch; watch and tremble with rage and impotence. She was dying. A red haze flashed across his eyes, but he shoved the Change that threatened aside almost carelessly. Nothing could distract him now. He could taste the Sorcerer's magic in the air, raw power like he had never felt, and he rejoiced and prayed and silently begged that it would be enough, that he could save her.

Jack gasped and his face tightened, and Daemon knew he had found the tear. The ghost looked grim as he read the extent of the trauma from Jack's mind.

Across the circle, the vampire moved. Daemon had crossed to it and crushed its ribcage again before he realized he intended to move, and he shook as he stood over the thing, forcing himself not to kill him. He closed his eyes and tested the gossamer cord that bound him to Deirdre more strongly than chains.

"Too fast! Slow down!" Shasta hissed, and Jack froze and huffed a panicked breath from his lungs.

"I can't—she'll die!" he spat back.

"If you go too fast she might as well," Shasta warned harshly, and Jack's eyes leaked tears of frustration and his power amped up another few notches, contained by the power of the dome until it was so thick it sparked and burned along Daemon's skin. He didn't care. The thread of her mind grew brighter; her pain was lessening, the pressure slowly fading as Jack siphoned the tiny puddle of thickening blood away from the area. Daemon could feel the tender, meticulous way the Sorcerer knit the walls of the blood vessel back together, sealing the tear as though it had never been, and sighed in relief along with Jack and Deirdre, all three of them at the same time, the same breath, as her breathing eased from its rapid shallow pant to a more natural rhythm.

"Check her again—make sure I got it all," he murmured to the dragon, not really leaving the trance as he shifted his power to the ugly purple hand-shaped bruise across her jaw. It disappeared swiftly beneath his fingers, and her skin was again perfect and unblemished. He floated his hands down her body, treating the bruise from the counter across her back and forearms, the hot red welts on her wrists, her ankles. Daemon knelt by her head and placed his hands at the sides of her face; her skin was warm and smooth beneath his fingertips, and he could feel the steady rhythm of her pulse. Her scent and the Sorcerer's—hot sunshine and meadow grass—filled his nose, and he breathed deeply. Foreign magic skittered across his skin, leaving dark hair-thin burns on his arms and face. He ignored them; they healed nearly as fast as they appeared. He went into her mind, easier now that he knew the way.

He felt carefully, using the sensitivity his father had taught him with the bone magic, casting his senses wider and wider, until he could feel every molecule of her body. He felt her breathing, her heart, the blood flowing smoothly through her veins, the spark that was *her*. It was intoxicating, being this close, and he lingered longer than he should have. Her mind flickered with images as she began to awaken, but he couldn't really see them, caught up in the sensation of feeling fragile, small, the memory of the graceful way she moved, of what it felt like to be her. He withdrew slowly, careful not to leave anything behind, like a surgeon counting his scalpels before he closed up.

"She's waking up," he told them, dropping his hands reluctantly from her face and moving away, back toward the vampire. It hadn't moved again, he noted with detached satisfaction. Jack's hot gaze found his, and he nodded slowly. The tension in the Sorcerer's jaw eased and he blinked back the moisture that filled his eyes, bending over her in shaking relief, cradling her head in his hands as he buried his face in her shoulder. The magic that filled the dome vibrated like a sound wave, marking the instant she regained consciousness. It flowed to her almost visibly, sucked into her skin, and she gasped, "Jack!" in an intimate crooning whisper. He quaked in reaction to the drain, and held her more tightly.

"I'm here, honey, you're okay." Jack took a deep, shuddering breath, and whispered again, almost to himself, "You're okay." Daemon looked away, feeling suddenly like an intruder. The ghost

Sorcerer was watching him. It nodded its head at him in a gesture like respect, and Daemon stared at it in astonishment as it vanished. He shook his head at the odd exchange and looked back at the pair on the floor. Jack had sat up a little, and they were staring into one another's eyes, holding the wordless conversation held by lovers everywhere, where a simple touch could communicate an entire paragraph. She nodded slightly and her expression softened; the corner of her lips lifted in a faint smile. He wondered what it would feel like to have her look at him like that, and he turned away again.

Jack rose slowly and lifted her to her feet, handling her as though she were made of glass. He came over to Daemon and looked up at the dragon, his gaze still hot with the echo of his power, his face gray with fatigue. Dark circles smudged the skin beneath his eyes, and his shoulders were hunched against the exhaustion that battered at him from the inside. Daemon wondered how much of his weariness was from the complicated healing and how much was from the emotional toll of nearly losing Deirdre.

"Thank you," he said, his voice thick with emotion. Daemon inclined his head solemnly in acknowledgment. Jack looked down at the vampire on the floor and held out his hand. A sparkling golden web of power flowed across the creature, binding it securely. Jack turned away.

"Let's go heal Alastair," he said. Daemon raised his eyebrows. Just how much power did the Sorcerer have? In spite of his exhaustion, or maybe because of it, Daemon could feel magic pulsing inside the boy, full and heated like a volcanic hot-spring, impossibly deep. He followed when Jack collapsed the circle with a touch, glancing back at the body on the floor.

"Leave him," Jack instructed, and re-invoked the circle as they left the room, trapping the vamp further. Daemon watched him pull Deirdre with him, holding her close with his arm around her slender waist as though he intended to never let her go again.

He closed the door behind them as they made their way down the hall to another room, turning in there abruptly. Daemon saw him glance at the little sink just inside the doorway and consciously dismiss it.

"What happened to you guys?" the boy who could only be Alastair asked, fighting to keep annoyance from his voice. He sat on a hospital bed that was raised to support him, and wires and diodes were connected to his skin, monitoring him carefully. He turned his sightless eyes toward Daemon, and the dragon stopped in the doorway, staring for a moment. On Deirdre, the face was impossibly lovely and the essence of feminine; her brother had the same arresting features but would never be mistaken for a girl. He radiated an almost electric current, a magnetism far stronger even than Jack's, and Daemon understood then why they were here. Alastair was a Sovereign, one of those rare people who others were drawn to, would follow, even worship. Alexander, Napoleon, Stalin, George Washington, Hitler, Christ. Sovereigns tended to burn bright and die young, and Daemon shivered as Alastair looked over at him, pinning him with his blank gaze. Except he wasn't really looking; his eyes were tracking the sounds he heard, Daemon realized.

"Sorry," Jack said, his voice clipped and short. "We ran into some trouble. We're doing this *now*," he said. Deirdre put her hand gently on his arm, turning him toward her. She paused until she had his full attention, then she stroked her hands across his face, tracing the circles under his eyes.

"I'm not arguing, but Jack, are you sure? You're exhausted," she said, her voice low and intense with concern. She dropped her hands to his shoulders and he took her head in his hands. He looked at her a moment and then kissed her deeply, desperately, with an edge in it she had never felt before, frightening her. He pulled back and sucked in a ragged breath and leaned his forehead against hers.

"They've found you, Deirdre. Found *us*. It's now or never, and I can't protect Al, or you, like this. It's only a matter of time now before more *others* come for you. We *have* to—I have to," he said. Her eyes widened as his words sank in. Daemon could feel her subconsciously tug on the line between them as she tried to control the raw terror that clawed at her insides as she realized there would be more attacks like the one she had just been through. He sent reassurance along the connection—it was deeper now, and somehow more immediate, since he had wandered around in her mind—and she took a breath and with it, a hold on the panic, but she never looked away from Jack.

"What do you need?" she asked, and her voice held a quiet note of determination. Jack smiled faintly and kissed her again, and when he pulled away this time his shoulders had a more relaxed set and his eyes were less haggard.

"I'm making a circle. Daemon, you check on the nurse—and don't get caught," Jack instructed, already turning away. With a long measuring look at the Sorcerer, Daemon nodded, wondering when exactly he had been drafted into Jack's ragtag army. He shook his head and made his way down the hall, where he could smell the nurse. He used his magic to remain unseen as he entered. She was napping in a chair, a romance novel lying face-down on her chest. The circle would have caught any noise they had made, he realized. He decided that this was a good place for her, and reinforced her sleep with a light touch on her forehead. She wouldn't wake easily, now.

He stopped in the hall outside Deirdre's room and looked inside to check on the vampire. He was awake, glaring at him with cold, glittering green eyes. They flashed hungrily; no doubt it was starving as his body used its dark magic to heal so swiftly as to be almost observable. Daemon couldn't get through the circle to knock him out again, but he didn't like that the vamp was conscious.

His eyes surveyed Deirdre's bedroom quickly, lingering on the closet. She would have to leave tonight, maybe forever. He swallowed. She would be torn from her life and shoved into a new one, always running, never safe. He walked over to the closet and flipped on the light. He smiled; it was just so…Deirdre. It was enormous, and full of her things. His eyes lighted on a shelf that ran along the back of it, which held an assortment of purses, bags, and backpacks. He picked up a large sturdy-seeming backpack and put a pair of her jeans into it and two long-sleeved T-shirts, and added a thick sweater. He picked up a coat that looked warm, and smelled as though she had worn it fairly recently. He took the things back out into the room and went to the dresser.

He felt like a creeper, reaching into her underwear drawer, but she would need those as well. He tried not to look, and even harder not to imagine, as he grabbed a couple sets and shoved them into the bag with her other clothes, and went for the socks; suddenly remembering her bare feet, he returned to her closet for a pair of tennis shoes. He passed her mirror on his way out and her hairbrush caught his eye. He snatched it up and tossed it in, too, hoping there weren't any other toiletries she couldn't do without. He went down to the kitchen and raided the cupboards, adding easily packed traveling foods—a box of granola bars, a couple of apples, water bottles. The bag was full to bursting as he zipped it up. He looked around one more time, and the cookie jar on the counter caught his eye. He smelled the cash from here. He opened it up, surprised at the amount—it held several hundred dollars. He took it all, stuffing it inside the front pocket of her backpack. He held the pack by the loop on top. Her coat draped over his arm, and he eased through the living room and out the back door, into the rain.

He cloaked himself in magic, moving unseen around the house, surveying carefully. The storm was escalating, and wind whipped rain into his eyes, soaking him before he even reached the front of the house, but he sensed nothing lurking in the shadows. He went to his car and put her things inside. If she didn't need it, he would return it. He hoped the Sorcerer wouldn't try to take her away by himself. No matter; he could find her anywhere, even Moenavi, the Sorcerer's sky-city. Lightning flashed in the distance, and after a moment, the thunder crashed after it, reverberating through the night. He jogged all the way around the rest of the house, checking the grounds, and let himself back inside.

He shook himself off and wished for a towel, and padded softly across the living room and back up the stairs to Alastair's room, leaving dripping footprints to mark his passage. He entered the room and found them with the circle already up and the ghost in attendance again. They didn't hear or see him and he tapped on Deirdre's line to get her attention. He didn't want to disturb Jack, already deep into the healing. She tore her eyes away and looked over at him.

All's quiet, he sent, and she acknowledged him with a nod. He went to the window and opened the curtains, staring out into the storm. Lighting forked through the sky, and thunder shook the house immediately after it; the storm was getting closer. The lightning flashed again and the lights flickered for a second as the thunder crashed in response. He turned back toward the circle, catching the edge of Deirdre's surge of emotions, wondering what had caused it. Jack was standing over her now, watching her reactions, but she had eyes only for her brother. It was like watching a silent movie without subtitles.

The moment when her brother met her eyes and he could see her, her face filled with incredulity, shock, and transcendent joy; she embraced Alastair so tightly he winced. Jack was drawn and tired but smiled as he watched them; his hair and shirt were damp with sweat. He looked somehow thinner after his exertions, as though using his power this extensively was whittling away at him. The ghost looked smug as he observed his protégé. Jack looked up and saw Daemon standing over by the window and collapsed the circle.

"Come on, this is the part I need your help with," he said. Daemon swallowed his irritation at being ordered around and stepped into the circle.

"The vampire is awake," he said. Jack frowned and Daemon continued. "The nurse is asleep and she'll stay that way until someone awakens her. There's no one outside," he finished. Jack nodded.

"What do you think about the vamp?" Jack asked him. Even his voice was tired. Daemon raised his eyebrows in surprise—a Sorcerer asking a Shapeshifter's opinion?

"We should keep our eyes on him," Daemon advised immediately. Jack stepped toward him, then looked back over his shoulder.

"Deirdre. I'll be right back," he said. She nodded, still talking in a low voice with her brother. Daemon followed him from the room and he sealed the circle behind them with Deirdre and Al inside. They walked down the hall and Jack collapsed the circle and they approached the vampire. He was whole and hissing inside his golden net, completely healed; his eyes were glowing, insane with thirst. Daemon bent to pick him up but Jack stopped him with a hand on his arm.

"The net will burn you," he warned. He bent and picked up the struggling vamp himself, staggering under the creature's weight and his exhaustion. He slung him over his shoulder and Daemon steadied him with a hand on his arm as they went back down the hall. Jack made it to Alastair's doorway before he dropped his twisting and bucking burden. Daemon stood helplessly as Jack grabbed the edges of the net and dragged him the rest of the way. He stopped at the edge of the circle and reached out and collapsed it, then lifted the vamp over the threshold, careful not to disturb the salt. He dropped him just inside, and staggered over to the chair that sat by the bed, dropping exhaustedly into it.

Deirdre looked over at him, watching him with worry in her eyes. She crossed over to him and laid her hand on his shoulder.

He raised his head to look up at her, and the tightness in his eyes unwound as they filled with warmth for her. She touched his face, her eyes full of love, and Daemon turned toward the vampire at his feet. Jack stirred.

"We should question him," Jack said. Deirdre looked at Alastair. Jack shook his head.

"I need to rest a little more," he admitted reluctantly. She squeezed his shoulder. He stood up, walked over to the vamp and dragged him to his feet. He dissolved the net down to his shoulders with a touch, so that it held the creature's arms pinned to its sides and fully encased the rest of his body, and looked over at Daemon.

"Will you hold him for a second, please?" he asked. Daemon stepped forward and reached for the vamp, and at that moment of inattention it lunged for Jack's arm with its teeth, snapping wildly. Jack threw it into the barrier and it fell to the floor where it writhed for a moment, screeching. Daemon kicked it in the face to shut it up, not hard enough to do any real damage, and dragged him back up, careful not to touch the net. The vampire snapped at him, but even its undead strength was no match for the giant Shapeshifter. Jack returned with the salt and poured it in a circle about two feet wide. Daemon held him awkwardly within it, away from his own body as the Sorcerer touched the salt circle with his fingers and invoked his spell. Golden vines sprung from the salt, twining in and around each other, creating a net-like barrier that grew up from the floor, weaving a shining living prison of golden magic around the creature.

Daemon released him when the vines threatened to touch him, stepping back and allowing Jack's magical prison to take over. The vamp struggled and twisted to stay upright, trying not to touch the vines as they wound up and around his head, closing over him like a cocoon. Jack reached through one of the spaces between the vines and touched the rest of the original net so that it fell away, barely snatching his hand back in time to avoid the vampire's lunge. He crashed into the vines and screamed as they burned into his undead flesh, jumping back into the center of his loose but deadly prison with his arms held stiffly at his sides.

"Who are you working for?" Jack asked tiredly, returning to Deirdre and his chair. The vamp laughed at him.

"Why should I tell you? You'll just kill me anyway," he snarled. Jack's eyes darkened and his face turned to stone. Daemon was glad he wasn't on the receiving end of the Sorcerer's expression.

"I would very much like to," Jack growled. Deirdre's hand tightened on Jack's shoulder. "However, I am actually not in the habit of killing people—or things—unless they force me to," Jack smiled, and the menace in it was chilling. "If you tell me what I need to know, I'll let you go," he said, and leaned back in the chair. Daemon looked at him in disbelief. Jack met his eyes without flinching. He was serious. The vampire stared at him.

"Yeah, right…." he muttered. The ghost shifted as though he wanted to say something, but Jack pinned him with a glance.

"Suit yourself," Jack waved his hand and the vines began to move. Daemon watched them for a moment before he realized the circle was getting smaller. He swallowed, disconcerted by this latest display of the Sorcerer's power. He remembered the stories his father had told him, but this… this was something else.

*This is what he can do when he's resting up from the **heavy** magic?* he thought to himself. He folded his arms across his chest as Jack continued.

"You have two minutes before the vines touch your skin. Five minutes until they crush and burn you to ashes. Your choice," he said, and closed his eyes. Deirdre exchanged a glance with her brother, whose expression was stiff with shock. Her own was more unreadable. He tested her feelings through the link. A confusing mix of righteous anger and reluctant compassion for the vampire, fierce joy and aching hope for her brother, a sense of safety and security and a little bit of awe in her thoughts of him, twisting anxiety and serene trust and love for Jack trickled through the link; she looked over at him with a raised eyebrow.

He shrugged, chagrinned at being caught, and she pressed her lips together. Her eyes weren't angry, though, and he smiled at her; her lips twitched and she looked away. Her gaze was drawn back toward the vampire, though, and all her reluctant amusement vanished. Al observed the exchange with a curious expression.

The seconds ticked by, and the vines danced death. The vampire hissed when his shaking hand brushed against one of the leaves and his skin smoked at the brief contact. The unpleasant odor of burning vampire seeped into the dome. The two minutes were almost up when he shouted. Jack sighed and almost negligently stopped the vines, opening his eyes reluctantly. The vampire stood frozen in his custom-made prison, unable to even shake in fear without touching one of the bright golden strands.

"What is your name?" Jack began. The creature answered sullenly.

"Peter," he growled.

"Who sent you?" Jack asked.

"David," the vampire answered, his voice tight with resentment and defeat.

"Who else?"

"Jacob, and one other whose name I don't know. He's the one who found out who you are, though," the vampire said, suddenly eager to please. Jack's eyes narrowed.

"How did he find that out?" Jack asked. Peter sneered.

"Saw you do your thing, a'course, what'd'ya think?" he mocked.

"Why did you attack her?" Jack asked next. Daemon's eyes flickered. Smart not to name her, he thought.

"What I was told. Get the girl, get to you. Never heard of one breaking the thrall though. How'd you do it?" he asked Deirdre curiously. She looked at him, through him, utterly aloof, and didn't answer, and Daemon stifled a laugh at the sudden rage that engulfed the vampire and made him forget the vines. Jack's hostility didn't incite the vamp to move an inch, but Deirdre did it with one look. It was a few moments before he was still enough again to talk to. Jack just watched, waiting with seemingly infinite patience.

"What did they plan to do with her?" Jack asked, and his voice was low and dangerous with this question. The vamp shrugged, not hearing it.

"How should I know? They promised me a taste, though, and I doubt she'd be wearing a crown, y'know. Prob'ly one of those dirty cells your kind always have lying around," the vamp baited Jack. Daemon tried not to let anything show on his face, but his relief was intoxicating. *They don't know. They only know about Jack*, he thought. If they had known about her, they would never have promised a vamp her blood. They wouldn't take any chances with a Seer.

"Are they working with the guild?" Jack asked, redirecting the vampire's thoughts.

"Don't think so. They wouldn't need local talent if they were, would they? I could be at the bar right now, picking up chicks, having some dinner," he sighed wistfully.

"What will they do now that you're late?" Jack asked. The vamp growled.

"How should I know? I'm not exactly part of the inner Circle," he said scornfully, as though the question was unintelligent, but the vines flamed green for an instant and began to writhe and close in again. "Okay! Okay!" the vampire shouted in pain. Jack waited one extra second before he stopped the vines again.

"More are coming," Peter said, vibrating with rage and relief and causing a leaf to brush against his cheek, a vine to sear his hand.

His eyes flashed with the sting and his breath hissed from his throat in a pain-filled gasp.

"How many? When?" Jack sat forward, power coming off him in waves.

"Five or six, I'm not sure," the vampire admitted grudgingly.

"*When?*" Jack repeated, almost ferociously. The vamp actually cringed.

"Midnight! Midnight," he cowered.

"All vampires?" Jack asked, sitting back in his chair.

"Don't know for sure. Some, at least." A light flickered in his eyes and the vines trembled. Jack raised his hand threateningly. "If I'm trapped here I'm supposed to invite them in when they come!" the creature said quickly. Jack lowered his hand gradually. He sat back in the chair, thinking. He looked over at Daemon, and his question was clear: anything else? Daemon shook his head slowly. He didn't know enough about Sorcerers or their politics to ask questions about them, and it appeared that Jack didn't either. Or perhaps he did, and so he didn't need to ask questions about them. He couldn't think of anything else that could help. He wondered who the third Sorcerer was who had identified Jack. Three Sorcerers…a full Circle, if small. Why were they here, in this out-of-the-way place? They generally liked big cities, where power could be most easily brokered and used, or the luxury of the legendary hidden city in the sky. And they apparently wanted Jack. Why?

"Why do they want him?" Daemon asked carefully. The vamp cut his eyes to him, startled that the giant Shapeshifter would speak out of turn, then back at Jack, as though for permission. Jack nodded infinitesimally.

"I told you. They know who you are. That's some kind of big deal, apparently, some Prophecy. I wouldn't know. Not a member, remember?" He grinned ferally and a vine brushed his cheek, causing him to hiss again in pain. Jack frowned and looked at Daemon again. The dragon shrugged.

Jack held out his hand and the vamp cried out, "You promised!" Jack rolled his eyes.

"Yes. And I will, but not until we're gone," he said, and closed his hand. The vines thickened and put out leaves, covering the spaces, sealing the vampire into his living magic cell, effectively cutting him off from what else they did in that room, allowing them to work freely.

"Okay, Al, are you ready for the rest?" Jack turned toward Deirdre's brother. Al only nodded, gazing at his friend as though he hardly knew him. A shadow passed over Jack's face.

"What is it, Al?" he asked, and he looked like he knew what was coming.

"It's just… I had no idea you were such a badass," Alastair said, wary embarrassment clouding his expression. Jack blinked in surprise, and then his face cleared and he laughed out loud, clutching at his sides and falling back into his chair. Al grinned with him, a little hesitantly at first, then more naturally, until he was almost laughing too. Daemon looked at Deirdre and she shrugged, unable to clarify the joke. He shrugged back at her, but he couldn't help smiling at the Sorcerer's mirth. Jack's laughter turned to chuckles, and finally he calmed enough to wipe his eyes and stand up again.

"I'm sorry, man, but don't you remember watching *Die Hard* that night, and…" he began to laugh again, and this time Al joined in wholeheartedly. Deirdre put her hand on Jack's arm and he covered it with his own and squeezed it reassuringly.

"You remember that night, don't you, Deirdre?" he asked her. "Al was parading around like Bruce Willis? He even did the voice," he reminded her. She grinned.

"Al does a terrible Bruce Willis," she teased.

"Better than yours," he retorted, and Jack chortled again. Daemon tried to picture the serene Deirdre goofing around like that and couldn't help grinning along with them.

"Yippy-kie-ay," she muttered, and the boys chuckled again.

"Anyway," Jack pulled them back on task as he clapped his hands together. "Let's finish this party. I've got things to do," he quipped, and for some reason Deirdre blushed. Jack grimaced and shook his head at her slightly in mute apology and she laughed again. He turned toward Daemon.

"You ready?" he asked. Daemon spread his hands.

"I guess so. What am I doing?" he replied. Jack frowned.

"Oh, yeah. I didn't tell you," he said. Daemon raised an eyebrow in annoyance. "Sorry. You're going to tell me what exactly is wrong with his back and help the bones move correctly once I fix them," he explained. Daemon nodded.

"Can do. But it would help if he could lie down on his stomach. I use my hands, not just my magic," he said. Jack held up the bed control.

"Way ahead of ya." Jack raised his eyebrows at Al. "Ready?" he said. Al clenched his hands around the guardrails and nodded sharply, his eyes full of fierce determination and hope.

***

Deirdre

Sunday Evening

They lowered the bed and helped him roll over, and he lay on his stomach with his head pillowed on his hands, flat on the bed. Deirdre moved, resting her hand on her brother's head while she watched them, explaining what she saw as they went.

The ghost hovered over them as Daemon went first. They did it in stages; their magic couldn't mix much, or they might do more harm than good. Daemon felt out the shapes of the bones with fingers and magic and pointed out the problems to Jack. Jack went in carefully, pulling the fused and damaged vertebrae apart, re-making their shape, one careful millimeter at a time, stimulating the marrow, healing. Finally, he was finished, and he withdrew from the trance, swaying with fatigue.

Daemon went in, double-checking, manipulating them carefully into place, lining them up, strengthening the ligaments and muscles that held them together. Then Jack took the final turn, stimulating the nerves, the spinal column, the atrophied muscles of his legs. At the very end, haggard and gray though he was, he made Alastair lie on his right side and ran his hands down the side of his body, healing the jagged scar until it was no more than a faint white line that probably wouldn't tan under the sun.

Finally, hours later, it was done.

Deirdre handed her brother a pair of pants. He put them on while she averted her eyes, and when she turned around Daemon was helping him down from the bed while Jack watched, gaunt with fatigue. Suddenly Alastair was standing before her, whole and healthy. Gone was the sickly pallor of his skin, gone the jagged white scar. His eyes focused and dilated naturally when he looked at her, and he looked down upon her from a height that just barely topped Jack's. Amazing that she could have missed looking up at him.

She threw her arms around his waist and crushed him to her, crying and sniffling into his shirt, making a scene but unable to help herself. He stroked her back and hair, holding her while she cried. Finally, she released him and let him step away, watching him with overjoyed eyes as he walked—*walked!*—around the edge of the circle. Shasta inclined his head respectfully toward Jack, and Jack nodded back as the ghost disappeared.

***

Daemon

Sunday Evening

Deirdre startled Daemon into stepping back when she threw her slender arms around him and hugged him tightly in gratitude. He barely had a chance to squeeze her gently back when she was away again, making her way back to Jack. She looked up into his exhausted eyes with something like adulation as she hugged around his waist, and Daemon looked away, watching her brother enjoying his new-found freedom. He wondered how the Sorcerer was planning to explain all this away. A miracle? Injuries not as severe as they thought? A new experimental drug? Struck by lightning? Even as Daemon had the thought, lightning flashed outside and the lights flickered again as they had before.

Deirdre shifted uneasily when they came back on, suddenly nervous again for no reason Daemon could detect. She exchanged a long look with Jack, and Daemon walked casually over to them, not wanting to alarm the brother, but sensing something was wrong.

"What's up?" he asked them softly, watching Alastair pace slowly past the cocoon. They hesitated, exchanging another glance.

"It's nothing," Deirdre began. "Only, in my vision, right before everything hit the fan, the power went out during a storm..." she told him quietly; the barest shadow of anxiety trickled down the link. The next few moments would be forever etched in Daemon's mind, burned there in fire and blood and adrenaline.

Jack took a little wooden box out of his pocket and turned it over in his fingers. Deirdre watched his hand from where her head rested on his chest and frowned. He stepped away from her, over to the chair and sat down, drawing her with him with a hand on her waist, so that she stood next to the chair with her hand on his

261

shoulder. He opened the box and took out a tiny blade, no bigger than his finger; Daemon could smell the silver and bone and the faintest trace odor of old blood and death magic. Deirdre's eyes went distant, and her hand tightened on Jack's shoulder as Daemon felt her swift surge of alarm.

"Jack, wait—" she gasped as he sliced his finger with the knife and his magic surged. Lightning flashed outside the window and Jack shuddered and clenched his fists and panic filled his eyes as he realized his mistake—like the straw that broke the camel's back, the magic was finally too much for his flesh; his eyes rolled up into his head and he fainted, slumping in the chair. The little box tumbled to the floor, and the ring and the knife skittered, clattering beneath the chair as they slipped from his limp fingers.

The vines that contained the vampire flickered and withdrew swiftly back into the salt, and the wide protective circle flickered and went out as thunder crashed through the room, rattling the windows. The electrical power died with Jack's spells and an ominous snap-crackle, and the distant sound of shattering glass, plunging them into darkness lit only by random flashes of electric lightning, like a demonic strobe.

The vampire screamed in sudden triumph and Daemon jumped at him as he flew to the nearest warm body. Crazed with thirst he jumped on Alastair, tearing at his throat. Deirdre screamed as they all three crashed to the floor, sliding on the slick linoleum to smash into the wall. Daemon dragged at the vamp and pummeled him with his fists, trying to knock him off; bones crunched, but Peter was locked around the boy with his entire body, latched on with teeth and claw-like fingers, and he wouldn't let go. Desperately, with an inarticulate cry of rage, Daemon grabbed the creature's head and twisted, ripping it away like a melon from a vine. Gore splashed everywhere, and Daemon wrenched the rest of the now-lifeless corpse off Deirdre's brother and picked him up, limp with shock from pain and sudden blood loss.

He laid him on the hospital bed and tried to stop the bleeding, but the damage was severe; blood seeped from between his fingers and Daemon hissed as the hot iron scent and his own adrenaline made him see red and the hungry dragon clawed at his insides to get out. He stamped it down ruthlessly—he must stay human if he were to help at all. In a flash of lightning, he grabbed Deirdre's hands and dragged her over to him. He made her press her hands into the wound, showing her where to put pressure to slow the bleeding. He ripped a sheet into squares and strips, and knocked her hands aside as he pressed a square of cloth into the wound instead. It soaked through almost immediately, but he held it there and added another on top of it as he tied a strip carefully over them, firmly enough to hold it in place, loose enough to not restrict Alastair's neck. The boy moaned softly as the vampire's soporific venom took hold, finally killing the pain of the bite and sending him from shock into unconsciousness.

Deirdre's hands were covered in gore; shaking with shock she wiped her brother's blood on her jeans, then clutched at his hand, feeling for a pulse. Daemon thought furiously as he watched her, and glanced at the clock. Only minutes to midnight. Five or six *others*, here already or on their way, vampires among them. Would the Sorcerers come too? He could not fight them all and protect Deirdre, Jack, and her brother at the same time. Especially not in such close quarters—he couldn't Change here. If even one of the attackers got inside, they could invite in the vampires, and while Daemon could make a protective circle, he couldn't hold it long. If he was to have any chance of protecting her—them—he needed space. With the Sorcerer weakened, they had to run—there was no other option. Deirdre could *not* be captured; if they found out what she was.... He stamped down the panic as the dragon looked out through his eyes. At least he could see in the dark now—he left the Change as it was.

"We have to get out of here, Deirdre," he told her softly. She turned wide eyes on him, empty and shocked. He felt her distant surprise at the silver sheen that coated his eyes in the darkness and the vertical irises that stared out at her from his face. He took her shoulders and rubbed them gently, worried at the chill he felt in her body.

"Come on, honey, come back to me. You have to help me get them to the car," he said. She blinked and took a deep shuddering breath. Still shaky, but more focused, she nodded.

"What can I do?" she asked.

"Try to wake Jack," he instructed, as he checked the bleeding at Alastair's neck. It still seeped, but it had almost stopped, the venom at work again, helping it to clot. Moving him was insane, but leaving him would be murder.

"Jack!" he heard Deirdre call softly in the Sorcerer's ear as she shook him. She got no response and repeated the call in his other ear, louder, more panicked. Still, he did not stir. Daemon would have to carry them both.

"All right, never mind," he told her. He lifted her brother over one shoulder, and kneeled at the base of Jack's chair.

"Help me, Deirdre!" he said, and she tipped Jack's body forward and dragged him over Daemon's other shoulder, trying to help him balance the dead weight as he stood. The burdens were awkward, but manageable, and he turned carefully toward the door, praying they would have enough time to get away before the *others* came. She slipped on something on the floor as she followed, and gasping, bent and retrieved the ring and the knife, glinting in another flash of lightning, throwing them into the little box and tucking it into her pocket. Daemon was already at the door and he growled at her impatiently to stay close. She opened the door, hissing and crying out when the metal doorknob burned her hand severely, and they stepped back reflexively from the light that flickered from the doorway and the smoke that poured into the room.

At the bottom of the stairs, the entire first floor was in flames. She choked on her sharp intake of breath as she caught smoke into her lungs and Daemon winced at the sharp sting of fear she sent along the link. He grinned at her reassuringly, and she stared at him like he was insane. But really, what did a dragon have to fear from a little fire? Even the smoke barely bothered him. She took faith from his nonchalance and covered her face with her sleeve as she took another breath. He knelt to the floor again, and told her, "Climb on. I'll have to carry you through too, but you have to hold on by yourself—my hands are full," he joked. She choked out a single note of laughter that was more like a sob and wrapped her arms around his neck and her legs around his waist, latched on like a little child. She tucked her head into his collarbone and breathed against his neck.

He lurched to his feet and focused his magic on the fire. It hissed and sizzled angrily, trying to bite at his ankles but shied away from his icy aura as he made his way carefully down the stairs, praying the wood had not already weakened and would hold their weight. He felt a tremor and he jumped the last half-dozen steps to the floor, landing like a cat in spite of his burdens and almost jarring Deirdre loose. The stairs collapsed behind them with a roar and a tornado of ash and sparks, and he ran for the door.

Deirdre jumped down and reached for the door, hesitating this time at the heat that came off the doorknob, hissing from Daemon's magic. She hitched the sleeve of her sweater over her hand and turned it quickly. He clenched his jaw at her cry of pain as it burned through the fabric, scorching her palm again. She wrenched the door open and ran through the short burst of flames on the other side and out into the pouring rain and thunder; Daemon stayed hot on her heels. They barely made it to his car before the vampires came. They materialized out of the thick shadows, six of them, gliding through the rainy night, bringing death. He dropped Jack and Alastair next to the car by Deirdre and threw the keys at her as he moved in front of them.

***

Deirdre

Sunday Evening

"Get them into the car if you can, Deirdre. I'll take care of *them*," he spat, and his words held such menace that the creatures actually paused for a moment—but only for a moment. Then they laughed softly and flitted forward. Daemon didn't wait, but leapt, catlike, to meet them. He ripped through one, dismembering him before they even realized he had moved, and they screeched in anger at the trick and converged on the Shapeshifter.

Daemon chuckled softly and began to fight in earnest. He ripped the head off another and Deirdre didn't watch any longer. She turned the key in the ignition and illuminated the drive in twin swaths of light, vying with the growing light of the fire behind them as the house burned brighter. The agony of her hand she pushed into the very back of her mind. *Not my hand, not my pain, it belongs to someone else*, she told herself, even as tears streamed down her face and the blisters burst and wept at her exertions.

She opened both the passenger side doors in Daemon's massive old sedan as wide as they would go and dragged first Alastair, then Jack, up to the edges of the doorways. Their dead weight was agonizing, impossible, and she had to lever herself almost to horizontal to move them an inch, straining muscles she didn't know she had as she pushed her bare feet against the ground; she slipped twice in the slick puddles that formed in little dips on the driveway, bruising her hips and biting her tongue. Blood ran thick down her throat and she gagged, but she finally had them positioned where she needed them.

She ignored the burning in her thighs and shoulders and back and the icy ache in her feet as she stepped inside the car and bent down to lock her hands around her brother's chest, screaming

266

with frustration and the tearing strain in her muscles as she dragged him into the car with all her strength. She fell down on the floor with him on top of her as Daemon's roar of pain echoed in her mind and in her ears, and she pushed and struggled to lever him up more onto the seats. She scrambled to her feet and out the other door to drag him the rest of the way, panic making her stronger. When his head was at the end of the seat she shut the door on him and ran around to the passenger side again to lift his feet in. She heaved the dead weight of his legs up, forcing his knees to bend, and wedged his bare feet onto the seat. She slammed that door on him as well and glanced back to see how Daemon fared, her chest heaving for breath, her hand throbbing and burning distantly, her heart racing with the adrenaline that still flooded her body.

There were three vampires left. He stood in the center of their loose circle, his eyes glowing silver and slitted like a cat's, his massive chest heaving, bleeding from a dozen wounds all over his body, but he had taught them respect, and they were bleeding and broken, though they healed before her eyes. As she watched, one of them darted in and slashed at him with a knife that dripped rain and blood and flashed in the stark lights. He screamed and she fell, hearing the agony in that strike through her ears and through the bond. *Silver.* Its touch was unbearable, and he retched. The dark shadows that surrounded him smiled, gloating already, but Daemon wasn't beaten yet.

Give me Jack's magic, Deirdre, he *called* to her, and she answered, *Take it*, opening herself up to him from where she had fallen. It left her in a rush of swirling sensation, she could feel him inside her mind, all immense physical power and uncanny sensory awareness, and he pushed up to his hands and knees on the concrete, the rain washing blood from his wounds until the ground beneath him ran red. Two breaths he took, she took, two matched heartbeats, and his eyes flashed gold and the dragon exploded from him, Changing impossibly fast; in the space of a single breath he lunged and killed two of the vampires with claws and teeth, and the other turned and ran.

He twitched his tail and trapped it between his enormous feet, almost as though playing with it for a moment, then he roared as it stabbed the silver knife into the softer flesh between his claws, sealing its fate as Daemon lunged and tore it in two with his teeth. She fell again with the burning pain of the knife in his flesh, then pulled herself up and ran to him, barely dodging his thrashing feet as he tried to shake the deadly splinter free. She calmed him through the link.

*Stop! I'll get it out, but you have to **hold still**!* She screamed the command through the acid fog of the pain in his mind. He obeyed, his tail thrashing instead with the effort of resisting the fire of the spreading poison in his veins. She located the knife and tried to yank it out, and he screamed in her mind when her hand slipped instead. She slapped him mentally and when he froze in surprise she gripped it with both hands and yanked it out of his foot with all her strength. She held up the smoking blade in shock, noticeably thinner than it had been and tarnished with his dead blood. The silver still burned in his veins, but no more poured in and he had overcome the panic, now.

More magic, Deirdre, he said. She put her hand on his massive jaw and leaned into him in acquiescence, and he took a little more of the Sorcerer's fiery magic through the link. It blazed through him, burning the silver away and leaving only ashes in its wake. He shuddered and sighed, bathing her in his icy breath, and together they turned toward the car. Deirdre lifted her hand, somehow still holding the silver knife, to shield her eyes from the too-bright glare of the headlights, trying to make out the shape that rose behind them. At first she thought that perhaps Jack had awakened at last, and her heart leapt in her breast, but then the man walked forward. He clapped his hands together in a slow mocking rhythm in time with his steps as he did so. His hair was dark and fell straight and shining to his shoulders. His eyes flashed with a ruthless intelligence, and he wasn't getting wet though the rain fell in curtains all around them. He stood tall and straight, and wore black slacks and a dark button-down shirt crisply ironed, everything tailored to a perfect fit.

"Quite an impressive show," he praised them condescendingly. His voice held the rich timbre of an orator, carrying effortlessly across the pavement, even in the downpour that continued to soak the earth. Deirdre moved closer to Daemon, sheltering beneath his massive shoulder, her sudden surge of renewed fear and adrenaline scenting the air, making him hungry. He stamped down the feeling ruthlessly.

"My Sorcerer is keeping awfully odd company. Two humans and a Shapeshifter—a dragon, no less. Extremely peculiar. I just *had* to come see for myself," he said.

Ask him what he wants, Daemon prompted her.

My Sorcerer? she questioned the man's phrasing. Daemon shrugged warily in her head.

"What do you want?" she asked, and her voice shook only a little. The surge of adrenaline was wearing off and she felt the now-familiar hungry stirring in her that meant her magic was low. Her attention riveted on the newcomer, and she *knew. Sorcerer…* she warned. Daemon's fear made her shiver, skittering across the link and crawling up her spine.

"I have what I want," he said, and gestured toward Jack, still unconscious, bound now by glowing magical chains to the ground. With a cry, Deirdre ran forward before Daemon could stop her and threw herself on Jack, pulling at the chains, hissing and crying when they wouldn't move and burned her fingers. The man watched her with amusement.

"Now really, my dear, you're making a scene," he chided disdainfully. The dragon growled, and the Sorcerer held out his hand. To her shocked dismay, Daemon flinched, and, as it had in the kitchen earlier tonight, Deirdre's terror quieted as it began to turn to rage. Oblivious, the Sorcerer nodded at the stillness of the dragon.

"That's better," he said. Then he did something with his hand, and chains similar to the ones that held Jack closed around Daemon's four feet and his neck, pinning him to the ground. Deirdre screamed again as Daemon roared in pain and impotent rage, real and inside her mind, and she fell to her knees in agony. Her burned hand stung as grit from the driveway rubbed into the raw patches left by the torn blisters and her nerves shrieked. The Sorcerer approached her casually, walking around her as though she were an interesting specimen in a thick glass jar. She scrambled to her feet, closing Daemon's pain and her own ruthlessly out of her mind, turning with the Sorcerer as he circled her like a snake that had spotted his dinner, unwilling to turn her back on him. He ignored the knife in her hand. He rightly knew there was nothing she could do with it that would harm him.

"Interesting. You care so much for them *both*, my dear? How very… modern," he mocked, misinterpreting her scream, unaware of the telepathic bond she shared. He walked so that her face turned into the light. "My my, you are a pretty one," he observed, and his eyes looked her up and down, lingering where they shouldn't. "I can see now why they were slumming. Perhaps you can still be of use after all. I'm sure these two fine gentlemen wouldn't want you to be… hurt," he observed nastily. Daemon growled at him again, and again he roared in pain as the chains tightened and burned with a flick of the Sorcerer's fingers. All she could feel from his link was pain, and her hands closed into fists so tight her fingernails cut into her skin and blood trickled down her knuckles and dripped onto the pavement. The knife handle grew slippery in her good hand. The wind whipped rain around her head, and her hair danced like snakes around her shoulders. She glared at him murderously and took a step forward.

He chuckled in amusement at her audacity and raised his hand, ticking his finger at her, "Ah, ah, my dear, that won't do. You wouldn't want them to be hurt, either, now would you?" He flicked his wrist and Jack's body twisted and he groaned in pain even in unconsciousness. A low whimper passed her lips and tears clouded her eyes, dripping onto the concrete as she turned her head away from him, averting her eyes before he could see the idea she had just had when she looked at Jack.

A little closer, she thought, her rage growing with every passing second. She knew what happened to a Sorcerer's spells when he lost consciousness. And, thanks to Shasta, she knew how to make any other Sorcerer but Jack unconscious. But he had to be closer—close enough to touch. Daemon quieted as he saw the plan in her mind.

*Be **very** careful, Deirdre,* he warned, his mind a whirlwind of fear and hope and pain. The Sorcerer was speaking, imagining he had her cowed. "There we go. Everything will be much better if you cooperate," he stepped closer and reached for her. She flinched at his touch as he took a tight grip on her chin and forced her face to the light again. His other hand twisted the knife easily out of her limp grasp and dropped it carelessly to the ground.

"The face that launched a thousand ships," he murmured, almost to himself, his eyes betraying his sudden desire; the Seer's hunger had reached out to him as to Jack. She swayed a little closer, and the move was hardly contrived, as the hunger and a wave of hatred swept over her. *Now, Daemon!* she called. The dragon began to thrash and the Sorcerer lifted his hand almost negligently to constrain him even more closely, never taking his eyes from Deirdre's face. She closed both her hands around his wrist and held on as she seized his magic and drew it hungrily into herself, gasping as it bit through her, sharp as a knife at first with the after effects of the spell aimed at Daemon.

He gasped and tried to pull away, but she held on grimly, and his eyes dilated with pleasure as he fell to his knees, staring at her, his expression thick with disbelief, and she drew harder. Compared to Jack, his magic was thin and slightly bitter, but it still tingled hotly

271

under her skin, and her tears flowed freely at the necessity of having any part of him inside her. She felt him weakening, his magic drying up, and finally truly realizing his danger, he began to fight her in earnest. His free hand slapped her across the face and battered her side and hips, impossibly strong even without any leverage. His other hand gripped at her throat and clawed at her soft skin. She gritted her teeth against the pain and held on, draining every last drop, and suddenly he moaned and shuddered in ecstasy and pain and fainted to the pavement, nearly dragging her down with him. She threw him away from her, revolted, and ran to Jack as his manacles disappeared, melting away into the pavement, washed away by the icy rain.

Daemon, free as well, lunged at the man, tearing him in half and dropping the pieces on the pavement as Jack began to stir. She threw herself on him, clutching at her side with her injured hand curled into a loose fist, the icy rain stinging the scratches at her neck. Her tears mixed with the rain falling on his shirt until Jack woke enough to be surprised at his surroundings. He lay on the pavement, still too tired to get up, and raised an eyebrow at the massive silver dragon whose scales reflected the fire that raged inside the house behind them. She laughed, a little hysterically, at his bewildered expression, relief at their narrow—if temporary—escape, making her giddy.

Chapter 7

Deirdre

Early Monday Morning

"What happened?" Jack asked her, and she just stared at him for a moment, not even knowing where to begin to answer that question.

"We have to get out of here," she told him, and helped him into the passenger seat. She turned back to Daemon, and he told her telepathically about his extra clothes in the trunk. She retrieved them for him, carrying them inside the nearby garage so he could change as he threw all the torn bodies into the raging inferno that had been her home for the past fifteen years. She wondered what her father would do when he found out about it—and discovered that she and Al were missing. She couldn't imagine it.

Magic, Deirdre? Daemon requested again when he was finished with the macabre cleanup, interrupting her reverie, and she nodded wearily, urging him silently to take all of it. She felt sick with the evil Mage's magic inside of her, burning and greasy. Daemon denied her request sympathetically, and he took it gently this time, a long slow trickle that felt like kisses along her skin.

Stop it, she told him, wondering what it felt like to him when he did this, wondering how much Sorcerer magic he should really be using. She kept her back turned while he Changed, lifting her face to the rain that still showed no sign of slacking.

Couldn't Change so soon or so quickly without it, he said, keeping quiet about how it felt to draw magic through her, and about how much was too much. He was dry for only moments before he emerged from the shelter and touched her shoulder. She turned and he grinned down at her, unrepentant, his shoulders straining the T-shirt he wore as it swiftly soaked up the rain. She looked at him, vital and so *real*, standing in front of her, and gasped as she remembered his injuries. She touched his chest where one of the knives had cut him deepest, and felt only solid muscle beneath his shirt. She lifted the fabric away to look and he laughed when she stared up at him in amazement. His wounds were gone, gone as though they had never been. She traced his chest where the deepest cut had been and he caught her hand and held it there for a moment, looking down at her. She wondered what she must look like as she stared up at him, feeling somehow both lost and nearly giddy with relief, and as he gazed down at her his expression sobered. He reached for her, touching her bruised face with his hand, tracing her jaw with his cold fingertips, and she allowed it; the rain spattered on her face.

We make a good team, he sent. She just closed her eyes and leaned slightly into his icy caress, needing comfort. After a moment she reached up and took his hand from her face, and turned away, toward the car. She eased into the back seat, cradling Alastair's head on her lap and shutting the door softly, finally out of the rain.

Hospital? Daemon asked her silently, cranking up the heat when he felt her chill. She swallowed. What *should* they do with Alastair? Jack needed time. And Al needed help. But would he be safe there? How much did the other Sorcerers know? At least they didn't know she was a Seer. Not yet, anyway. That Sorcerer would never have treated her so carelessly if he had known. No, they had been after Jack. After a moment she nodded at Daemon.

Hospital, she agreed silently. *He'll be safe there?* she asked, biting her lip, wanting desperately to keep him with her. Daemon winced at the distress in her eyes as he put the car in gear and drove down her driveway.

I think so, he agreed, trying to send reassurance with his words. *No one would hurt a Sovereign unless they were desperate,* he said.

????? she sent. He looked at her in the mirror, then shook his head.

You didn't know? he asked. She shook her head. He sighed.

We can tell you later, he sent, including Jack with a nod of his head. She nodded and stroked Alastair's hair again. She didn't look back at the burning house as more tears joined the raindrops on her face. She felt like she had been crying for hours; her eyes were irritated and scratchy but she couldn't seem to stop. She stared unseeing out the window as Daemon drove into town through the storm. Then she stared at the back of his head, his broad shoulders, watching his eyes in the mirror as he drove.

Since when had they been able to talk through the link while Daemon was human? she wondered, suddenly bothered. *What would Jack think? Jack.* She looked over at him. He was asleep again, his head leaning against the window, his body supported by the seatbelt Daemon must have fastened over him. His face was still gray with exhaustion from healing Alastair; even the bumps in the road didn't stir him to waking. She stroked her brother's hair, noting the pallor of his skin, unable to feel him breathing, and she felt again for his pulse. It was getting weaker. But he had walked tonight. *Walked.* And he could *see.* This other injury was nothing, compared to that.

The End

CPSIA information can be obtained
at www.ICGtesting.com
Printed in the USA
FSOW02n1225220117
29917FS